THE RELUCTANT QUEEN

Books by Molly Costain Haycraft

THE RELUCTANT QUEEN
TOO NEAR THE THRONE

THE RELUCTANT QUEEN

▽ ▽ ▽

MOLLY COSTAIN HAYCRAFT

J. B. LIPPINCOTT COMPANY

PHILADELPHIA AND NEW YORK

2

Copyright © 1962 by Molly Costain Haycraft

FOURTH PRINTING

Printed in the United States of America
Library of Congress Catalog Card Number 62-11333

FOR DORA

A very special sister

PART I

CHAPTER I

THE KING'S PHYSICIANS, who had been talking softly to Prince Hal and the small group of nobles gathered near the door, fell silent for a moment; the only sounds in the vast, wainscoted bedchamber were the irregular, labored breathing of the dying man, the rattle of Lady Margaret's beads, and the low mutter of her prayers for her son.

Thomas Wolsey stepped closer to the bed. As Henry's chaplain, he had already done everything in his power to ease the King's heart and conscience; but, he thought, there might be one last confession— He was finding it difficult to believe, even now, that the man who had made him, Thomas Wolsey, a mere butcher's son, his personal chaplain and confidential courier, would soon be dead.

That gaunt, wasted figure, looking more like his own effigy than a living man, had succumbed so swiftly to the lung rot that was killing him; only a few months earlier, Wolsey remembered, his royal master had sent him to France to discuss a possible marriage with the recently widowed Duchess of Savoy, and had given him private instructions to notice whether the lady had beautiful breasts.

"The doctors say he cannot last much longer."

Prince Hal's whisper startled the older man. He turned to find the lad just behind him. "I'm afraid not," was his answer. "A few more hours, perhaps. He's in God's hands now, your Grace."

The Prince said nothing more. Until this moment he had half believed that his father might, by some miracle, recover. Even

9

when he had watched Wolsey administering the last rites, earlier in the day, he had told himself that the physicians could be wrong. He had heard of men hovering on the verge of death and mysteriously winning their way back to health; but the grim faces around him and the quiet way in which Wolsey had agreed with the doctors convinced him at last, and he sought refuge in a shadowy corner.

On the other side of the room, little Mary Tudor tried desperately to keep her eyes from the ghastly countenance on the pile of pillows. She studied, instead, the pattern on the Turkish floor covering, so much more pleasing than the usual thick layer of rushes and herbs; she counted the Tudor roses on the plaster ceiling high over her head, she looked down into the garden below the mullioned window and watched one of the royal gardeners digging around a bed of flaming red tulips—but it was no use. Her father's sunken features were all she could see.

The thirteen-year-old princess sat crouched in a deep window seat, fighting the tears that insisted on slipping down her cheeks and spotting her bodice. Although death was no new thing to her—she had, in her comparatively short life, lost her oldest brother Arthur and her much-loved mother, the gentle Elizabeth of York—it still frightened her. When her father was gone, she realized suddenly, she and Hal would be orphans, and terribly alone.

Swallowing a sob, she turned her attention to the venerable lady kneeling beside the large carved bed, her sober black gown and white linen hood making her seem the nun rather than the mother of the King of England. This was a sad vigil for her and an intolerable burden on her poor thin old body; but why, Mary asked herself, must her grandmother kneel on the hard floor? That, at least, was not necessary.

Choosing a soft embroidered pillow from the seat beside her, she tiptoed to Lady Margaret's side, touched her slightly on the shoulder, showed her the cushion, and pointed to her knees. With a grateful smile, her grandmother rose stiffly while Mary slipped it into position, then sank down on it and continued her prayers.

King Henry opened his eyes. He stretched a white, emaciated hand toward his youngest child.

10

"You here, daughter?" His voice was barely audible. "Come kiss me, Mary, then leave me to finish this sorry business." As Mary bent over him, he caressed the bright smooth hair, offered his cheek for her kiss, and called feebly for the Prince.

Mary knelt, watching her brother hurry around the wide, curtained bed, his face drawn as he pressed his lips on the King's thin fingers.

The dying man looked from his pretty daughter to his tall, wide-shouldered son and heir, now only a few weeks short of his eighteenth birthday. They were a handsome, healthy pair, children of whom he could be truly proud. He was even willing to admit to himself that he loved them more than he had ever loved his other son and daughter—poor, delicate Arthur, who had died back in 1502, and selfish, greedy Margaret, wed these several years to King James of Scotland.

But Mary and Henry were still very young. And death is ugly.

"Take your sister to her own apartments, Hal. This is no place for her." His eyes went to Lady Margaret. "Go, both of you. I would like to be alone with my mother, now. As alone," he added bitterly, "as it is possible for a dying king to be."

The group near the door were murmuring together, their backs politely turned on the royal family.

The Prince took Mary's hand and raised her from the floor.

"You will send for us, dear lord, if you—" He swallowed and stopped.

"No, Hal. I won't be sending for you again. This is farewell." He touched Mary's head again. "Be good to your sister. I had hoped to see her safely wed—but, there, never mind that. When you are King, son, England must be first. Remember—England—" A paroxysm of wracking coughs shook his whole body. The Lady Margaret was beside him instantly, a linen napkin in her hand. She pressed it to his lips just in time to stanch the bright red blood.

Mary shuddered and turned faint. Her brother squeezed her fingers and made a move to lead her out of the room.

"Wait, Hal," the King gasped. "One more thing. Marry Catherine now. We've kept her waiting long enough."

"I will, Sire; I promise. At the first possible moment."

His father made no answer, speaking softly instead to Lady

11

Margaret, who was still hovering over him. "Ask our God to forgive me, Mother. Surely a king's sins are not all his fault. God knows they cannot be! So often, I had to choose between the good of my people and the peace and comfort of a quiet conscience—" He choked. "But I'd be a changed man, Mother, if God would send me life. I would reconcile both, somehow." However, it was too late to bargain with God, and Henry knew it. When the seriousness of his condition first became apparent he made pilgrimages to Our Lady of Walsingham and Thomas of Canterbury, and he began building the Savoy hospital for the poor, hoping that Heaven would repay these gestures with a miracle cure. As these good deeds were of no avail, he had little hope that promises, now, would save him.

As the tortured voice whispered on and on, young Henry bowed in the direction of the bed, Mary dipped a deep curtsey, and they backed carefully out of the dim chamber. Still hand in hand they ran past the guards and down the long stone corridor that led to their part of Richmond Palace.

"God help me," said Hal, pulling Mary into the sanctuary of her withdrawing room, "but I am grateful to our father for dismissing us! A bit more and I would have bawled like a new calf!"

The girl sank into the nearest chair. "I almost swooned when he bled. Is he really going to die, Hal?"

"The physicians say so and so does Master Wolsey. At any moment. Mother of God, this waiting is hard on a man."

He began prowling around the room, a restless and uneasy figure in his faded tawny velvet doublet. Mary, watching him, decided that he could very well be one of the lions she had seen the last time they had been at the Tower of London. Even his step, slow and deliberate, reminded her of the large golden animals; just so had they paced back and forth in their cages, paying no attention to the royal party gathered on the other side of the heavy bars.

If the Prince forgot, for a few minutes, that he was not alone, it was because he was, suddenly, strangely and uncomfortably torn between sorrow at the thought of losing his father and the triumphant knowledge that he would, before very long, be the King of England, the eighth Henry to wear the crown. It was going to happen at last. He would be King! He would rule England, as had his father before him, and, inevitably, sometime in the dim mists of the future, he, too, would lie on his deathbed while *his* eldest son waited for the moment when his breathing would stop.

He halted at last to stare hungrily out of the window. The late April landscape, spread below the wide casement, was lovely to see; the lawns and hedges had turned a vivid green in the soft spring sunshine, and the shining Thames curved widely here at Richmond, its banks fringed with lacy willow trees. "I'd give a hundred crowns for a good gallop," he said wistfully, "or an hour in the meadows with my gerfalcon."

His sister shrugged her shoulders. They both knew perfectly well that he must remain in the Palace while their father lay in the shadow of death. Nor could they turn to the card table or backgammon board to pass the time. They could only wait.

"*Must* you marry Catherine?" The question had been on Mary's mind for so long that it popped out. "I suppose I shouldn't say this to you, Hal, but I've been hoping that the long delay over her dowry might mean a younger and fairer bride for you." She hesitated, then went on. "Spanish women don't wear well, you know. They turn into fat, greasy old puddings. With mustaches, more often than not."

"You paint a pretty picture."

"But she's twenty-four already, Hal! And you aren't quite eighteen."

He nodded. "I know. I don't mind that. As a matter of fact, I think we'll do very well together. Kings can't marry for love, after all; I'm fond of her and," he smiled smugly, "she's made no secret of the fact that she's even fonder of me. It would break her heart if I cried off now."

"Not if you plead your conscience. She's your brother's widow."

"Well, of course, Mary! There are many things I could do if I misliked the match. But I don't. And as for my conscience"—he spread his hands wide—"it's quite clear. I'm convinced that Arthur never consummated their marriage."

Mary stirred in her chair and frowned. She had heard this important question discussed very often and although she had not, at first, understood the matter, she did now. For the last year or so the ladies of the royal household had considered her old enough to hear their most intimate conversations and some of the talk had been very intimate indeed.

Her brother, misunderstanding her frown, laughed. "Now don't ask me to explain, sis. Ask Mother Guildford or wait until Prince Charles is old enough to show you. What is he now? Nine? Ten?"

"I'd rather not even think about it." She shuddered. "If you suppose I'm in a hurry to wed that shovel-chinned ninny, you're very much mistaken!"

"Then why did you simper over his portrait when the Spanish ambassadors were around?"

"Because I was *told* to! Everything I said and did from the beginning to the end of that long, wearisome betrothal ceremony was nothing more than a well-learned lesson. 'Smile at Prince Charles's proxy, wear his portrait around your neck, tell our guests from abroad that you find your betrothed pleasing—' Pleasing!" Mary spat out the word like a cherry pit. It was true that she had obeyed the King's orders, and with good grace; but in her heart she had rebelled against every vow, every smile, every curtsey, every dutiful lie.

Surely, she thought, when Hal is King he will arrange my future more pleasantly and not send me off to Flanders to marry Charles. It was too soon, of course, to say anything to him. She looked up at him from under her gold-tipped eyelashes. My brother, the King. King Henry VIII. Sire. Your Majesty. Odd as it still seemed to think of her sportive, romping Hal as King, she admitted to herself that he would make a handsome one.

"What are you staring at?"

She chuckled. "I was thinking of you as King."

The Prince bridled and his round face flushed. A true redhead, he changed color easily and often. "You find the thought something to laugh at?"

"No, no, no! It was just that you're my brother. As a matter of fact, Hal, you should carry the robes extremely well. There's not a man in England with your inches and shoulders." Except Sir Charles Brandon, she corrected herself. "And you're still growing. Of course," she tossed her head and twinkled at him,

14

"there are people who don't like thick, curly red-gold hair, but *I* think that gaudy mat of yours is going to show off the crown of England to perfection!" She was glad that her own hair was more gold than red, but her brother's suited him, and, except for the fact that his eyes were a bit too small, he was a strikingly handsome young man.

"I wonder," Henry said thoughtfully, "how long it would take the royal tailors to make me a new suit?" Mary's remarks had pleased him, but they had set him thinking of his appearance. "Have you ever noticed what a miserably shabby pair we are, for England's Crown Prince and his sister?"

He strode over to a long mirror of highly polished steel and studied his reflection. "God—*how* shabby!" He swung around and pulled her to her feet, looking from her worn hood to her scuffed slippers.

"How could our father's Grace have treated you so badly?" He sounded actually angry. "The very first thing I shall do, Mary, is order new clothes for us both. Gowns, hoods, slippers. You need dozens of them. I won't have my sister dressed like a ragpicker! And as for me, I must have velvets, satins, brocades, cloth-of-gold—jeweled and furred, of course, in the latest fashion. And ostrich plumes. My people will see a real king for a change—"

He stopped abruptly as a scratch on the door heralded Lady Guildford, followed closely by a lackey bearing a tray loaded with cold meat and fowl, bread, ale, and a flagon of wine.

"My lord Prince, Lady Mary," she sketched a curtsey before turning her attention to the setting out of the food. "Your grandmother left his Majesty's bedside to order this supper for you. You missed your dinner and she feels that the King's family should not appear in the dining hall tonight."

Lady Guildford, for many years the Princess Margaret's governess and now Mary's, had almost taken the place of her dead mother in the girl's heart.

"Is he any better, Gilly?"

Lady Guildford shook her head, her plump, goodnatured face sober. "He's sinking fast, God rest his soul." She took Mary's hand in hers and patted it comfortingly. "Now, come, child, and you, too, your Grace—eat. You'll both be needing your strength."

Although it seemed heartless to consider food at such a time, Mary and her brother realized that they were extremely hungry. Surely, if their grandmother had ordered their supper it must be seemly for them to eat. It was late afternoon now, and the shadows were deepening; they had been summoned to their father's bedchamber that morning and had not dared leave it until he had roused and dismissed them himself.

While Mary was settling herself in her chair a page sidled in and announced in a shrill, excited voice that the Archbishop of Canterbury and the Earls of Surrey and Shrewsbury would like audience with the Prince.

"Quick!" At Lady Guildford's gesture the serving men whisked away the table again and rearranged the chairs. Mary and young Henry straightened their garments and stood, the Princess slightly behind her brother, facing the door.

It opened slowly to admit the three men, the Archbishop leading the two nobles. The Prince stepped forward to meet them, holding himself stiffly.

"Yes, my lords?"

"The King is dead." Canterbury's tones were round and ringing. "Long live the King!" He fell to his knees, Surrey and Shrewsbury following his example.

Mary heard her brother gulp and saw his face flame as he extended his hand to the kneeling men. After he had received their kisses of homage, she knelt, too.

"Your most loving servant, Sire," she said, and, in her turn, touched her lips to the large, hairy paw that she knew so well.

As she rose to her feet, the Lady Margaret Beaufort joined them, walking slowly, her eyes stricken, her mouth set and strained in her thin face. Mary and the nobles turned aside, leaving the new King alone in the center of the room; the feeble old woman faced her strong, towering grandson.

"My dear lord—" She was trembling so much that her words were almost inaudible. "Your Majesty—" At her first move to kneel he bounded forward, caught her in his arms and kissed her.

"No, no, you shall not!" He looked over her bowed head and

met the eyes of the waiting group. "Could you return to us in an hour, my lords? May we have a little time, now, to be alone with our sorrow?"

CHAPTER II

WHEN THE SMALL GROUP had climbed aboard, the royal barge moved swiftly away from the water steps. It was one of those quiet moments that often occur around dawn when the night breezes drop suddenly and everything is absolutely still. No ripple disturbed the wide glassy surface of the Thames and the dangling leaves of the large willow on the opposite bank hung straight down like limp, uncurled ostrich feathers. Near the river's edge huddled the flock of sheep who would soon be ambling contentedly around the flat meadow cropping the lush grass while their new lambs played close by; now they were an irregularly shaped mound of grayish white, keeping each other warm in the cold April morning.

As the black-draped barge neared the bend in the river that would take them out of sight of the Palace, Mary looked back at the oriental minarets topping its towers. The short lull was over; a chill wind moved the sable pennants flying from the spires and set the gloomy awning and barge hangings to flapping. Shivering, she tried to forget that her father's body was lying, stiff and cold, back there at Richmond.

Perhaps at this very moment he was being disemboweled and embalmed—a horrible thought! Although her grandmother had dismissed her to bed quite early the night before, Mary had heard enough of the talk to know that this must be done immediately and that the finest waxworker in the kingdom had been summoned to prepare an effigy to lie on Henry VII's coffin.

"The funeral," Lady Margaret had said, "cannot possibly take place for at least a fortnight." The nobles, she reminded her grandson, must first have their mourning robes made, then travel to London over roads churned into soft mud by winter thaws and spring rains. The funeral guests, she continued, would gather from all over England, from the borders of Scotland to the white cliffs of Dover. Lords and ladies on horseback, in litters, in whirlicotes, their great bands of servants on mules, pack horses, in jolting baggage wagons.

"Your father's body, of course, remains here at Richmond until all is ready for him in his new chapel at Westminster Abbey. How sad," she sighed, "that the chapel is still so far from finished. I know he hoped to see it completed before he died."

"We'll give orders that they work day and night." The new young King gave his grandmother a loving pat. "We—you and I. Thank God, dear lady, that my father chose *you* for my Regent!"

"If I can be useful, my son, I shall be proud and happy."

"Then tell me, must I retire to the Tower until after my father is buried?"

Lady Margaret nodded. "It is the custom. A—a final gesture of love and respect from the new ruler to the late King. The people should have time, Hal, to mourn for your father before they cheer for you."

"But you will come with me?"

"Of course I will. There are many things you and I must decide in the next few days, Sire. Choosing your Council is the most pressing business, and I'm afraid we should be considering the matter even now."

"First let me send word to the Tower to ready apartments for us. And for Mary," he added, indicating his sister, sitting quietly nearby.

It was then that Mary was shooed off to bed. To reach the Tower unnoticed, her grandmother told her, would mean leaving for London shortly after daybreak.

Lady Guildford had wakened her charge while it was still dark and hovered over her while she ate a hearty breakfast and dressed in her warmest gown. As the royal party was small, consisting only of the Princess and her governess, Lady Margaret and two of her ladies, the King and his favorite gentleman, Sir Charles Brandon, there was no delay in setting out from Rich-

18

mond. Their personal servants and the other lords and ladies of their suites were already on their way, having gone ahead with some of the hurriedly packed boxes and hampers.

The two tall young men—for Brandon was built very much like his friend and royal master—stood quietly watching the oarsmen. It was the first time, Mary realized, that she had ever seen them in such a sober mood, for they were usually the merriest of companions, joking, laughing, singing, wrestling, working off their high spirits and bounding energy with and on each other. A matched pair, except for their coloring, and closer than most blood brothers, their association was of so many years' standing that Charles seemed to Mary like a member of the family.

Actually, the little Princess was only five when Sir Charles, a lad of sixteen, came to Court to join her brother's household. His father, Sir William Brandon, had carried Henry VII's standard at Bosworth, the battle that won Henry the crown of England; his oldest son was one of those slain that memorable day, and young Charles's appointment, made many years later, was the King's reward for Sir William's loyalty and grievous loss.

He never regretted it; a royal prince has all too few playmates and devoted friends, and although the dark-haired, dark-eyed Brandon was the senior by six years the boys soon formed an attachment for each other that was to last the rest of their lives. It was based on a similarity of tastes and interests, the healthiest possible foundation for an enduring friendship, and as Sir Charles seemed to know instinctively when to remember and when to forget that he was only a squire's son, the vast difference in rank had never been a problem.

When they had left the lonely stretches of the river behind them, Mary, feeling the need to ease her cramped legs, rose and joined them at the rail, her cloak blowing around her ankles. Before long the barge was skimming by the rambling old buildings at Westminster, and a few minutes later passed the great houses that sat in their gardens between the Strand and the water's edge. As they neared London Bridge she noticed that the Thames was beginning to fill with wherries, skiffs and other small craft, intent on beginning the business of the day before the river grew crowded.

A little fishing boat tacked so close to the black-draped barge that its skipper could peer curiously at its occupants. Swearing under his breath, Henry glowered at it and stepped over to where Lady Margaret was sitting.

"Come into the cabin," he said. "London is waking."

With most of the morning light shut out by the hangings, the small enclosure was oppressive. Lady Margaret, tired and white, chose a corner where she could resume her prayers, the soft drone making Mary drowsy enough to lean her head against Lady Guildford's shoulder and close her eyes.

The barge began to pitch in a most uncomfortable fashion. "Ah," said Brandon, "we must be under the Bridge. The currents are even worse than usual today."

As the Tower lay just beyond London Bridge Mary roused herself and straightened her hood and cloak. In a very short time the barge veered to the left, bumped something solid, and stopped, rocking gently.

"The King's Steps." Sir Charles turned to help the ladies, and Henry left him to it, hurrying up the short flight of water stairs to acknowledge the obsequious welcome of the Governor of the Tower who was waiting at the top on the wide wharf, flanked by rows of Tower attendants.

Brandon handed Lady Margaret from the barge, but Mary, after a hasty, shivering glance down the river at the Traitor's Gate, its closed portcullis looking like evil teeth grinning in the rounded arch, was too quick for him. She was off and up on the wharf in a flash, her skirts held firmly in one hand.

"We are housing you and the gracious ladies in the White Tower," the Governor was telling the King. "I would have liked to find a few carpets for your Majesty, but the best I could do, in the time at our disposal, was to spread fresh rushes and hang some heavier tapestries. We are cold here in April. The stone walls are damp and the lightest river breeze seems to find our chinks and cracks."

Assuring him that he and his party would do very well, Henry indicated a desire to move on to his destination. Mary, after a look at the two litters provided for her and her grandmother, turned to her governess.

"Take mine, Gilly," she said. "It's a short walk and I won't mind the cobbles. Litters make me queasy."

The rooms in the huge old Keep were gloomy and uninviting; it was almost impossible for the sun to find its way in through the narrow Norman lancets, and the leaping fires had not yet dispelled the damp that their apologetic host had so aptly described. However, the wide beds had been fitted with handsome hangings and the finest coverlets the Tower could provide, every seat had a soft cushion or two, the steel mirrors were highly polished, the carved oak chests and court cupboards gleamed with beeswax, and there was the pleasant smell of crushed herbs sifting up from the rushes on the chilly stone floors.

Her energy soon restored by hot food, a short sleep, and fresh clothes, Mary prowled around her apartments in search of amusement. Finding little to interest her there, and suddenly aware that her chatter was of no help to the busy maids and ladies-in-waiting, she sought out her governess.

"Come, Gilly dear," she said. "Fuss with these boxes later, and adventure with me now as far as the Green. If we stay inside these clammy stone walls we'll forget that it's April."

Lady Guildford hesitated, not sure what Lady Margaret's wishes would be. Should the Princess Mary remain closely indoors during these days of mourning, or might they feel free to stroll in the open air? After a moment's indecision, she made up her mind to risk a scolding; she must not disturb her ladyship now, for her ladies said that she was sound asleep, oblivious for a while of her sorrow and the nagging pains that had bothered her recently.

So, catching up light wraps, they hurried down the stone stairs and over to a wide stretch of grass, shaded here and there by a few tall trees. It was a beautiful afternoon, the sun shining warmly and the sky a vivid blue. The two companions strolled slowly around, talking contentedly together about the King's probable marriage to the Princess Catherine of Aragon, the coronation that would take place soon after the late monarch's funeral, and how best to keep busy during these quiet days in the Tower.

Turning the corner of the Keep, they saw that Henry and Sir

21

Charles were apparently occupied with the same problem. They were pacing off a long level portion of the greensward and calling out orders to a group of scarlet-clad Yeomen warders and two or three gardeners in plainer green livery.

"Here, lads." The new King's voice was loud and cheerful, his face pink and happy. The change of scene had raised his spirits to their customary high level. "There's length enough for our bowls—and to spare. Trim it close and smooth, and," he added, catching sight of his sister and her governess, "set up a bench or two for the ladies."

He hurried over to kiss Mary on the cheek, greeting Lady Guildford with a question. "This weather is too fine to waste, Gilly. Don't you agree that if we are to be mewed up here we must amuse ourselves as best we can? Brandon and I are seeing what games we can contrive. The days will be deadly tedious if we don't arrange something."

Lady Guildford shook her head dubiously. "As you've asked my opinion, Sire, I think it would be wiser if you came to our rooms for cards or backgammon. This is not the time to enjoy yourself in public."

"Nonsense, Gilly! Who is to know what we do here?"

"All London—and in an hour!" It was obvious that she was very much in earnest. "I can hear the gossip now: 'The new King plays at bowls while his father lies on his bier.' No, Hal." She forgot for a moment that he was no longer the boy Prince who could be scolded when necessary. "You will, believe me, undo all the good of retiring here to the Tower."

"The Lady Guildford is right, my lord." Brandon spoke for the first time. "We must give up our game of bowls." He smiled down at Mary, who was standing nearby, her face showing her disappointment. She had round blue eyes, and a little tiptilted nose, and the young man realized, for the first time, that she looked exactly like a charming kitten. How odd, he thought, that he'd never noticed the resemblance before; it gave him an almost overpowering desire to tickle her gently under that soft, dimpled chin.

The days at the Tower slipped by more easily than Henry had feared. There was much to be done, he discovered, when a new king mounts the throne. His first task was one he set himself, to convince his new Council that he should wed the Princess Catherine as soon as possible. He summoned them to the Council Chamber and, while he awaited their arrival, he paced around the vast apartment wondering what could be done to bring in more sunlight. Making his way through a rough stone arch to one of the Norman lancets set in the thick walls, he pondered a moment, then shook his red head over the narrow slit. The first William, he decided, had built this portion of the Tower meaning it to remain exactly as it was; it would be much too difficult to alter the enduring work of the Conqueror's stonemasons.

The sound of voices and footsteps behind him drew him back to his place at the table. He welcomed his advisers with a warm smile, and, when they were all seated, he informed them of his intention to marry and stated his three reasons for doing so without further delay. First, he had promised his father on his deathbed; second, such a ceremony at this time could, and, indeed, should, be performed privately; third, and most important perhaps, if he and Catherine were man and wife they could be crowned together, thus saving England the cost of separate coronation ceremonies.

The Councilors whom Lady Margaret had helped her grandson choose argued the matter thoroughly before letting him have his way. Many had served on the old Council, and those who were added were equally wise and able, advisers who could be trusted to think first of England. William Warham, Archbishop of Canterbury, Richard Fox, the Bishop of Winchester, and Nicholas West represented the Church; the Earls of Surrey and Shrewsbury, Sir Harry Marney, Sir Thomas Lovell, and Sir Edward Poynings the nobility.

Realizing that the King's marriage was a weighty problem, they produced objections to be balanced against Henry's three reasons, but the determined young monarch fought each point, winning his opponents over to his side, one by one; and when even Warham, reluctant to see Henry marry his brother's widow, finally agreed, he softened the Archbishop's defeat by asking him to perform the wedding ceremony.

Neither the wedding nor his coronation could take place until

23

his father was entombed but Henry found planning for his coronation especially delightful, and the hours passed by almost unnoticed. Actually, he was deep in a welter of guest lists and a tangle of velvet and brocade samples when Mary ran in to tell him that the funeral procession was nearing the city and that the Lord Mayor of London was waiting for it on London Bridge.

He stood up, scattering the small pieces of fabric on the floor. "And here we are, shut up like prisoners!" Almost snorting with irritation the young King strode to the nearest window. "It will be dark in a short time. I wonder—"

Mary shook her head. "No, Hal. I asked our grandmother but she was very firm. We must stay here at the Tower. But we might climb up to the top of the building and watch from there."

"Why not?" Up and up the spiral stone steps they went, down a passage, through an arched doorway, up more steps, and past a sentry who dropped his halberd in astonishment as the royal pair swept by. On the flat spread of rooftop at last, they hurried over to one of the gun embrasures in the stone parapet and looked eagerly down in the direction of the Bridge. They were so high that they could see right over the irregular roof lines of the higgledy-piggledy houses that lined the Tower side.

"There they come!" Mary pointed excitedly to the far end, where the long cortege was just beginning to cross the Bridge. As it moved closer, and darkness fell, the hundreds of mourners, dirge singers, and royal attendants lighted wax tapers and torches and turned the somber, snakelike column into a dazzling contrast of light and shadow, the tapers seeming to dance in the air, and the flaring torches gleaming on the carved and gilded death chariot, slowly drawn by seven black horses.

To the brother and sister on the summit of the White Tower, it looked like a toy procession, an illusion that prevented them from feeling much grief. Long before it disappeared in the direction of Westminster, Henry moved restlessly around the rampart, showing Mary the mass of ships anchored in the Thames, their night lanterns reflected on the surface of the dark river, the dim spire of St. Paul's, piercing the evening sky, the wide moat and stout towers that encircled the great fortress in which

24

they were living. Finally he paced back and gave the cortege a last glance.

"He was good to us, Mary," he said, "but I shan't do things his way. I think our people like a king to be a *king!* Well, he'll soon be laid to rest and I can begin—"

Almost immediately after the solemn rites were concluded, the royal party made its way to Greenwich where Catherine of Aragon awaited her youthful betrothed. Henry was all the eager bridegroom now, hot to start wooing the woman who had waited so long for him and, much to her astonishment, Mary found herself watching what seemed to be the courtship of two true lovers. The Spanish Princess bloomed now that she had gained her heart's desire; as the May sunshine turned the green hedges white with snowy hawthorn blossoms, so did the King's promises and boyishly ardent kisses change the rather plain, dark-haired woman into a radiant girl. For the first time in her twenty-four years she had some real claim to beauty; dainty, slim, and graceful, she walked beside her handsome Henry, her step light, her face adoring.

"I hardly know her Grace these days," said Mary to Brandon one morning. She had been in sole attendance on the older Princess, when, a few minutes before, her brother had joined them and taken Catherine off to stroll in a little wilderness nearby, thus leaving her alone with Sir Charles, who had followed his master into the garden.

"What has become of that almost painful air of dignity?" she asked. "And those constant trips to her prie-dieu for one more prayer? To say nothing of the sharp words, the frowns, the gloomy silences." She dimpled up at the tall man beside her. "I tell you, Charles, if this is love, love is truly a wonderful thing!" She lifted the small mirror that hung from her girdle and peered into it. "Could it do as much for me, do you think?"

"Ask me in a year or two, minx. You're much too young to fish for compliments." He looked rather dolefully after the royal lovers, and sighed. "Your brother makes me his Esquire of the Body," he said, "then takes that body elsewhere." Hearing a footstep on the graveled path, he turned. "And here comes your good Mother Guildford, her mouth set to scold you."

25

Mary nodded, then chuckled. She ran to meet her governess and began to speak the moment she reached her, not giving the elderly woman the opportunity to utter a single word.

"Yes, my lady," she said, "yes, madam, quite right, my lady. It will not happen again, I promise you." She shook her head mockingly. "And a shocking business, too, my lady, for a princess of the blood to be in the gardens unattended and talking—yes, actually *talking* to one of the King's gentlemen!" She finished up her torrent of foolery with an exaggerated curtsey, bending her right knee so close to the ground that she overbalanced and sat right down on her round bottom, her small, square-toed walking shoes sticking straight up in the air, framed in the circles of her bell-shaped skirt and her stiff canvas underskirt.

"Mary!" If Lady Guildford managed to sound reproving, it was with difficulty. Her charge's expression had changed so suddenly from one of impish delight to pained, youthful embarrassment.

But Brandon was not as successful in concealing his amusement. He burst into laughter as he helped the girl to her feet, his bellows of mirth bringing his royal master and Princess Catherine out of the shady copse. As they approached the little group, still standing in the garden path, Sir Charles succumbed to a fresh explosion; when his eyes met Mary's, he tried to apologize. "Forgive me, your Highness, but—but—" He gestured with his hands, still too helpless with laughter to speak.

"Forgive you!" Mary sounded like a small, angry cat. "I will *never* forgive you!" And before the King and Catherine could reach them, she turned and ran back to the Palace, the long linen lappets of her hood streaming out behind her.

Now Lady Guildford could laugh, too, as did Henry when they described his sister's upset. "Nevertheless," added the governess, "I must punish her. Her Highness knows very well that she should not have been here unattended. But I must say, Sir Charles," she said sternly, "that you are quite as much to blame. Although the maid is very self-willed, I know. Since her betrothal she thinks herself a full-grown lady of the Court. Which she will be, only too soon." She shook her head and primmed her lips. "I'm afraid I must work doubly hard to teach her decorum and curb that restless spirit."

Catherine, who had thought for some months that Mary needed discipline, opened her mouth to say so—then closed it again.

"Oh, come, Gilly," answered the King. "You are forgetting that she has several more years of girlhood ahead of her. Mary won't be wed at fourteen as our sister Margaret was." He smiled. "Don't be too hard on the lass, for all our sakes. I want my Court to be a merry one, and I must confess that I like my little sister just as she is."

CHAPTER III

MARY GAVE HER GRANDMOTHER a furtive glance, saw that she was asleep at last, and closed the prayerbook. When Lady Margaret's regular breathing turned into a gentle snore she crept quietly over to the open casement and sniffed the sweet, perfumed air. It was too bad, she thought, to be shut up on such a perfect June day, and with the rose gardens in full bloom.

Could she slip away? She looked again at her grandmother, still napping in her big cushioned chair, and decided to remain; there would be other summers and other roses—but not, she was beginning to fear, for the Lady Margaret. It was obvious to everybody that she was growing frailer each day and although she refused to consult her physicians, and never complained of any pain or discomfort, her ladies had confided to Mary that they sometimes heard her groaning in the night.

Climbing into the high window seat, the girl rested her bright head against the wall, waiting to take up the prayerbook again when the old lady roused. Her own eyelids were drooping when the door opened and the King and Catherine entered, unannounced and unaccompanied by any of their suites. Startled, Mary shook her head in warning, pointed to Lady Margaret and put her finger to her lips.

But it was too late. She had heard them, too, and was trying to struggle out of her chair. Henry led Catherine over, pressed his grandmother gently back against the cushions and fell to one knee.

"We've come for your blessing, dear lady—" The young King's voice was brimming with pride as he bent his red head under her thin old hand. "Bless your grandson, if you will, and his bride."

"Your bride?"

"My bride and queen!" He kissed Catherine's hands, then put them in Lady Margaret's. "We stole a march on everyone this morning and slipped around the Palace wall to our favorite chapel. Canterbury was waiting there to make us man and wife —until death do us part." Henry beamed first at Catherine, then at Lady Margaret. "I had no idea that you could tie such a lasting knot so swiftly and simply."

Lady Margaret kissed them with trembling lips. "God bless and keep you both," she said, "and give you many years of happiness together. This is wonderful news you bring me."

"I do think you might have shared your secret with *me*," protested Mary. "I could very well have crept into the back of the chapel and watched from behind a pillar with no one the wiser."

"I'm sorry, Mary." Catherine's dark eyes met Henry's and she blushed deeply. "Perhaps we were a little selfish."

But of course, thought Mary, suddenly understanding. It was quite natural for the Spanish Princess to want this second ceremony different in every possible way from the lavish royal wedding that had made her Prince Arthur's wife eight long years ago. And, remembering with distaste her own elaborate betrothal rites, she decided that a man and woman deeply in love might feel more truly joined together in the sight of God if they could avoid the customary parading and posturing, feasting and ribaldry, and prying eyes and sniggering comments.

"Now that Kate and I are wed," said the King to his grandmother, "we must choose a date for our coronation. I thought, perhaps, Midsummer's Day." He looked rather anxiously at the fragile woman who still held the reins as Regent. "That would give us a fortnight in which to make ready. Is it too little time?"

Lady Margaret patted his hand, a shadow dimming her face.

"Nay, lad, not if the Queen's Grace will take the arrangements and decisions off my weary shoulders. Will you, Catherine, to spare an old lady? My only wish, now that you are married, is to see you crowned."

The trumpets sounded, the crowd roared, the King swung his high-stepping mount into place, Catherine settled herself in her cloth-of-gold litter, the noblemen shifted on their horses, the carefully chosen little boys lifted their banners, each noble woman tried to find a comfortable position in her carved and gilded whirlicote, and the great procession moved on its slow way from the Tower of London to Westminster.

Mary, riding immediately behind the Queen, watched the elaborately draped little vehicle swaying between its two handsome white horses and thanked God that she was riding on her own gentle palfry. She saw Kate stiffen her back and reach for another gold cushion; the poor woman, she knew, must sit absolutely erect the whole time, nodding and smiling, the side curtains open wide so that all London could see the new Queen.

She was lovely to look at, certainly, although her sumptuous gown of embroidered white satin was almost hidden by the cloud of glossy dark hair that hung to her knees. That curtain of tresses was the symbol of virginity, her pledge to the people that she had come to the King a maiden, and as this was her first appearance since their wedding, it was right and proper that it should be unbound.

Catherine, Mary realized, would never look as enchanting again: from now on she must hide that shining, luxuriant hair under tight-fitting hoods and headdresses, a fashion decidedly unbecoming to the Spanish lady. But today—ah, today—today all Westminster and London would cheer their throats hoarse for the King's bride, convinced that their Queen was a great beauty.

The girl stroked her own gown with her free hand, content in the knowledge that she, too, was appearing at her best. Every lady in the long procession, except the Queen, was dressed in gold satin and decked in her richest jewels, but the Princess, having studied them all with a critical eye, was positive that her costume was the most becoming. The deep square neck was cut a bit more cunningly, she thought, and the large milky pearls that outlined it and her gold hood brought out the whiteness of her skin as their glittering diamonds and emeralds never could. Let the countesses sparkle. . . . The ride through the narrow crowded streets seemed endless. By the time they reached their destination Mary's back was aching, she had a crick in her neck, her smile was stiff, her fingers cramped from holding the reins, and she was sure she would never again be able to straighten her bent knees. But for all that it was a triumphant day for the family of the new King and Queen; for Mary, who took part in it, and for the Lady Margaret, who was waiting at Westminster Palace. The enthusiastic response of the crowds, their obvious love for the young Tudors—"I'll never forget today as long as I live," Mary said to her grandmother.

Later, when they were seated side by side in Westminster Abbey, watching and listening to the ritual that made England's eighth Henry its anointed ruler, Mary was still bursting with sisterly pride. "He's truly a king," she whispered to her grandmother. "Every inch!"

Mary saw only the regal picture her brother presented, broadshouldered and handsome in his raised gold coat and his sweeping mantle of crimson velvet with its wide border of ermine; Lady Margaret looked, instead, at the face under the jeweled crown and her lips moved in prayer. "Bring him wisdom," she begged, "and humility. Help him to be kind and understanding. Prevent him from falling into the thoughtless and cruel ways that come with power."

Her last few words reached Mary's ears and she wondered why her grandmother thought them necessary. Hal would never be cruel. Not Hal!

When the long ceremony finally drew to a close, the Princess made sure that Lady Margaret was safely settled in her litter before joining the other noblewomen who were readying themselves for the coronation banquet. She found Lady Guildford and Bess Howard waiting for her in the anteroom to the white hall, where the great feast was to take place. As they unfastened her heavy ermine-edged robe and lifted it from her shoulders, she sighed with relief.

"Bless you both! I'm numb from the weight of it."

The Countess of Shrewsbury, having just surrendered hers, strolled over to discuss the ceremony. "I hear it's the longest and most elaborate coronation ever held in England," she said. "Excellent planning, excellent. But I was glad to see it end!" While she talked, she used one hand to mop her damp face and the other to wield a small fan.

A moment later she excused herself and disappeared in the direction of the nearest necessarium. At a word from her governess, Mary followed her; there would be no time later to attend to such matters. Once the King and Queen were seated at the High Table on the raised dais, everyone must remain in their seats until the banquet was over.

She returned to find her brother and Catherine standing together at the entrance to the hall, the trumpeters in position and the guards waiting for the signal to throw open the great doors. She sped over to the group of lords and ladies who were forming a line behind the royal couple, nodding her thanks to Lord Mountjoy as he made room for her at its head. A page, at his elbow, roused Mary's curiosity; he held a pillow in his hands, covered with small objects, all carefully arranged. She was leaning forward, trying to see what they might be, when the Chamberlain spoke to her again.

"Your Highness," he said, "will sit under the table at the Queen's feet. The Countesses of Derby, Surrey, and Shrewsbury will sit there with you." He turned to the page and began lifting things from the satin cushion. "It will be your privilege, your Grace, to hold her Majesty's purse." He handed a small embroidered pouch to Mary, who was looking at him with disbelieving eyes. "And you, my Lady of Derby, the royal handkerchief—and you, the fan—" He went from one noblewoman to another distributing Catherine's pretty possessions.

Mary summoned him back with an imperious gesture. "I'm afraid I misheard you, my lord. I thought you said I would sit *under* the table."

He bowed. "That is quite correct, your Highness."

"*I*—sit *under* the table?" Her voice rose to such a pitch that the King turned around and frowned.

"If you please, Sire." She caught his eye and beckoned to him.

He strode to her side, obviously annoyed and impatient.

31

"What in God's name is the matter? Our guests are waiting!"

She pulled his head down and whispered urgently in his ear. "It must be a joke, Hal. Tell that ass Mountjoy that there is some mistake. He says I sit under the table at Kate's feet and hold this!" She waved the purse in his face.

"Mountjoy is absolutely right." Her brother threw an uneasy glance at his wife's white satin back, his broad face a little pinker than usual. "Those are Catherine's orders, so behave yourself and do as you are told. It's a custom at her father's court, and a great honor. She tells me that the Spanish noblewomen quarrel for the right to sit at the Queen's feet."

"Well, you go and tell *her* that *English* noblewomen do not! The Princess Mary of England and Castile sits at nobody's feet!"

Henry took her by the shoulders and gripped her hard. "The Princess Mary of England and Castile does exactly what her King says—and she never, do you hear me, sister?—she never, never tells *him* what to do!"

The two young Tudors were glaring at each other by now, their cheeks flushed and their angry words only too audible to the nobles behind them. A complete hush fell over the room. Queen Catherine looked back to see what was causing the sudden quiet.

"Is something amiss, Sire?"

He shook his head. "Our sister thought for a moment that she was too ill to attend the feast. The heat made her feel faint. Am I right, Mary, in thinking you have quite recovered?" His question was asked slowly and sternly, his eyes fixed on her in a menacing way that was new and a little frightening.

The girl swallowed hard and forced herself to curtsey despite her trembling knees. "Quite recovered," she answered grimly. "Thank you—your Majesty!"

The story of Mary's tilt with her brother reached Lady Guildford's ears long before the banquet was over and, from her place at one of the side tables, she watched her charge's stormy face with trepidation. The moment the Queen rose, the older woman hurried to Mary's side, leading her quickly out of the room on the pretext that her gown needed a stitch before the dancing began.

When they reached the farthest corner of the nearest retiring room she insisted on hearing exactly what had happened. She sighed after Mary finished her story, and fell silent for a few minutes.

"I think I'm rather glad," she said at last, "although I wish you'd chosen a smaller audience for your quarrel. I was sure that sooner or later you would forget that Henry is now the King, and try to match your will with his."

"But, Gilly, all I said was. . . ."

"You lost your temper and made him lose his in front of the Court. Now listen, Mary, and don't interrupt me." She chose her words with care. "The King loves you and enjoys spoiling you. If you wish to keep your place in his favor, you must learn to control that temper and show him a smiling face no matter what it costs you. I mean it! And—please—never be fool enough again to make him side with either his wife or sister. Don't you know that men hate being put in such a position?"

She shook her head at Mary, hoping with all her heart that the Princess was heeding her words. "You may be sure that *you* will lose every time. Certainly now, when Catherine is his bride and he's eager to please her."

Leaning forward, she twitched Mary's gown into place, making sure that it hung evenly around her slipper tips. "There! Now go. Smile, and show his Majesty your dimples. Tell him a joke and dance with him. Be merry. Laugh! Kiss the Queen—!" She gave her charge an affectionate hug and pushed her toward the door.

Mary walked slowly down the corridor. Gilly is right, she decided, remembering that menacing look in her brother's eyes when he said she must never tell him what to do. If she herself hadn't been in such a rage it would have terrified her. He'd always been so kind and affectionate; apt to turn a little ugly to other people who crossed him, but never to her. . . .

As she neared the hall she heard the musicians playing a galliard, and she smiled to herself as the infectious triple-time tune lifted her spirits and set her toes tingling. It wouldn't be so hard to do what her governess suggested. She might even manage a moment alone with Hal when she could tell him she was sorry.

With this in mind she entered the vast room through the door nearest the gold-canopied throne and, seeing that everyone was watching the King and Queen dance, she slipped quickly across the floor and hid behind the arras that hung across the back of the dais.

When the music stopped she heard her brother and sister approach their thrones, their voices mingling happily together as they climbed the steps. She peeked around the edge of the curtain, hoping to whisper a word of apology before Henry sat down, but, when their eyes met, she suddenly realized that his broad shoulders hid her from the rest of the room.

On an impulse she changed her mind and said nothing. Instead, she fixed him with a wicked smile and, remembering a delightfully vulgar gesture she had caught a page using some weeks before, she placed one thumb on the tip of her small nose and waggled her fingers at him.

He bounded to her side with a roar of laughter and dragged her out of her hiding place.

"Here—" He beckoned to Lord Compton, who was standing nearby. "Tell the musicians to play a lavolta," he said. "Lead it with the Queen. I'm dancing this one with my sister."

As the festivities continued, day after day, Mary could see that Henry's greatest desire at this time was, as Lady Guildford had told her, to please his new wife. Nothing was too much trouble, no detail too small for his attention if he thought it might add to her happiness, with the result that the old palace became a hive of activity. Lavish decorations were constantly being replaced by fresh ones, new and gayer tunes were practiced on the royal instruments, and harried cooks spent hours inventing sauces and more elaborate desserts.

He and Mary were better friends than ever, and she found it easy to join wholeheartedly in everything he planned, showing him, rather than telling him, how much she loved him and her sister-in-law. The only cloud in their sky was Lady Margaret's illness; every day found her weaker and in more pain but her orders were that all should go on as usual.

On June 28 the young monarch would be eighteen years old and his grandmother's regency would come to an end, another excuse for special festivities. Brandon, Compton, and the rest of Henry's suite were called in for a very private conference and urged to think of some wonderful and original sport to make the day memorable for his Queen and their court. If there seemed to be an extraordinary amount of bustle and secret talk, and an unusually large flow of orders issuing from the royal apartments, her Majesty discreetly saw and heard nothing as she alternated between her prayerbook and her needlework.

By late morning on the day in question all apparently was in readiness, because Henry asked Catherine in a much too casual voice to stroll with him in the June sunshine. "Bring your ladies," he added, his boyish face clearly announcing that she was about to be surprised. Hearing Catherine accept his invitation in her most placid fashion, her demeanor indicating that she expected nothing but a quiet walk in the Westminster gardens, Mary laughed to herself. Catherine, she decided, was really the finest actor at court and should not be allowed to play audience only when the others were mumming.

No one mentioned the fact that the King and his gentlemen, who joined them in the lower hall, were all in hunting clothes, bows over their shoulders and knives in their belts. As a matter of fact, his Majesty talked so loudly and constantly of everything and nothing that little was said by anyone else as he steered his Queen and her ladies out the wide doors, across the courtyard, and along the path toward a stretch of lawn shaded by a few trees.

"Why, Harry!" Catherine's voice held such genuine astonishment that Mary and the other women pushed eagerly forward. There, actually only a few yards from the Palace, was a miniature park, railed in on all sides and filled with soft-eyed deer. The braver of the animals were cropping grass but most were nervously trying to find shelter in the sparse stand of trees.

Mary clapped her hands and beamed at her brother. "Magnificent, Hal! How did you ever manage such a feat? Are we truly in the heart of Westminster still, or have you moved us on a magic carpet to the country?"

While Henry chuckled delightedly over the success of his achievement, a band of lackeys was occupied in turning a half dozen hunting dogs into the enclosure. The hunters now hurried toward the little park, but before they could pass through the gate the dogs had begun to harry the deer, and the terrified bucks were leaping over the fence and galloping in the direction of the Palace.

The ladies screamed and scrambled out of the way of the distracted animals and the madly barking dogs, but when the King and his companions, their lackeys at their heels, pelted along the path after the deer, Mary and Catherine and the other ladies fell in behind them and ran, too.

It was a wild chase; into the ancient Palace and past the amazed guards streaked the panic-stricken game, the pursuers in full cry. Down the passages they fled, their sharp hoofs ringing loudly on the stones, until, in a last desperate attempt to escape the baying dogs, they plunged through the open archway that led into the dining hall. The long tables and benches were already set up for dinner, and as Mary neared the doorway she could hear the splintering of wood and the crash of falling plate and glass.

"Oh, no, no!" Catherine gave a sick little moan and hid her eyes. The Princess, looking over her shoulder, shuddered, then put her arm around the trembling Queen's waist. In all her life, Mary decided afterwards, she had never seen a more ghastly sight.

The trapped deer, after blundering helplessly into the tables, overturning them and strewing the floor with silver platters and shattered goblets, were caught in the welter of bench and trestle legs, brocade tablecloths and other fallen objects. As Mary stared, too horrified to say anything, the dogs leaped on their prey, ripping and tearing their soft quivering flanks, snarling, snapping and growling among themselves as the blood ran down their jaws.

"Mother of God!" She heard Charles Brandon swear loudly and saw him dash recklessly into the melee, pulling at the dogs with his bare hands. "Here, Thomson, Jackman—you men! Help me! Call off these hounds, for God's sake!"

At his frenzied summons, the lackeys ran to his aid, and after a lively tussle which included a great deal of whipping, kicking, shouting and whistling, the dogs were controlled and driven out of the hall.

Mary gave a gasp of relief. "It's all right, Kate," she whispered to the Queen. "You can open your eyes." But she spoke too soon. Instead of giving orders to round up the deer and take them to safety, as she assumed he would, her brother, his small eyes flashing with excitement, was charging in for the kill, loudly urging his small band of companions forward, his knife in his hairy hand.

A wave of nausea swept over her so that she had to press her hand tight against her mouth. Hunting and hawking were one thing; this was hideous, gory slaughter.

"Come away, Kate," she managed to mutter through clenched teeth. They retreated, but had only taken a step or two when the King called them back.

"Wait, Kate!" His voice rang out proudly. "Here, my sweet, the spoils of our chase are for you!" And before the Queen could escape or stop him, he and Compton laid a warm, quivering body at her feet, a fountain of bright blood gushing from its throat and its eyes just glazing over in death.

"I—I thank you, my lord. A truly"—she swallowed hard—"a truly noble prize. Save me the antlers, if you will." The soft hissing of her Spanish esses was perhaps more noticeable than usual, but except for that she succeeded so well in hiding her revulsion that Mary stared at her in admiration, wondering if she herself would ever learn such dignity and control.

She was thinking frantically how she could best excuse herself when she heard quick footsteps in the stone passage. Turning, she saw one of her grandmother's ladies, her face white and agitated.

"It's the Lady Margaret, your Grace," she faltered. "She—she —oh, please come!"

Mary's heart sank as she realized what this sudden summons probably meant. "One minute," she said. "I must tell the King and Queen."

The Lady Margaret died the next morning. Everyone had loved her—the "venerable Margaret"; so was she known then, and so she would be remembered in all the years to come. Her grandchildren mourned her sincerely, their grief eased a little, perhaps, by the knowledge that she had had her wish: she had seen the coronation and lived out her short period as England's Regent.

Not long after her passing the dread word, *plague,* began to be whispered around London. It was only a rumor at first, but when the red crosses appeared over dozens of doorways and the death cart was heard at night, rattling over the cobbles of the dark, deserted streets, the King realizing that he should leave the city as soon as possible, arranged for his grandmother to be buried hastily though with all due reverence. The moment the sad rites were concluded he and his Court fled back to Richmond.

Once safely there he put his sorrow behind him and resumed his honeymoon, the summer months slipping swiftly by as the Court hawked, rode, danced, feasted, masqued and jousted. Catherine, a deeply religious woman, saw to it that their prayers were not neglected; no less than three masses were heard each day, and every evening the young King hurried to her chamber for vespers and complines. His conscience easy, the new ruler threw himself into the pursuit of pleasure, finding the days and nights all too short.

"If I were still free, I would choose her for wife before all others," he wrote of his Kate to her father, Ferdinand of Castile. And Princess Mary, keeping tactfully in the background, fell into wistful daydreams as she watched her brother making open love to his wife. She looked often at the portrait of her betrothed, hoping to find some hidden charm in the long-faced little boy. Would he, by some miracle, grow into a man she could love? And if he did, would he love *her?*

The Queen's greatest delight was her morning ride with her husband, for she was a fine horsewoman; nothing but bad weather was allowed to interfere with that precious hour together. But there came a day, late in August, when she sent Mary in her place, and for the happiest of reasons; Catherine was pregnant. Now it must be the sister who cantered and galloped with the King, her small merlin on her wrist; now it was Mary, not Kate, who opened the evening's dancing as his Majesty's favorite partner.

Knowing that her sister-in-law was content to have it so, Mary made the most of her days in the sun, spurring her lively mare to keep up with Henry's large mount, and matching her small hawk against his gerfalcon. When dancing time came there was no leap too high, no measure too swift, no step too intricate for the nimble feet of the royal pair, spurred on as they were by Catherine's applause and affectionate smiles.

Affairs of state and foreign problems must soon claim a large share of Henry's time, but for this first year of his reign he was free to play, his most serious task the composing of songs to sing to his Queen. When the evenings grew chill, and the pregnant woman found her own fireside more inviting than the vast banquet hall, he brought his friends and his musicians and his lute to her apartments to dance for her and to sing her his newest tune.

> *Pastance with good company*
> *I love and shall until I die*
> *Grudge who will, but none deny*
> *So God be pleased this life will I*
> *For my pastance,*
> *Hunt, sing, and dance,*
> *My heart is set:*
> *All goodly sport*
> *To my comfort*
> *Who shall me let?*

Who, indeed? wondered Mary, slipping into the room as he finished the first verse. It was a charming bit of rhyming, set to light-hearted music, and as stanza followed stanza she thought each better than the last, her brother's voice this night unusually clear and true, his fingers on his lute never more sure and skillful.

"Sing it again, please, Harry." Catherine was leaning forward, her eyes alight with love and pleasure, when suddenly her face twisted and her hand tightened on the arm of her chair. "Oh!" She clutched her belly and rose unsteadily to her feet, throwing her husband a frightened, appealing glance. "Perhaps another time. I think, ladies and gentlemen, that you must excuse me—"

The King was beside her instantly. He picked her up and carried her to the door of her bedchamber. "Call the physicians!" he shouted.

There was a moment's stricken silence as he disappeared with his burden, then Brandon rushed off to find the royal doctors and Catherine's favorite ladies hurried after their mistress. Mary tried to follow them, but the oldest of the women barred the way.

"No, your Highness, let us first see what ails her Majesty. If it is what I fear, it will be better for you to remain out here."

The horrified girl retreated to a cushioned chair, avoiding the cluster of lords and ladies who still hovered near the door, whispering and shaking their heads. To her great relief the Queen's physicians soon arrived and passed quickly into the inner chamber. A few minutes later Sir Charles Brandon re-entered the antechamber. After a word or two with the others, he walked over to the Princess.

His smile was comforting as he drew up a chair by her side. "The doctors say it may be nothing," he told her.

Mary nodded, listening to the sound of rapid footsteps in the other room and an occasional half-smothered groan from Catherine.

But the groans grew louder and more frequent. When an hour had dragged by, the King appeared in the doorway, looking white and miserable. "She is miscarrying," he said. "It will be a long business, they say. Better leave us to it, my lords and ladies."

The door closed behind him and the withdrawing room emptied slowly until only Mary remained. Glancing around the pretty chamber, which had been, such a short time ago, so full of song and laughter, she saw her brother's lute, lying where he had tossed it on the floor, its crisp green ribbons half untied. She picked it up and made a fresh bow, then placed it on a nearby table before creeping back to her chair.

Another hour passed, and another. The door opened at last and Henry came out, his eyes wet.

"The baby was stillborn," he said. "It was a girl."

CHAPTER IV

"OF COURSE, KATE DEAR," said Mary, smiling her sunniest smile. "I'll be more than happy to do anything you suggest."

The King, entering the room at that moment, sighed in pleased content as he heard this evidence of accord between the two women. This was the way things should be, he told himself: his wife, well and strong again, smiling at him from her cushioned chair, his sister on a stool at her feet. Indeed, the whole room breathed peace, from the beeswaxed oak wainscoting and the soft light that streamed through the mullioned windows, to the Queen's drowsy confessor, nodding over his prayerbook; even the gossiping, giggling maids-in-waiting, circled around the leaping fire with their needlework, blended harmoniously into the peaceful, charming picture.

"I have been telling Mary," Catherine said, "that our visitors from Spain will be very disappointed if she remains in the background. Because of her betrothal to Prince Charles, I mean. I think we should overlook the fact that she's over-young for such formality and arrange for her to have a place of honor at all the festivities."

"On my faith," announced Henry, "the King's sister shall be second only to his Queen. If," he added, striking a pose, and giving Mary a teasing glance, "she behaves herself."

The girl answered him by thrusting out the tip of her tongue and crossing her eyes, and they were still laughing when they excused themselves a few minutes later and strolled out of the room together.

"Tell me, Hal," Mary turned serious suddenly, "why should Kate think me 'over-young'? I'll be fourteen in less than a fortnight now. After all, Margaret was *married* at fourteen, and a mother before the year was out."

"And," answered her brother, "has been wretchedly unhappy ever since. If she is telling me the truth, I should say. She writes me one complaining letter after another. You should be grateful that Kate thinks you over-young!"

He put his arm around her and gave her a squeeze. "Order a new gown, chuck. Don't think of the cost. I know Kate wants to put on a great show for all these foreigners. I'll pay for it."

"But, Hal, you've been spending so much!"

He laughed. "Wake up, Mary, wake up! I'm not my father. Let me tell you something—" He lowered his voice as they passed a group of guards. "I bearded our accountants in their stuffy old den the other day. I wanted to know what was in the treasury. They wouldn't tell me at first." He frowned, remembering their stubborn protests. "But they sang a different tune when I said they might lose their heads."

Until Mary saw the quick blood rise in his face and the hard set of his jaw, she thought he was joking. Her laughter died suddenly. He had meant every word of it, he told her, and he had jerked a cowardly, sniveling scribe off his high stool by one ear, sending him to bring Thomas Wolsey.

" 'Fetch my Chief Almoner,' " I said, and he scuttled off like a frightened hare. Wolsey had the figures for me in a moment. And what figures! Our father left me thousands and thousands and thousands—"

Struck by a fresh idea, he changed the subject. "Make them find you some marigold velvet," he suggested. "Band it with sable, Mary, and trim it with hundreds of those tawny gems, whatever they are."

"Topaz?"

"Yes. Topaz. And work on your languages between now and then, puss. If you could talk French and Italian and Spanish to these envoys it would please Kate. Let them see what a clever sister we have." With a pat and a kiss, he moved away. "I must find Brandon. We're planning a masque for our foreign guests and another little surprise for after the banquet."

"Could I take part?"

He halted, considering her question. "Well, not in the masque, I'm afraid. Our lords and ladies have been given their lines and I believe Kate will want you by her side. But why couldn't you be one of our Oriental beauties? Let me tell you our other scheme, Mary." He bent over her and whispered enthusiastically. "A group of us plan to slip away soon after the dancing begins and disguise ourselves. . . ."

42

The Queen and the chief Ambassador from Spain were dancing the lively coranto, their running steps so graceful and their coupees so agile that no one saw the King and Princess leave the Great Hall. "Don't primp too long," he told her as he made his way to one retiring room and hurried her off to another. "I expect the other ladies are ready and waiting."

A few minutes later, six heavily veiled women joined a half-dozen masked men clad in rich Oriental robes. They greeted each other with hoots of delighted laughter.

"They may recognize you, Sire, because you are so tall," said one of the women, "but I don't imagine even you know which one of us is her Highness." Turning to Mary, she pulled down the black gauze headdress so that it more completely hid her head and neck. "What a brilliant plan to have us all garbed alike!"

There was no fanfare of trumpets to announce their entrance; the King and his playmates simply made their way into the hall as unobtrusively as possible and mingled with the other guests, the fantastic blue and crimson costumes of the men and the somber, sable robes of the six Egyptian ladies adding a bizarre note to the whole assemblage.

For Mary it began as an hour of pure delight. Never before had she been free to dance with any man, regardless of his rank. Protected by her disguise, she might even dare to flirt a little—if, that is, she spoke seldom and laughed less.

So when, after a romping pillow dance, one of the younger French visitors suggested a stroll in search of fresher air, she hesitated only a moment, then nodded recklessly. Why not, she asked herself? Looking around the room she saw that two masked ladies were missing. If two could disappear for a few minutes, why not three? Who would know, now or later, which of the Egyptian women had been absent?

Her companion talked gaily as they passed through the first antechamber, pushing aside a crowd of students and apprentices who were allowed, as was the custom at Westminster, to stand quietly and watch their monarch and his guests making merry. As they turned into the vaulted stone corridor beyond, he pressed her to lift her veil or at least whisper her name. She shook her head, answering his protests with a chuckle and a murmured refusal.

The air was indeed fresher in the hallway; in fact, the drafts were so chill around Mary's velvet-slippered feet that she soon wished they had remained in the stuffier hall.

She shivered. "Come, sir," she whispered, "It's much too cold here. Take me back, please."

He drew her into a deep window embrasure and slipped an arm around her waist. "No need to be cold, *ma petite*," he said. "I know the sweetest way to warm you. But first"—he held her a little tighter—"first, we must rid you of this dark entanglement—" As he reached for her veil, Mary, frightened now, pulled herself free and turned to run away, holding the gauzy covering closely over her head. But he caught her again, this time in a firmer grip.

"No, no, my lady! Not without a kiss and a glimpse of your face!" Although he laughed as he said it, there was something about the look in the Frenchman's eyes, the sound of his voice, and the touch of his hands that made Mary's heart beat faster. It was madness, of course, but for a moment she wished he would carry out his threat. Then sanity returned and she began struggling frantically, pounding at him with her fists and kicking hard at his ankles.

"Let me go! Let me go!" Her muffled wail reached the ears of one of the other maskers, just emerging from a retiring room farther down the hall. A second later she was free, her rescuer standing between her and the Frenchman. Before he spoke, she had the dreadful thought that this tall, strong man in blue and crimson must be her brother; she shrank back into the shadows, hoping desperately that he would not insist on knowing who she was.

"You must forgive me, monsieur, for interfering in your sport." At his first word Mary heaved a sigh of relief. Thank God, it was only Charles Brandon! "But our customs here in England differ, I see, from yours. We don't force our attentions on unwilling ladies, masked or unmasked." His voice was icily courteous. "May I suggest that you return to the hall? I will be happy to see that your partner reaches her friends without further annoyance."

The young man bowed and hurried away, suddenly remembering, no doubt, that the first rule for an ambassador in a foreign court is to avoid trouble.

"Thank you," Mary whispered faintly.

"You may well thank me, your Highness," Brandon answered sternly. "What, in God's name, possessed you to do such a rash thing? A pretty tale that Frenchy would have taken home to King Louis. The English Princess is such a light-skirt that she invites kisses in dark halls!"

"He thought me one of the ladies. He won't ever know, Charles."

"But he would have, if I hadn't happened by when I did. And you may be sure that when you and the King unveil with the rest of us he will wonder."

Mary shuddered. "Yes, I suppose he will. You are right, as you always are. It was stupid of me and I am truly grateful. Truly, Charles." As they started back, she tried to explain how it had come about. "I meant no harm. Just a stroll in search of fresh air. You have no idea how delicious it was to feel free for a little while, free to come and go, without trumpets and ushers and maids-in-waiting!"

Sir Charles's voice softened. "But I do know, child. For all our sakes, though, be more careful another time."

When they reached one of the side entrances Charles swung Mary right onto the floor among the other dancers without missing a step.

"Your gallant is at the far end of the hall, with his back to us," he told her. "Seek out some of the other veiled ladies when the music stops, and mix with them for a while. If he is still watching for you he will never be sure which Egyptian maid is which." A sudden thought struck Mary as she agreed. "But how did you know it was I, Charles? Back there in the corridor, I mean?"

His answer came slowly. "Your littleness. Your scent. Something told me it was you."

By early summer the Queen was pregnant again and under strict orders from her physicians to avoid any exertion, orders which she obeyed to the letter. Nothing must endanger *this* baby.

45

If necessary, she said, she would remain in bed for the whole nine months.

The doctors smiled and assured her that she need not guard herself quite that closely but agreed that the Princess Mary should take her place even oftener than she had before. Much as the girl enjoyed playing companion to her brother, there came a time in late July when her bounding energy and blithe spirits showed signs of flagging.

The spring months had been warmer than usual, and the fourteen-year-old princess found herself making excuses to stay in her cool apartments at Greenwich, leaving Henry to hunt and hawk with his gentlemen; and at night she fell into the habit of slipping away to bed while the rest of the Court was still dancing, often crying herself to sleep. No one understood her, she felt, and her future looked bleak.

After watching her with a knowing eye, Lady Guildford asked for a private audience with the King. "I think, Sire," she said, "that the Lady Mary would benefit by a change of scene and a rest from the gaiety of the Court. With your permission, I would like to take her to Eltham, perhaps, or to Wanstead, to rusticate for a few weeks."

He looked alarmed. "Is she ill, Gilly?"

"No. Merely changing from girl to woman, a process that tends to cloud the sunniest disposition." She shook her gray head ruefully. "I shall always remember how difficult it was to please the Lady Margaret in that year before her marriage. But you, my lord, were too young to notice such a thing."

"Oh, no, Gilly!" The King laughed. "Indeed I was not. Meg turned into a shrew. But she still is, if what our Scottish friends say is true."

"Don't forget that the poor child was thrust at a very early age into what appears to be a most unhappy marriage. And she was never the merry little grig our Mary is—or was."

She leaned forward and patted Henry's large hand. "Let me take the lass away for a while. I promise to bring back the giddy companion we both have been missing recently."

When Lady Guildford told Mary that they were to retire to the old palace at Eltham for the rest of the summer, the girl first answered flatly that she would not go, then agreed, rather sulkily, to try a few weeks there with her governess.

"The whole idea is ridiculous," she fretted. "Why should we leave Greenwich where we do have a few fresh breezes from the river? Eltham will be intolerable!"

Lady Guildford admitted to herself that her charge was not entirely wrong. Eltham was encircled by woods and marsh; but she knew that what Mary needed most was rest and quiet and one could not be sure of either at Greenwich, Richmond, or Windsor, as the King and Queen moved from one to another of their country homes with little warning. As for London, that was impossible; only those unfortunate people who could not afford to leave it were willing to endure the smells and flies that came with July and August.

But much to Mary's surprise, she was so completely content at Eltham that she almost dreaded the thought of leaving it. The beautiful gardens, planned by her late father, and the unusually handsome Great Hall, with its exquisite windows, lofty roof, and delicate stone tracery, became home to her; she let the hours drift by as she wandered around the old quadrangular building, free to go wherever she wished. There was no "Queen's House" and "King's House" as there must be when the Court was in residence. It was merely a quiet, almost deserted palace, with a wide moat and a surprising view of the spire of St. Paul's, the roof of Westminster Abbey and, nearer at hand, the trees of Greenwich park.

Her bubbling spirits and glowing health returned long before the summer was over, and Lady Guildford was pleased to see that they were slightly subdued by a new and most attractive air of dignity. She much preferred this gay, charming, well-mannered young lady to the romping, reckless tomboy, and it was her hope that the King would, too. That he had been missing his sister was clearly evident; the gifts that arrived every week or so made that apparent—a hart he had killed himself, a pair of red shoes with enchanting toe roses, a copy of his latest song, peaches from the walled garden at Greenwich, and, best of all, or so Mary thought, a new little merlin to take the place of her favorite, killed that summer in a battle with a wild hawk.

When she rejoined them at Richmond early in September, the

King and Queen greeted her with open arms. "We have been dull without you," said Henry, kissing her loudly. "The months have been hot and tedious."

The Queen gave him an odd, veiled glance that puzzled Mary. For the first time since their marriage she sensed a restraint between them, a slight coolness. And although Catherine seemed well and strong in this sixth month of her pregnancy, she was no longer the starry-eyed bride.

Later that evening, having returned unattended to her bedchamber to have a rent mended in the hem of her gown, Mary overheard a short conversation that explained the change in her sister-in-law. At first, deep in her own thoughts, she had paid little attention to the gossipy talk in the next room beween Lady Guildford and one of Catherine's ladies. Then, without really meaning to, she found herself eavesdropping.

"You and the Lady Mary," she heard Señora de Casseris say, "missed the very large scandal while you were at Eltham. A very large scandal! Lady Stafford was caught all alone in a bedchamber here at Richmond with one of the King's gentlemen."

"Lady Stafford?" Gilly sounded to Mary as if she couldn't believe her ears. "The Duke of Buckingham's sister? Surely not, Señora!"

"But surely yes, milady! There was no concealing it, I promise you, for the whole palace was in what you call an 'uproar.' Her husband dragged her off to a convent and the King had her innocent sister dismissed from Court." She paused, as if she were savoring her little tale. "And the anger of the Duke was something to behold—he shouted that his Majesty had been unfair and stormed away from the palace, vowing he'd not spend another night under the royal roof."

"Who was the guilty man?"

Mary had been wondering herself and hoping, for some reason, that it wasn't Sir Charles Brandon. She moved a bit closer to the half-open door to hear Señora de Casseris answer Gilly's question.

"It was Lord Compton who was discovered with her that night, but we think now he was not the lady's lover. He was playing go-between. *Royal* go-between, if you know what I mean!"

There was a horrified gasp from Lady Guildford, then a burst of indignation. "How dare you repeat such a story to me, Señora? You, one of her Majesty's ladies! You must be mad or a fool! Certainly I would be a fool to listen to any more of your vicious insinuations. Pray excuse me!" And before Mary could move from her listening post, Lady Guildford had swept into the bedchamber and slammed the door behind her. Startled at finding her young charge close beside her, she stopped abruptly.

"You here, Mary? Alone? And listening, I suppose?"

The Princess nodded miserably, too upset by what she'd heard to defend herself. She pointed to the tear in her gown. "I came back to have it mended."

The older woman studied Mary's flushed face for a moment, then drew her to a chair. "I wish you hadn't heard that distasteful bit of gossip, child, but you did, and a scolding won't change that. So you must simply take my advice now and forget it. Put it right out of your mind. It may be true, or it may be false; I don't know. I do know it isn't our business. Just tell yourself that the King wouldn't be the first man to seek other company when his wife is pregnant. . . ."

Mary said sadly, "I suppose not."

One of the tiring women joined them at that moment, a threaded needle in her hand, and nothing more was said. But it took the Princess some time to regain her tranquillity and to convince herself that Gilly was right. It was *not* her business if Henry was unfaithful to Kate at this time, or any other time, for that matter.

Nor, she told herself firmly, would it have been any concern of hers if Sir Charles Brandon had been Lady Stafford's lover. The doctors said that poor Lady Anne Brandon would never regain her senses, so neither she nor anyone else could blame him if he took a mistress. Shuddering, Mary remembered the day when Charles's wife had been thrown from her horse in the paved courtyard at Westminster; it had seemed impossible, then, that she would live more than a few hours, but that was over a year ago, and she still lingered on, a feeble body to be fed and cleansed.

It was a tragedy, of course, but it would have been an even sadder story if her marriage to Charles had been a love match.

49

As it was, he had immersed himself in the busy life at Court soon after her accident, more than ever grateful for his duties there and for the King's constant demands for his companionship. As she had preferred living in the country, Anne Brandon had been rarely at Court anyway, so she was not much missed. Charles had visited her when the King was willing to excuse him from his duties, but it was obvious to all their friends that Sir Charles and Lady Brandon had been quite content to live apart.

Thinking back over Charles's matrimonial situation, Mary wondered how one man could become so entangled in problems and difficulties. Of course, he was only a child when his parents betrothed him to Anne, the little daughter of Sir Anthony Browne, and still a very young man when the Lady Margaret Mortimer, a voluptuous widowed kinswoman, seduced him into wedding her instead. That Lady Margaret had taken advantage of the lad was common knowledge; no one at Court had a good word to say for her, and when Charles, pleading a previous contract and consanguinity with his wife, had their marriage annulled, everyone felt he had done the right thing.

And perhaps he had been right, too, in making good his contract with Anne Browne; at least, Mary told herself, his conscience was then clear. What if they didn't love each other? Many a marriage flourished when there was nothing but mild affection between husband and wife, and if Anne had not been thrown from her horse they might have gone on very comfortably together.

At this point Mary admitted that, as far as she was concerned, it was extremely pleasant to have Charles still living at Court as a virtual bachelor. She and Henry would miss him if, after all these years of close and constant companionship, he should ever choose to retire to the country. But there was little fear of that; gay, delightful, energetic Charles had apparently put his troubles behind him and seemed as happy as any of the King's gentlemen. If his difficulties had made him kind and thoughtful —and he was always at hand when you needed him—they had not broken his spirit or turned him into a dullard. Mary smiled. No, Charles could never be called a dullard!

As the autumn waned, the atmosphere at Court grew easier and the royal couple were almost as affectionate as they had been before the Stafford affair, although Catherine, Mary was sorry to see, never recaptured her happy radiance. But she and the King seemed determined to celebrate Christmas that year even more merrily than usual, giving orders that no holiday custom must be forgotten. Yule logs were dragged in and burned in the wide hearths, wassail bowls steamed on every table, mummers danced and sang, bands of carolers roamed the halls, and every room in the rambling palace at Richmond was trimmed with bright-berried holly and branches, garlands, and wreaths of fragrant greens from the nearby woods. Mistletoe hung from doorways and rafters, and any maid who walked through a hall or chamber without being kissed at least once had cause to feel sadly slighted.

Shortly before the end of December, the Queen retired to her apartments to await her baby. New Year's Eve came and went and no little prince or princess had arrived to make memorable the passing of 1510. Mary went to bed disappointed; she had been sure, somehow, that the infant would be born that night. She was, as it happened, not too far wrong, for Catherine's pains began early the next morning, and everyone whose privilege it was to witness the royal birth was roused and summoned to the Queen's bedchamber.

Mary decided to remain in the adjoining room. It was painful enough to hear the muffled sounds of Catherine's agony; she found she had no desire to watch it. Lady Guildford joined her there, the two women talking quietly together as the hours dragged by. The withdrawing room filled, the halls outside the royal apartments were crowded with nobles awaiting news, and, in a courtyard below the windows sat a messenger on a swift horse, ready to carry word to the Tower of London, where loaded guns would boom out to inform the city of the birth.

"Hush!" A gentleman standing nearest the bedchamber door held up his hand. In the silence that followed, Mary distinctly heard an infant's wail and the murmur of excited voices. Five minutes passed. Ten—

Suddenly the door was thrown open and the King stepped proudly over the threshold, a small bundle in his arms. He stood there, his feet planted wide apart, his red head high and his small eyes gleaming.

"A prince," he announced loudly. "A prince for England!"

CHAPTER V

INSTEAD OF WATCHING the King, as he and his gentlemen danced with the six beautiful masked ladies, the laughing crowd of apprentices, students, seamen and peddlers, who had been allowed in to see the evening's entertainment, were staring with fascinated eyes at the elaborate golden arbor which had been drawn back to their end of the long banqueting hall. When Henry and his five young men had pulled it up to where the Queen sat on her throne, their six dancing partners were sitting in it, framed becomingly by the silk and satin flowers, which looked amazingly real twined around its glittering pillars. Now it was empty and abandoned; it had served its purpose.

It was understood, here at Westminster, that a certain number of townspeople would always be given permission to view the royal frolics, as long, that is, as they were quiet, orderly, and remained in the places allotted them. A much coveted privilege, of course, and the Palace rules were always scrupulously obeyed.

But tonight the proximity of the unguarded arbor was too tempting and a shabby arm reached out and plucked a silken hawthorn, another snatched a velvet pomegranate, a third tore loose a strip of gilt ribbon. It was stealthily done and stealthily finished, and by the time the dance was over the little building was bare.

"Sir! Sir!" A frightened lackey pulled at the sleeve of the Palace Steward, who was standing contentedly in a place of honor near the royal dais. "Look, sir! They've stripped the arbor and we can't make them move back."

Muttering threats of dire punishment, the Steward hurried to the far end of the hall and did his best to shoo the milling mass of Londoners into their accustomed place. When he saw that it could not be done without interrupting the entertainment—and this was a very special festivity tonight, planned to celebrate the birth of little Prince Henry—he threw up his hands in a gesture of despair, stationed several guards in front of the troublemakers, and returned to his post, flushed and angry. His careless staff would suffer for this tomorrow; tonight the gaiety must go on.

His Majesty, happily ignorant of what was happening at the far end of the room, was enjoying himself thoroughly. This was no casual performance. Every bit of it had been carefully rehearsed, and he and Mary and the ten other ladies and gentlemen were fully and completely occupied in following the intricate steps and figures, and in making sure that they began each dance with the correct partner.

When the final and most complicated dance of all was finished, the King, panting and red-faced, blew his Queen a kiss and bowed low to his shouting, applauding, stamping audience.

"Here!" He beckoned to a group of young and pretty noblewomen who were seated nearby. "Come pluck a letter from my doublet!"

As they rushed to obey him, he leaned forward, ripped a golden C that had been basted on Mary's gown, and tossed it to a lady on the other side of the room. "Keep it to remember this happy evening," he called to her.

In a moment the floor was crowded with lords and ladies all reaching for the royal initials which trimmed the maskers' costumes, ruffling, and even tearing the satin gowns and doublets as they pulled them loose. The King, throwing back his red head, roared with laughter, obviously delighted at the bedlam he had created.

Turning from side to side, as he submitted himself to the eager fingers of his courtiers, he waved more and more spectators over to join them, still not aware of the mass of townspeople, herded together at the far end of the hall. The guards were holding them back with great difficulty now, their orders and threats lost in the shouting, laughing, and cheering of the nobles.

"Come on, lads!" suddenly called out a tattered street urchin,

53

his eyes on Henry's waving arms. "His Majesty means us!" And the impatient Londoners, made reckless by their success in pillaging the arbor, were past the guards in a flash. A moment later it was *their* fingers jerking at the golden letters, pushing aside the bejeweled royal guests.

Before the stunned Court quite realized what had happened, the mob was completely out of control. When the initials were gone they tore off the ladies' necklaces and the gentlemen's gold chains, then they began on their satin gowns and doublets. The King, still laughing, was soon stripped to his drawers, and Sir Thomas Knevet, who, after resisting hotly, had climbed far up the scaffold nearest him, found himself trapped there and at the mercy of ten lusty apprentices.

"Hoy—here's his shirt for you, Tom!"

"A stocking—a stocking!"

"Save half those drawers for me, George boy!"

Mary, hopelessly engulfed in the seething mass, looked up through her mask to see a completely naked man standing alone at the top of the scaffold, trying to cover his genitals with his hands. She gave a gasp of horror, then forgot Knevet's plight as a leering face loomed in front of her and five strong fingers ripped her gown all the way down to her waist.

She screamed. Her assailant cursed and ran, and a moment later someone behind her scooped her up, lifted her high over the heads of the crowd, and carried her swiftly out of the hall. She clutched her bodice together, then bent down to see her rescuer's face.

"Charles." It was a statement, rather than an exclamation or question. With what sounded strangely like a purr, she leaned back, settling herself more securely in his arms. Brandon said nothing as he strode quickly through the anteroom and down the outside corridor. He apparently did not even see the startled faces of the palace guards, as he passed them.

"Where are we going?" There was a ripple of laughter in Mary's voice that showed she sensed the absurdity of the picture they must make—the tall, angry-faced nobleman carrying a masked girl in a torn satin gown.

"As far away from that madhouse as possible," he answered. "Mother of God, Mary, this masking nonsense has gone too far!

Hal must be crazed to subject you to such indignities! A princess of the Blood being stripped by the rabble—"

He turned a corner and headed for a small writing closet, sure to be empty at this hour of the evening. "First you risk your honor at the hands of that Frenchman, and now this—this horror happens!" He was almost shouting at her by the time they reached the doorway.

When he had carried her inside Mary ripped off her mask. As she did so she felt something brush against her cheek. There, dangling from a low rafter, was a withered branch of mistletoe, forgotten, dry, and dusty.

She chuckled. "Look, Charles, mistletoe!" On impulse she lifted her face to his and watched the angry expression fade out of his brown eyes as he bent to give her the casual kiss she expected. His lips met hers lightly, then, as she drew away, they sought hers again, hotly this time, fiercely. Without quite realizing what she was doing, Mary's kisses answered his. Lost in the rapture of this delicious new sensation, she threw both arms around his neck and drew his face even closer, completely forgetting her torn gown.

"Great God!" Charles suddenly raised his lips from hers and wrenched her arms free. He thumped her down on the nearest window seat with such force that he hurt her small, rounded bottom.

"What in the name of all that's holy am I doing?"

"Kissing me, Charles," she said dreamily. "And I liked it. Very much. Oh, very much. Must we stop?"

Charles stared at her, aghast. "Of course we must stop! Hasn't anyone told you that kissing is no sport for princesses? Here." He handed her the mask. "Tie this on again, and for God's sake do something about your gown. I'll fetch one of your ladies."

Mary sat very still for a moment or two after Brandon strode out of the room, then she replaced her mask and hurried away, holding the edges of her torn bodice together in one trembling hand. Deeply shaken by his lovemaking, she decided to seek the seclusion of her own rooms. Let them look for me, she told herself, as she sped through the corridors and up the stairs. She would not, no, she would *not* go back and be forced to talk and laugh and eat—

She opened the door to her bedchamber and stepped quietly inside. Her tiring woman was crouched on a stool by the fire, so sound asleep that Mary hated to wake her. Poor old Dorothy, she thought, she had probably counted on at least two more hours in which to rest. As she discarded her mask, the Princess coughed. The woman opened bewildered eyes, then jumped to her feet, horrified.

"Your Highness, I—" Her voice was frightened and apologetic.

"It's quite all right, Dorothy," Mary said. "You certainly had no reason to expect me at this early hour. But, as you see, my gown is ruined. Some of the townspeople set on us in the hall and spoiled our clothes. It was all in fun, of course, but it frightened me and I want to go right to bed. Help me disrobe, and send anyone away who comes to inquire for me." She began stripping off the satin garments, dropping them on the floor for Dorothy to pick up. "And I don't want you to go and rouse Lady Guildford. She retired early tonight and I see no reason to disturb her."

The maid had just helped her mistress into her bedrail when there was a knock on the antechamber door. While Dorothy hurried off to see who it was, Mary climbed quickly into the large carved bed, drawing the curtains on the side nearest the other room. She heard the murmur of voices, then the sound of the door into the outside corridor closing.

"It was Lady Anne Howard," Dorothy reported. "His Majesty has ordered supper served in his own apartments and everyone is to sit down in their tattered garments. She said to tell you it will be a very gay frolic."

"I'm sure it will," answered Mary. "But, for all of that, I shall stay right here in my comfortable bed. Send a page with my excuses, say my head aches," ordered the Princess. "Draw the rest of these curtains, Dorothy, and leave me. When my ladies return, ask them to sleep in the other room as I don't wish to be wakened."

Alone at last in the quiet, darkened bedchamber, Mary settled back on her silken pillows and snuggled deep in the covers, reliving those moments in Charles's arms. Tomorrow, she exulted to herself. Surely, tomorrow she would see him alone, somehow. She must! And he would forget that nonsense about not kissing her again.

A princess, she knew to her sorrow, must wed for state reasons; but fortunately that dreaded event would not happen for some time. Why should a princess not, she argued, enjoy herself a little in the meantime? All the other unmarried maids indulged in a bit of lovemaking now and then; there could be no harm in it. Everyone must have something happy to remember in the difficult years to come, the years when you are tied to a stranger, sharing his bed and bearing his children. Charles would understand, and agree that there was really no reason why they should not be happy while they could; she would explain it all to him tomorrow.

Falling asleep at last, she wakened the next morning with a smile on her lips. The day ahead seemed full of wonderful possibilities, and she chuckled as she asked Dorothy to bring one of her most becoming gowns, thinking of how she would tease Charles into admitting that kissing *was* "sport for princesses."

It was unusually early. Her ladies were still asleep and there was no sign of Lady Guildford when the young Princess left her rooms and slipped down the stairs, hoping to find her brother and Brandon up and planning some morning ride or game. Too early, she soon decided, for the long halls and huge rooms were almost deserted, the guards yawning in the doorways and the scene of last night's excitement not yet restored to order. She peeked in at the white hall, and saw the scaffolds being dismantled by a crew of workers; a dozen maidservants were clearing up the littered floor, and the naked arbor was just being wheeled out of sight.

A sudden impulse took her into the writing closet. She smiled to herself as she glanced around it, one hand rubbing the still tender place on her bottom. A second later she was standing on a chair under the shriveled sprig of mistletoe. The dried berries had almost all fallen off, but some of the leaves remained; Mary broke off a piece and tucked it quickly inside her velvet bodice before she replaced the chair and returned to her rooms.

At first she settled down with a book, but after a few minutes she tossed it aside and sat quietly, looking dreamily into the fire.

When Lady Guildford joined her, followed by Anne Howard and Lady Bess Percy, she was half asleep.

"I've been hearing a pretty tale of last night's doings," said Lady Guildford, after they all exchanged greetings. "Our ladies tell me you were so roughly used that you retired before supper."

Mary nodded. "My gown was completely ruined, Gilly. I was too tired to change so I went right to bed."

Bess Percy laughed her infectious laugh. "You missed a merry meal, your Highness. The King had us all sit down in our tattered finery and I've never seen such a disheveled group! Tom Knevet borrowed somebody's cloak and his Majesty bound it around his middle for him with a curtain cord—" She turned to Lady Guildford to explain. "The rabble stripped poor Tom to the buff, madam, and there he stood—stark naked! He *couldn't* come to the table as he was—"

"It may seem a great joke to you, Bess, but I find your story shocking." Lady Guildford looked extremely distressed. "The King's own sister, and his lords and ladies, mauled and mishandled—"

"Fortunately," said Mary, "I was still masked."

"Well, masks or no masks, I must see that such a thing never happens again. I suppose I'm partly to blame. I should have been there."

"Nonsense, Gilly dear. You couldn't have prevailed on that wild mob. No one could!"

"It was a costly adventure for me," added Anne Howard, ruefully. "My best pearl necklace was snatched off my neck and carried away. The King just laughed. 'Think of it as largess to the commonalty,' he said."

Lady Guildford shook her gray head and pursed her lips, wondering if she might risk a private talk with the young monarch. He had, in the past, taken her scolding in good part; but he was King now, after all, and could well resent even the best intentioned interference in his pleasure. Later, perhaps. She would decide later.

The day having now begun for the nobles residing at Westminster, a stream of visitors kept Mary busy for the rest of the morning, all eager to discuss the events of the preceding evening and curious as to why she had deserted them so early. As she listened and answered, she watched the door, waiting to see a certain tall, broad-shouldered, dark-haired young man. When her brother popped in to call her a faint-heart, she peered around him. Where was Charles? He was usually at his royal master's heels.

In her sudden disappointment she fell silent, finding it impossible, for once, to laugh back at her brother and cap his jokes. He looked at her with astonishment, then concern.

"Is something amiss, Mary?"

She flushed. "No, no, Hal. I'm feeling a little weary, that's all."

He rose immediately and swept everyone out of the room. "Then rest until dinnertime, sis. We're tilting this afternoon and Kate will want you by her side. It's a fine sunny day—a perfect day for a tournament!"

Mary's heart rose at the thought. She was sure to see Charles at the tiltyard; he always played a leading part in the jousts. A word from him, a smile, a meaning glance—all she craved was the assurance that he, too, was remembering those wonderful moments in the writing closet. Then, later, they would arrange to meet in some deserted corner. . . .

It was, as the King had said, a perfect day for a tournament. As Mary and Catherine took their places on the royal dais, both women agreed that they hardly needed their fur-lined underskirts and capes. For the middle of February it was unusually warm, an afternoon of bright sun and no wind, with that soft hint of spring in the air that makes everyone forget how chill March is apt to be.

When Mary was settled comfortably on her cushioned bench slightly below the Queen's carved and gilded chair, she took advantage of the few minutes of noise and bustle around her to whisper a question in Catherine's ear.

"How is our little Prince, Kate?"

"The doctors say he's stronger today and that it's nothing but a bad cold. All infants have them in this chilly weather, I hear." But the Queen's face was worried and her voice hesitant. "Every time I ask Hal to let me return to Richmond the news turns encouraging, and I tell myself I'm a fool to fret. Still, I do think it might help the child to have his mother by his side, don't you?

How can I enjoy these celebrations when my heart is so torn?"

"I find it difficult myself. Let's both urge him to move the Court back there soon. If all is well with the babe we can be just as gay at Richmond as we are at Westminster. Gayer!"

Before they could say anything more the heralds blew a loud blast on their trumpets to open the tournament, and silence fell over the scaffolds packed with spectators; but when a strange, shabby figure appeared and made his way on foot across the tiltyard, instead of the customary challenger on horseback, a ripple of excitement ran over the crowd. He was tall, and dressed in the gray robe and lowly weeds of a poor hermit, his face concealed in the hood of his gown, his broad shoulders more than a little bent.

As he neared the dais Mary heard dozens of whispered questions and bewildered comments from the nobles seated around her. Was he a wandering religious, come to beg from the Queen? Some mad monk who had slipped by the guards? An assassin? Amused, she sat and watched them lean forward, all trying to see the cowled face; it would take more than a gray gown with a close hood to fool *her!* Her leaping pulse had warned her that this was no monk, no hermit, no religious. It was Charles, and this was some new mummery of her brother's. A happy thought occurred to her suddenly; he must be the first challenger, come in disguise to approach the lady of his choice. She steadied herself for his question, her answer ready on her lips. She stripped off one embroidered and jeweled glove and laid it in her lap. It would be her favor; he could wear it on his helmet.

The gray-clad figure was standing directly in front of her now and she smiled warmly at him, waiting for his dark eyes to meet hers. But when the hooded head was raised, it turned, instead, to the Queen. Charles's glance passed over the little Princess as if she was not there at all.

"I beg, your Gracious Majesty, the boon of tilting in your honor," his voice rang out so clearly that it could be heard from one end of the field to the other. "Will you allow a lowly hermit this great and much coveted privilege?"

Mary felt her upper lip trembling as Kate made a graceful answer and scolded herself for being so silly. Of course Charles had to choose Kate! All these tourneys were in the Queen's honor. How could she have been so stupid? She clapped her hands vigorously as Brandon stripped off his long robe and showed himself, already clad in his armor, to the applauding audience. And she was smiling delightedly when, as her Majesty's champion of proof, and wearing a ribbon from Catherine's sleeve, he challenged all comers in her name.

It was a fine and exciting tournament, with Brandon and King Henry, as usual, winning most of the matches. No one was seriously wounded today; the sun remained out, the bright trappings of the horses and the rich habits of the contestants made a brilliant picture, and the Queen was so well amused that she forgot her sick baby for a little while.

Her face was genuinely happy when the winners lined up before her, and she made a gay ceremony of awarding her prizes, reaching forward to give some with her own fingers, and handing the rest down to Mary. Several were for the King. These she delivered herself, with a proud smile. When Brandon stepped forward she had saved one for him, then indicated that the Princess would bestow the rest.

This was the moment that Mary had been waiting for, and, as she handed him several small packages, she managed to squeeze his gauntleted fist, her round eyes fixed expectantly on his strong-featured face.

"I thank you, your Highness." His voice was polite but distant and his eyes seemed to be intent on some point over the top of her head. He bent to kiss her hand, his lips barely touching it as he bowed, stepped aside, and made way for the next champion.

As the last man received his award, the heralds marched to the middle of the field and closed the tourney by crying out in chorus: "My lords, for your noble feats in arms, may God send you the love of the ladies you most desire!"

Somehow these familiar words, an echo from the days of chivalry, hurt the bewildered girl, and she followed the Queen from the dais with listless step, taking little part in the chatter of the other ladies, her mind busy with the problem of Charles's cold attitude. A headache was her answer when Lady Guildford asked what was making her so quiet, and it won her an hour alone in her bedchamber to think the matter out. When her governess came in to help her choose a gown for the evening's dancing, Mary had fully regained her usual high spirits, having convinced herself that Charles had been discreet, not indifferent. Tonight they would dance together, and then—

But they did not. While Henry danced with Mary twice, as did Lord Howard and young Percy, Sir Charles Brandon seemed to be kept busy on the other side of the hall, laughing and talking merrily as he danced, his dark head bent over first one fair lady and then another. He was especially attentive to pretty, honey-haired Bess Percy, and, when Mary saw him lead her out for the third time, she experienced her first agony of jealousy. "I'll have her sent from Court," she raged to herself while she tried to look happy.

She spent a wakeful night and was still tossing around on her pillows when Lady Guildford entered, her face set and anxious. "Get up, Mary, at once," she said. "Prince Henry is much, much worse, and we are all leaving for Richmond the moment the Queen is dressed."

That was the beginning of a long week of horror for everyone. The doctors fought desperately to save the infant's life, and the frantic mother spent most of her waking hours on her knees, praying, praying, praying. When Henry wasn't closeted with her, he paced around the palace by himself, having made it known that he was in no mood for companionship. The servants kept out of his way during these difficult days, too, having soon discovered that he was apt to behave like a wounded animal, lashing out at anyone who crossed his path. Even Mary wasn't safe from his tongue, so she retreated to her own quarters to weep and pray for her little nephew, her romantic troubles forgotten in the face of this real sorrow, this looming tragedy.

On February 22 the Prince died and much of the young King's boyishness died with him. The Court moved back to Westminster for elaborate funeral services, and Mary found herself wishing that she might never have to return to Richmond; the halls, she felt, would always echo with the Queen's screams and her brother's uncontrolled sobbing.

London was little better, but as March, April, and May dragged away, the worst of the grief seemed to have passed, although the Queen still spent most of her time at her prie-dieu, and Henry, more man now than lad, forgot his fancy tournaments and maskings as he turned to the serious duties of kinghood. War with France was on the horizon, and Scotland, despite its close family tie with the Tudors, was threatening to side with the French.

Mary changed, too. That romantic interlude with Brandon was now as if it had never happened, and, as she listened to her brother discussing the tense foreign situation, she rebuked herself for having been a silly child, going into daydreams and heartbreak over a casual kiss and caress. And if, perhaps, she and Charles had not quite regained their easy, brother-and-sister relationship, they were good friends again, dancing often together as before, meeting with a smile, parting with a pleasant word.

When the warm weather was imminent the Court went to Greenwich. A few days later Mary and Lady Guildford continued on to Eltham—this time at the girl's suggestion. They made the two-mile trip south from Greenwich with high hopes of enjoying this summer as much as they had the last, and found the old palace waiting for them, the gardens as breathtakingly beautiful as before, the Great Hall just as handsome, the moat as wide, the air as peaceful, and the whole place as completely at their disposal.

But the young Princess soon learned that it is almost impossible to repeat a happy experience: the contentment never came, somehow, and nothing seemed the same. There was, she thought, the suggestion of a foul smell from the moat; there were wasps in the garden and the sun was too hot. When she wandered into the Great Hall her eyes, instead of going to the lovely roses and foliage adorning the ceiling, were drawn to the hideously deformed men and beasts which someone had carved, many, many years before, over the northern cornice. For some odd reason she didn't want to have a palace all to herself this summer—Eltham was lonely instead of peaceful, and she was a lonely girl.

Often she was a disagreeable girl, so disagreeable that Lady Guildford sighed with relief when it was time to return to Greenwich. Much as she loved Mary, she had been wondering if perhaps some younger and stronger lady should not take her place.

But once back with the rest of the Court, their days were so full that the uneasy weeks at Eltham were forgotten and life returned to normal; Mary's voice regained its old happy lilt, her dimples were in evidence, and Lady Guildford laughed at herself for having thought she might relinquish her mercurial charge to anyone else.

Henry, Mary soon saw, was still absorbed in the thought of war. King Ferdinand, Catherine's father, had promised to join England in an invasion of France, and the young English ruler was impatient to know when and where it should begin. Messages and ambassadors streamed back and forth from one king to the other but it was apparent to Henry's most perspicacious advisers that the wily Spaniard was sending his more important information in letters to his daughter, relying on her to convince her husband of his sincerity and wisdom.

Henry listened to Ferdinand's evasions and asked blunter questions. He had sent his father-in-law many bands of archers to harry the French in Flanders and to use against the Moors; this was *his* pledge that he and King Ferdinand were allied in a mutual cause. What, he wanted to know, were they waiting for? Why could they not invade France now?

It was November before Don Luis Caroz, Ferdinand's ambassador, received orders from home that he might sign a treaty with Henry for a joint invasion of Gascony, beginning the following spring.

Why Gascony? asked the English. Because England, wrote the Spaniard to his daughter Queen Catherine, had long claimed Guienne, the adjacent duchy; and the citizens of Bordeaux, he assured her, would like nothing better than to be ruled by the British. If all this was not quite true, if Ferdinand had his own selfish reasons for this odd plan, neither Henry nor Kate suspected him of double dealing. It was good, they agreed, to have everything settled at last.

Christmas came and went with the usual festivities, but New Year's was celebrated very quietly by the royal couple for the anniversary of their little son's birth brought back only too vividly the sadness of the year before. To have had their much desired heir and then to have lost him was such a bitter memory that Catherine was, once again, the prey of grief, and spent long hours over her beads and prayerbooks.

During these holiday weeks Mary was extremely attentive, doing everything in her power to amuse the Queen and raise her spirits, and when Catherine, early on the day of Twelfthnight, announced that she was feeling too miserable to leave her apartments, the young Princess sent an order down to the kitchens that a special Epiphany cake must be baked for the occasion. There would be a huge one cut in the dining hall, as always, and whoever found the bean would be king or queen for the evening. This second, smaller cake was for Catherine and whatever guests she might have gathered around her.

When it was ready, Mary decided to carry the gaily decorated confection there herself, walking with greatest care over the uneven stone floors of the passages that led to the Queen's rooms. The King, Sir Thomas Knevet, Don Luis Caroz, the Earl of Surrey and his wife, Sir Charles Brandon, Compton, and six or seven ladies were clustered about the royal lady when she entered. Sir Charles leaped to his feet and took the cake out of Mary's hands, placing it, at her direction, on a table near the Queen. There was no opportunity, in the little bustle of arranging it and finding a knife, to express her surprise at seeing Sir Charles back here at Westminster. Lady Brandon had finally died two days after the New Year and he had been absent from Court, attending to all the unhappy details that follow death. As she watched him helping Catherine divide the cake among her guests, she decided that he seemed unusually serious and a little thinner than before; a natural result, of course, of the somber errand that had taken him away.

To the Queen's great delight, it was Don Luis Caroz who found the bean and Catherine herself explained the English custom to him and settled the hastily contrived crown on his head. Both quick-witted and inventive, the Spaniard made a most amusing king of their little revels, demanding such ridiculous attentions from his subjects that Catherine actually had tears of laughter in her dark eyes when she finally dismissed them all to go and join the merrymaking downstairs.

Content with the success of her surprise, Mary let most of them go on ahead. She descended the wide staircase slowly, almost wishing she need not now take Catherine's place at the other banquet. An unusually dim landing brought her to a sudden halt; it was much too dark for safety. A branch of candles had guttered out on the wall overhead, she noticed; a lackey must replace them immediately or someone might fall.

A footstep sounded behind her and, a moment later, Charles Brandon appeared at her side, smiling down on her.

"That cake was a most happy thought, Mary," he said. "The Queen was truly pleased, and so was Hal. He said to me, as I left the room, that he was a lucky man to have such a sister."

His words were sweet and so unexpected that Mary's eyes filled. Not wanting Charles to see her tears, she moved ahead of him, and, forgetting to watch where she was going, she missed the top step. With a frightened oath, he leaped forward and caught her.

"Good God, Mary," he said, lifting her back on to the landing, "you could have been killed!" His arms tightened around her and she began to tremble, her heart beating wildly. Closer and closer he held her until her cheek was pressed against his chest and she could feel *his* heart, pounding too. The long months that had elapsed since their first kiss melted away and Mary's conviction of Charles's indifference melted with them. She was in his arms again and nothing else mattered. With a rapturous sigh she raised herself on tiptoe and lifted her face for his kiss.

For a long, bewildering moment Charles still held her close, then he released her, suddenly, and stepped away. "What a lucky thing," he said, clearing his throat slightly, "that I was here. But why is it so dark?" Glancing around the landing, he noticed the burned-out candles and shook his head. "It's no wonder you stumbled! We must report this carelessness, Mary, or someone else will fall. And whoever is responsible should be beaten so severely that it won't happen again. Here," he held out his hand. "Let me guide you down."

Mary said nothing until they reached the hall below; when she felt the solid stones of the hallway under her feet she pulled her fingers away and tried to smile gratefully. "Good night, my lord," and her voice was almost natural. "Thank you for catching me. I would have had a nasty tumble."

"Good night?" Charles sounded puzzled. "But aren't you coming to the banquet?"

"Oh. Of course." Mary gave a shaky little laugh. "How stupid of me! For a moment I thought I was on my way to bed." As I would like to be, she said to herself; as I would give anything to be! Could she plead a headache, she wondered? No, the King and all his guests expected her in the banqueting hall and there would be too many questions tomorrow. Besides, what good would it do to run and hide and play the lovesick fool again?

And looking up at the tall, dark-eyed man who was walking by her side, Mary resolved that, for her own sake, she must see as little of him as possible from now on. There had been much speculation about him when his wife died; she had heard all the maids wondering whether the handsome Sir Charles Brandon would marry again. She had wondered herself until Henry had more or less settled the question. "If he listens to me," the King had said, "Brandon will wed that rich ward of his. The Grey child. She won't be old enough for some time, of course, but Charles won't mind that. He's heart-whole, he enjoys playing the bachelor, and with her great fortune she's a wife worth waiting for."

Well, why shouldn't he "enjoy playing the bachelor"? It would not be with her, certainly; he had made that abundantly clear, and a painful sob rose in her throat as she pictured him flirting with Bess or Nan or—anyone. If she could only go away, have a house of her own, perhaps. Would Henry give her one and allow her to leave his Court?

Her heart lifted a little at the thought. She would wait for just the right moment, she decided, and ask him.

It was easier now to smile at Charles. "Well, Charles," she said, "we should have a pleasant evening. I wonder who will find the bean in Hal's cake?"

CHAPTER VI

MARY PULLED HER CHAIR a little deeper into the shadow cast by the barge's striped awning and tapped her foot, her patience wearing thin. Was Hal going to blow another blast on his absurd gold whistle? *Must* he have one three times larger than the Lord Admiral's and stuck all over with lumpy jewels? And couldn't he see how he was slowing the workmen on the dock, that they were so awed by his presence that they were neglecting their tasks? How could they possibly keep on with their hammering and scraping and painting while he was strutting up and down like a gaudy parrot in his scarlet hose, cloth-of-gold breeches, and that odd, long, gold brocade vest?

"Galley-fashion," he had said when he had first appeared in it. "As supreme head of the Navy, I must dress galley-fashion."

Galley-fashion! Mary's sense of humor returned, and when he blew his whistle again she merely smiled indulgently.

As a matter of fact, she reminded herself, she was grateful for these daily visits that the King insisted on making to London's busy dockyards; they took his mind off his worries. She sighed. It had been a wretched winter and the spring had been no better, with Hal fretting day and night because Ferdinand was not using the ten thousand archers sent from England to help him take Guienne. Instead, he was keeping them in dangerous idleness, cooped up under the blistering sun of San Sebastian. Even Mary knew that this could result in serious trouble.

In the circumstances, it was better for him to be here, content in the thought that he was being useful, than back in the Council Chamber, harrying his advisers. Most men, Mary knew, found everything about ships and shipbuilding fascinating, and Henry was no exception. The piles of lumber, the coils of rope, the bales and boxes and waiting guns, the barrels and hogsheads; all the supplies and materials standing around on the dock spelled adventure. And the ship itself, with its high, elaborately decorated forecastle and poop deck towering over the little royal barge made Mary herself yearn to be at sea instead of in stifling, stinking London.

She watched an agile young man climb the masthead and begin regilding the huge crown, then turned her attention to the crew of workmen who were touching up the carved bowsprits with gold and copper. It was finicky work, to be sure, but more rewarding, certainly, than the dull task of covering the huge hull with Henry's favorite green paint. Dozens of men were painting away at it out there in the broiling sun, some hanging from ropes, others standing on flat rafts tied to the side of the ship; all were stripped to the waist, their bodies glistening with sweat, and here and there among the brown shoulders and chests, Mary noticed a few that ranged from pale pink to bright red. Their first day on the dock, she surmised, and a day that was going to end in masses of painful blisters.

A breeze rippled the surface of the Thames and set the barge rocking from side to side, but it was still so warm on board the flat vessel that the girl was relieved when she saw her brother approaching, followed by his gentlemen. As they leaped onto the deck, her eyes met those of the tallest of the young men; her heartbeat quickened for a moment, but she forced herself to look away and speak casually to the King, commenting on the handsome ship he had been inspecting.

"It will be Howard's flagship," he told her, pleased at her interest. "My Lord Admiral must have the very best we can provide." Beaming down at her, he wiped the sweat off his red face with the back of one hairy hand.

Mary leaned forward to read the name on its stern. "The *Mary Ann*. For our Lord Admiral, Hal? I don't like it. It sounds like a fat fisherman's wife with a babe at her breast."

Henry laughed. "We'll change it. Why not the *Mary Rose*? For my favorite sister and favorite flower. I'll give the order tomorrow."

Before Mary could thank him, he turned away and began talking to his Esquire of the Body. "Hot work, eh, Brandon? But we'll ready them, lad, we'll ready them!" He pointed to Thomas Wolsey, a stocky figure in his priest's robe, still moving purposefully from dock to shipside and back again, a long roll of parchment in his plump hand. "That Almoner of mine is a

69

wonder. On my faith, Charles, he's doing the work of ten men, or twenty. He has everything in hand—everything. Guns, biscuits, cod, beef, uniforms, sails, ale; that list he's carrying would make your head split! And believe me, he wastes no time in discussing how things should be done. Not Wolsey. He does 'em. If we need more breweries, up they go. When our windmills don't grind fast enough he builds water mills. One of the wisest things my father ever did was to give him a place in his household. Lowborn he may be, but I wouldn't trade him for half a dozen earl's sons."

As the barge pulled away from the wharf, Mary's two ladies, the Lady Anne Howard, sister of the Lord Admiral, and the Lady Elizabeth Percy, left their seats to stroll around the deck with Charles and Lord Compton. The young King, left alone with his sister, fell into his chair with a sigh of relief, stretching his long legs out on the small piece of Turkey carpet.

"I suppose," he said, "that when I send my fleet out to harry the French navy all my friends will ask for a ship. Brandon's been after me already and our other hotheads are sure to follow suit. Well, why not? I'd like nothing better than to captain one of them myself." His velvet-shod feet stirred restlessly, like those of a dog dreaming of rabbits, and he touched his foolish whistle with wistful fingers.

While Henry paced an imaginary quarter deck, Mary fought down the dread that rose in her at the possibility of Charles sailing away to be drowned or killed in a naval battle. If she must worry about someone, she told herself, it should be Anne's brother Henry; England's Lord Admiral would be a great prize in the eyes of the enemy, and the Howards were a brave and reckless lot.

She watched Charles, bending down to smile at fragile, enchanting little Bess Percy; Bess, with the oddly set brown eyes that made her pale honey hair so striking; Bess, demure and sober on the surface, but with a well of bubbling laughter always ready to burst through. They were a striking couple, he so dark, she so fair. Was he thinking he might not wait for the Grey child to grow up? Bess was wealthy, too, and what more suitable, after all, than a match between the King's best friend and a Percy? Without realizing what she was doing, Mary pressed her

70

hand over her heart and gave a small, half-smothered groan.

"What's wrong, Mary?" She saw the King looking at her with sudden concern.

She made herself laugh. "Nothing, Hal, nothing. This heat stirs up the bilgy smell and makes me a little queasy."

Jolted out of his preoccupation with his own problems, Henry studied her face. Mary was thin, he decided, and there were shadows under her eyes. Well, it *was* hot, devilishly hot for June, the kind of unusual weather that breeds disease. And she probably wasn't any too comfortable at the Tower, but since most of Westminster had been gutted by fire in February, there was no other place for them to stay in London.

"Would you like to go to Richmond, chuck, or Greenwich? Shall I send you back to Eltham with Gilly? Or better yet, sis, why not come on progress with me?" Just the thought of going on progress made Henry happy; he loved moving from one great house to another with his huge retinue, to be feasted and fêted by his hospitable nobles, each trying to outdo the last in the magnificence of their entertainment. That he would leave their gardens stripped and cupboards bare, and, in most cases, his hosts deep in debt, did not worry the young King. This was how England's monarchs spent their summers; this was the way they kept in touch with their people, taking advantage of the few months when the weather was pleasant and the pitted and rutted roads were dry.

But this year it could not all be visiting and amusement. He must carry on his war preparations from wherever he happened to be.

"You've been a damned good lass this year, Mary. You shall do exactly as you wish." Struck by a sudden thought, he slapped his forehead. "I forgot your birthday. You were sixteen in March! Most sisters would have whined and cried and made me feel a dog—"

"You were so busy then, Hal, and so worried about the war."

"Busy or not, I should have remembered. Come, name your gift. A sable cloak? Diamonds, emeralds? Make me pay for my thoughtlessness."

Mary came to a quick decision. Now, she told herself, now. When would she ever have a better opportunity to speak her mind and extricate herself from a situation that seemed to grow more difficult every day?

"Not furs or jewels, please, Hal. But there is something. . . ." Leaning forward, she put her hand on his knee and looked pleadingly into his face.

"What could a pretty maid want instead of gems or furs?" Henry was puzzled.

"Now that I'm sixteen I want to be—settled."

"You want to marry Prince Charles now? But he's only—what? Twelve?"

"No, no! Mother of God, Hal, haven't I made it clear yet that I loathe the very thought of my marriage? I don't want to leave England—and you—ever!" Doubling up her fist, she pounded on his knee.

"Then what—?" He was frankly bewildered.

"All I want," Mary said firmly, "is my own household."

"You *do* want to leave me," he said in a hurt voice.

"Try to understand, Hal. Leaving you has nothing to do with it. It's because I'm a woman now, and restless. A home of my own would keep me busy, content." How could she explain without telling him the truth? "Isn't there a house some place nearby, so that I could come and go?"

Henry grunted, but his face had softened and his small eyes were thoughtful. Hadn't Kate said, not too long ago, that it was time he set his sister up in a home of her own? And he'd brushed the suggestion aside, being reluctant to part with her?

He leaned over and kissed her on the cheek. "All right, Mary. I told you to name your gift, and you have named it. But I'll miss you. Promise that you'll come back to us for holidays."

"Gladly."

After a moment's thought he spoke again. "Wanstead might be the best of our houses for the purpose. Convenient, and it has a lake, parklands—I could ride over and hunt with you." He brightened up at the prospect. "It needs work, but I'll tell my good Wolsey to put it in order. He'll be glad to see to it."

Within a few days the King's Almoner had inspected Wanstead Manor, given the necessary orders for its repair, and informed the eager girl that it would not be habitable until sometime in

August. "But I think," he said, smiling at her, "that you will find the delay well worth while. His Majesty told me to spare no expense in making it comfortable for you, your Highness, and I was happy to obey him. It's a beautiful house, but it's been sadly neglected."

Mary thanked him, and turned to her brother. "In that case, Hal, may I come with you when you go on progress? Do you still want me?"

Instead of answering, he pulled her over to a table littered with papers and maps. "Here," he said. "Sit down and help me plan our route. Let's make it a good one, Mary. Who knows where we will be by next summer— I may be fighting in France." A moment later they were both following his finger on one of the maps. "If we leave from Windsor," Wolsey heard him say, "there's my hunting lodge at Easthampstead for the first night. And Sandys will welcome us to the Vyne—"

The Vyne. When the slow progress was over, some weeks later, it was the house that Mary remembered best. Set in the deeply wooded Lodden valley, not far from Basingstoke, with its handsome diapered brick front reflected in the wide moat and its mullioned casements open to the warm July air, it was indeed a lovely place to visit. But so were all the other houses on their way, and it was not the beauty of the Vyne that made it stand out in Mary's mind. It was because it was here that she found the faces of her father, mother, and sister Margaret looking at her from the lower lights of the chapel windows, distorted but recognizable; and it was here, when the King's suite were strolling around the peaceful garden, that she heard her brother tell Charles Brandon to set his affairs in order and prepare to leave England.

"I'm giving you your ship," was what Henry said. "Word came from Wolsey today that the *Sovereign* and the *Regent* will be ready to sail from Portsmouth when we arrive there. You and Guildford will captain the *Sovereign*, Brandon, and Knevet and Carew the *Regent,* with orders to do as much damage to the French navy as possible. On my faith, I envy you!"

Without waiting to hear anything more, Mary crept away to try and regain her composure. Charles, Gilly's son Henry, and her two dancing partners, Tom Knevet and Jack Carew—all sailing away to risk their lives for England. Although the news was not unexpected, it shook her. It was then that she sought sanctuary in Lord Sandys' chapel and was somehow comforted by seeing her mother's face and figure in the colored glass window.

When she tried to re-create the rest of her travels for Catherine, who had remained at Richmond, she found it almost impossible. Oatlands, the royal manor at Guildford, Bess Percy's family home at Petworth, Cowdray, Halvenake House: they were all a blur of great halls, long galleries, gardens in full blossom. Which one was it that had the elaborate, castellated front? Where had they watched that interminable masque? On whose velvety bowling green had Hal and Jack Carew played their memorable game of bowls, a game so hotly contested that it was discussed in detail for days afterwards?

"Now, Stanstead," said Mary, "Lord Lumley's place at Portsmouth, I shall never forget. The view over the harbor and of the Isle of Wight was so magnificent. We actually were able to stand at the windows and watch the *Sovereign* and *Regent* sail for France." She was quiet for a moment. "Hal gave his captains a great farewell banquet the night before," she continued, "but I hardly need tell you, Kate, that no ladies were invited. I wonder why the very thought of war makes men shut us out?"

The Queen shrugged. "War is their own private world and they like to keep it so."

"Leaving us to our needlework!" With a grimace, Mary threw her piece of tapestry down on a table. "I'm more grateful than ever that I asked Hal for my own home. I will welcome the bustle of settling in."

By the first week in September Mary was living at Wanstead, feeling truly the custodian of her new establishment. It was delightful, she found, to meet daily with Sir Ralph Verney, her chamberlain, to set tasks for her ladies, to discuss plans with her head gardener for a knot garden all in herbs to be set out next spring, and to entertain the stream of lords and ladies who rode over to see how she was faring. Lady Guildford was still her guide in these matters but, for the most part, she remained

74

wisely in the background and allowed her royal mistress to make her own decisions and mistakes. Anything that Mary learned here at Wanstead would make life easier when she married and moved away to Flanders.

Everything was in such good order for the King's first visit that Mary was exceedingly proud and her brother equally appreciative. The dinner, he said, was superb, and she had made sure that the house was in immaculate order.

After he had eaten greedily and sent his compliments to the kitchen, Henry rose from the table. "Show me everything, puss," he said. "Is there any little thing that Wolsey overlooked?"

A tour of the principal chambers soon convinced the King that his Almoner had, as usual, been meticulous in carrying out his orders. "And with so much else to think about, too," said Henry in a pleased voice.

This gave Mary the opportunity for which she had been waiting.

"Is there any news of the *Regent* or the *Sovereign?*"

"You mean you haven't heard?"

"We are out of the way here, you know."

"Well, they threw a great scare into the Frenchies, I am glad to say, and we captured their largest carrack. The entire French navy fled from us." But his smile had faded as he told the story and there was something in his tone that warned Mary all was not well. "We"—he swallowed—"we lost a good friend, you and I."

The girl's heart stood still. "Who?"

"Knevet. A brave lad, sis, a very brave lad. He was drowned trying to board one of the French ships."

Even in her relief, Mary was saddened. Poor Tom! Poor Tom!

"And Charles?" she managed to sound casual.

"Safe, and back in England. He's off on some family business now. Rode as far as your gates with me, then turned and took the road to Suffolk."

Mary said nothing more for a few minutes, then, as much to distract her own thoughts as to interest her brother, she changed the subject by asking him what had been happening in Spain. Disturbing rumors had reached her and she hoped he could tell her that they were not true.

But it was obvious, from his flushed face and the way he began pacing up and down the room, that Henry was not going to deny them. If anything, matters were worse than she had heard. Ferdinand, he told her, had played the part of a treacherous dog.

"I see now," he said, "that he's been using our men to protect his flank while he takes Navarre for himself. I sent them over there to help him invade France, not to sit in Spain and swelter in the heat. You know how discontented our soldiers grow when they are idle, Mary. They want to come home, and they're making all kinds of trouble. Wolsey reads me grim reports of drunkenness on Spanish wine, raids on the commissary, demands for higher pay, deaths from the flux. It's bad, very bad! Their officers write Wolsey, not me."

Seeing his red, angry countenance, Mary told herself that his officers could hardly be blamed for trying to avoid his wrath. She doubted that she herself would have the courage to write him such dreadful news.

"The men are determined to leave Spain before Michaelmas, but I've settled that. A courier is on his way now, with orders that our troops spend the winter where they are. I'm going over next spring and lead them myself." He was standing still now, with his feet wide apart and his broad shoulders thrown back, looking like a young bull smelling blood. "Parliament will have to see that there's no other solution to this problem. I'm tired of Ferdinand's excuses and evasions."

Mary's first feeling was one of fear. It was bad enough to be sending their men and their ships across the channel to harry the French; to face the prospect of her brother's risking his life and throne on foreign soil was much more terrifying.

But how ridiculous, she suddenly decided. Hal would be a superb leader and their brave English soldiers would make mincemeat of the French. Without realizing what she was doing, she assumed the same belligerent stance, all her doubts falling away as she caught his war fever.

"By our Lady, Hal, you are right! And I'd give anything to ride at your side." With shining eyes and flushed cheeks she imagined herself dashing into battle on a mettlesome mount. "Take me with you, brother, take me with you! I could cut my

hair and dress like a man. That French maid did it—that Joan!"
The young King laughed and pinched her chin. "Aye, chuck, and be burned for a witch? No, no, home is the place for you."

CHAPTER VII

NOT LONG AFTER the King's visit to Wanstead his sister received a most unusual gift, a gift that was to bring her a great deal of pleasure in the months to come and, eventually, some pain. She looked up in astonishment when he was ushered into her winter parlor and fell on one knee in front of her. A messenger from the King? In jester's motley and bells?

She saw, immediately, that he had a badly twisted and humped back, made even more noticeable by the tightly fitted striped suit, and an unusually handsome face, framed by the belled cap. It was a sensitive face, and Mary felt a twinge of pity as she noticed the haunted expression in his deeply set, darkly shadowed blue eyes. Before she could question him, he rose to his feet and handed her a letter.

"From his Majesty," he said. "To explain why I am here, your Highness." Mary's bewilderment grew as he spoke; this was no strolling player turned jester. His speech was that of a gentleman born and bred.

She broke open the royal seal and scanned the short note.

"A present for you, sweet child, to make your new home merry and tuneful. I send you Thomas Gillespie, a lad with a keen wit, a skillful way with a lute, and a voice to charm the birds off the trees. Be kind to him, Mary; he's been badly treated and must earn his bread by using his God-given gifts. Crippled, orphaned, cast penniless on the world by a greedy older brother —a dreadful story, but one that will appeal, I know, to your tender heart."

Mary's first impulse was to make the poor lad welcome and

comfortable. With her warmest smile she said how happy she was to have him at Wanstead, then she turned to her ladies and explained his presence. "My brother the King," she said, "has sent us Master Gillespie to"—she referred to the letter—"make our new home merry and tuneful."

Knowing that Nan Howard had a penchant for rescuing stray dogs and befriending homesick page boys, Mary chose her to conduct Tom to the steward. "See that he houses him with my other gentlemen." She stressed the word, wanting Gillespie and everyone else in the room to know that he was not to be treated as a servant.

He flushed, casting her a grateful look as he bowed his thanks. When the door closed behind him and pretty, dark-haired, gentle-tongued Nan, the Princess wasted no time in repeating his sad history to the other members of her suite. It was customary for jesters to be kicked, petted, allowed many familiarities and little or no comforts, like the mongrel curs who fawned around the royal table; if Tom was to have kinder treatment, she decided, everyone in her household must be told why.

Only one thing happened to upset the Princess's newfound serenity and that was an unexpected visit from Charles Brandon. The King, he explained to Mary and Gilly, had made him the Viscount Lisle and appointed him the Keeper of Wanstead Manor. It was now his duty to see that the park was kept in order and that the game didn't multiply too swiftly. "A chore any man would enjoy," he told them.

Mary was stunned at first, for her most important reason for leaving her brother's Court had been to spare herself the pain of constant meetings with Charles. But he soon reassured her. "I will not be able to spend as much time here as I would like, however," he added. "The news from abroad is so disturbing that I feel I should not leave his Majesty any oftener than is strictly necessary. Our men refused to obey his direct orders to winter in Spain, practically forcing their leaders to provision ships and bring them home. It could very well be called mutiny, but I think the hardships they suffered over there will excuse their conduct—heat, flies, hunger, pestilence—two thousand dead and the sick bays still crowded. . . ."

What he didn't tell them was that the young King and his Almoner were being blamed both at home and overseas for the humiliating failure of the Spanish expedition. Two thousand stout archers lost, two hundred thousand ducats spent for nothing. No battles, no foreign possessions gained for the crown; no booty, no glory, no victories eased the pain of this shameful scurry for home. King Henry, they said, was Ferdinand's dupe; Wolsey, an incompetent upstart.

"And so," Brandon went on formally, "I will, with your permission, spend a few hours in your park and woodlands, then ride directly back to Richmond."

After that, life at Wanstead settled into a tranquil pattern. There was nothing to bring the Keeper of the Manor there during the winter months, the King was too much occupied in planning his spring campaign to visit her—he had finally succeeded in persuading Parliament that he should go to France himself—and the roads were so bad that even her neighbors stayed at home.

Thrown on their own resources, Mary and her little household grew very close together. For the first time in her life she was able to enjoy uncounted, uninterrupted hours with her young ladies-in-waiting, and she and Nan and Bess became the best of companions. Freed from the restrictions and duties of Henry's Court, the three girls passed their mornings and many of their afternoons in quiet harmony, their heads bent over their books or their needlework, their voices carefully lowered when the talk between them grew intimate.

It was wistful talk, most of it, for they realized that a Tudor, a Percy, and a Howard could have little say in what their future lives were to be; like Mary, Nan and Bess would almost inevitably have their marriages arranged for them. But occasionally, when demure-seeming, honey-haired Bess described one of her harmless love affairs, making it sound like romantic adventure of the highest order, their laughter would drown out her funny little bubbling chuckle and the tiring women, busy nearby, would smile indulgently at each other.

Nan had no such stories to recount; gentle and kind-hearted, she had grown up among several brothers, all willing to take

79

advantage of their little sister and to let her shoulder the blame for their wild schemes. But Mary enjoyed Nan's tales of family life almost as much as she did Bess's fascinating confidences and was often surprised at how swiftly the hours slipped away.

The gentlemen of Mary's suite joined the ladies when the weather was fair enough for walking or riding in the park, and were always present at dinner, supper, and the pleasant interval in the winter parlor that preceded bedtime. Playing games, dancing, singing, or just gossiping the long evenings away, sharing jokes that became more amusing the oftener they told them, their laughter rang through the fire-warmed rooms and formality was set aside. Even Lady Guildford, clucking and scolding them for behaving, as she put it, like "a crowd of apprentices on May Day," joined in the hilarity more often than not.

A practiced hand with young people, the elderly noblewoman knew how to keep the inevitable flirtations to a minimum, and if she noticed that Tom Gillespie sometimes followed his royal mistress with a mute and desperate adoration in his deep-set eyes, she said nothing about it to anyone, respecting what she hoped would remain his sad secret.

Had the jester not been a misshapen cripple, she would have been extremely concerned. And with good reason, for it was obvious, from the moment that he arrived at Wanstead, that there was a bond of sympathy between Mary and Tom—a meeting of minds, an instant understanding and appreciation of the same things, whether it was a jest, a song, or a well-turned phrase in one of the many books they read aloud that winter.

One nail drives out another, and if Tom had been as straight and tall as he was handsome, he might very well have stolen Charles Brandon's place in the Princess's secret thoughts. Had he not been a hunchback, of course, he would not have turned jester and the King would have found someone else to send his sister.

As it was, the warm-hearted girl felt quite free to enter happily into what was, for her, a real friendship with Master Gillespie, never suspecting that he had fallen hopelessly in love with her.

"Look here, Gilly," said Mary one day, spreading four or five pieces of brightly colored silk on the table in front of Lady

Guildford, "tell me which of these I should choose. I'm ordering a new suit for Tom."

"A new suit?"

She nodded. "A gentleman's son should not wear fool's motley. It's demeaning. I thought something like this." She handed her lady a sketch. "Long hose, and a short, loose, silk jacket, a kind of surcoat. To hide his hump. He will be our troubadour, now, instead of jester."

After a moment's hesitation, Lady Guildford decided that there was no good reason to object to Gillespie's change of attire. The Princess's design was not unlike the livery worn by the royal trumpeters and quite suitable for the purpose; it would set Tom apart from the gentlemen of the household without naming him "fool."

When it was finished, both women took satisfaction in the young man's obvious pleasure in it, and Mary assured him that he need never wear his bell-trimmed motley again. "I'm sure his Majesty will approve of this new habit, too, Tom, and that he will agree with me that it is much more becoming and appropriate."

She indicated a letter on her table. "Word has just come that his Grace plans to visit us tomorrow, so we will soon know. Practice 'Green Groweth the Holly.' That will please him."

Mary and her household stood waiting in the high-ceiled, wainscoted hall, listening for the sound of horses' hoofs on the courtyard cobbles. Everything was ready for Henry's arrival —the sideboards gleamed with silver, the stone floor was strewn with fresh rushes and fragrant herbs; the fireplaces at both ends of the long room were burning fiercely, for the April evening was cool, and a tall, carved throne chair had been set in place at the high table. Tonight the King would dine with his sister. There was no need, he had written, to set up a table in his private apartments. "We will dispense with ceremony—my stay must be short. I come to see that all is well with you, to spend a merry evening with your lords and ladies, and to ask a favor."

Mary was wondering, as she had been doing ever since the letter was handed to her, just what her brother wanted of her. A faint sound interrupted her thoughts and she turned to Lady

Guildford, an excited smile on her face. "There, Gilly, listen! I'm sure I hear horses now."

At first the older woman shook her head, then she nodded vigorously as the clatter of hoofs and the cheerful babble of men's voices grew louder and louder. A few minutes later there was a great bustle in the courtyard, heavy footsteps rang out on the stone corridor leading to the hall, and a breathless lackey threw open the door to announce his Majesty's arrival.

Before she had time to straighten out the folds of her silken gown, the girl was in her brother's thick arms, being kissed on both cheeks.

"Here we are at last, chuck," he boomed, his flushed face evidence that he had not been dawdling on the way. "A late start and a swollen ford delayed us, but the thought of the good supper waiting for us here kept us hurrying on. We are so famished that we hope you will forgive us our dirt and let us sit down in our riding clothes."

Mary laughed up into his eyes. "This magnificent velvet and satin suit is your 'riding clothes'? Sit down as you are, by all means, dear lord. All is ready in the kitchen." With a signal for her head steward, she then turned to welcome her other guests.

"Master Wolsey, how good to see you here at Wanstead. And Sir Charles—" A curtsey for the royal Almoner, a hand given to the Keeper of her Manor, a smile and a word for the other gentlemen who were standing behind them, and she was leading them to the supper table, where they were soon seated according to their rank.

Mary had a cushioned stool set close beside her brother's chair; tonight she planned to wait on the King herself. Before sitting down, she lifted from the table a handsome jeweled goblet, filled to the brim with spiced hippocras, and dimpled at Henry. "I am your wine bearer," she said, "but if I go down on one knee, as I should, I will spill this delicious drink. So—" She held it out at arm's length, very steadily, dipping him the merest suggestion of a curtsey as she gave it to him.

This was the kind of attention that always pleased the young monarch, and he beamed happily at his sister as he grasped the cup and took a deep, satisfying, rather noisy draught that all but emptied it.

"Excellent!" While he thumped it back down on the table, Mary cut him a fat piece of venison and set a flakey eel pie under his nose.

"When do you leave England, Hal?"

"June." He spoke thickly through a mouthful of meat. "Brandon goes first with four thousand men—my advance guard—then I follow with the major part of the army. We sail from Dover, Mary, and Kate has promised to see me on my way."

The girl gave him an amazed glance. "But Kate is pregnant again!"

"I know. But we plan to travel only a few miles each day and she will ride in a horse litter. The doctors say it may even do her good. The morning sickness will be over by then and she tends to spend too much time indoors, praying and worrying."

Sighing, Mary said nothing more until she had refilled his cup. "I wish Kate could be more active. Remember when she rode with you every morning and showed us all how to dance the Spanish dances?"

"Things will be better when we have our son," was his answer. He always says "when," Mary thought. Never "if." Before she could change the subject, he said quickly, "If you want to please us both, sister, you will return to Greenwich with me. I came here to ask you and to take you back to Kate. My mind will be easier if you two are together when I am off fighting."

So that was the favor? Well, there could be only one answer, and when the last sweetmeat was eaten, Mary rose to her feet and waved her hand for silence.

"We accompany his Majesty when he returns to Greenwich in the morning," she told her lords and ladies. "And it is uncertain just when we will come home to Wanstead again. As there are many arrangements to be made in the short time left to us here, I will take my ladies away now, with his Grace's permission. Linger over your wine, Sire, and join us later in the winter parlor."

It took longer than Mary expected to give her orders, and she and the other ladies hurried frantically to the comfortable little retiring room, thinking to find the King already there and waiting for them.

"Well," said Bess Percy, when they entered the empty parlor, "we may as well retire for the night. They must be under the table by now."

"I couldn't sleep." Nan Howard's face was white and drawn. "I found out from Sir Charles Brandon at supper that my brother Edward sailed on the *Mary Rose* with our fleet, his heart set on avenging poor Tom Knevet. I suppose he didn't have time to write me or see me before he left England, or perhaps he didn't want to worry me. Well, I *am* worried. He's always been so reckless."

"I'm afraid we are all going to have many anxious days before we sit in this peaceful room again. Perhaps months!" Mary looked around the pleasant chamber, where reflections from the fire danced on the waxed woodwork and the silver sconces. "But it will be better for you, Nan, as it will for me, to be at Court where we shall hear the latest news from across the Channel. Ah!" As Tom Gillespie entered, she gave him a smile of welcome. "Are our guests still at the table, Tom?"

"They are coming to you now, your Highness. It was not the wine that delayed them, it was a long discussion of their invasion plans. They turned to it the moment you and the ladies retired."

That Tom was speaking the truth was soon evident, for when the men appeared their eyes were clear and their steps steady.

"Now, lass," said Henry, settling himself by the fire, "we have conducted a fine lot of business at your hospitable board and we are ready to be amused. Where is that jester I sent you?"

Mary beckoned Tom to her side, where he took his usual place at her feet. "Here, Sire, and eager to sing for you. But," she indicated his costume, "not my jester any longer, if it please your Majesty. I call him my troubadour now. We ask him for music these days, not foolery."

The girl's eyes were on her brother as she spoke, so she failed to notice the look of passionate devotion that Tom gave her and the way his hand was trembling on the throat of his lute. Brandon, standing slightly behind the King's chair, missed no detail of the tableau in the soft circle of candlelight; the royal

84

Princess in her velvet and fur, her jewels gleaming on her white throat and slender fingers as she pleaded the cause of the sad-faced, twisted young man, crouching at her slipper tips.

"Then give us a song, lad." Henry was relaxed and well-fed. He smiled indulgently at them both. "We will make our own jests tonight."

Tom was plucking at his lute strings almost before the King stopped speaking, and the young ruler, recognizing one of his own melodies, gave a pleased nod as the hunchback began to sing.

> *Green groweth the holly, so doth the ivy*
> *Though winter's blasts blow never so high.*
> *As the holly groweth green and never changeth hue*
> *So am I—ever hath been—unto my lady true.*

Tom's eyes strayed to Mary's face as he finished the first verse and stayed there while she and her ladies chimed in to sing the chorus with him. Henry boomed away in the background, beating time on the arm of his chair.

> *As the holly groweth green with ivy all alone*
> *Whose flowers cannot be seen and green wood leaves be gone*
> *Now unto my lady, promises to her I make*
> *From all other only, to her I me betake.*
> *Adieu my own lady, adieu my special*
> *Who hath my heart truly, be sure, and ever shall—*

"Oh, green groweth the holly," roared Henry, "so doth the ivy. . . ." The ladies were singing softly in the background now, the King carrying the tune so loudly that even Tom's clear notes were almost drowned out. But Brandon, watching closely the intense way the young cripple sang the love song to his mistress, fidgeted in his place, his face growing grimmer and darker with every note and every word.

When the last bit of melody died away Henry gave a bellow of approval. "Well done, sirrah, well done! You sing my song as I like it sung. Bring him to Court, Mary, and he shall have another fine suit from me."

The girl clapped her hands and beamed first at her brother and then at her troubadour. "Thank you, Sire, thank you. And now, Tom, suppose we show his Grace how well we know 'Pastime with Good Company.' "

The evening was almost spent when the singers tired at last. "To bed," said the King. "A brisk start in the morning should take us to Greenwich in good time. And tomorrow night we will sing for the Queen."

As there was still much to be thought of, Mary dismissed her lords and ladies, telling them to see to their own belongings. Lady Guildford was, she knew, working busily with two or three tiring women, sorting out what should go with them on the morrow and what must be carried to Greenwich later.

She lingered for a moment or two in the deserted parlor, making sure that her favorite books and music had not been forgotten, then started off down the hall toward her bedchamber, humming softly to herself. "Adieu mine own lady, adieu my spec-i-al. . . ." A sweet song, she thought, and Tom sang it like an angel.

"Mary!" a husky whisper froze her in her steps. Charles Brandon, with fingers that bruised her through the heavy velvet of her gown, jerked her into a dark window recess, drawing the silk arras over to hide them.

"I won't keep you long." He sounded so savage that the girl shrank back into the shadows, staring at him in astonishment. "But I must tell you—I've been waiting here to tell you—" He broke off and began again. "Damn it, Mary! This Gillespie nonsense must stop! Have you gone completely mad, letting him moon over you in front of everyone?"

She gave a startled gasp of protest, but he paid no attention. "And instead of whipping him, as you should, for his impertinence, you dress him in silks and satins and call him your 'troubadour'!"

Torn between hurt and indignation, Mary finally found her tongue. "So I should whip Tom, you say? A poor crippled lad, a gentleman, who has been forced to earn his living in a most demeaning fashion, grateful for any little kindness or understanding word!" Her voice was shaking as she turned on him. "Let me tell you this, Sir Charles Brandon, you could learn a lesson or two from Tom Gillespie! You, who dared to maul and kiss me when I knew no better than to let you. . . . Tom has

served me as a gentleman should, and if there is more than gratitude in his starved heart, why, he has never said a word, hinted a
hint, or betrayed himself to me in any way."

Bursting into a storm of tears, she beat on Brandon's chest
with two clenched fists. "Tom and I are friends—friends! You
can't understand that, can you? Animal! Beast! It was comforting and wonderful to have a friend, and now you've spoiled
even that for me. Whether you are right or not, I shall have to
find Tom another post—another home. How many ways can
you find to make me miserable? Oh, damn you, Charles! Damn
you! Damn you!" And before he could answer her, she was gone,
running blindly down the corridor.

CHAPTER VIII

GREENWICH WAS A HIVE of activity. The halls were thronged with
England's noblemen soon to leave for France, their wives come
to bid them farewell, tradesmen seeking interviews with the
Royal Almoner on the chance that the army could use more
meat, biscuit, guns, powder, ale, uniforms—any of the long list
of articles and provisions necessary for the campaign; and as
always, there was the scattering of the curious, who were simply
wandering through the palace hoping for a glimpse of the King
or Queen.

As a rule, May is England's most beautiful month, and May
of 1513 was no exception, with one soft, sunny day following
the last, interrupted by just enough rain to keep the lawns and
bowling greens a vivid emerald and the carefully tended gardens
at their best.

It was the kind of weather to lure everyone out of doors and
Mary, having escaped from Catherine's stuffy apartments after
a long, dutiful hour on her knees in prayer, hurried off to her

own rooms to change into a gown more suitable for walking in the sunshine.

"Way, way for the Princess of Castile!" shouted her usher as he preceded her down one winding corridor, up a short flight of stairs, and around three sides of a galleried courtyard. The milling men and women fell back to allow her through, some bowing and curtseying, some just staring stupidly with open mouths and envious eyes. As the girl acknowledged the obeisance of strangers and answered the greetings of her friends, she felt the irritation that always rose in her when she was called Princess of Castile. At Wanstead she was the Princess Mary; but here at Court she must reassume the hated title.

Now that she was at Greenwich, it seemed as if she was always being reminded of the future she so dreaded. There had been that letter from the Lady Margaret of Savoy calling her "my beloved niece," and enclosing patterns of the gowns worn at her court. How Mary had loathed answering it in kind— "Thank you, dearest Aunt, for the patterns. They are charming, indeed, and I shall try to introduce these new fashions at Greenwich." What a lie; they were hideous and she wouldn't dream of wearing them.

"Way for the Princess of Castile!" A group of seafaring men from a ship anchored nearby in the Thames doffed their knitted caps and nudged each other as she passed. She held her head high and pretended not to hear the lewd remark one of them made to his nearest companion but she quickened her step, thankful when the door of her apartment closed behind her.

It was strangely quiet. The pretty sitting room, with its wide casement windows overlooking the river, was empty. A soft breeze brought in the smell of salt from the sea, not too far away; a lute tossed on a pile of pillows reminded Mary sadly of poor Tom, now a member of the Howard household at Arundel. A piece of needlework with its needle still stuck in it was the only evidence that the room had been occupied that afternoon.

Someone had filled a large bowl with pink roses and, as the Princess paused to bury her tiptilted nose in their fragrant petals, Nan Howard came out of the bedchamber, a book in her hand.

"We are deserted," said her mistress. "Where is everyone, Nan?"

"Gilly's gone to London with Sir Henry, and Bess"—she pointed to the inner chamber—"is busy with one of the sewing women. Shall I call her, your Grace?"

"No, no." Mary shook her head. "Let her finish whatever she's doing. Ring for some wine and cakes, Nan, and then walk with me in the garden. This sunshine is too precious to waste."

Before the young lady-in-waiting could obey her mistress's orders, there was a scratch on the door and Sir Charles Brandon entered. When he saw Mary standing there he bowed stiffly and began to apologize for his unheralded entry.

"Forgive my intrusion, your Highness. I understood that you were closeted with the Queen's Grace and that I would find the Lady Anne alone."

Mary raised her eyebrows, looking coldly from one to the other. "If you two have private business together then *I* am the one who is intruding."

Brandon flushed. "No—please! Believe me, your Grace, I'm more relieved than I can say that you *are* here. I have a message for Nan from the King, news that his Majesty felt should not reach her when she is in company," he explained hurriedly. "He sent me from the council room with orders to find her without a moment's delay or I would have sought you out first, your Highness. Your presence will be comforting."

By this time both Mary and Nan were frightened. Mary moved closer to her young attendant and took her hand. "Are you trying to tell us, Charles, that you have bad news for Nan?"

Charles gulped. "I'm afraid I do. Bad for her and for us and for England. Our country has lost its gallant Lord Admiral, Nan, and the King and I have lost a brave and good friend."

Nan burst into a passion of tears and Mary took her in her arms. Brandon would have told them more, but Mary waved him aside.

"Later, my lord, later." She led Nan toward the bedchamber. "Wait here for me, if you will."

Bess looked up as they entered the room, gave a gasp, and rushed to meet them.

"What is it, your Highness?"

"Sad news from abroad, Bess. Sir Edward Howard—" She said no more, giving Bess an expressive glance over Nan's bent head.

"Oh, Nan!" Without another word Bess took her sobbing friend in her arms and she, too, began to weep.

"Put her to bed," Mary ordered. "Give her some wine, and stay by her side. I will be in the sitting room if you need me."

Charles rose as she rejoined him, but she motioned him back to his seat and sat down by his side. "Now, Charles, tell me what happened. Was it a battle?" She and Brandon had had little to say to each other since their quarrel the night before leaving Wanstead, but this tragedy made his outburst and her angry response to it seem foolish and unimportant.

"I didn't wait to hear all the details," he said. "We were so afraid Nan might hear of Howard's death from someone else that Hal hurried me off before I could listen to the complete reports. But as I understand it, the French fleet retreated into a bay too shallow for our ships, and Sir Edward, having listened to some bad advice from a Spaniard named Charran, rowed across in galleys, thinking to make a surprise attack. Unfortunately, the French were waiting for them. They had guns and men with crossbows planted in bulwarks on both sides of the little bay, so although Howard and his men succeeded in boarding the enemy craft, and began fighting bravely and fiercely, they were caught in a devastating crossfire."

Mary shuddered.

"Couldn't they have been rescued?"

"Apparently not. Howard shouted for his galley, ordering it back to the side of the French ship, but either one of the enemy had cut the cable or it had come untied, and the tide had already carried it out of reach."

"But are you sure that Sir Edward is dead? Perhaps he's a prisoner of war."

Brandon shook his head. "No hope of that, Mary. A boy on the galley saw him thrust against the rail by a band of Frenchmen with morris-pikes. He says that Howard took his gold admiral's whistle—you know, the jeweled one that his Majesty himself put around Sir Edward's neck—and tossed it overboard.

A moment later the pikemen killed him and our Lord Admiral's body followed his whistle into the sea."

Suddenly remembering her brother so happily blowing on that same absurd whistle, Mary began to cry. Before long he and Charles would be on their way to France, too. She buried her face in her shaking fingers.

Two strong hands pulled them away and held them comfortingly.

"Come now, kitten! This is sad news, I know, but Howard died a hero. If we are to fight a war we must all be brave."

"That," she wailed, "is just what I fear the most. I know my brother and you! Always the first into the lists, challenging all comers! How many times have I watched you? Hal will ride into battle at the head of his men, with you by his side. A perfect target, you two tall fools, for those French arrows!" Her voice choked with sobs but she struggled on. "Then you will be the dead heroes, and I shall have to be brave and Kate will have to be brave. . . . Last summer it was Tom Knevet. Today it is Nan's brother. Tomorrow it will be *you!*"

Before she could say anything more she was in Brandon's arms, being soothed and tenderly kissed. He tried to quiet her as one comforts a sorrowing child, pressing her head into the hollow of his shoulder and stroking it with clumsy fingers.

Ashamed of her show of emotion, Mary moved to free herself, unaware that the rope of pearls wound through her coronet of hair was caught on a chain around Brandon's neck. As she pulled away it broke, the pearls scattering on the floor and her hair falling loose in a red-gold cloud.

At that moment the door opened and the King came in, alone. He stared at the startled, disheveled girl and the tall young man who was still bending protectively over her. His jaw dropped, then he closed it with an angry snap, only to let out a bellow of rage a second later.

"Body of God! Mary, you little slut! Brandon. Traitor! Dog! I'll have your head for this!" He spread his legs wide and placed his hands on his hips, as if to brace himself against the force of this blow, his face turning almost purple as he looked from one to the other.

Before he could say anything more, Brandon stepped away from Mary.

"No, no, Hal! Believe me, I was merely comforting her Highness. Poor Howard's death—"

"Poor Howard's death! Do you take me for a fool? Comforting!" Henry snorted and pointed to his sister's hair and the dangling, broken string of pearls. "Seducing is a better word, Brandon, and treason another!" He snorted again. "And as for you, Mary, behaving like a light-skirt, a doxy. . . ." He raised his clenched fist as if to strike her and Mary shrank back, her heart turning to ice.

Her initial feeling had been embarrassment at being caught in such a disordered state, and she had not blamed her brother for his first angry words. But surely Charles's perfectly understandable—and true—explanation should be enough? What had happened to Henry that he could so easily assume the worst of her, his sister, and Charles, his best friend?

"If you won't believe Charles, Hal, you *must* believe me." Mary spoke firmly although her voice was shaking. "The news about Nan's brother made me worry about you—and my pearls got caught. . . ." As it grew harder to explain, Mary's cheeks flushed and the set of her head and shoulders became more defiant.

The young King gave a jeering laugh. "You worried and 'your pearls got caught'! Well, my girl, I see that one of the first things I should do when I reach France is to set your marriage ahead a year. If you can't be trusted to behave, the sooner you are wed the better."

"No, Hal, listen to me!" Charles strode forward and put his hand on the King's shoulder. "The Lady Mary is as dear to me as if she were my own sister. You must know that, after all the years that we three have been together. Her honor—and yours— are more important to me than my life."

"Fine words, Brandon, and nobly spoken. I'd say the same, in your place. But as your ward is even younger than Mary's prince, I think I'll find you a bride of a more suitable age, too, just to be sure that you keep out of mischief. You *may* be telling me the truth, but my eyes tell me a different story. After all, I've 'comforted' a few girls myself and I know what it leads to." He was silent for a moment, then spoke again.

"I've just appointed Tom Howard Lord Admiral in his brother's place. You and your men will sail with him as soon as his ships can be provisioned for another voyage. So make your farewells today and be gone. Kick your heels at the dockside or in London. Any place but here in Greenwich. I don't like your ways of passing the time."

Brandon parted his lips as if to protest, but Mary caught his eye and gave her head a little shake. He bowed, instead, and backed out of the room.

When they were alone, the King turned to Mary. "And now, for God's sake, Mary, pin up your hair before anyone else sees you. You look every inch the slut I called you."

Mary walked to the bedchamber door, then paused, her temper rising.

"Oh, I do, do I?" She spat out the words like an angry cat. "Then let me tell you what you look like, Sire! *You* look every inch the bully!" And stepping quickly inside, she slammed the heavy door in his face.

CHAPTER IX

MARY RODE ALONGSIDE the Queen's wide, swaying litter, trying to forget the noise and confusion surrounding them. When she had accompanied her brother on progress the summer before she had thought nothing could be more unwieldy than the King and his Court, now she realized how simple that had been compared to this expedition. Preceding and following her slow little palfrey was an endless mass of horsemen; six hundred archers in white gabardine capes and caps, the Yeomen of the Guard in new green and white livery, and uncounted hundreds of knights all brightly clad and on their best mounts, their plumes nodding as they trotted over the ancient Roman road.

As far as she was concerned, this unbelievably tedious trip to Dover was a nightmare. It seemed to her that no sooner had the interminable procession set out each day than the word was given to halt for a long nooning, then, after a few more miles, for the night. She counted on her fingers: two more days to Dover, at least a week there probably, waiting for wind and tide. Then the long journey home. Even without the hampering presence of the army, it would be close to mid-July before she and Kate saw Greenwich's towers and turrets again.

She began brooding over her own problems as she rode along. Somehow, before Henry set sail for France, she must see him alone and make her peace. There had been no opportunity before they left Greenwich, and if he set off thinking her still in need of punishment he might very well carry out his threat to hurry her marriage. No matter what it cost her, she decided, their parting must be a loving one.

Just before they reached Dover, the King sent word down the long, straggling column that those on horseback and in litters should follow him to the town itself, and ride through the high street before proceeding to the great castle set high up on the chalk cliffs. The baggage wagons and personal servants should go directly to the castle to prepare for the arrival there of their masters and mistresses.

While the cumbersome vehicles rumbled slowly away up the hill, the Lord Chamberlain did his frantic best to align the weary travelers according to their rank and to restore order among the soldiers and archers. Tired as they all were, they must give Dover the pageant it was waiting for. This was a great day for the town and its inhabitants.

With a fanfare of trumpets and much shouting from the crowds that lined the road, the procession wound its way down to the heart of the little seaport, pacing slowly between the docks on one side and the row of houses and seaside shops on the other. Banners, tapestries, and lengths of rich fabrics had been hung out of the windows in honor of the King's arrival, and the bright colors made a gay frame for the excited faces jamming the open

94

casements. Dozens and dozens of heads filled every window, or so it seemed to Mary.

But these were the luckier spectators. Hundreds of other on-lookers crowded the narrow street itself; townspeople who were not fortunate enough to live or have friends who lived in the houses facing the harbor, and scores of countryfolk who had come from miles around to gather there long before daylight, bring-ing their day's food and ale with them. Dogs barked, sea gulls swooped and screamed, infants wailed, the men and women and children cheered and laughed and sang while King Henry passed by, bowing his acknowledgment of their welcome, his well-trained mount neither shying nor missing a step amid the mad noise and confusion.

Mary walked her palfrey close behind the Queen's litter, one firm hand on the reins and the other waving to the populace, her eyes moving from time to time to Catherine's stiffly held back and regally nodding head. Heartwarming as was this enthu-siastic reception, she hoped for the Queen's sake that they would soon reach that huge stone pile that towered over them at the top of the beautiful white cliff. It must, she told herself, be almost impossible to smile and nod when you are suffering the double torture of nausea and exhaustion.

The sky clouded over as they finally turned up the road to the castle but luck was with them and most of the King's party was safely inside the ancient stone building before it began to rain. While the Governor of Dover Castle made the usual pompous speech to his royal guests, Mary thought a little sadly of all those fresh white gabardine capes and caps and the hun-dreds of new plumes still seeking shelter.

Within an hour the shower was over and Mary, snugly ensconced in her own apartment in one of the castle's tallest towers, leaned far out a narrow lancet window that overlooked the harbor. It was such a glorious sight that she called Bess Percy to her side.

"Come here, Bess," she said, "and leave those boxes to the women. I thought the view at Stanstead was magnificent, but this is even better."

It was Bess Percy's first visit to Dover, too, and she gasped with delight when she reached Mary's side.

Looking to the right, they could follow the coastline as far as Folkstone; to the left, the view stretched to Ramsgate, probably twenty miles away as the crow flies. Below them spread the town, the docks, and the harbor, dotted with hundreds of royal ships, their pennants fluttering in the freshening breeze that had swept the rain clouds out of the sky, leaving it a vivid blue.

The girl pointed across the Channel. "Can you see it, your Highness? That must be France!" As Mary agreed, they fell silent, thinking of the sad things that might very well happen on that far shore, in the weeks to come, to those they loved.

Later that night, when everyone else was asleep, Mary lay awake on her pillows, her mind full of Charles at Calais. On impulse, she crept quietly down out of the large carved oak bed, being careful not to rouse Bess, who shared it with her.

An arras had been drawn across the window on the harbor side, but she was able to push it partly aside and crawl into the deep embrasure. The night was wonderfully clear. The lanterns on the rigging of the ships turned the scene below into a fairyland of twinkling lights, making broken little paths of gold on the dark, rippling water, and as she looked past the harbor and over the dim strait beyond, she was sure she could see faint lights on the other side.

Was Charles wakeful, too, as she was tonight? Thinking, perhaps, of home and even possibly of her? She began puzzling, as she had done often recently, about what his behavior could mean, adding together all the things that had happened between them, remembering his first kisses, his anger over Tom Gillespie, his words to Henry at Greenwich.

He had said she was as dear to him as his own sister and her honor more important than his life. That last was true, certainly; Mary knew that. He'd been watching over her for years, protecting her from amorous gallants, her own young ardor and—yes, from himself. Was all this because he loved her as a brother, or could something deeper be creeping into his affection for her?

She sighed and moved restlessly on the window seat, trying to see those distant lights more clearly. If Charles *was* falling in love with her, why had his kisses of comfort before Hal surprised them been so gentle? Why had he patted and caressed her as if she were a child? She confessed to herself now that although she had moved resolutely out of his arms that afternoon, it had taken every bit of her will power. As always, when Charles touched her, she had wanted to cling and kiss and be kissed. . . .

A sudden chill breeze stirred her hair and made her shiver. She might as well return to bed and go to sleep! There could be no happy ending to her problem, anyway. Why should she sit here hoping Charles loved her when such a thing could only mean dreadful unhappiness for them both? Giving one last glance at the harbor and Channel, she slipped back across the room and crawled in beside Bess. Lucky Bess! A Percy couldn't marry just anyone, but at least she didn't have to wed an ugly little shovel-chinned prince.

"Her Royal Highness, the Princess Mary of England and Castile," announced the guard at the King's door. Henry looked up, glared, nodded permission for his sister to enter and turned back to Wolsey, who was standing at his side with a sheaf of papers in his plump hand.

Mary came in a little hesitantly making a low obeisance to the King. She smiled at the Chief Almoner.

"Shall I retire, Sire," Wolsey asked, "and return later?"

"Certainly not." The King sounded testy as he frowned at the girl. "These matters must be dealt with *now*. Mary can wait. Sit down." He waved her toward the far side of the audience chamber. "I'll hear you shortly."

Mary gave an imperceptible shrug and chose a cushioned window seat. She tried to hear what the two men were discussing but they seemed to be going over long lists again, as they had been doing for so many months now. It was a dull business, she decided, being the royal Almoner. She discovered that she had a fine view out of the windows of the busy castle courtyard, bustling with soldiers, noblemen, and townspeople; it was a fascinating sight, and she was soon so engrossed in watching a quarrel between two archers and a tradesman with a cart full of cheeses that she paid no more attention to what was passing at her brother's work table.

The cheeses changed hands at last, apparently to the satisfaction of all parties in the dispute, and she turned away. How much longer must she wait? Her private audience had been arranged for ten, and the clock on the wall was about to strike eleven.

"But the Earl of Surrey's boxes are on board one of your ships, your Majesty. He expects to sail with you." Wolsey had raised his voice.

"Unload them, then, but say nothing about it to the old firebrand. Isn't it enough for him that he's lost one son for England and that I've made young Tom our new Lord Admiral in his place? His duty lies here, and I have too much to do before we embark to listen to his long-winded arguments. I'll give him his orders when I make Catherine. . . ." Henry rattled one of his papers and Mary missed the rest of his sentence.

"Just as you say, your Majesty."

"You will be glad of the space, I know. Most of my lords plan to fight in comfort. Listen to this." The King began to read from a document in his hand. " 'The Earl of Northumberland: one feather bed and mattress, silk cushions, hangings of fine worsted, twelve dishes, six saucers, twelve silver spoons—' " He looked up and laughed. " '—one folding table, three folding stools, a carriage and seven horses, two chariots with eight horses, four carts each with seven horses.' " He turned it over. "And here's the list of his household: 'a steward, chamberlain, a treasurer, a treasurer of wars, two chaplains, a gentleman usher of the chamber, a master of the horse, carvers, cupbearers, a herald and a pursuivant.' "

Wolsey smiled rather grimly. His royal master would not have thought this such a lengthy list had he read the pages and pages of articles already packed for his own comfort not to mention the long letter of instructions dispatched many weeks ago to Sir Gilbert Talbot, deputy at Calais, telling him what wines to lay in for the King, and just how the royal lodgings must be arranged for his arrival in France.

Instead of commenting, he put his hand on a pile of small books. "Did you find *The Statutes of War* satisfactory, Sire?"

"Splendid, Wolsey. Exactly what I had in mind. See that every commanding officer has his copy and studies it carefully. I feel very deeply that a war should be fought as much like a tournament as possible, and I'm sure that the rules you have set forth in your little book will keep our battles clean and chivalrous. Thank you, my friend, thank you."

"I'm happy that it pleases you, your Grace. And now, if that is all?" His eyes strayed over to where Mary sat waiting.

"I think so, for the moment. If you have any more questions about that final ceremony, I'll answer them later."

As Wolsey bowed his way out of the room, Mary rose and approached the table, her courage almost failing her. Was she foolish to do this? There was nothing reassuring, certainly, in her brother's glowering face.

"Well, Mary?" He tapped one foot and stared over her head.

She gave a little sob and fell at his feet. "Please, Hal, don't be angry anymore. Don't leave me with this cloud between us. . . ." A tear rolled down her round cheek. "I've been terribly unhappy."

"And how do you think I've felt? Unable to trust my sister and my best friend." His voice was so cold and his eyes so hard that Mary flinched. Where was the Hal she had loved for so many years? Had she lost him entirely to the throne? Suddenly, she heard once more her lady grandmother's prayer at Henry's coronation, begging God to bring him humility as well as wisdom, to keep him kind and understanding, to prevent him from falling into the thoughtlessness and cruelty that come with power.

She remembered Gilly's advice, too. "Show him a smiling face, no matter what it costs you."

A smiling face! Pulling herself to her feet, she turned away. But despite a desperate attempt to regain control over her emotions, another sob escaped her and she stumbled on the uneven stone floor.

A moment later a big arm encircled her shoulders, steadying her, and a large, hairy hand lifted her chin. For the first time in weeks, the eyes that looked down into hers were those of her brother, not those of King Henry, the eighth ruler of that name. As she realized it, she tried to follow Lady Guildford's wise suggestion. It was, however, a weak and watery smile, not the merry, dimpling one that Henry loved to see, and his arm tightened around her as he watched it flicker bravely then disappear.

"There, there, chuck, don't cry anymore." He patted her head clumsily in an effort to be comforting, and his voice sounded kind and loving. "Be a good friend to my Kate while I am gone, behave yourself, and you and I will be as we were."

"B-bless you, Hal." Mary's dimples were in full play now, but she still sobbed a little. "I'm miserable when we're out of sympathy! And I don't know why, but when you shout and glare I just grow more and more stubborn."

The King laughed. "Two redheaded Tudors, that's what we are. Now leave me, sis," he waved a hand at his disordered table. "If the wind stays fair we must sail in less than two days, and I have hours of work ahead of me."

Supper on the evening of the day after Mary's interview with the King was a meal at which the food received less attention than usual and, by some, the wine even more, as the lords and ladies who were gathered at the long tables tried to be merry, knowing that it might be their last meal together on this earth. It was served early, at the King's orders, and, when the final toast to success in France was drunk, a royal herald announced that all those who wished to say farewell to the departing warriors should accompany them down to the waterfront.

Both Henry and Catherine had been openly affectionate to Princess Mary all through the meal, a sign that she had been right in healing the breach, and it was with a quieter and more peaceful heart that she followed the Queen to the beach. The ladies were carried in litters, as the distance was short, and when they reached the sands they found a handsome gold canopy set up on the edge of the strand, sheltering a pair of gilded throne chairs for the royal couple. The breeze was still blowing fair, the evening warm and pleasant, and the daylight just turning to dusk when Henry led Catherine to her place under the gleaming awning and turned to speak to the expectant crowd.

"My lords and ladies," he said, pitching his voice so that it would reach every one of the nobles clustered around the dais. "As you see"—he waved a hand at a long string of bobbing boats, manned and waiting—"our sturdy oarsmen are ready to row us out to the ships that will take us to France. We sail with the morning tide and, God willing, should arrive safely, willing and eager to acquit ourselves bravely and win many glorious victories for England. In our absence, I now proclaim my beloved wife, Queen Catherine, as my Regent, and Governor of the Realm, to protect and rule our kingdom in my place."

Taking her hand, he raised her from her chair and led her to the front of the platform.

"But I must tell you all that this is no easy task I set her Grace. We have just recently received disquieting news from Scotland. Despite his union with my sister, Queen Margaret, King James is lending comfort to our enemy in this impending struggle and it is more than possible that Queen Catherine may be called on to see that our borders are not violated. In anticipation of such an emergency, I hereby appoint her Captain-general of the forces for home defense; I appoint my Lords of Canterbury and Lovell to head a council to advise her, and I appoint the Earl of Surrey, the father of our two brave admirals, one lost to us and one now in his place, to lead the army in the north. We will miss my good friend of Surrey's strong right arm on the other side of the Channel, but we will fight with an easier mind, knowing that he is doing his difficult, and perhaps dangerous, duty here at home."

He smiled in the direction of the elderly earl, then spoke again. "Kiss your husbands farewell, my ladies, for we must leave you." Embracing the Queen, he kissed her not once but many times, then stepped down on the sand to take Mary in his arms. "See that our Kate keeps well and is not too unhappy," he whispered, "and I will be grateful."

She smiled mistily up at him and raised her mouth for his kiss. A moment later she had made her curtsey and was beside the Queen, her warm young fingers holding Catherine's chilly, shaking hand in a comforting clasp.

As they stood there, watching the men embark, she noticed that three of the King's minstrels were clustered together in the stern of one of the largest boats, facing the men and women who remained on the shore. As the crowd fell silent, Dick Rutter, the singer with the strongest voice, began to sing. "Departure—" His sweet notes rang poignantly across the water now separating the boats from the land's edge.

101

Departure is my chief pain
I trust right well to return again.

Before he had finished the couplet, another of the minstrels began it, then the third, and the round went on and on as the oars cut through the swelling waves.

"Hal's own song," said the Queen to Mary. "When he wrote it, I never thought to see him leave me thus."

"Departure is my chief pain—" As the King's boat drew up beside the waiting ship, the words, once again, drifted back on the soft night air. "I trust right well to return again. . . ."

PART II

CHAPTER X

BRANDON PACED UP AND DOWN the quay at Calais, watching the
fleet of ships sail into the harbor, drop their sails, and begin the
tedious business of unloading men and supplies. A calculating
glance at the sky told him that there must be two hours still
before sunset. Surely ample time for the King to disembark,
ride through the waiting town, take part in the planned ceremonies, and still reach, by daylight, the handsome house where
his quarters had been so carefully prepared.

The port had been a busy place for weeks, with one shipload
after another of green-and-white-clad soldiers pouring in. The
quiet inhabitants, mostly descendants of Kentish colonists who
had settled there more than a hundred and fifty years ago, welcomed them with broad smiles and loud cheers, finding these
strong young Englishmen an agreeable change from the staid
merchants and traders who had been their only link with their
mother country. They were reluctant to see the marching troops
depart through the streets to the camp outside the city walls,
where their tents and next meal waited; small boys clung to
them with eager questions, and town and country folk of all
ages and rank followed at their heels, staring with curious eyes.

But this was another day. The King was arriving and the
horses who had been chosen to carry the royal party began to
whinny and stamp restlessly, making the silver bells on their
cloth-of-gold and crimson velvet housings tinkle. Brandon, strolling over to quiet Henry's broad-backed mount with a gentle
hand and a soothing word, turned to speak to the grooms. They

were looking extremely hot in their elaborate liveries; the late afternoon sun had been beating down on them for some time, now, and it was obvious that they felt like stamping and whinnying, too.

"See there?" Charles pointed to a large ship that had just entered the harbor, its sails of cloth-of-gold gleaming against the bright blue sky. "The King, at last." As they watched, the sails dropped and a heavy anchor plopped overboard with a splash they could see but not hear.

A word from Sir Gilbert Talbot, waiting farther out the jetty, sent a boat covered in figured silk arras out to the side of the royal ship. It returned to shore, a few minutes later, and Henry stepped out, a picturesque figure in his light suit of armor, made in the German fashion. A red cross on his coat front and the Cross of St. George pinned to his crimson cap symbolized the fact that the King considered his invasion of France a holy business, a crusade, in fact, and as his noblemen followed him out of the boat, the onlookers saw that each and every one of them wore the same cross somewhere on his person.

"Thank God for your safe arrival, Sire." Brandon fell on his knees beside Sir Gilbert Talbot, and although the sudden, deafening shouts from the pushing, excited crowds all around them drowned out Henry's answer, his smile set Charles's mind at rest. They were friends again, apparently; the King's hand pressed his warmly when Brandon helped him mount, and there were no signs of anger or coldness on his broad face.

The young man was so relieved that he found himself actually amused as he watched Master Wolsey, clad in a sober, simple cassock, move quietly over to a scrawny mule, settle himself in its saddle—a saddle as plain as his priestly vestments—then take complete charge of the whole unwieldy group. Messengers were sent off at his bidding, the procession was reformed several times before he gave the signal for it to start off toward the Lantern Gate of the fortress, and a missing box had to be opened in his presence and its contents checked. He might be a lowborn man of God, but he made it clear that he was, in this campaign, the King's true right hand.

Sweating in his armor, Henry nevertheless bore the ordeal ahead of him with grace and good humor—the ride between the rows of ancient timbered houses, whose second-story windows projected so far over the street that he could have touched the cheering, excited faces in them, and the dull and wearying speeches of the Mayor and the Merchants of the Staple, as they welcomed him at Staple Hall.

Darkness was falling when they at last arrived at the Church of St. Nicholas, their final halt before reaching the King's lodgings, and Henry dispatched his errand there with all reverent speed. He strode up the aisle of the dim, candlelit church, knelt carefully in his creaking armor, and intoned his prayer of thanks to God and His Saints.

"For the safe passage of myself and my armies across the perilous seas," he prayed, "I dedicate both to the services of the Almighty and of His Church, in the great enterprise I now enter on in vindication of the rights of the Holy See against the sacrilegeous insolence of Louis XII."

Henry would have been happy if it had been possible to set out to war immediately. He had arrived, he had dedicated himself and his men to fighting France, and he had been waiting, he said, for months and months now. But there was a practical side to fighting a war, it seemed, and it kept the eager warrior in Calais for three long weeks.

While the King spent his days practicing with his archers, and his evenings poring over maps and campaign plans, Wolsey attended to the unromantic details, seeing to the unloading of ships and the loading of supply wagons; allotting ammunition, food, ale; arranging for the care of the horses, the health of the men; moving the artillery, the large culverins and the smaller sakers and falcons, dangerous iron monsters, all of them, that would either wipe out a large group of the enemy or backfire and kill an equal number of good English soldiers. If the King had had his way, these new weapons would have been left in England. "A war," he grumbled, "should be a series of skirmishes. Advances and retreats, with the leaders of each side meeting in single combat."

They were still in Calais when a letter arrived from Maximilian. Brandon could see that Henry was disappointed and bewildered; he expected the Emperor himself, and large bands of soldiers—not a letter. He ripped it open and began to read, his Council clustered around him.

"What is it, Sire?" Buckingham spoke first.

Henry swallowed and threw the scroll on the table. "Maximilian's treasury is empty, he says, but he has arranged for us to hire German *Landsknecht,* Burgundian cavalry, and all the artillery we can afford. We must first take Therouanne, then Tournai, before proceeding farther into France. If we will pay him a hundred crowns a day for his personal expenses, and add a bit more for his household troops, he will serve as adviser and fight under my banner."

There was a silence as the nobles digested this disheartening information, the wiser of the group wondering to themselves if the Emperor could be using Henry to further his own schemes, as Ferdinand had done the summer before. Therouanne and Tournai were towns heavily fortified by the French that protruded into the Habsburg holdings, interrupting trade in the southern part of the Netherlands. It would be a fine thing for Maximilian if the British took these towns—but would it advance Henry's plans?

But the King, glum at first, was beginning to see advantages in the Emperor's suggestions. And, inexperienced as he was, he was afraid to quarrel with his powerful ally, for Ferdinand refused to join him, saying that he would harry the French in Italy instead, and Henry was not eager to invade France without support.

"It's not what I hoped," he said. "But I suppose we should do what Maximilian wants." He bent his red head over the map and traced a route with a thick finger. "See, my lords—here. Why *not* begin with Therouanne?"

It was a ten-days' march to Therouanne, for they were traveling with twenty thousand men—Wolsey had spread the rumor around the country that their army actually numbered sixty thousand—and they arrived at their destination on August 1, setting up their cannon and tents in the shadows cast by the city's walls.

After a long session at the council table the King and his commanders, Brandon, Percy, Herbert, Shrewsbury, and Buckingham, accompanied by Wolsey and the Archbishops of Durham and Winchester, climbed a little knoll to survey the camp and the town beyond. It was a pretty scene, strangely peaceful in the circumstances; gay pennants fluttered from the tent tops; groups of soldiers and archers, in comfortable undress, moved busily around the camp; smoke drifted lazily from the leaded rooftops and peaked towers visible behind the high stone walls; and off in the distance, farmers and their wives could be seen bending over their fields.

They were discussing how the first attack should be made on the apparently impregnable walls when a messenger approached with word that Maximilian was nearing the camp.

Henry and his nobles had changed into their most elaborate armor and the King was standing under a hastily erected canopy when the trumpets sounded and the halberdiers came to attention. Across the grass walked a rather insignificant figure, clad in sober black frieze. Henry looked at him in astonishment. Could this be the Emperor of the Holy Roman Empire, this snub-nosed, gray-bearded man with an affable, almost conciliatory smile on his plain face?

Before he could say the formal words of greeting that hovered on his lips, the stranger fell to his knees.

"A humble soldier, Sire, at your service. A soldier who will be proud to serve his son, his brother, his King!"

Henry's eyes gleamed with delight, his young vanity fed by such unexpectedly servile homage from a descendant of the great Charlemagne. Strutting and beaming, he raised Maximilian to his feet and kissed him on both cheeks, bidding him welcome, more than welcome. From that moment on, all Henry's plans for entertaining his guest with pomp and ceremony were forgotten, and the two men ate, drank, and strolled around the camp together.

Maximilian's arrival was the only interruption in the twenty-two days of skirmishes and minor hand-to-hand combat that passed for warfare. Therouanne made merely a passive resistance to the siege of the English. Neither Louis XII, the ailing King of France, nor young Francis of Valois, the heir-apparent, appeared to defend it, and, on August 22 Therouanne surrendered to Henry's standard, the first French city to do so since the Maid of Orleans rallied her countrymen against the British.

It was a day that the English ruler would never forget, a day that he often referred to in later years as one of the happiest in his life, although, when he sat down to breakfast that morning, neither he nor his commanders were aware of the town's imminent capitulation.

"Well, my lords," he said cheerfully, "I hope someone will give us a fight this forenoon. I think we all—" The sound of excited voices at the door to the tent caught his attention and he interrupted himself to ask what had happened.

"A courier, Sire, from one of our outposts. A large troop of French cavalry is marching this way, bringing supplies for Therouanne."

"By God!" Henry leaped to his feet. "I asked for a fight and I shall have one. Come, my lords, to arms! This is one battle I myself shall lead and they will not get through. I promise you, they will not!"

He strode from the table, then turned to see why his companions were not following him. To his surprise, they were clustered together, whispering and shaking their heads. Finally Percy, the Earl of Northumberland, stepped forward and fell to one knee.

"You must trust us, your Majesty, to see that the enemy do not supply Therouanne. It would be folly to risk your precious life," he said earnestly. "We are all agreed that it would be too high a price to pay for any victory."

The King's face darkened; before he could protest, red-headed Buckingham handed him a map. "Here, your Grace." He pointed to a spot on it. "You and your guard take a position on that rise. The French approach from the direction of Guinegate —here. Percy and his men will await them here, Brandon and his there, Herbert, Shrewsbury, ap Thomas. . . ." He sketched in their hastily made plan. "You will be perfectly situated to direct our operations and to rally our men in the unlikely possibility that such a thing should be necessary."

Henry glared around the circle, grunted, shifted heavily from one foot to another, hooked a thumb in his belt, then studied the map. "Well, my lords," he said finally, "I don't like it, but I

suppose I must submit to you all. But it must be clearly understood that if the French reach this point"—he indicated it
firmly—"I shall leave my hilltop and ride against them myself."

When he saw the enemy cavalry approaching, Brandon waited
only long enough to make sure that Henry was safe on his knoll
before sweeping his men forward. Over a stripped cabbage field
they galloped, almost choked by the clouds of dust stirred up by
their horses' hoofs, and down the road to where the French
seemed to be waiting for them. It should be a good fight, he told
himself exultantly; the fight they had all hoped for. As he neared
the enemy, so did the other English commanders, charging in
from all directions with shouts of encouragement to their men
and a great waving of swords.

Suddenly realizing that they were surrounded, the French dug
their spurs desperately into their horses' flanks and tried to run
away, breaking first into a canter and then a full gallop.

From the King's hilltop came a mighty war cry: "England
and St. George! St. George and England!" And down the slope
catapulted Henry, his armor flashing in the sun as he bent forward on his horse's neck, urging him on. "Faster, faster—!" A few
minutes later he was in the middle of the fray, shouting like a
boy as he rode from one little skirmish to another, using his
sword when necessary, and pausing only to take prisoners. As
they knelt before him, surrendering their weapons, he could
hardly believe it—the Chevalier Bayard, the Duc de Longueville!
What prizes for England!

Late that night, still glowing and happy, Henry sent for pen
and ink and wrote his wife a hasty note. "Therouanne fell this
day, my love, after we defeated a desperate attempt to supply the
town. I shall never forget the way the French turned tail and
ran—we are calling it 'the Battle of the Spurs.' I am able to report, thank God, that we suffered practically no casualties and
that we took many prisoners, among them the Chevalier Bayard
and Louis d'Orleans, the Duc de Longueville. De Longueville I
send you with this letter, to be held for ransom. We besiege
Tournai soon, and Wolsey, fearing wet weather, has a marvelous
scheme for housing our men in wooden huts. What a man he is!
If I had my way we would ride directly to Tournai and take it

without delay, then press on to Paris; but Maximilian is urging me to break our march at Lille, where his daughter Margaret and our Mary's young betrothed are eager to entertain me. I must confess that it does seem a splendid opportunity to meet these good friends and allies of England and to see what can be done to hasten my sister's wedding day."

CHAPTER XI

"MOTHER OF GOD!" exclaimed Mary. "Must we do nothing but stitch these banners and badges?" She threw down the heavy piece of silk and looked over at the Queen, working patiently in her tall carved chair.

"It's a dull way of passing the time, Mary," answered Catherine quietly, "but our men may need them very soon. My lord of Surrey writes that the Scots have massed a huge army on the border—forty, fifty, it may even be as many as a hundred thousand men. They could cross the Tweed and invade us any day now." She sighed and brushed a bead of sweat off her high forehead. "Is it hotter than usual? I can barely breathe!"

"I'll open a window." Mary sounded a little apologetic as she leaned forward and pushed the casement beside her as wide as possible. The late August sun had been pouring into the round tower chamber all afternoon and the hope of a breeze from the river was a pleasant thought. For the last hour the Thames had been smooth and glassy, but now the surface rippled a bit. She sniffed. Yes, the tide must be turning; there was the smell of fresh salt in the air and the sails on a ship some distance down the river flapped, then filled, carrying the vessel nearer the Palace.

"I feel a breeze, Kate." The Queen rose at Mary's words, and moved clumsily toward the window.

"Is that ship on its way to London or could it be heading this way?" The Queen was beside Mary, watching the large sailing vessel plow along between the smaller craft dotting the river. The Thames, here at Greenwich, was a busy stretch of water; there was always something to see—merchant ships, with their exotic cargoes from the East; fishing boats, dirty but picturesque; gayly painted barges or plainer wherries, carrying men and women to and from London; or, often, just a family of swans, skimming majestically to some unknown destination, their manner suggesting that they owned the river.

Before Mary could answer Catherine, the ship dropped its sails and rolled out a heavy anchor. A small boat set out from the water steps and two women saw a man in green and white climb down into it from the ship's deck.

"It may be news from France!"

The Queen was back at her seat on the dais when the door opened to admit an excited page leading a tall man in Tudor livery. "A messenger from his Majesty the King," the boy announced shrilly.

"You are most welcome, sir," said Catherine to the courier, extending her hand for the scroll he was carrying. "Did you leave my lord the King in good health?"

"Very well, your Grace, and very happy. Therouanne is ours at last. A great victory!"

Mary's heart was in her throat and her knees began to shake under her as she waited for Catherine to read Henry's letter. Her brother was alive and well, but what of Charles?

After what seemed an interminable time, the Queen raised her head and smiled around the room. "We can all rejoice, ladies. Apparently we captured the town without losing any of our friends." She read a little further, then paused, her forehead wrinkling. "His Majesty writes that he is sending me some of his noble prisoners. Did they accompany you?"

The messenger bowed. "They did, your Grace. The Captain is holding them, awaiting your orders."

"Oh." She frowned, and brushed a fly off the arm of her chair with an impatient hand. "Well, tell him he will hear from me very soon."

When the courier was gone, she turned to Mary. "My lord has landed us with the Duc de Longueville! An awkward respon-

113

sibility just now when I may be called north at any time, you know."

"And we plan to move back to Richmond, in any case."

The Queen nodded grimly. "I can hardly carry him around the country like a monkey on a chain. Perhaps we might give him an elaborate welcome here, then see him comfortably established in one of our own apartments at the Tower? Such a noble prisoner is a heavy burden."

Mary agreed before pointing to the letter still clutched in Catherine's hand. "Is there any other news from France?"

The older woman studied her sister-in-law's face. Should she show her the bit about Henry's visit to Lille, and her impending marriage? It would make her unhappy, she was afraid. But what purpose would be served if she kept Mary in the dark? With an almost imperceptible glance of sympathy, she handed her the scroll.

The Princess took it over to her seat by the window and read it in silence. When she had finished, the Queen saw her drop it in her lap and turn away, her face hidden from the other occupants of the room; Catherine sighed to herself as she noticed how rigidly Mary was sitting. How many times had she, Catherine, braced her own back under some new blow from Fate?

In the hustle and bustle of the next few days Mary had little time to brood over her brother's letter; but it was, nevertheless, always in the background of her thoughts. Nan and Bess watched her with worried faces, whispering questions to each other behind her back; this subdued, almost somber girl was utterly unlike the Princess Mary they knew. What had happened to Mary's dimpling smiles, her ready chuckling little laugh, her gusts of Tudor temper? When they went to Lady Guildford with their queries she was sharp with them. Wasn't it natural for their mistress to be disturbed at this particular time, with her brother at war, the Queen pregnant, the Scots ready to attack?

As Mary had run to her with the news that Henry was hoping to hasten her marriage, Lady Guildford was well aware of what was worrying her. She had tried to soothe the girl with the old proverbs; there's many a slip, she'd suggested, and why cross your bridges until you reach them?

To her surprise, Mary found her greatest comfort these days

in being with Catherine. Catherine's courage and tranquil demeanor made her own problems seem smaller, somehow, and she spent long, quiet hours at the Queen's side, sewing, reading, praying, or just chatting serenely.

It soon became obvious that Catherine felt the same need, for she kept Mary with her even while she conferred with her councilors, and, although the Princess made a point of remaining in the background, there came a day when she forgot to efface herself.

"The Scots," she heard the Archbishop of Canterbury announce, "have crossed the Tweed and taken Norham Castle." With a gasp, Mary left her secluded seat and pulled a stool up to Catherine's feet.

"Well, then, my lords"—the Queen looked from Canterbury to Lord Lovell, her other adviser—"it is time that we move to support the Earl of Surrey. Send word to our southern and western counties that I need the thousands of loyal men who are ready and waiting my summons. I will leave London as soon as possible and lead them to York. Tell the gentlemen and yeomen of our home counties to join me in London."

"But your Grace!" Lovell was the first to raise his voice in protest. "You must not risk your health! I will carry out your orders, that I promise you, but we cannot allow you to embark on such a long journey at this"—he hesitated—"er—moment."

"Thank you for your concern, my lord." Mary noticed that Catherine placed one hand on her belly as she spoke, as if to reassure herself that all was well with the babe she carried. "But I am not expecting England's heir for more than two months, and my physicians tell me that I have nothing to fear this time. And if, as I hope, fifty or sixty thousand men answer my call and join me along the way, our progress will, of necessity, be so slow that I cannot come to any hurt."

The Archbishop shook his head gravely. "With the King overseas, I think it would be most unwise for our Queen to endanger her person as well. Move back to London, by all means, your Majesty, and take up residence in the Tower until we have driven the Scots back where they belong. Send your banner with us and we will rally an army for Surrey in your name."

"I think, my lord Archbishop, that the Queen herself could rally a larger one." Catherine looked steadily from one man to another, as if daring them to refute her words. "Have you forgotten that the King named me Governor of the Realm and Captain-General of our forces? My place is with my armies!"

"But a woman—alone—"

Mary sprang to her feet. "Her Majesty will not be alone. Wherever she goes you may be sure that the King's sister will be at her side."

"Thank you, your Highness." Catherine stressed the title purposely. She rose and took Mary's hand in hers. "Do not let us wrangle any longer, my lords. We have too much else to do. My sister and I will decide which of our household will travel with us, and you must speed my messengers on their way. Tell our people that the Queen of England and her Highness, the Princess Mary of England and Castile, go north to defend our beloved country."

Mary's impulsive gesture melted the last of Catherine's natural reserve and from that moment on they were truly sisters. As they made their slow progress toward the north, they talked as they never had before, and the younger woman asked the Queen many questions about her earlier life. Had she dreaded her marriage to Arthur? Was it a frightening thing, leaving your home for a foreign court? Must she, Mary, really marry Charles of Flanders?

Catherine's answers came slowly, and there was little comfort in them. Of course she had been reluctant to leave Spain and wed a stranger. But she had known all her growing years that it must be so, and God had given her courage. As he would give Mary courage, when her time came.

The Princess changed the subject by pulling open the curtains of the wide, horse-drawn litter she was sharing with the Queen.

"I believe the rain is over," she said. Then, as the litter swayed and jolted to a sudden stop, she leaned as far out of it as she could, trying to see what had happened. "I thought," she said, puzzled, "that our nooning at Leighton Buzzard was to be our last halt today. We can't have reached Ampthill already."

A moment later she turned back to Catherine. "No, something *has* happened. Lord Lovell is riding back with two of the sweatiest, dustiest horsemen I have ever seen!"

When Lovell reached the litter, his face was alight with joy and excitement. "Great news, your Majesty! A magnificent victory at Flodden Field—but here, I should let our couriers tell you themselves. They have been riding day and night to bring you word!"

He moved aside and the two messengers dismounted to kneel beside the litter.

"Rise, gentlemen," said Catherine. "I hear you have good news for us."

"It could not be better, your Grace." One of the two handed her a letter as he spoke. "The Scots have suffered a crushing defeat—they are completely routed, your Majesty—over ten thousand of them slain to less than fifteen hundred of our soldiers. And"—he paused a moment as if he were savoring his next words—"his Majesty, King James of Scotland, was one of them! We found his dead body on the battlefield."

Reaching into a pouch that hung from his belt, he drew out a piece of checked silk, ragged and stained an ominous dark-brownish red. "Here is a piece of his coat, your Grace."

Catherine took it in steady fingers. "A memorable day for England, gentlemen. I shall write our King this very night and send him this—silk—for his banner." With a smile and a nod, she tugged off two of her rings and handed one to each of them. "Wear them, if you will, to remember my gratitude and England's triumph. Come to me at Ampthill," she finished. "I would like to hear more of the battle."

CHAPTER XII

SHORTLY AFTER HENRY wrote Catherine telling her of his victory at Therouanne, and Maximilian's suggestion that he visit the Archduchess Margaret at Lille, letters came from that lady herself, one to the King and one to Charles Brandon, the Viscount of

Lisle, urging them to "come and repose after the fatigues of battle."

"Well, Brandon," he said, "shall we accept this extremely pressing invitation? Lille is not more than twelve miles from Tournai, after all."

Wolsey spoke up before Charles could answer him. "Do, Sire. Ride ahead to Lille and visit the Archduchess and young Prince Charles while we proceed, in our slower fashion, to Tournai. The army will be some days on the road, as you know; then, when we reach our destination, there will be much to do before we are ready to attack the town. If our couriers keep you informed of our progress, you should be able to join us there with little or no loss of time."

The King looked at his Almoner with obvious approval. This was what he wanted to hear; the fighting had been a great adventure, but he was tired of camp life, for the moment, and Margaret's note had hinted at banquets and tournaments. "We'll do it," he said.

Once his mind was made up there was little reason for delay, and he and Brandon were soon thundering down the road to Lille. "On my faith," shouted the King to his companion, "but it is good to gallop freely again. I'm heartily sick of traveling at a slow trot. Do you think we could reach Lille today?"

Charles laughed and shouted back. "We could, Sire, but we'd meet our hostess dusty, travel-stained, and unescorted."

With a grimace, Henry slowed his mount and turned his head to locate the rest of his entourage. A cloud of dust was all he could see, some miles back. It was obvious that they must stop for the night and allow the baggage wagons to catch them up; he grudgingly admitted as much. "We'll arrive at the appointed time, then. In our most elaborate trappings. A fine and handsome pair, eh, Brandon?"

That they were indeed a fine and handsome pair was clearly the opinion of the crowds at Lille and of the Duchess Margaret herself. As the two men, one so fair and one so dark, and both well over six feet tall, led the English entourage in through the city gates and down the gaily decorated street the admiring throng crowded closer and closer around them, forcing the procession to move at a snail's pace.

118

As a result, it was so late when the formal greetings were concluded that the Lady Margaret led them directly to the banqueting hall and seated them at the table, placing Henry on her right with young Prince Charles on his other side. Brandon, as the second guest of honor, sat on her left, and the moment she saw that the King's wants had been attended to and that he was busy with her nephew, she turned to him.

For a moment they studied each other in silence. She was a pleasant enough woman, he decided, warming instantly to her genial, friendly smile, her inquiring blue eyes, and particularly her button nose, the one feature in her plump face that reminded him of Mary. She resembles her father, he thought, seeing in his mind's eye Emperor Maximilian's plain visage and remembering his easy, informal manners.

While Brandon was scrutinizing her, Margaret of Savoy was thinking of a letter she had received some weeks before from Philippe de Bezilles, a confidential courier she had sent to Therouanne with messages for her father. It had concerned this attractive young man, sitting now at her left hand. "I think you are well enough aware," it said, "that the grand esquire, my Lord Lisle, is a second king. It seems to me that you would do well to write him a courteous letter; for it is he who does and undoes."

"A second king"? Margaret admitted to herself that he looked the part. She sighed wistfully. Why couldn't either of her husbands have resembled dark-haired Charles or red-headed Henry? Lucky, lucky Cousin Catherine to be wedded to Henry! And Lord Lisle? A widower, she had heard, and for some years before his wife's death virtually a bachelor.

"This," she finally said in French, "is a great day for us."

"I have expected for a long time," answered Brandon in the same tongue, "that the day we met would be, no matter when or where, a great day."

She laughed delightedly. "A pretty answer, my lord, and just what I hoped to hear. I will warn you that we lead a rather dreary life here at Lille and we are hungry for compliments and other gallantry. No flattery is too extravagant for us," she said, twinkling at him. "In truth, we are plain and simple, though we like to pretend otherwise."

119

"I refuse to accept the words 'plain and simple,'" answered Charles. "I think, however, that I must call you cruel. What answer can I give you now? Any pretty speech is killed at birth and I must sit here like a dumb English ox."

"The English ox," said Margaret thoughtfully, "is a remarkably handsome beast. Large, strong, and with beautiful, soft dark eyes." Pausing, she tilted her head. "The handsome and large we find fitting, and the beautiful, soft dark eyes—"

They both laughed. "And slow," added Charles, "and clumsy."

"You must prove that to me tomorrow," she said. "If the fair weather holds—even if it doesn't—we shall ask you and his Majesty to joust for us."

Before he could say anything more, she turned back to Henry, and Brandon, instead of talking to his other neighbor, took the opportunity to stare down the table at Prince Charles.

He watched the thirteen-year-old boy frequently all afternoon, picturing him as Mary's husband. As he looked at him now, he found that his emotions were mixed; it was extremely difficult to think of the frail, undeveloped lad as anyone's husband, and the idea of Henry hurrying Mary into his arms, was, Brandon discovered, peculiarly painful. He remembered her sweetness, her softness, her ardent and exciting response to his kisses. Was all that to be wasted, or thrown away? Must Mary suffer what he had suffered in his loveless marriage with Anne, the bleak disillusionment that comes with a union between a dutiful man and a reluctant woman?

Henry loved Mary dearly; how could he treat her cruelly? Charles gulped down his wine and reached for more, trying to close his ears to the sound of Prince Charles's thin voice answering some sally of the King's.

"His Highness has a quick wit," he heard Henry boom to Margaret.

It was obvious that England's young monarch was determined to like his sister's betrothed, Charles decided. In fact, he had probably already convinced himself that the match was a good one. And perhaps it would be. Who could tell? It seemed unlikely that Mary could be happy with this ugly little princeling, but what choice had she, after all? Better Prince Charles, no doubt, than any of Europe's other eligible bachelors.

120

Brandon sighed heavily as he came to this conclusion and made up his mind that he, like Henry, should do his best to see only the likable side of the boy. And he must try, also, to be grateful to Henry for sending him about his business, that disturbing day at Greenwich. He was beginning to realize that Henry had been right, although he still hated to admit it even to himself. If he hadn't burst in on them at just that moment! Charles remembered Mary standing close to him, her cloud of red-gold hair on her shoulders and her eyes raised to his. Yes, if he and the Princess were to remain on a brother-and-sister footing, and nothing else would ever be possible, the less they saw of each other from now on the better. Mary was too young and inexperienced to see the dangers ahead; *somebody* must look after her, protect her. . . . As usual, he'd have to be the one.

Later that evening, when Charles Brandon was helping Henry disrobe, he noticed that his master was regarding him with a speculative eye and that an odd little smile tugged at the corner of his pursed mouth. Almost instinctively, Brandon braced himself for something unpleasant.

"You and the Lady Margaret seemed quite merry at the banquet table," Henry said, pitching his voice so that only Charles could hear him.

"She is a very pleasant woman, Sire. Unusually easy and friendly for an archduchess. I suspect she patterns her manners on those of her father."

The King nodded. "While we are her guests, we should do the same. Don't disappoint her, Charles, if she invites you to play the gallant." He gave his companion a glance that just missed being a leer. "But who knows better than you, my lord, the many ways to please a lady?"

Brandon forced himself to smile and make the bawdy answer that Henry expected of him. For the second time in their long years of friendship he felt uncomfortable. It was usually almost too easy to guess what the King was thinking and planning, but tonight it was not. Why, for instance, had he thought it necessary to tell him to make much of their hostess? The rawest young courtier would do that as a matter of course. Could Henry be fool enough to think that Margaret of Savoy was looking for a lover? Impossible! There was nothing in her charming manner that suggested the wanton—quite the contrary, in fact.

He leaned over to untie the points that held up the King's hose, glad of an opportunity to hide his face. It might show the distaste he was feeling at the very thought of making love to stout, plain, matronly Margaret, however gay and pleasant she might be. Stifling a groan, he handed Henry's small clothes to the waiting lackey, slipped the warm bedgown over his ruffled red head, and signaled to the other gentlemen of the bedchamber to join him for the making of the royal bed. As it was Compton's turn, tonight, to sleep on the pallet in their master's bedchamber and Brandon's to sprinkle the holy water on the bed, Charles and the King had no further opportunity to continue their conversation. He wished his Majesty a good night's sleep and made his way to his own quarters, still wondering what Henry had on his mind.

He awakened early the next morning to hear a heavy rain drumming steadily on the leads over his head. How would they amuse the King? Then he realized that this was the Lady Margaret's problem, not his, and turned over for another hour's sleep.

When he woke again it was after six o'clock and he had to hurry with his own dressing in order to reach the King's bedchamber by seven, the hour when the Esquire of the Body helped his master into his clothes. His duty done, he and the other gentlemen were about to retire for breakfast when a message arrived from their hostess.

"If his Majesty is in the mood for jousting," it said, "we will hold a tournament after dinner. The contestants will not be damped by the rain."

This was the kind of thing that Henry most enjoyed—an entertainment with an element of surprise. How could they joust without getting wet? He turned to the messenger. "Tell Lady Margaret that we will be most happy to joust," he said.

"Then if your Grace will don his armor, and my lords, too, of course—we will, when the field is ready, send a guide to show you the way."

Henry nodded and dismissed him. "We will be as handsome

as possible," he told his companions. "Our finest armor, our richest plumes. . . ."

Along a corridor, down a winding staircase, and around a corner clanked the Englishmen, following a little band of pages in matching green satin suits, and waiting while the lads lined up at the entrance to the hall, their trumpets in their hands. As the trumpets blew, the great doors opened.

"His Majesty, the King of England," the pages shouted in chorus.

Henry strode across the threshold, his mailed feet ringing out on the stone floor, then stopped, letting out a surprised oath. "Mother of God!" he said. "See here, my Lords!"

Brandon and the others stepped forward, their visors open and their lances in their hands. To their amazement, they found themselves in a miniature tilting yard, complete in every detail, even to flower-trimmed scaffolds full of cheering, gaily garbed ladies and gentlemen. In the middle of one side sat the Lady Margaret, with young Prince Charles beside her, a bevy of her most beautiful maids-in-waiting clustered at their feet. The ceiling over their heads was hung with bright banners, the black stone floor had been polished until it looked like slabs of dark mirror, and, at the far end, stood the waiting horses, their hoofs wrapped in thick felt so they would not slip.

The King paused there only long enough to notice every bit of the surprising scene, then he marched down the hall to his hostess. As he passed, the crowds on the scaffolds rose from their benches and tried to kneel, a most difficult feat on the narrow boards.

He waved them up. "No, no, my lords and ladies. No formality in the tiltyard, if you please."

Beaming at Margaret, he complimented her on the amazing transformation, thanking her for the pleasure he and his companions were about to enjoy. "It should be my privilege to wear your favor today, dear lady," he said loudly, "but I have in my train a knight who is so eager to be your champion that I could not refuse him—the Viscount Lisle." With one hand he waved Brandon forward and with the other he held up a piece of ribbon. "If you will grant him that honor," he added, "I will carry the colors of your cousin Catherine, my own good lady."

Henry's announcement caught Brandon off guard. At first he stood as if frozen, then, as he started obediently down the hall, he stumbled and almost dropped his lance.

"Damn Hal!" he swore to himself. "What in the name of God and all the angels is he trying to do to me?"

Much later that night he found the answer to his question. Exhausted by the afternoon in the lists and an evening of strenuous dancing, he fell into his pallet beside the royal bed (it was his turn to sleep in the King's bedchamber) and waited impatiently for the candles to be snuffed out and for the other occupants of the room to stop talking. When it was dark at last, and there was no sound but the heavy breathing and occasional snores of the pages and grooms curled up here and there on the floor, he drifted off into a sound slumber.

"Charles! Charles! Brandon—" Henry's whisper woke him. Still half asleep, he fumbled his way to the large bed.

"Shall I light a candle? Is there something you want, Sire?"

The King patted the fur coverlet. "Ssh. Softly, softly. Don't waken anyone. No, Charles, all I want is a word with you. Sit here."

Smothering a yawn, Brandon did as he was told.

"I have great news for you, lad, great news." Brandon could tell that his master was pleased and excited. What news could he have that wouldn't wait till morning? No messengers had arrived, no letters.

"I talked privately with the Lady Margaret tonight," Henry went on, keeping his voice very low, "and I must tell you, Brandon, that she is so taken with you that I think, if we go about it the right way, that I will be able to arrange a match between you."

Charles gasped. "Impossible, Sire! The Archduchess of Savoy and *me*?"

Chuckling delightedly, the King leaned forward in the shadows and nudged Brandon in the ribs. "I told you I had great news! You can't believe it, can you? The truth of the matter is that the lady was wed twice to please her father and now she wants a husband of her own choosing, someone young and strong and handsome. You, in a word."

"But, Hal, my rank—"

"Am I not King? I can take care of any objections on that ground. And I will, I promise you. When the time comes you will not be merely the Viscount Lisle. . . ."

The room spun around Brandon for a moment. To make such a marriage possible, he, Charles Brandon, would have to be a duke or an earl. A knight's son, to become a duke? Never in his wildest dreams had he imagined such a thing. It would mean another loveless union. Was it worth the price? Could he be happy with Margaret? She was pleasant, certainly—but as a wife, to love and cherish?

Again, unbidden, the picture of Mary crept into his mind. He pushed it resolutely aside and tried to keep to the question Henry had raised. It was probably, he decided, one of the young King's mad schemes that would, after a few days, be forgotten. Besides, wasn't he supposed to marry the Grey child?

He mentioned it now. "Isn't it more or less understood," he asked Henry, "that I am to wed my little ward when she is old enough?"

"The only thing that is *understood*"—his Majesty underlined the word in a way that held a hint of menace—"is that I want you married as soon as possible. If Margaret will have you, you are her man."

Before he could continue, the outside door opened quietly and a guard roused the nearest page with an urgent foot. After a whispered colloquy, the boy lighted a candle and looked for Brandon; no one but the Esquire of the Body was allowed to awaken his Majesty, no matter how great the emergency or important the message, and that was why one of them must always sleep in the royal bedchamber.

The page moved over to the bed and handed Charles a sealed scroll. The King was obviously awake, but a rule was a rule. "It's a letter from the Queen's Grace," he said, "to be delivered to his Majesty without delay, no matter what the hour."

Brandon took it and placed it in Henry's outstretched fingers. As the young King opened it, a stained piece of checkered silk fell out onto the bedspread. Both men looked at it in puzzled astonishment. The page gaped at it, too, then at a gesture from the King moved closer to the bed so that the light from his candle would make it possible for his master to read the Queen's long scrawl.

A moment later Henry's face flushed and he let out a shout of triumph, waking everyone in the room. "Magnificent! Oh, this is truly wonderful! England has defeated the Scots in a crushing battle at Flodden and King James is slain." He picked up the silk and waved it in the candlelight. "Kate has sent me a piece of his coat!"

Soon after the arrival of the Queen's letter, word came to Lille that the army had reached Tournai and would be ready to attack the city when the weather cleared. Rain continued to fall, however, giving the King the best of excuses to remain at Margaret's gay court enjoying the plays, masques, banquets and dancing. The good news from England must be celebrated, of course, and in the continuous revels Charles Brandon tried, at first, to obey his master's orders. Only a fool, he told himself, would reject such a dazzling future; he and the Lady Margaret had liked each other immediately—they would do very well together. But after a day or two of playing the eager suitor he discovered that the task was not such an easy one, after all. Even when he was warmed with wine and food and stimulated by the constant laughter, music and dancing, he was repelled by the lady's response to his gallantries.

He was beginning to feel like a fly caught in a spider web when the skies finally cleared and the King rushed his suite off to Tournai. To everyone's surprise, the town fell within the first week of their siege: an easy, almost dull victory.

"And now," announced Henry firmly, "we will press on to Paris."

No, said Wolsey and his other advisers, equally firmly. Yes, insisted the King.

"The sun is shining now," said Wolsey, "but there are many more rainy weeks to come and then the cold weather will set in." Having once lived in Calais, he knew the country and its climate well. "The roads will be impassable, Sire, and if we are not to be trapped here for the winter, we must leave Tournai by the middle of the month."

The arguments were long and stormy; but as common sense was on the side of his Council, the hot-headed ruler reluctantly agreed that the army should return home. The campaign would be renewed in the spring and he would use the time between now and October fifteenth to further his other schemes. If he must halt the fighting, he could entertain Margaret and Prince Charles and settle Mary's future once and for all.

The royal aunt and nephew accepted Henry's invitation with flattering alacrity and the night before they arrived the young King said to Brandon that he expected him to ask the Duchess for some sort of pledge or promise. Charles avoided answering, and when the gay visit drew near its close without Henry's saying anything more, he began to hope the King had changed his mind about playing matchmaker. Returning to the royal apartments, soon after dinner on the last day, he was summoned to Henry's side.

"Here it is," the King announced, cheerfully. He showed Brandon a treaty, all drawn up and ready for the royal signature. "The Lady Margaret and I thrashed it out this forenoon while you were fencing with Percy. Kate and I are to bring Mary over to Calais next summer. The wedding will be on the fifteenth day of July. His Highness will be fourteen by then, old enough, certainly, to be wed in name, if not in fact." He scribbled his "Henry R.," shook sand over the wet ink, and reached for the wax. "God, but I'm happy to have this business arranged at last. I had to promise that if Kate and I have no children, Mary and her heirs will succeed to the throne."

He smiled grimly. The mere suggestion that he and his queen might not produce a living child was always painful, for it touched a festering spot that he called "conscience." "Actually," he continued, "I was glad she asked it of me. After this trouble with Scotland, you can be sure that our people would resist accepting my sister Margaret or any child of hers."

Mary to wed so soon—and perhaps, some day to be Queen of England. Charles thought he detected something malicious in Henry's eyes and voice. Was his master playing cat and mouse with him, watching to see if this announcement hurt Brandon in some way?

"You'll have your son one of these days, Sire." Charles kept his voice matter-of-fact and his manner easy. "But, in the most unlikely event that you should not, I know her Highness would be a greatly loved ruler." As he spoke the conventional words he could see Mary's small hands holding the heavy scepter, her head bowed under the crown; he thought of her at the mercy of all the unscrupulous power-seekers, both at home and abroad. His heart contracted with a sudden spasm of pain. Not *that,* for Mary!

And now, he was sure, the King would call him to task about the Lady Margaret. He waited, his face impassive, while Henry pressed his seal into the blob of hot wax and handed the treaty to a waiting page. But before either of them could say anything more, Wolsey rushed into the room, looking hot and harried.

"If you will forgive me, Sire, for intruding, a matter has come up in the town here that must be settled without delay."

A wave of the hand dismissed Charles, and the young Esquire of the Body thankfully backed out of the presence chamber. If he were lucky, Wolsey would keep the King busy all afternoon. Still, it might be wise to send for his horse and spend the rest of the day in the saddle; tonight was the farewell banquet for their guests, and if Henry said nothing to him before then. . . .

Brandon remained carefully out of reach until it was time to dress for supper. No messages had come from his Majesty, said his valet, helping him out of his dusty riding clothes and into his silver and sapphire velvet doublet and hose. But even though this was not Charles's evening to attend Henry in his official capacity, he realized that he could still receive a last-minute summons. When his servant left the room, he began pacing up and down. Body of God, would the time never pass? If it were only this hour tomorrow! He looked at the clock and swore again. One more evening of flattering speeches and soft glances, one more evening of torture, wondering what the King might do or say to force him into an understanding with the Lady Margaret. . . .

He stood still and stared at the far wall. If it came to a royal command he would, he knew, have to obey Henry. On the other hand, hadn't he outwitted his slower-thinking young master many times in the long years of their friendship?

After rejecting several ideas as too similar to tricks he and Henry had played together in the past, he suddenly laughed out loud, stripped off his elaborate court costume and dropped it on the floor. He untied his hose and threw them and his small clothes into a corner, climbed naked into bed and shouted for a page.

"Go immediately to his Majesty's apartments," he ordered him, "and tell one of the gentlemen that I have the flux and dare not leave my room. Then find someone to take a message to the Lady Margaret—say that I am indisposed but will hope to see her Grace in the morning, before she sets out for Lille."

As the door closed behind the lad, he settled back on the pillows. A woman's dodge, this, but it might be successful. He was hungry after his long ride. Dared he send for food? What did one eat when ill with the flux? Anything? He couldn't remember. He'd suffered from it only once, a long time ago.

He was reaching out a hand to ring for Devlin, his valet, when Compton entered hastily and strode over to the bedside.

"So you really *are* ill, Brandon? I thought you might be arranging a private farewell supper with one of Margaret's ladies. There's a honey-haired minx I've had my own eye on these last few days." He shook his head and smiled. "Well, I'm sorry, my friend, but I must say it's a fortunate thing for you that you aren't lying to our Henry. He's coming to visit you with his own physician in tow."

Brandon sat up. "Before supper?"

Compton nodded. "He sent for Ramsey a few minutes ago. I'll call your man, Brandon. This place looks as if you'd been stirring it up with a spoon." He turned and was gone, leaving Charles staring after him.

A moment later he threw back the covers and jumped out of bed. He ran to a window and threw it wide open, letting the chill, damp October air play over his naked body. When his valet opened the door, he beckoned him inside.

"Quick, Devlin, I need your help. I have a mild case of the flux, understand?" He winked one eye. The young man smiled and nodded. "His Majesty is bringing his doctor to see me," he went on, "so go and watch for them. Tell me the moment they appear in the corridor."

Devlin glanced around the bedchamber. "But, my lord—"

"Not now. Leave everything as it is. When they enter the room you can seem to be straightening it up. I want it to look as if you'd been too busy attending me. . . ."

The servant nodded again, dashed to a cupboard for a familiar vessel, and placed it close to the bed; he rumpled up several towels and tossed them near it, then ran to the anteroom to take up his post. Brandon hung out the window until he heard him call.

"His Majesty is coming, your lordship."

With a leap, Charles was back in bed; at the sound of heavy footsteps in the adjoining room, he pulled up the coverlet and flopped back on the pillows, trying to look wan.

"I've brought you Ramsey," said the King as he neared the bed, the royal physician at his heels. "A sudden attack, this, Brandon. You were well enough at midday!" he studied his friend with his sharp little eyes, then looked around the room, taking in the tangle of discarded clothing and the bustling servant, who was just beginning to gather up the welter of towels.

"I was out riding, Sire," explained Brandon. "Sudden is the right word, I assure you! It was a close thing. . . . I just managed to make my way back here before the worst of it struck me."

The doctor leaned over him, touching his chilled body and forehead with gentle fingers. "Feel him, your Majesty. Cold! A nasty business, isn't it, my lord? Leaves you weak as a cat, I know! How is it going now?"

"Much better, thank you, sir." Charles made his voice thin. "The griping and purging seem to be almost over. I just want to sleep."

Ramsey turned to the King. "Nothing to worry over, Sire. A light case, obviously. I have a draught here that will have him on his feet by morning." Calling for a goblet and water, he mixed a powder into a thick liquid. "You won't like this, I'm afraid." He handed it to Brandon.

Charles swallowed it obediently, gagging as it went down. "Now keep warm, my lord, and sleep as long as you can."

Henry thanked him and sent him away, then turned back for a word or two with Brandon, his eyes still suspicious. "You chose an awkward time for this, Charles. The Lady Margaret's last evening with us."

Brandon groaned, retched, and pressed his hands to his belly. "By God," he said, "I hope the damned thing isn't beginning again! Sorry, Sire. The Lady Margaret, you say? I sent her a message," he explained feebly. "I shall try to be on hand to wish her farewell and godspeed in the morning." He closed his eyes, as if the effort of talking had been too much for him.

"Tcha!" Almost convinced at last, Henry was now both annoyed and impatient. "That won't do at all. I haven't had a chance to tell you, Charles, but I arranged for her to see you in private tonight, as a favor to me. Well, I will have to act for you, I can see that."

"No, no, Sire!" Brandon sat up abruptly. "I can't let you do that!" Trapped, he tried to find a way out. "Surely there will be time for me to have a word or two with her tomorrow. I'll try."

"That's not good enough, Charles." Henry shook his head and pressed Brandon back on the pillows with a firm hand. A small smile tugged at the corners of his mouth. "No, my boy, if you are too sick to join us this evening, I will be happy to play the proxy suitor. Why not? If your King cannot speak for you, who can? You have nothing to worry about, I assure you. Just leave everything in my hands, and sleep well!"

CHAPTER XIII

"THE KING!" Catherine dropped her pen and rose to her feet, her eyes fixed on the door. "Please. . . ." She succeeded so well in steadying her voice that only Mary heard it shake. "Please, my lords and ladies. I would like to welcome his Majesty alone."

But as Mary made a move to hurry away, too, she spoke again. "No, sister, you stay. For a moment, at least."

The last of Catherine's ladies was bowing herself out of the door when Henry brushed past her and caught his wife in his arms. "Kate! Kate! Dearest Kate!" He rained kisses on her white, upturned face and Mary saw the lady-in-waiting give the royal couple a smiling glance before she hurried away, shutting the door behind her. Good, thought the Princess; she's rushing to tell everyone of the King and Queen's loving reunion. Should she leave them to it herself, and return later?

But Henry suddenly released Kate and stood away from her, staring at her body.

"Why, Kate!" he said. "What. . . ."

The poor lady flushed, then paled again. Mary held her breath.

"We had a stillborn son, my lord. A few weeks ago, at Ampthill."

"Mother of God! Another dead son!" He groaned and buried his face in his hands. When he dropped them, she could see that he was angry. "I begin to think God is punishing us, Kate. Were we wrong, after all, to wed? What a horrible homecoming!" He raged up and down the room, then stopped and glared at her. "Why didn't you write me? Why was I kept in the dark?"

Kate made an inarticulate sound and bowed her head as if to avoid a blow. Mary spoke quickly. "It was a difficult decision, brother, but we both thought it kinder to wait and tell you. So that you could comfort each other." She caught his eye and indicated the Queen's woebegone person. "My sister has been sick at heart. Yes, and sick in her body, too. It was a most painful birth and she should not have left her bed so soon. But we heard that you were sailing for home and she insisted on returning here to Richmond. I have been scolding her for her foolishness."

The girl ran to the Queen. "See how white she is, Hal? And look." She grasped one of Catherine's arms and held it out. "Her hands tremble with weakness still." She turned back to her brother. "Thank God you are home to take care of her!"

By the time Mary finished speaking the anger had faded out of the King's countenance, leaving only concern. He put a protective arm around his wife's thin shoulders and led her to her chair, fussing for a minute or two with the velvet cushions as he begged her pardon for his harshness.

When the younger woman tried to slip away, Henry stopped her.

"Don't go, Mary. Why, I haven't kissed you yet." He left the Queen and gave his sister a bear hug. "Stay, child, and we three will sup together. We must have a great deal to tell each other."

Some food, wine, and a harmonious hour spent discussing the taking of Therouanne and Tournai and the great victory at Flodden Field brought a little color back to Catherine's cheeks and some animation into her voice. As she told of her adventures during his absence she let him see how close she and Mary had grown and how grateful she was to the girl for her loyalty and affection. "If it hadn't been for Mary—" she said; and "I could not have done it if Mary hadn't helped me—"; and "As I had our sister with me, all went well."

The King beamed on them both. He finished a large, thick slab of beef, reached for the leg of a roast peacock, and tore at it with his sharp teeth.

"God, but it's good to taste English meat again!" He belched appreciatively and swallowed half a goblet of red wine. "Your cousin Margaret sets a good table, Kate, but I don't really like foreign messes and kickshaws. Not that I'm complaining. No, she fed us well, housed us well, and entertained us *very* well!" He paused, gave Mary an odd, furtive glance, then busied himself with his knife. There was a moment's silence, then he said, abruptly, "We settled that matter of your wedding date, Mary. Next July fifteen will be the great day and Calais the place."

Mary turned cold. "Must I, Hal?" Her voice was low and pleading. "*Must* I?"

He nodded, refusing to meet her eyes. "The treaty is signed and I shall order your clothes and choose your household just as soon as possible. So don't waste my time with tears and tragic scenes, sister, because it won't change my mind. And, as a matter of fact, I see no reason why you shouldn't be a very happy woman. I found your Prince Charles a delightful boy—gentle, eager to please, and with a keen wit and a ready tongue. You will like him, I know."

Mary said nothing more. This was not the time, obviously.

"By the way—" Now Henry's voice was so overly casual that both women instinctively braced themselves. "Your cousin Margaret, Kate, may wed again too, before long." He laughed. "Our handsome Brandon seems to have won her heart. There's no formal betrothal, but they both promised not to marry anyone else between now and next spring, when we plan to resume our campaign over there."

The Queen gasped. *"My cousin—*and Charles Brandon? I don't believe it!"

"Why not?" Henry sounded resentful. "She told me that she's married twice to please her father and this time she intends to please herself. And I've assured her that Brandon will soon be more than Viscount Lisle. I'm making him the Duke of Suffolk at the New Year. He'll be a great match for any woman then."

"I don't care what rank you give him, Hal. You can't change his birth. My uncle will never allow his daughter to marry a knight's son!"

"Don't be so sure, Kate. The Lady Margaret has been arranging her own life for some time now."

Although they went on arguing the point, Mary heard little of what they said. She remembered afterwards that Charles was to be Duke of Suffolk and that her brother had made some statement about his being a great match for any woman, but it meant nothing to her at the time. The thought of Charles wooing and marrying the Lady Margaret was a blow to the heart, and the second that she had suffered in almost as many minutes. She had been telling herself for a long time that what Charles did was no concern of hers, but she knew now that it was.

"I never want to see him again!" In her anguish, she almost said it aloud. "I must go away and hide until July." Suddenly she welcomed the prospect of marrying the Prince of Flanders and leaving England forever.

"I want to go home to Wanstead." This time she did speak aloud, not knowing that she had interrupted the King in the middle of a sentence. "Let me go. Please let me go."

Even Henry's insensitivity was pierced by the misery on her face, and he wondered again if he had been right in suspecting her of a tenderness for Brandon. Well, it didn't matter now;

her future was settled. At the moment he knew that she dreaded leaving England, wedding a stranger. All right, he decided, let the girl rusticate for a while. She would soon recover. When she saw the jewels and gowns and furs. . . .

That was late in October. With the King's permission, Mary managed to set out from Richmond on the day following his return, and without having seen Charles Brandon. Wanstead had never seemed so much her own home as it did now, for here she hoped to be safe from any more emotional upheavals, here she could protect herself from any chance encounters. If Charles rode down to inspect her forests and parks she was determined to plead illness and remain in seclusion. A word with her chamberlain would be enough to ensure her privacy.

After a few weeks of broken nights and restless days life slipped back into its peaceful pattern; the Princess began to sleep again and to move through the waking hours in a numbness that passed as content. She forced herself to think of each day as an entity, to live it, as best she could, brooding neither over the past nor the future. An empty, futile sort of existence, perhaps, but bearable. Lady Guildford, after several unsuccessful attempts to gain her confidence, wisely decided to leave her alone.

She was sitting staring into a roaring fire, one chill November afternoon, when Henry arrived unexpectedly, striding into her presence unannounced. The moment he crossed the threshold, it seemed to her that the quiet house woke up, and she found herself, albeit reluctantly, responding to his vitality, good humor, and affectionate solicitude.

He and Kate missed her, he said. They were planning a great Christmas celebration at Windsor and Mary must share it with them. No, he would not let her be excused. Didn't she realize that it would be their last Christmas together?

Poor Mary realized it only too well. She burst into a flood of tears, remembering the happy holidays they had enjoyed in the past, when she and Hal had been just a merry, loving brother and sister, their hearts free and their skies unclouded.

"There, there." Henry hated to see women cry. He patted her bowed head awkwardly and thrust a long list into her hands, pointing to several items. "Here, this will cheer you up. See all the wonderful things I shall order for you, Mary. The Princess of England will not go to her husband empty-handed. Look—"

Mary looked, marveling that Hal could be so unimaginative. Did he really think she could read descriptions of brocades and velvets and cloth-of-gold for elaborate gowns, gilded chariots and litters, rich bed furnishings, chairs, tapestries, cushions, jewels, silver and gold plate, chapel articles—God knows what all—with actual enjoyment? Must she be delighted by the fact that her household was to consist of more than a hundred people?

"Add anything you wish," her brother said. "Wolsey and I have spent hours over this business and I've consulted with Kate. But you and Mother Guildford may find some omissions, although I think we've done very well with the furnishings and vehicles. Oh, and the jewels. See, coronals, rings, necklaces, chains, girdles. . . ."

Mary tried to smile and sound grateful. "I'm sure you are being more than generous, Sire. Leave it with me and I'll study it later."

Henry rose and stretched. "Summon Gilly now, chuck, and I'll ride around the park while you two discuss it. It must be sent off to the Lady Margaret without delay."

"The Lady Margaret?" Mary was surprised and hurt. "Why should it concern her?" Was Charles Brandon's new love to decide what she, Mary, was to bring to Flanders?

"She knows what you will need, Mary, even better than we do. And, at Catherine's suggestion, we plan to send her all the silks and velvet and stuffs so that your gowns can be made by her women in the fashion of her Court."

Mary threw the list on the floor. "But I don't like the Flemish fashions! I'm English and I want my gowns made here at home. It will be time enough to wear their ugly things when mine are worn out."

Henry opened his mouth to argue with her, then shrugged his wide shoulders. Why make a fuss? It was easier, he had discovered recently, to agree with women and then to go ahead and do what you wanted.

"I won't have it, Hal," Mary went on hotly. "You must admit that I've been very good about this distasteful match. Surely I can at least have my gowns made the way I want them."

"Just as you wish," he answered, hurriedly. "Just as you wish. Let's not quarrel, sister."

Mary assumed that the King would be as good as his word; but when she arrived at Windsor for Christmas she found out that he was proceeding with his original plan. It was Catherine who mentioned it to her, knowing nothing of Mary's objections, and she looked extremely surprised when Mary flushed and began to protest.

"But he promised me, Kate," the girl said, her voice rising. "I don't want the Lady Margaret to make my gowns. I told Hal so when he visited me at Wanstead, and he said it should be as I wished!"

The Queen shook her head sadly and reached for her needlework. "It's too bad, child, and I'm very sorry if you are disappointed. But you will learn, as I have, that you cannot always trust your brother in these matters. Too often lately he has said one thing to me and then done another." She spoke softly, not wanting her ladies to hear what might be considered a criticism of the King. "He usually has a good reason, of course. In this case, I think it's because he's extremely anxious to please my cousin. He's still determined to wed her to his beloved Brandon but now she wants the whole affair forgotten."

"How do you know?"

Catherine laughed. "Hal had a frantic letter from Margaret the other day which he let me see. She says that rumors of the match are being spread around the Low Countries by our merchants, and she is terrified that they may reach her father's ears. If you remember, I told Hal that the Emperor wouldn't allow such an alliance, but he wouldn't listen to me. Now Margaret wants him to scotch the story by wedding my Lord Lisle to the little Grey child this winter. Apparently she doesn't know the girl is only nine years old."

"And what does Hal say to that suggestion?" Mary's emotions were distinctly mixed, but she was reluctant to close the subject.

"Oh, you know how he is! He refuses to admit that his plan is impossible, and he's going ahead in his most stubborn fashion. Brandon is still to be the Duke of Suffolk, he says, and then he will send him to Lille as our resident ambassador, to woo the

137

lady at his leisure. I wonder what Margaret will do when she hears that?"

Mary's heart sank. It would be unbearable, living at Lille as the Prince's wife and being in constant association with Charles. If he were there as ambassador their paths would cross every day—they must dine often together, dance, confer—

Too miserable to talk about it any longer, she managed to change the subject. What did Kate think of the Duke of Buckingham's fifteen-year-old sister Elizabeth marrying Thomas Howard, a widower? "Our new Lord Admiral looks high for his brides," added Mary. "First my mother's young sister Anne, and now a Duke's sister. Nan tells me she is a pretty little thing."

Mary woke the next morning still tormented by the thought of Charles living at Lille. If she had an opportunity during the day she would, she resolved, ask him whether the matter had yet been arranged. Better to know now, and become accustomed to the idea, than to keep on worrying about it; she could make her question sound very casual. But Brandon was busy with the King all morning and most of the afternoon, and the only time when she might have been able to speak to him he was whispering in a corner with the Queen's youngest and most beautiful lady-in-waiting, his dark head bent over hers and his laughter making it obvious that he was finding her good company.

The Princess watched them for a few minutes; then, as he seemed oblivious to the fact that she was nearby, she gathered a merry group of her own around her. When suppertime came she retired to her private apartments and sent her ladies down to the dining hall without her, pleading lack of appetite and a small but nagging headache. Actually, Mary was suffering from a large and nagging heartache, combined with a feeling of disgust for her vacillating self-deception.

She confessed to herself that she had been making excuses for Charles's behavior, for his careful avoidance of her during these holiday weeks and even for the talk of his wooing of Lady Margaret. But this little tableau that she had just witnessed added the final featherweight to the scale and Mary saw him suddenly as a gay blade who could not resist dallying with the nearest available woman. And it brought her own behavior

138

clearly into focus; she realized that she had been doing nothing for months now but make and break resolutions. Well, she decided, she would make just one more, but this one she must keep, for her own sake.

The shadows deepened around her as she sat and stared into the fire, forgetting to ring for candles. January, February, March —she counted them on her white fingers—April, May, June. She had six months left before she must wed Prince Charles; they would be short months, she was sure of that. She looked at the dim face of the little clock on the table. The hands pointed to six—and today was January the seventh.

Her resolution must begin from this very moment. Now. From six of the clock on the seventh day of January she was calling a halt to all the useless, sentimental foolishness that had made her increasingly wretched. Instead of moping away the months that lay ahead she would return to Wanstead and try to enjoy them. After all, she had one more English winter and one more precious English spring there before she must say farewell to everyone and everything she loved.

Why not savor them, she asked herself, in the hope that before spring had turned to summer she would have regained her peace of mind and taught herself resignation. Gilly would help her. And Nan, and Bess. Together they would all read about Flanders and its customs, together they would discover what her duties and prerogatives would be, together they would prepare her for her new life. Rebellion had been futile, and submission was not good enough; no, for an hour or two each day she must actually work at conquering her fear of the future, leaving herself free, when that was done, to enjoy the time that remained.

Feeling virtuous, sensible, and amazingly hungry, the girl rose to summon her chamberwoman. She had her hand on the bell when the door into the outside corridor opened and Lady Guildford came in, followed by a maid with candles and a lackey carrying a loaded tray.

Mary laughed delightedly. "Oh, Gilly—my dear, dear Gilly! How do you do it? I send you away, swearing that food would make me ill and that I want to be alone. Suddenly I am hungry and I want to see you, to talk to you. The door opens and you are here, bringing me my supper!" She shook her head, in mock wonder. "Sit down with me while I eat. I've been making plans for our winter."

The cold months slipped by even more swiftly than Mary had expected, and if she failed to live up to all her resolutions she did, at least, try. By the time the daffodils were blowing in the fresh spring breezes and the catkins gone from the willow trees, she could think of July without actually shuddering, although deep in the farthest corner of her heart she still prayed for the unlikely miracle that would postpone or prevent her marriage.

Letters and visitors arrived frequently at Wanstead, bringing the news from Court. The plague had broken out again in London, but it lasted only a short time; and on the Day of the Purification of Our Lady Henry celebrated its passing by making the elderly victor of Flodden Field the Duke of Norfolk. His previous title of Earl of Surrey now passed to his son Thomas Howard, the Lord Admiral of England recently married to the Duke of Buckingham's sister. On the same day Charles Brandon became the Duke of Suffolk, but as Henry had received more letters of protest from the Lady Margaret, he did not dare send him back to Lille as ambassador.

Mary also learned that her brother was gathering together men and supplies for continuing the war with France, but no date had yet been set for their departure as neither Ferdinand nor Maximilian seemed in any hurry to answer his questions or make the necessary plans. Henry, Mary was told, was fuming with impatience. Knowing this, it was with the greatest reluctance that Mary set out for Greenwich to spend Easter with the King and Queen. When Henry was angry with Ferdinand he was prone to take it out on poor Kate and then everyone suffered.

And although she was quite convinced—yes, quite, quite convinced—that her feeling for Charles Brandon had been merely the natural response of an impressionable girl to a handsome, experienced older man, and not love at all, still it would be easier not to encounter him again. As her palfrey picked its careful way over the rough, rutted road she consoled herself with the thought that Easter was a time of prayers and church services, not feasting and dancing. With luck she might see very little of the new duke.

As it turned out, she had her first glimpse of him while he was helping the King with the foot washing of the poor on Maunday Thursday. Henry was twenty-three years old in this year of our Lord, 1514, and so, according to ancient custom, he, as England's King, must wash and dry the feet of twenty-three poor boys, using herb-scented water in a silver bowl and the softest of linen towels. Suffolk and several other high-ranking noblemen attended him in the chapel; they handed him the towels, carried the basin from one frightened lad to the next, and, when the washing was finished and the last trembling foot dried, it was their more pleasant privilege to assist their royal master in the distribution of food, clothing, and money.

Mary watched from the gallery, finding it difficult to restrain her laughter. Hal was so serious—so overwhelmingly noble as he dabbed awkwardly at all those bony toes! And that row of sad little ragged boys, looking absolutely terrified, their eyes round and wide in their dirty faces! She knew, from other years, that someone had scrubbed their feet before they were sent in to the King's presence—but why, she wondered, had no one thought to wash their faces?

She turned to whisper to Bess Percy and found that the girl had slipped away, leaving her alone. Feeling a bit squeamish, Mary decided; Bess never could stomach odd sights and smells. She leaned farther over the railing and, as she did so, a small bunch of wood violets fell out of her corsage and landed at the feet of the tallest of the gentlemen beneath her. He looked up, startled. The Princess, recognizing Charles, ducked back out of sight, but she was sure he had seen her. She blushed hotly, realizing that he might think she had dropped her flowers on purpose and take it as an invitation to seek her out when the ceremony was over.

She should return to her own rooms—immediately. But she didn't. As she crouched down on a stool, away from the railing, she heard the service end and the participants leave the chapel, the young men talking and laughing together as they walked away down the corridor. She was still there when heavy footsteps sounded on the stairs up to the gallery. She was still there when Charles strode over and looked down into her eyes.

"May I have my violets, my lord Duke?" said Mary, holding out her hand. "They fell out of my bodice. . . ."

Instead, Charles took her fingers in his and kissed them, then seated himself on a stool beside her. "I'm glad they did, Mary," he told her, "because I have some interesting news for you and I've been trying to think of some way to see you in private." He glanced around the dim gallery. "Will we be safe here, do you think?"

Mary nodded. "The chapel is always empty at this time of day."

"And you? Won't someone come looking for you?"

She thought quickly. Gilly was with the Queen and would assume she was walking or riding with Bess. "Not for a little while," she said. "But what is it, Charles? Am I to wish you and the Lady Margaret happiness?" She swallowed hard and tried to smile. "I do, of course. It will be a brilliant marriage for you—"

"No, no, Mary! Never, believe me! The whole thing was the King's idea. On my honor! He ordered me to woo the lady, but I couldn't do it. And when Hal saw my reluctance he took matters into his own hands and acted for me." The memory of it made Brandon flush darkly. "I never said one word of love or made one promise!

"However," he went on, "the lady has repented of her share in the distasteful business and the King is in honor bound to punish anyone who spreads the story. But God, Mary, you will never know how trapped I felt!"

"How do you think I feel right now?" asked Mary. "He's forcing me to wed Margaret's nephew in July."

He nodded, then rose and walked first to the railing, looking from one end of the chapel to the other. Next he turned and surveyed the corridor outside the gallery. When he was sure there was no one around, he returned to Mary's side.

"Now that I have you here," he said, "and can speak freely, I find myself afraid to tell you what I have heard. It could so easily be nothing but rumor, and then you would be hurt and disappointed."

"Tell me," Mary ordered him. "I promise to remember that it may not be true."

"It's this, although no one has dared mention it to Henry. . . ." He paused, then hurried on. "I have good reason to believe that the Emperor may postpone your marriage to Prince Charles. In fact"—he dropped his voice even lower—"there is talk that Ferdinand and Maximilian are making a secret peace with France and that young Charles will wed a French princess instead of you."

"Charles!" Mary jumped to her feet and began dancing around the balcony. It was almost too much. Charles had *not* wanted to marry the lady Margaret and *she* might not have to marry the Prince of Flanders. "Oh, Charles, Charles, Charles!"

She swung back to him and took his hands in hers, pulling at him to get up and dance with her.

"Ssh!" Hearing a footstep in the chapel below, Charles drew her into the shadows and held a finger over her lips. They stood there, hardly daring to breathe, until they heard whoever it was leave the chapel and walk away down the corridor again.

Mary gave a delighted chuckle and nibbled Charles's finger. The ridiculous and endearing gesture was more than he could stand and he swept her into his arms, kissing her hungrily. "Oh, my love," he whispered in her ear, "my little, little love!"

Mary gave a sob of rapture and crept even closer into his embrace. "Yes, Charles, yes. Always, always! I will *always* be your love!"

He kissed her again, but tenderly this time, and for a little while they were content merely to look at each other. Mary's eyes were like stars and her whole face was radiant with happiness. As he realized what he had done, Charles felt his heart turn over.

"You *do* love me." She made it a statement rather than a question.

"Yes," he answered. "I do. I do love you, Mary."

"And I love you. Isn't it heaven?"

Charles shook his head. "No," he said quietly, "it isn't heaven. It's hell, my darling. There's no hope for us, ever. Surely you know that as well as I do."

"But, Charles"—Mary sounded impatient—"let's not think of

that now. If I don't have to marry that—that boy, who knows what will happen?" She reached out and tugged at his sleeve. "Kiss me again and tell me—tell me properly, I mean—that you love me."

"Oh, God!" Brandon groaned and moved away. "No, Mary, no. Listen to me. You *must* listen to me! Don't you see that we shall have to forget today ever happened? What a weak fool I am! I've tried, though; God knows I've tried. I've been fighting my love for you ever since I returned from France, hiding it from you and trying to make you hate me by flirting with anyone handy."

"If it's any comfort to you, Charles, you almost succeeded. You certainly made me completely miserable. Well," she said complacently, "there will be no more of *that!*"

Charles was silent. How could he explain the danger of their situation? Her danger—not his; for he realized—to his own surprise, that he didn't greatly care about his own fate. It was Mary who mattered; the need to protect her, look after her, ensure her happiness, if such a thing were possible, meant more to him than his place in the sun, even than his dukedom. He was a man; he could take whatever came. But his little Mary—his love! So many rebellious princesses had, in the past, been shut up in remote castles or immured in convents to waste their lives away; it had always been the royal solution to the problem of troublesome sisters and daughters.

From the moment Charles had faced the fact that he loved Mary, he had been haunted by this nightmare. Knowing the King as he did, it was only too easy to picture him peremptorily ordering his sister into some distant place of incarceration. His anger if he discovered their love for each other would be doubly violent this time, because he would be sure they had lied to him that day at Greenwich. Could he convince Mary that her brother was capable of treating her so cruelly? Perhaps not. But he could, at least, point out the need to be discreet at this particular time; that he could, and must, do.

"No," he agreed, at last, "there need not be any more of 'that,' as you call it. But now that we have confessed our love to each other, Mary, it is even more imperative that we hide it from everyone else. Hide it and try to conquer it. Especially while

144

your immediate future is in doubt. There could come a moment in the next few weeks when the right word from you, or just the way Henry feels toward you at the time, might make all the difference about what decision he makes about your betrothal to Prince Charles. Do you understand me, Mary? Do you see what I mean?"

"Yes," she answered slowly, "I suppose I do. If the Emperor tries to nullify it, I must see that Hal has no excuse to force him into going through with the marriage. No excuse of my making, at any rate."

Sighing, she stood up. "Well, Charles, it isn't as if I hadn't been practicing discretion! I've been on my best behavior for months and months. Or is it years?" It was her turn to peer over the railing and inspect the corridor. She came back and put her arms around him.

"I promise to be good. There! And I can assure you that there's no one near. So kiss me once more and tell me. . . ."

CHAPTER XIV

"IT MAKES ME LOOK A STUPID DOLT for ever trusting your father, Kate. Tell me, are all Spaniards liars and tricksters? Do promises and contracts mean nothing to them? Well, they will soon discover that the King of England can defend himself; Maximilian can whistle for that thirty thousand pounds he's waiting for!"

Henry's voice was so loud and angry that Mary hesitated in the doorway, afraid to enter. As she stood there, wondering if she should retreat and come back later, her brother stalked around the corner of the carved screen, his face purple and his eyes bloodshot.

"Eavesdropping, sister?" He stopped short and glared at Mary. She dipped quickly down in a deep curtsey, bending her red-gold head. When she raised it she was smiling, and a dimple flashed beside her mouth.

"Why, Sire? Were you and Kate telling secrets? And to think I missed it all!" Pursing her lips regretfully, she gave him her sauciest look. "Pray, do go back in and tell them again, Hal, and I will do my best to overhear you. But talk loudly, please, and hurry. It's wretchedly drafty in this doorway!"

As she had hoped, Hal's frown faded.

"Baggage!" He looked her up and down. "I'm glad to see that you are dressed and ready. Now don't delay Kate with your chatter, Mary. The barge is waiting for us at the water stairs."

He turned on his heel and disappeared down the long corridor. Mary shrugged her shoulders, watched him go, then hurried in to join the Queen. She found her standing listlessly in the center of the room with her eyes full of tears, paying very little attention to the ladies who were circling round her, preparing her for the morning's trip to the docks.

To help her regain composure, Mary talked of anything that came to mind—the beautiful June weather, the new ship they were to inspect that day, her delight that the Court was moving to Eltham, the becoming color of her Majesty's new boat cloak. By the time the ladies-in-waiting had been sent ahead to take their places in the barge, Catherine was calm enough to venture a few commonplaces of her own and to follow the royal usher through the palace and out to the water stairs.

"Way, make way for the Queen's Grace!" he shouted. "Way for the Princess of England and Castile!" Over and over again he called out, clearing a path through the bowing and curtseying nobles who thronged the corridors and garden paths.

"What was Hal quarreling about?" Mary whispered, just before they reached the water's edge.

Catherine shook her head, warningly. "We will meet my Uncle Max's ambassadors on board the new ship," she said, "and my lord is very angry. But I can't tell you why, Mary. I'm sorry."

"Does it concern me in any way? Come, Kate, just say yes or no."

The Queen hesitated for a moment. Then she nodded, quickly. "Yes, it does. But don't ask me anything more. It was wrong of me to say so much."

As the gaily painted water craft skimmed along the blue Thames, the girl sat quietly in her place, trying to fit Kate's answer in with what she had overheard. Her brother had shouted that the Spaniards were liars and didn't live up to their contracts and treaties—and it did concern her.

This, she decided, was the first hint that what Charles had told her at Eastertime was not merely gossip. For two months she had been waiting patiently, not daring to question either the King or Queen. It had seemed to her, however, that the preparations for her wedding were not progressing as swiftly as they should, with July 15 less than a month away.

If there had only been another opportunity to discuss it with Charles—but their encounters had been rare, and always in company. A whispered word or two during a dance, a smile; meager fare, Mary found, for lovers. But she knew that Charles was right and that this was as it should and must be. He was standing talking to the King, now, as the barge neared their destination, and she studied his face, wishing she could read his thoughts. She could see that he was listening intently to what Henry was saying, but his expression told her nothing.

A moment later they were alongside the dock and everyone was caught up in the ceremonious business of first inspecting a new ship, and then welcoming the foreign ambassadors who came on board following the royal inspection. Both Mary and the Queen eyed Henry closely as he greeted Maximilian's envoys, noting that he was courteous but not friendly. When it was their turn, the two women were careful to follow the pattern set by his behavior, keeping their own remarks impersonal and their smiles cool.

The meeting was so pointedly brief that the foreigners, obviously distressed and ill at ease, asked for a private interview. To discuss some matters, they said, that concerned them all.

Planting his feet apart in the position that was becoming familiar to everyone, Henry gave them a raking glance. "If," he said coldly, "you mean what I think you do, the discussion is long past due between us. Come to Eltham on Saturday and I will see you there."

When they arrived at the old palace on the day designated,

147

the King was on the tennis court, engaged in a hot contest with the new Duke of Suffolk. The envoys were shown to seats near Mary and Catherine, but neither lady did more than smile and nod. It was a hot afternoon, and Henry's silk shirt, soaked with sweat, clung to his broad pink chest and back as he bounded back and forth after the ball. He presented such a picture of glowing youthful health and vigor that the foreigners openly exchanged glances of admiration; Mary smiled to herself, thinking of the portraits of Maximilian and young Prince Charles.

On the other side of the rope his Grace of Suffolk looked even handsomer than his royal opponent—at least to Mary—and she joined enthusiastically in the applause when he returned a fast drive to tie the score. The two men were evenly matched; and if, a moment later, Charles missed the winning stroke on purpose, he did it so cleverly that even Mary, who herself often let her brother win at cards, couldn't be quite sure.

"Game!" Henry threw down his racket and walked off the court with his arm around Brandon's shoulders. As he passed the row of spectators, he paused to greet his guests from across the Channel. "Give me a few minutes to change this wet shirt," he said, "and I will join you in the hall."

Mary asked Catherine's permission to retire, and slipped away to her own rooms. She was sure that this afternoon's meeting concerned her approaching wedding, but she realized that she might never be told what was said or decided. She took up a book and tried to read, telling herself firmly that worrying and fussing would do her no good.

"Mary!" Lady Guildford rushed in and closed the door behind her. "The King wants you immediately. You are to go directly to the Presence Chamber—" She was panting, her face red and beaded with perspiration. "I ran almost all the way," she confessed, sinking into a chair. "I was afraid you might have taken off your gown." Fanning herself with one plump hand, she inspected her charge's appearance, nodding approval as her eyes ran from the smooth hair, tucked tidily under the pearl-rimmed hood, to the tawny silk gown, opening to show a rich cream silk kirtle, and, finally over the tips of her velvet shoes, just visible under the hem of her skirt.

"You look neat and charming, my love," she said, "and now,

if you will excuse me, I think I will wait for you here. Those stairs are almost too much for me on a day like this! Go along now. Your usher is waiting in the corridor."

"Gilly, pray for me!" Both women knew very well what there was to pray about; Mary did not need to explain.

Lady Guildford nodded. "I promise. Now hurry. This is no time to keep his Majesty waiting."

Mary hurried away, her usher walking swiftly ahead of her. She could hear her brother's familiar bellow long before she reached the door and she paused for a moment to listen.

"—nothing but evasions and excuses. For weeks now it has been the same story! Your master is afraid of the plague, Calais is too small for my sister's wedding, September is a better month than July— Has the Emperor no regard for the contracts we signed? Does he think the King of England will stand by and see his sister slighted, and all the large sums of money spent on her marriage preparations wasted? Believe me, my lords, he will soon find that I am not without power, and that I resent being insulted and ridiculed! I am not deaf, you know; I've heard that all Europe is laughing at us—"

Mary motioned her usher forward and he stepped inside the door to announce her.

"If it please your Majesty, the Princess Mary of England and Castile!"

Holding her head high, Mary walked slowly toward the dais, the skirt of her gown sweeping the sweet herbs and rushes that were spread thickly over the stone floor. She was much too preoccupied to notice it, of course, but the Great Hall at Eltham had never looked more beautiful than it did that afternoon, and everyone who had ever seen it agreed that it was one of the loveliest rooms in all England. The strong June sunlight flooded in through the double oriel windows, lighting up the whole chamber so brightly that the delicate stone tracery around the windows themselves, the exquisitely sculptured cornices over the doorways, the handsome linen-fold paneling, and the enchanting roses and foliage on the high white plaster ceiling, were all free of shadows and showed to their best advantage.

She saw that her brother and the envoys were the only people in the hall. Henry had, indeed, granted them a very private audience. He leaned forward quickly and raised her to her feet, kissed her, then turned her toward the three foreigners.

"I sent for her Highness," he said, "to give you a better opportunity to see the bride I promised to bestow on your young Prince. Examine her carefully, my lords, and tell me if it is some fault or lack in her that is causing this rupture. She is, perhaps, too ugly? Too old? Fat? Clumsy? Cross-eyed? Bald?" He reached over and jerked off Mary's hood, unpinning her hair with rough fingers.

As it fell to her waist, a cloak of red-gold satin glinting and rippling in the sunlight, the girl met the startled, admiring eyes of the Flemish ambassador; she blushed hotly and dropped her own.

"There!" Leading her to a small carved chair set beside his throne, the King glared truculently at his visitors. "Now, I think, you will understand why I am so angry. Is there any princess in the world today who can match my sister for beauty, virtue, and accomplishments?"

The answer came swiftly from the highest ranking ambassador. "Believe me, Sire, no one could admire her Highness more wholeheartedly than we do. I wrote the Lady Margaret some time ago, telling her of the Princess's excellent qualities—that I had never seen a lovelier, more beautiful girl; and that her grace, her charming manners, her education, and her skill at games and dancing were even greater than we had been led to believe." He bowed deeply to Mary. "I beg of you, your Majesty," he continued, "that you will be patient during these extremely annoying delays. They are due to unforeseen occurrences, I assure you, and the marriage contract must not be considered broken. Indeed, Sire, I will personally do all I can to hasten its completion."

"Is this all you have to say to me, my lord?" The King's face had flushed an even deeper red during the Ambassador's apology. "I had hoped for something better than another evasive speech. Why, I don't quite know! It is all of a piece with the treatment I have been receiving at your hands for the last few months."

Tapping his fingers on the arm of his chair, he waited a moment in silence. "No? Then you have my permission to retire."

By the time they had bowed themselves out of the room, Mary had her hair pinned back up under her hood. After the first shock of Henry's behavior and speech, she had soon recovered her composure, and now she felt nothing but elation. Everything that Charles had told her was true.

She rose from her chair and approached her brother, who was still sprawling morosely in his throne, his legs thrust out in front of him. Perching on the edge of the dais, she put a tentative hand on his ankle.

"What do you think they mean, Hal? Am I to marry the Prince or not?"

Henry stirred uneasily on his gold cushions. "I think the traitorous dogs plan to betray me in every way possible, that's what I think. Now Ferdinand has Navarre and we have cleared the French out of Therouanne and Tournai for Maximilian, they both seem quite content to drop our campaign to invade France. I've even been warned recently that they may be making a secret peace with France behind my back—God damn their conniving, treacherous souls!"

"Would they dare? Would Kate's father really stoop to such a thing?"

"Stoop? He'd enjoy it! Have you never heard what he said when Louis of France told someone else that Ferdinand had deceived him twice?"

Mary shook her head.

"Ferdinand's answer was this: 'Louis lies, the sot! I've deceived him *five* times.'"

"Poor Kate! Is she still trying to defend him?"

"Not any longer. Oh, she makes excuses, but her heart isn't in it."

"Hal—" Mary looked pleadingly up at her brother, her own heart in her eyes. "You won't force me on Prince Charles, will you? I couldn't bear it if everyone said that the King of England had to use threats to make Charles of Flanders marry his sister. And they would, you know they would! I can hear them now— jeering, laughing—" She let her voice break and covered her eyes with her handkerchief. "The shame would kill me! Let me stay here with you and be an old maid!"

She peeked carefully through the lace. Had she said the right or the wrong thing? To her relief, she could see that his anger was directed at his allies, not at her.

"If I find that they have been lying to me, Mary, we will be the ones to cry off, that I promise you." He reached out and cuffed her ear gently. "And as for being an old maid"—he smiled —"we'll see about that!"

Instead of returning to her rooms to tell Gilly what had happened, Mary slipped out of the Palace and strolled up and down on the grass beside the wide moat. The last of the afternoon sun filtered through the trees that lined the far bank, making lacy shadows on the still water and the masses of flat green lily pads; a good place to be, she decided, when you have some serious thinking that must be done. She was only vaguely aware of the buzzing of distant voices, an occasional burst of laughter, and the sound, drifting softly out of the open casements nearby, of one of the Queen's ladies practicing on the virginals.

There was to be no wedding in July; that at least was clear. And the forced smiles and indefinite promises of the envoys, to say nothing of her subsequent conversation with her brother, had left Mary with the strong impression that she would not be marrying Prince Charles in September or at any other time. She had, so far, followed Brandon's advice to the letter—she had behaved herself, she had said the right thing at the right time. . . .

Would it not be wise, perhaps, to return to Wanstead now and wait there for the question to be resolved? If she stayed here at Court there was always the risk of disturbing the harmony between herself and her brother, and she had already taken advantage of the important moment when his anger had made him ready and willing to listen to her.

She paused for a moment to watch a fat carp rise to the surface of the moat and swallow a water beetle. How much better to be living at Wanstead, enjoying her new fish pond, her rose garden, and all the improvements both indoors and out that she had planned the winter before; they must all be finished by now. If only she could confer with Charles! But at eighteen, she told herself, she was certainly old enough to make her own decisions. She would return to Wanstead and have all news good or bad brought to her there without a moment's delay.

She smiled as she made her plans, and, as she began to walk back to the Palace, her cheeks flushed a soft pink, her step lightened and her eyes were brighter than they had been for some days. Brandon, watching her from one of the windows, thought he had never seen her look so lovely.

At another window sat the Duc de Longueville, with a letter to King Louis half-finished on the desk in front of him. His release was, even now, being arranged between Henry and his own royal master, but before leaving England there was something he must write Louis. He, as well as Suffolk, watched Mary pace up and down beside the moat. Not for the first time, he studied the Princess with a speculative eye; she had been the object of his close scrutiny and secret interest for many weeks.

The sight of her this afternoon drove him to a sudden decision. Yes, he told himself, he would hesitate no longer. He reached for his pen and set to work.

"My lords," Mary smiled warmly at the nobles gathered around her. They were an imposing group, certainly, and she was happy to see them: England's two new dukes, elderly Norfolk, the victor of Flodden, and Suffolk, her own Charles Brandon; plump, sympathetic Thomas Wolsey, now the Dean of Lincoln, and the Bishops of Winchester and Durham, reverent and responsive men; and, finally, earnest and helpful as always, the Earl of Worcester, Lord Chamberlain of her brother's household, squinting and frowning as he peered at her with his near-sighted eyes. Here before her were the men who could influence the King, and she thanked God they had all seen fit to answer her summons.

"Let me first bid you welcome to Wanstead," Mary said. "I am more grateful than I can say for your prompt response to my invitation. I hope Sir Ralph"—she glanced over at her gray-headed Chamberlain, Sir Ralph Verney—"made it clear to you I need your help?"

A murmur of assent rose from her guests. "Then let me tell you," she continued, "why I sent for you today." Turning to a nearby table, she picked up a sheet of paper. "This"—she held it out toward the waiting group of nobles—"is a formal declaration in which I announce that I no longer consider myself betrothed to the Prince of Flanders. I want to sign it in your presence, my lords. But first, I think I should explain why I am taking this rather drastic step."

She paused, looking from one to another, her eyes softening involuntarily as they met those of Charles Brandon, who was standing quietly behind Thomas Wolsey. He made a move as if to speak, then checked himself; Mary could see, from the color rising in his cheeks, that he was restraining himself with some difficulty. This action of hers was as much of a surprise to him as it was to the other lords assembled there because she had had no opportunity to see him alone.

"This is the twenty-ninth day of July," she went on, "and, as you all are aware, I was supposed to wed Prince Charles on the fifteenth day of this same month—and was prepared to do so. You know as well as I do of the delays, excuses, and evasive answers received by his Majesty in the last two months. Now I hear that King Ferdinand and the Emperor Maximilian have signed a secret peace treaty with France in which it is stipulated that my betrothed will wed a French princess instead of me."

She looked at Wolsey, her brows slightly raised; he nodded, as if in answer to a question, and she sighed with relief, then continued speaking. "I have also been informed that certain relatives and councilors of Prince Charles have so prejudiced him against both me and my brother the King that he is now as reluctant to marry me as I am to wed him. In fact," she smiled, "I am happy to stand here today and swear solemnly to you all that I hereby resolve never to fulfill my contract with Prince Charles of Flanders and Castile, and that my resolution was made independently of the persuasions or threats of any person whatever.

"I have said as much in my declaration." She indicated the paper in her hand. "This is my sole act and deed, and I ask you now to attest to it. Read it please." She presented it first to the Duke of Norfolk, as the oldest man present. "Every one of you read it, if you will, and then I will sign it." Sitting down, she folded her hands in her lap and waited quietly while the paper went from hand to hand and the nobles discussed it in low voices. Wolsey, who was the last to read it, asked the first question.

"His Majesty knows nothing of your decision?"

She shook her head. "Nothing."

"This is an unusual and, if you will forgive me, your Highness, a bold step for you to take alone." It was the Bishop of Durham who spoke, a kindly but nervous little man.

"My lord Bishop," said Mary, "that is one reason I wanted you with me today. I have prayed constantly for God's guidance in this matter, but I need your help. I realize, believe me, how greatly my brother respects the opinion of each one of you, and I ask you now to intercede for me. Will you tell him, please, that I have done this in good part, and ask him not to be displeased with me? Will you assure him that I am always ready to obey his good pleasure?"

Again she smiled at them in turn, her sweetest and most pleading smile. She held out her hand to Norfolk. "Will you help me, my dear lord?"

He knelt on one knee and kissed her hand. "With all my heart, your Grace."

"And you, my lord Bishop?"

Winchester took his place. "Gladly, my daughter."

"My lord Duke?" As she raised her eyes to Brandon, she shifted a small wad of paper from her left to her right hand. By the time he had finished his kiss of homage, the paper was hidden in his fingers. It was a delicate maneuver, but Mary was quite sure that no one had seen it.

When everyone present had promised to stand as her friend, the young Princess signed the document, they added their names, and she handed it to Wolsey. "I entrust this to you, sir, as I know you will choose the propitious moment to show it to the King."

He laughed. "I can but try, your Highness."

"And now some wine, my lords, before we part. But first let me thank you again. Pray for me, if you will, and remember I love you all."

It was a moonless night and the fragrant garden was already damp with dew. Mary, huddled on a stone bench in the farthest corner of the pretty walled enclosure, was torn between joy at the thought of seeing Charles alone and the fear that her careful plan might go awry. Nan Howard, who shared her bedchamber, was away at Arundel, but would Gilly spoil it all by making an unexpected visit to her room, even at this late hour, and discover the bolster in her bed?

She tried to reassure herself. Gilly had certainly been sound asleep for an hour or more and the corridors had been deserted when she left the house. Surely all was well. But where was Charles?

The gate at the other end of the garden creaked. A shadowy figure walked slowly down the path, Mary whistled softly. A moment later Charles was beside her, her cold hand in his.

"Now don't scold me," Mary spoke quickly and firmly. "I simply had to see you. There's something I want to tell you that cannot wait any longer." She stopped and began to tremble. Although she had practiced the words over and over they wouldn't come.

Charles pulled her cloak closer around her. "Why, you are shivering, my darling! And it's warm tonight. You aren't ill, are you, Mary? Was the strain too much for you today?" He leaned closer, trying to see her face in the dimness. "I was so very proud of you, love. It was a brave thing for a young girl to do—and you did it so beautifully. I shall never forget the way you stood there, really more like a queen, Mary, than a princess. Every man present commented on your dignity and on the excellence of the declaration itself."

His words acted like a glass of wine on the hesitating girl, giving her the courage to tell him her dream.

"Now that I am free," she whispered, "I shall try to win Hal's consent to my wedding *you*. After all, Charles, you're the Duke of Suffolk now and, as my brother said himself, 'a great match for any woman.'"

Charles lifted her hand and kissed it tenderly, holding it close to his cheek. "Oh, my darling," he said, his voice shaking, "my darling!" What could he say to her, this precious love of his? Must he put out the light that he could see in her eyes? Must he warn her now of Henry's probable anger and the dreadful things that might happen to her if she made such a suggestion? God in heaven, he swore silently, why hadn't he been *born* a duke? It was a bitter dose to wear the title and not have the rights that should come with it.

156

"You have put into words," he finally said, "what I have never dared say even to myself. A Duke of Buckingham—or Norfolk—might raise his eyes to the King's sister. But Charles Brandon? No, no, sweetheart; you're still much too valuable as a political pawn for Henry to give you to *me*."

"Has he mentioned any new alliance for me?"

Brandon shook his head. "No, thank God! Until a short time ago he still hoped to wed you to Prince Charles."

"Then he might very well listen to me, Charles. Truly, he might! If I hint to him that he could use our betrothal as evidence of how little he cares about the broken contract. 'My sister,' he could say, 'was always most reluctant to marry your Prince, and I am happy for her sake that it is no longer necessary. We would not have dishonored ourselves by failing to live up to our promises, but now that you have broken yours, I am delighted to give her hand to the man who has won her heart.' " Mary watched him hopefully. "Or something like that."

Although Charles was sure, in his heart, that the King would say no, he realized that Mary's idea was a good one. It was the kind of romantic gesture that would appeal to Henry at this time, when he was seeking a way to save his face.

"I have nothing to lose, you know," Mary added quickly. "If I can't marry you I don't care what Henry does to me. Let him send me to a nunnery! I'd welcome it." She sounded very positive. "Surely you must see that I'm right, Charles. There's never been any hope for us before, but there is now. It's small, I admit, but it's a hope. Why should we throw it away?"

"We would be fools to do so. You are right, Mary. But I wonder"—his voice was grim—"if you can imagine how I am feeling at this moment. It's a dreadful thing, believe me, to let my lady do the wooing and take on her little shoulders the burdens and risks that should rest on me."

Mary smiled in the darkness. "I know, Charles, and I'm sorry. But this, my dearest, is what comes of falling in love with a princess."

CHAPTER XV

MARY SPENT THE NEXT two days wandering anxiously around her house and gardens holding imaginary conversations in which she justified her independent action to her brother. Wolsey had warned her that it might be some time before the auspicious moment presented itself for showing her document to the King. "And even then," he said, "it may prove to be the wrong one. His betrayal by his allies has made his Majesty very testy, your Highness, and even small things throw him into a temper."

And when the expected summons came—Mary must ride to Greenwich immediately—there was no way of telling, from the wording of the royal command, whether she faced a scolding or, as she hoped and prayed, a commendation for her spirited decision. She wasted no time in covering the miles between the two palaces, changing into her most becoming gown, and following her usher to the Presence Chamber. She was shaking as she stepped over the threshold, but one glance at her brother's wide face, smiling warmly at her from behind a table covered with papers, set her mind at rest and slowed her racing pulse. It was obvious, thank God, that he was glad to see her.

"Here she is," he said, turning to Wolsey, who was standing close to his right hand. "Long before we expected her, my lord Bishop, and, if you'll forgive a fond brother's partiality, looking extremely charming."

He leaned forward. "Come kiss me, chuck!" He held out his arms, embraced her with enthusiasm, kissed her loudly and wetly on both cheeks, and pointed to a chair near his.

"Sit, Mary. We have a great deal to discuss today and you must be tired from your journey. Have a glass of wine with me as we talk." He reached for a flagon of wine and filled her goblet himself, then pushed over a silver plate. "Saffron cakes—good ones. Try them. The pastry cook here has learned how to make them at last. Light and plump and full of currants! Here—shove 'em back. I've made myself hungry." He took the largest on the plate and sank his teeth into it with relish, scattering crumbs down the front of his handsome brocade jerkin, a garment Mary hadn't seen him wear before. "My tailor just finished it," he said, when she admired it.

He gulped down the delicately flavored hippocras and ate another cake. "Delicious. But I didn't send for you to discuss saffron cakes." A long finger poked around the papers strewn in front of him. "That declaration of yours, breaking your betrothal. Here it is—no, that's something else—"

It seemed to Mary, as she watched her brother tumbling the heap of documents, that he was a trifle uneasy. Was his voice too hearty, perhaps, and those smiles forced? The right word escaped her for a moment or two, then she found it. Conciliatory . . . that was it; he was being conciliatory. But why?

"Now I have it!" Unrolling the long sheet of parchment, Henry showed Mary her own signature and those of her noble witnesses. "This was a bold thing for you to do, you know. A very bold thing!" He looked at her and shook his head, but there was pride rather than anger in his tones and the girl made up her mind swiftly to answer him in as spirited a fashion as she could muster.

"Well, Hal, I'm your sister, after all. Surely you didn't expect me to sit there at Wanstead and do nothing! Now tell me, are you giving me permission to send it to Maximilian and Prince Charles?" She leaned forward eagerly. "If the wording is faulty, I could alter it. I'd be happy to."

"The wording?" Henry turned to Wolsey. "It seems well phrased to me. An excellent statement, in fact. What do you say, Wolsey?"

"I wouldn't change a word, your Grace."

"Good. Good!" Henry beamed from one to the other, then settled back in his throne chair and ran his fingers through his short red hair. His face was slightly flushed, and something crept into his expression during the short, tense silence that made Mary's heart sink.

"No, Mary," he tapped the long document on the table. "I don't think we'll dispatch it for a while. Let them think, for a little longer, that they are deceiving me. Let them continue to lie and promise and evade. . . ." Clearing his throat noisily, he spoke again to Wolsey. "But have a copy of it made as soon as possible. For France. I want her Highness's new betrothed to see that his future Queen can think and act for herself."

So that was it. Mary flinched under the blow. Her "new betrothed"!

She was still reeling from the shock when something else that the King had said made her raise her drooping head to ask him a question.

"Queen?" she whispered.

Henry laughed triumphantly. "Yes, Queen! Mother of God, what I wouldn't give to see Maximilian's face—yes, and Ferdinand's, too—when they hear the news. They thought they were making a dupe of me with their secret treaties and broken contracts! We'll see who has the final laugh. It's not as safe as they thought to hoodwink Henry of England." He was talking so loudly and quickly that the words tumbled over each other. "Look." He reached for another document and handed it to Mary.

"You were not the only one who was busy on the twenty-ninth day of July. On that very day, sister, on that very day, I too was drawing up an important paper. God, what an important paper! Read it! Read it! We're at peace with France, chuck, and you are to wed Louis. Can you believe it? Isn't that magnificent? You will be the Queen of France!"

Queen of France? Marry Louis—?

"No, Hal. You can't do it! Not that decayed old man! You couldn't ask such a thing of me, your own sister." She burst into tears, remembering all the grim descriptions she had heard of France's King.

"He's not too old and decayed to fall in love," answered Henry with his usual obtuseness. "It seems that your portrait and what de Longueville wrote him about your beauty and accomplishments have made him mad to marry you. He's as eager to wed you as any young lover, Mary; can't wait for the wedding day, is happy to agree to all my terms and stipulations. He writes that he'll do anything to please you. Your wedding and coronation will unite England and France."

As he boomed on and on, describing the glories of the match, Mary felt actually ill. When he stopped at last, she controlled her tears and faced him.

"I won't do it. Listen to me, Hal—I simply *will not do it!* If you try to force me, I'll seek sanctuary in a nunnery. I'd rather take the veil than wed Louis!"

"What?" The young King doubled up his fist as if to strike his sister but instead banged it on the table. "You will not? You'll do exactly as I say! Now listen to *me*, Mary, while I tell *you* something—"

Before he could say another word, Wolsey laid his hand on his master's wide shoulder. "May I interrupt to suggest, Sire, that you allow the Princess a little time to think things over? And, if you will forgive a man who has known you both since you were little children, I would like to add that it might be wise for the two of you to finish this discussion when you are a bit—calmer.

"You love her Highness and she loves you; these quarrels must be extremely painful, I'm sure." He pressed Henry's shoulder, meaningly. "I see by the clock that the Duc de Longueville has waited more than an hour for his tennis game. Go, if it please your Grace, and leave me with her Highness. I will be happy to answer her questions and to point out some of the advantages that may not have occurred to her. She and I can talk it all over more coolly."

Henry grunted and rose to his feet. "You may be right." He made the admission grudgingly while he glowered at his sister. "Now try not to be such a damned fool, Mary." As he reached the door she heard him mutter, "Jesu—women!"

When the door closed behind him, Wolsey poured out another goblet of wine. "Drink this, your Highness," he said. "You look positively faint." Walking swiftly to the nearest window, he threw it wide open. "It's stuffy in here." When he saw some color creep back into her cheeks, he drew up a chair and began to talk.

"Believe me, my dear child, I know how repugnant this marriage must be to you. Any young woman with your sensitivity would feel the same. Although they do say that poor Louis is a very kind and gentle man—good to his daughters, faithful to his late wife, and an excellent king. His people call him their 'father.' But he has been ill for a number of years and I have heard that he is frail and prematurely old." Wolsey sighed. "Yes, despite his good qualities, we cannot claim that he will be the handsome and charming bridegroom that a young girl dreams of marrying."

"Even shovel-chinned Prince Charles would be preferable," said Mary, "and I dreaded wedding *him.*"

"In the heat of the moment," said the Bishop, "you forgot, and are forgetting, I'm afraid, that no matter what you say or do, your Grace, you are destined to wed for reasons of state. I admit that King Louis may seem, when you first think of him as a husband, the worst possible match for you, but he is not. Not by any means." He leaned closer and looked earnestly into her eyes. "May I point out a great advantage that this marriage would hold for you?"

Mary nodded, quite willing to listen to him. She liked this man and trusted him. Thomas Wolsey, she was sure, would not lie to her.

"It lies in the very thing that makes you shudder—his ill health. To be brutally frank, your Highness, I do not think you would be tied to him for very long. Marry a young Prince and you will spend the rest of your life with him; marry Louis of France—" He shrugged. "A year? Two years? Before too long, my dear lady, you will be his widow and, as the Dowager Queen of France, in a much better position to arrange a pleasanter future." He smiled meaningly as he said this, and it was obvious to Mary that he was trying to say something he dared not put into words.

"His Majesty is a great bargainer, you know. He rarely gives anything without demanding value in return. Why not play the game his way? Is there not some promise, some concession you would like to ask as a reward for your obedience in this matter?"

A light broke through the girl's confused thoughts as she realized what he was suggesting. Did he know, then, of her love for Charles Brandon? Or was he just assuming that there was someone, or could be someone? In any case, could she conquer her horror over the thought of being Louis' wife—?

She rose to her feet. "Your advice is good, my lord, and wise. I am more grateful than I can say. If I go to my own rooms now and pray perhaps the Lord will give me the strength and courage to heed it."

"God bless you, my child, and help you." He nodded, approvingly. "One thing I forgot to say to you is that your sacrifice will bring peace to England. Blessed are the peacemakers, you know."

"Well?" Henry looked questioningly at his sister, his whole attitude one of arrogant impatience. Still clad in his tennis costume, he had summoned Mary from her withdrawing room, giving the girl less than two hours to make up her mind. She saw that he was in no mood for further rebellion.

She sank to the floor in a deep curtsey, her mind busily choosing the right words. The next few minutes, she knew only too well, were the ones in which she would lose or gain her last chance of some day winning her heart's desire. "Help me, dear God!" She prayed silently.

"Well?" The increasing truculence in his voice warned her not to hesitate any longer. She pointed to her prie-dieu.

"I've been seeking guidance, Hal, and praying for the strength to do what you want." Grimacing, she shuddered openly. "Mother of God, you must realize, brother, how repulsive it is to me!" With a deep sigh, she touched the corners of her eyes with her lace handkerchief, then raised them to his. "Tell me, is it so very important to you and to England? Will it bring peace if I marry Louis?"

The hint that she was ready to surrender, and the pleading in her round eyes, softened Henry a little, and for a fleeting second he had to close his own thoughts to the unpleasant picture of his beautiful young sister in the arms of disease-ridden Louis. Every royal princess must marry for expediency, he consoled himself, and she would be the Queen of France, after all.

"I swear to you, Mary," he answered, "that you will be rendering our people a great service. You'll save the lives of thousands of soldiers—English and French, and your union with Louis should even prevent future wars between our two countries." He put his arm around her and kissed her. "And to tell you the truth, chuck, I'm glorying in the thought of my little sister as the Queen of France!"

Mary managed a wistful smile. "You know that it is always my pleasure as well as duty to obey you, Hal. But you are asking

163

something almost impossible this time." She drew away and paced slowly up and down the room, pretending to be deep in thought. Finally she stopped in front of him and clasped her hands tightly together as if to give herself courage.

"It would make it easier to shoulder this distasteful burden," she said, "if I had some hope of happiness in the future, no matter how distant." She spoke slowly and carefully, weighing each word. "If I knew that, when Louis dies, I would be free to marry as I please, without fear of your displeasure, I believe I could do it." Had she made him angry? No, he was looking impatient, perhaps, but not angry.

"Promise me *that*, Hal, and I'll wed old Louis for you as soon as it can be arranged." As she offered her bargain, she let her voice sound brisk and decisive. There must be no doubt in Henry's mind but that she meant it; she would marry Louis in exchange for his promise, not otherwise. "If you cannot give it me, I ask your permission to retire into any nunnery that you and Kate think suitable."

"It's Brandon you're hot for, isn't it, Mary?" Henry laughed. "Well, have it your own way, have it your own way. Marry Louis and do as you wish later."

Without another word Mary ran for the door, opened it, and called a page to her side. "Find the Dean of Lincoln," she said. "Bring him here immediately. Tell him his Majesty must see him without delay."

When she had closed the door again she found her brother looking at her in some annoyance. "What now?"

She gave him an impish smile. "I thought that if our good Wolsey knew what we had decided between us, he could begin drawing up my marriage contracts." During the silence that followed, she held her breath. Had she pushed him too far? But she must have a witness, she knew that; his promise to her alone would mean nothing.

For a second the King was torn between rage and admiration. With a roar of laughter, he caught her in his arms. "So you don't trust your old brother? Well, you may be right, you may be right! As a matter of fact, wench, I'm not sure I trust you either, and the sooner the matter is settled, the happier I will be. Now, before Wolsey reaches us, suppose we seal the bargain between ourselves. Will the future Queen of France condescend to bestow a sisterly kiss on the King of England?"

CHAPTER XVI

WOLSEY CAUGHT UP WITH Mary soon after she left the Presence Chamber. "Come into my sanctum for a moment or two," he suggested, "and compose yourself. This afternoon has been a hard one for you."

"Indeed it has. My knees are still shaking." Giving him a faint but grateful smile, she followed him into the small room that served as office and private devotional; a table littered with papers was obviously dedicated to one side of Wolsey's busy life, a beautiful prie-dieu to the other.

After seating her comfortably, he drew up a chair for himself. "Even with your brother's promise, you find the future frightening."

The kind understanding in his voice was almost too much for Mary. Fighting back the tears, she nodded. "You see," she said, "I came to Greenwich hoping that I might choose my own husband. Silly dreamer that I am, I actually thought Henry might listen to me." She threw up her hands in a gesture of despair. "And to find that it was already too late! That it was *always* too late!"

"But the King would never have allowed you to marry the Duke of Suffolk, your Grace." A startled gasp from Mary brought an amused look to his face. "Oh, I'm not blind, you know! Why else do you think I suggested that you bargain with his Majesty? After all, my daughter, I've loved you since you were a small child. I learned your secret some time ago."

"How could you? I haven't told anyone. Not even Gilly!"

Wolsey laughed gently. "I didn't need to be told. I read it in your eyes. However"—he turned serious—"I'm glad you've been so discreet. Continue to keep your secret, my child. It is safe with me, I promise you; and if you are ever free, you may be sure that I will do all I can to help you."

"If, if, if! I'll be an old woman and Charles married to someone else."

"Perhaps. In the meantime, you can at least hope; and you can pray for patience and guidance."

"Oh!" A sudden thought struck the Princess. "Charles must not hear this dreadful news from the King. But how can I—" Rising to her feet, she took an indecisive step toward the door. Should she simply seek out Charles and arrange a private interview? Why not? For the first time, she had the upper hand; she wasn't afraid, she discovered, of anything that her brother would say or do. Except for Charles. He might use Charles as a whipping boy.

"No, no." Wolsey put out a restraining hand. "Stay here, your Highness. I'll send for his Grace immediately."

When Brandon hurried in, a few minutes later, Mary could see that he was bewildered by the sudden summons. "You wished to see me, sir . . . your Highness. . . ." He looked from one to the other.

"The Lady Mary has something disturbing to tell you, my lord Duke. Some news that concerns you both, and that will soon be common knowledge."

Afraid of losing her courage, Mary spoke quickly. "The King ordered me here to Greenwich today," she said, "to inform me that I must wed the King of France."

"The King of France? Louis?" Charles's response was a cry of horrified disbelief. "He couldn't! Not even Hal. . . ."

Wolsey interrupted him. "But he has, my son, and for very good reasons. The marriage will insure peace with France, for one thing. And give his Majesty the opportunity to triumph over Maximilian and Ferdinand, for another; which means a great deal to the King, of course—and it means a crown for his favorite sister."

"A crown, yes, but. . . ."

"I know." The older man stopped him again. "We all know. Still, Princess Mary *will* be Queen of France. Louis is not young,

166

strong and handsome, but he is a good man and has been a fine king. As her Highness must marry to please her brother, I know of no other alliance that holds such advantages for England and for her."

Wolsey then presented the other arguments in favor of the match, the arguments that he had used earlier to convince Mary. When he was finished, he made his way to the door of an adjoining room. "I will leave you to tell his Grace what the King promised you," he said to Mary. "I shall return shortly."

As the door closed behind him, Charles rushed to Mary and took her in his arms. "Mary, Mary!" His agitation was so great that he could say nothing more. To her surprise, she found that this time she was the one to whisper brave words of comfort and reassurance.

Raising his head at last, Charles reminded her of Wolsey's final remark. "What could Henry promise you that would make this cross any easier to bear?"

"That when, and if, I am ever free, I may marry to please myself. I made a bargain with him, my darling, when I realized that there was no hope for us *now*. And I made him repeat his promise in Wolsey's presence."

A few weeks later, when Queen Catherine was leading Mary between rows of bowing and curtseying nobles to the large dais where the King and her proxy bridegroom awaited her, she heartened herself by remembering the tender scene in Wolsey's study. Once Charles had accepted the fact that Mary must, in any case, either marry Louis or go into a convent, he had sworn that he would wait for her—for years, if need be. It would be a small price to pay, he had said, for the happiness they might some day have together.

As she dropped Catherine's hand and took her position beside the Duc de Longueville, who was taking Louis's place in the ceremony, she saw Charles standing with England's other two dukes, elderly Norfolk and red-headed, laughing-eyed Buckingham. He gave her a smile of encouragement and she managed to answer it with a lift of her own lips before turning to her brother. Henry's kiss was the signal for the long elaborate ritual to begin, a ritual so similar to the one, seven years before, in

167

which she had become betrothed to Prince Charles, that her responses came easily. Once or twice she even had to remind herself that the King beside her was her brother, not her father, and that this time she was pledging herself to the King of France.

But when the exchange of vows and the signing of documents were over, the participants and the onlookers did not retire immediately to the banquet hall as they had done before; a new and unpleasant addition to the ceremony was considered necessary to bind the Princess to her absent husband-to-be, and she had to summon up all her courage to face it gracefully.

Stepping down from the dais, she made her way to a large carved and gilded screen, set across one corner of Greenwich Palace's state apartment. Lady Guildford, who was waiting behind it, welcomed her with a comforting hand and a loving whisper, then quickly stripped her of her overdress, helping her immediately into a gold velvet chamber robe. Although it was a most enchanting garment, embroidered all over with pearls and diamonds, and lavishly trimmed with glittering gold lace, the Princess turned away from the mirror in Lady Guildford's hand with a shiver of distaste.

"Never mind, love," said the older woman, "it will take only a moment. Let me have your stocking."

Mary held out her left leg and Lady Guildford untied her garter and pulled off the knitted silk covering, leaving bare her slim ankle and pretty leg. As she left the shelter of the screen and returned to the platform, she saw that the throne chairs had been removed and a wide divan, made up to look like a bed, had been put in their place. Henry, even handsomer than usual in a purple satin mantle, took her trembling fingers in his and escorted her to the cushioned couch, indicating the spot where she must lie.

The Duc de Longueville, still wearing a red stocking and boot on his left leg, but with his right one naked, stretched out beside her. The room was silent. Mary was shaking violently, and she could feel the hot color flooding her face as she forced herself to raise her robe. The Frenchman touched his bare leg to hers, she lowered the robe, and he helped her quickly to her feet. The proxy marriage had been consummated.

Rarely in history had a match between a king and a royal princess been arranged in so short a time. Only a few weeks had elapsed since the day when de Longueville and Henry first discussed its possibility and their messengers had begun crossing and recrossing the Channel. Now, in less than a month, the deed was done and Louis was clamoring for his bride.

While love letters and lavish gifts of jewelry arrived almost every day from Paris, scores of seamstresses were working around the clock on the new Queen's trousseau. Many of the things that Henry had ordered for her wedding to Prince Charles could be used, of course; her chariots, horses, tapestries, altar furniture, plate, beds, chairs, hangings, jewels. Initials and coats of arms must be altered, the fleur-de-lys of France embroidered here and there. But the gowns made in the Flemish style had to be discarded completely and thirty new ones finished to take their place, of which sixteen were to be in the French fashion, six in the Italian, as Mary would also be the titular Queen of Milan, and eight in the current English mode, with the deep square necks, slashed sleeves, tight, fitted bodices and full overskirts to which she was accustomed.

Immediately after the ceremony at Greenwich, the Duc de Longueville returned to Paris, accompanied by the Earl of Worcester, who had been chosen to be Mary's proxy in the French ceremony. There, on the fourteenth day of September, at the Church of the Celestines, King Louis and Worcester made the same vows and exchanged the same documents that Mary and de Longueville had a month earlier. Two days later, with a great sound of cymbals and trumpets, the King of France stood at a massive marble table in the great hall of the Palais Royal and proclaimed the fact that his country was now at peace with England.

The carefully guarded secret was out at last, and the Lady Margaret of Savoy was both hurt and indignant. She burst into a flood of tears when the news reached her at Lille, and dashed off an angry letter to Henry, accusing him of having broken his kingly word, and of having brought dishonor on his name. She would publish his promises, she said, and expose his infidelities to the world. She had (and this was indeed true) spent the previous spring and all that summer trying to persuade Ferdinand and Maximilian that they must not break the marriage contract between her nephew Prince Charles and the Princess Mary, and it was a bitter blow to discover, now, that Mary was irrevocably bound to Louis of France.

She had known that the kings of France and England were busy about something; her agents had kept her informed of the stream of couriers and noblemen who were shuttling back and forth across the Channel. But Henry, by cleverly spreading the rumor that his older sister Margaret, the newly widowed Queen of Scotland, was to be Louis's new bride, had taken her in completely.

Henry roared with laughter as he read her letter and wasted no time in composing his answer. It was a task he enjoyed thoroughly, the right words and phrases flowing into his mind and onto the paper before him:

"Make known my promises," he wrote her, "and I will publish yours. Yours will be the greater blame for, as you well know, I broke my faith because your father and uncle had betrayed me by signing a secret pact with France, and because they had delayed my sister's marriage until I could no longer delude myself that they had any intention of honoring our contract. I had no right, in the circumstances, to deprive the Princess Mary of what, you must admit, is a brilliant alliance."

This was the young King's revenge and revenge was sweet, feeling, as he did, that Margaret had made a fool of him over the Brandon affair, and that her powerful kinsmen had used him as a pawn in their private chess games, counting no doubt on his youth and inexperience to protect them from retaliation.

"I've beaten them," he told Wolsey now, showing him the lady's letter and his answer, "and I did it by using the methods they taught me. What a triumph—what a victory! The poor little pawn has captured their king!" He threw back his head and all but crowed, looking for all the world like a rooster, thought Wolsey, as he strutted up and down the room, his short red hair bristling on top of his squarish head just like a red coxcomb.

With England at peace, Henry's chief task these days was to see that his sister went to France with the most sumptuous and lavish equipment possible. Nothing was too fine or too expensive for his darling Mary; she must have the best of everything:

the largest diamonds, the reddest rubies, the longest strings of the most lustrous pearls obtainable, and the heaviest and most elaborate gold plate for her table. She must have cloth-of-gold hangings—throw away the damask ordered for her match with Prince Charles!—find richer altar cloths and chasubles, finer banners and banneroles for her litter, embroider her hatchments and scutcheons with gold, make her azure canopy of state the most beautiful ever seen!

Although Mary was glad to see the last of her hated Flemish gowns, she took practically no interest in the other preparations for her departure. If Henry wanted to deck his blood sacrifice in gold and precious jewels, let him; as far as she was concerned, it all made her feel ill. She forced herself to smile dutifully when he called her "my beloved sister, the Queen of France," but it grew increasingly difficult; he used the expression so often and so loudly that she found herself hating the very sound of it.

Whenever possible the unhappy girl slipped away to her own apartments to study her French, using a new grammar book written expressly for her at this time by John Palsgrave, her French master and chaplain. Hard work, she discovered, helped her to forget her troubles, while the company of her ladies made matters worse. All they could talk about, these days, was the imminence of their departure and the glories that they expected to enjoy in France.

Bess Percy and Nan Howard, her two maids who had been with her for so long, were to accompany her as her chief ladies-in-waiting. They were her own choice. The others were not: the two Grey girls were appointed because of their father, the Marquis of Dorset, was a member of the Joint Commission to attend Mary's wedding, and his wife, the Lady Margaret Grey, was planning to join the royal entourage. It followed naturally that their daughters should be asked to come along, too, as ladies-in-waiting to the Princess. Mary Boleyn was to be another, and young Jane Seymour, whose brother Edward was a page of honor. Mary, the daughter of Sir Thomas Boleyn, the granddaughter of the Duke and Duchess of Norfolk, and niece of the Earl of Surrey, had recently lost her mother, and so her elderly grandmother, who was, with the Duke, accompanying the new

171

Queen to France, suggested that she be the sixth of the royal maids.

"You will have more Howards than anything else," said Nan, when she scanned the list. "I see that my mother has arranged for little Anne Boleyn to be with us as a junior maid. I suppose it will be my duty to see that my two young nieces behave themselves, as my brother Surrey's new wife Betty is too close to their age herself to play the aunt with any authority."

Mary shrugged. "I expect Gilly will keep them in order, Nan. I thank God every night that Gilly has agreed to come with us. What would we do without her?"

Much as Mary loved Nan and Bess Percy, Gilly was really the only one of her attendants who gave her comfort and understanding, having learned, at last, the girl's secret. One night, when she heard Mary crying uncontrollably into her pillows, she came quietly to her bedside, drew up a chair, and sat there until her charge had told her the whole story. She held Mary's hand and said nothing while the girl confessed her love for Charles Brandon and talked of her hopes, earlier that summer, of winning the King's consent to their marriage. But she shook her head doubtfully when Mary had described the bargain she had struck with her brother.

"I wouldn't count too much on the King's promise," she warned. "When the good of the country is at stake, kings often change their minds and break their word."

Mary sat up in bed and faced her governess. "Now listen to me, Gilly. Much as I hate it, I'm marrying repulsive old Louis to please my brother and to help England. But when Louis dies I shall marry Charles *immediately*—I shan't give a tinker's damn for England, my brother, or anything! I won't give Hal a chance to change his mind. I have his promise and I shall see to it that he doesn't break it, king or no king!"

As September drew to a close, the King and Queen took Princess Mary and her suite to Dover, where they waited for a long spell of stormy weather to end before sending her off to France. The moment the seas subsided, English ships were posted around the Channel to make sure that it was free of anyone who might prey on the royal bride. Her costly belongings were sent on ahead and, by late evening of the first day of October almost everyone except Mary had boarded the small fleet of ships and were ready to sail with the morning tide. Knowing that she would sleep little or none that night anyway, the Princess had asked the King's permission to remain on shore until the last possible moment. Her reluctance to leave him and her sister-in-law, her lover, her friends, and the land of her birth seemed to grow greater as each hour passed.

Following Catherine to her bedchamber, she waited until the royal lady had dismissed her women for the night before bidding her farewell.

"Keep a stout heart, my dear," said the older woman. "Life is not easy for either of us, you know." Mary kissed the plain, thin face on the pile of silken pillows and silently agreed, hoping for Catherine's sake that a healthy heir to the throne would restore the old harmony between herself and the King, and remove the strained, anxious expression from her darkly shadowed eyes.

Too soon after Henry's return from the wars the warmth of their reunion was spoiled by angry words on one side and unhappy, patient silence on the other. Each new evidence of Ferdinand's double-dealing brought about another tirade from Henry against everything Spanish and, as was inevitable, his wife bore the brunt of his displeasure, withdrawing more and more into herself as her only defense against his noisy storming.

"Send me news of yourself, dear Kate, and guard your health. Believe me, dear sister, I shall be thinking of you often—and praying for you."

With one more embrace, the two women parted, the Queen to seek escape from her weariness and misery in sleep, the Princess to return to her own apartments where she waited, fully clothed and wide awake, for the dread moment when she must leave the old castle and embark on the short voyage which would change her life. The October night was cold, the high-ceiled bedchamber chill and damp despite the heavy tapestries covering the stone walls and the roaring fire on the wide hearth. At first she paced up and down the room, trying to keep warm, then she wrapped herself closely in her fur-lined boat cloak and huddled near the fire.

She had had hopes of arranging, somehow, a last moment

173

alone with Charles, but the proper opportunity never came. Mary's only comfort was her confidence in the understanding between them. Whenever their eyes had met even in a crowded room, she had seen it, and her ear caught its echo in his most casual greeting. But tonight, as she faced what might be years of separation, she found it necessary to quash a few small doubts by repeating over and over their vows and promises.

The hours passed all too quickly. Mary's heart sank even lower when she saw the dark lancet windows turn gray and heard a scratch on the door.

"So soon?" She tried to smile at Anne Jerningham, her chamberwoman, who entered hurriedly, carrying her mistress's gloves and her own boat cloak.

"The litter is in the courtyard, your Highness," was the answer. With gentle fingers, the woman who would soon be known as the Queen's femme de chambre, pulled Mary's hood over her red-gold curls and tied the long, dangling cloak strings.

Dawn was just breaking when the girl stepped outside the castle doorway. In the soft pink light, she walked toward her litter, swaying between two white horses. Waiting beside it was a small group of men on horseback—the King, the Earl of Surrey, and the Marquis of Dorset; Surrey, the spare, dark-haired son of old Norfolk, was out of his saddle and ready to help her into her litter long before she reached it, and Henry gave her a loud and cheery greeting, his breath showing white in the crisp morning air.

"The wind is favorable, sister, so off we go. We'll ride ahead to make sure that all is ready for you at the harbor."

By the time the little curtained conveyance began to move forward there was no one in the courtyard but the small open wagon in which Mary's chamberwoman sat, her feet propped up on a large bundle, and the usual scattering of soldiers going about their early morning duties. The litter and the wagon jolted over the rough cobbles, passed between twin towers guarding the inner bailey, then clattered across the drawbridge. Once they were on the chalky road that led down to the waterfront, the litter rode more steadily and Mary leaned out to look back past the wide, murky moat at the huge castle, now looming over her. Catherine was sleeping behind one of those long, narrow

174

windows. And Charles? Was he awake and sharing her despair, or was he sleeping, too?

She shivered, partly from cold and partly from the dreadful feeling of loneliness that was settling deep into her heart. Her bad time had come at last; no miracle would save her, she was sure of that. Within the hour she would see the last of everything and everybody that she loved best, and this fresh wind would carry her swiftly over the water to the arms of an aged, sickly bridegroom.

The sound of quick hoofbeats on the road behind her caught her attention and she craned her neck to see a lone rider galloping past the slow baggage wagon. A second later he reined up beside her, adjusted his horse's pace to that of the litter horses, and bent down to look into her startled eyes.

"Charles!" Already emotionally shaken, the unexpected sight of him was too much for Mary's composure. She burst into tears.

"Mary, Mary, sweet!" Brandon sounded a little desperate. "Come, love, don't weep. Please, don't weep! I must ride on after a moment or two, or the King will guess why I found an excuse to delay at the Castle. This is our only chance for a word or two alone. . . ."

Mary swallowed hard and dried her eyes, laughing shakily. "It was because I was feeling so lonely and thought you might be sound asleep, not caring. . . ." Her voice broke and a few more tears ran down her cheeks and dropped on the front of her velvet cloak. "Oh, Charles, how can I bear it? How can I bear it? I'm frightened."

He groaned and set his teeth. "I don't know, my darling. I don't know how I can, either. I wake up in the night and think of you married to Louis and I almost go mad!" They were speaking softly, not wanting the grooms on the litter horses to hear them, and both were aware that they must part shortly without a last kiss or caress. Finally the misery in Charles's voice awoke Mary to the fact that he needed comforting, too, and she pushed aside her fears and sorrows to give him a watery smile.

"If he's as feeble as they say, Charles, he may want more of a companion than a wife. At least I am praying that it will be so. But no matter what happens"—and she shuddered—"I shall cling to the hope that someday I may be free to marry you."

Brandon nodded. "That's my brave girl, my good girl! Even if it's years, Mary, we must close our eyes to all the time between now and then. Let Louis have today—tomorrow will be ours!" He straightened in his saddle and touched his horse. "I must leave you now, beloved. God bless and keep you until we meet again."

Without another word he was off and speeding down the road; a moment later there was nothing left to prove that they had had this brief precious time together but a slowly settling cloud of chalk dust, stirred up by his horse's hoofs. When Mary reached the beach, he was standing with her brother and the other lords, but although he moved quickly to the side of her litter to wish her a good day, it was the Marquis of Dorset who lifted her to the sandy ground.

"Well, your Grace," he said, pursing his thick lips and looking out over the harbor, "we will soon be on our way." He pointed to a small boat, already manned with sturdy oarsmen, then showed her a large sailing ship, anchored out from shore. "There's the galley to take us out, and there's our ship. The rest of our fleet is setting sail now—see?" His pudgy finger indicated several ships that were moving slowly out toward the Channel, their sails full and taut.

She was watching the sea gulls circling the water, diving for fish and chattering together, when her brother joined her and took her cold hand in his. "Come walk down the beach with me, Mary," he said. "Before you leave me, I must tell you some annoying news."

He waited until they were a good distance down the strand before speaking again. "It's that fool sister of ours," he sounded both angry and disgusted.

What could Margaret have done, Mary wondered, to upset Henry so much?

"She married the young Earl of Angus on the fourth day of August—and I've only now heard of it." He laughed grimly. "That's a long time to keep such a thing a secret, isn't it? But I don't imagine she was proud of the fact that the Queen of Scotland couldn't wait even a decent interval before rushing into marriage with a beardless boy of nineteen!" He leaned down and kissed Mary on the cheek. "I must say, Mary, that her rash behavior has made me more pleased than ever with you."

"I wonder," said Mary slowly, "if you have any idea at all, Hal, of the horrors I must undergo in the next few weeks? Margaret's marriage to James was an unhappy one—but mine!" She shuddered and raised her eyes. "I don't blame her for wanting to choose her own second husband and I want you to promise me again that I may do so when Louis dies."

The young King grunted a little uncomfortably. "I admit that Louis is a most unappetizing bridegroom and I promise that you will never be asked to make such a sacrifice again. There, does that satisfy you?"

Mary's voice shook with fury and despair. "No. No. It isn't the same thing at all! How can I go to France thinking you may break your word? Don't you realize that the hope of being happy some day could be my only comfort for years and years? Louis has been ill for so long already—he may go on this way forever!"

She turned and buried her face in her hands. "You promised, Hal, you promised!" With a despairing sob, she ran away down the beach and stood, alone, the picture of desolation.

After a moment of indecision Henry followed her. "There, there, chuck. Don't weep! Come, dry your eyes, Mary, and give me a kiss. If it will make you feel more content I will repeat my promise. Marry Louis, be a good queen to him, and if you are ever free you may marry as you wish." He looked up at the sky, then down at the surf breaking at their feet. "If you are not to miss the tide, you must leave me now."

By the time they reached the boat, Dorset and Surrey were sitting in the bow, shouting last messages to Brandon and the others who were remaining in England. Mary, her face still wet with tears, made her own farewells as brief as possible and took her place, clutching her cloak tightly around her.

"God be with you," said Hal, stepping back. "I trust you to His loving care. I hope you and our good friends will have a fair crossing, my dear sister, and that you will find happiness with your new husband . . ."

As the oars flashed through the water, taking the small craft swiftly on its way to the waiting ship, Mary strained her eyes to see the last of her lover, her brother—and England. "Departure," she sang softly to herself, "departure is my chief pain. But I trust right well to return again—"

PART III

PART III

CHAPTER XVII

THE SHIP GAVE A DEVASTATING LURCH, heeling over until Mary thought this time they were surely foundering. As she steadied herself by clutching the edge of the open door, she heard the crash and clatter of all the small objects that were loose in the overcrowded cabin sliding across the tilting deck. Her ladies, meanwhile, were seasick and moaning piteously. Bess and Nan were sharing a basin nearby; the elderly Duchess of Norfolk and thin little Lady Margaret Grey were stretched out on top of the two narrow lockers, the only secure resting places in the dark, low-ceiled, wainscoted enclosure; and Lady Guildford, her face the greenest of any, was huddled on a pile of pillows in a corner, trying to brace herself against the heaving wall.

The basin set on the deck beside her shot out of reach; pressing a towel to her white lips, Lady Guildford gave Mary an agonized glance. Mary, just barely able to control her own rebellious stomach, looked desperately around her, hoping to see someone who was well enough to attend to Lady Guildford's needs. Rank apparently was forgotten during a storm at sea. Tiring women and chambermaids were spewing beside countesses and Lady this and that; only the youngest and strongest seemed able to keep upright in the tossing ship.

"I'd come to you, Gilly dear," Mary shouted over the noise, "but the moment I let go of this door I know I shall lose my balance. Here, Anne—Anne Boleyn! Yes, girl—you!" A small, slant-eyed maiden with smooth dark hair tucked carefully under her hood, who had been watching the confusion around her with malicious enjoyment, now picked her way through the scattered wreckage and the vomiting women. She took her time, and the sharp, almost insolent look in her odd, tiptilted black eyes made Mary suspect that this Anne, at thirteen, was already a great deal smarter than her older, prettier sister Mary Boleyn, who was bending over the young Countess of Surrey, their new aunt.

"You called me, your Grace?"

"Yes, I did. Don't just stand around, Anne. You seem fairly steady on your feet, so make yourself useful. Hand Lady Guildford her basin. Can't you see it has slipped out of her reach? And fetch some fresh towels. The maids are all too ill to help us, girl, so do what you can."

Anne wrinkled her nose in disgust. "Faugh! The whole cabin stinks! Let Jane Seymour do it." She pointed to the other thirteen-year-old of the royal party, a serene-faced, quiet child who was assisting Anne's groaning grandmother, the Duchess of Norfolk.

A surge of anger swept over Mary. She reached out with her free hand to box the girl's ears. "Insolence! How dare you answer me in such a fashion! Do as I say this instant!"

But Anne had slipped past her to the open deck; by clinging to everything within reach and waiting for the few steady moments between pitches and rolls, Mary was able to retrieve Gilly's basin for her and hand her a fur rug. Then, deciding that she, too, would be happier in the fresh air, she followed her naughty young maid out of the cabin.

When she reached her destination, her first thought was that all her gentlemen must be ill, too. Only sailors were to be seen on the soaked, tilting deck, some busy with ropes, others just standing and staring out at the gray, whitecapped water. Then a shout of "Your Majesty!" made her turn, and two cloaked figures hurried to her side.

"This is no place for you, your Grace," scolded the Earl of Surrey, his black hair curled into damp rings around his thin face. "Here, Garnish! Take her other arm and we'll help her back to the cabin."

"No, no, my lords!" Mary laughed and tried to free herself. "I came for air and news. How are we faring? Most of my ladies are so miserable that they hope the ship is doomed—and the sooner the better. Your Betty, my dear Tom, is greener than that sea water."

"Poor child! She warned me that she was a bad sailor. However, even the worst seasickness is soon forgotten, thank God." He looked up at the sky, then back to Mary. "It's a bad storm, your Grace, but nothing unusual for this time of year. And, as you can see"—he pointed a long finger—"we are nearing the coast of France now. That's Boulogne over there. Finding our way into the harbor will be a pretty trick, but as the captain isn't worried, I don't see why we should be."

"Where are the rest of our ships?" Mary searched in all directions for a glimpse of other sails. They seemed to be alone on the vast expanse of grim water.

"Scattered," answered Sir Christopher Garnish. "The last we saw of them, they were being driven up toward Calais. That change of wind, so soon after we set sail, made Calais the easiest port to reach, but our skipper was determined to set you ashore at your destination. 'The Frenchies will be awaiting her Majesty at Boulogne,' he told me, 'and that's where she will land.' "

"I could have wished for a little less bravery. Or shall we say stubbornness?" She smiled from the young knight to Thomas Howard. "Better Calais with my lords and ladies beside me than Boulogne and a cabin full of spewing attendants. Are you my only good sailors, my lords?"

"The Bishop of Durham is still on his feet. He's praying for our safety in the men's cabin, and he seems well enough. But Dorset is as sick as a horse and Garnish, here, is the only knight who isn't prostrate. It's a shambles down there, I'm afraid, with the few lucky ones looking after the unfortunates."

They were so close to shore now that Mary decided to go below again. "If we are landing soon," she said, "I must tell my ladies. By the way"—she glanced around the deck—"have you seen that young niece of yours, Tom? Anne Boleyn, I mean. She ran away from the cabin and I expected to find her up here."

Surrey nodded. "She was around the deck a few minutes ago, deviling some of the sailors. Don't worry about her, your Grace. Satan takes care of his own, you know."

As soon as she reached the cabin, Mary told her suite the

good news. "The harbor is in sight," she announced to them all, "and we will be disembarking very soon. You will all feel better the moment—" Before she could finish her sentence, the ship came to a violent, shuddering, grinding stop, heeled over on one side at a perilous angle and then hung there.

Lady Howard, the Duchess of Norfolk, clutched the edge of the locker and screamed, her wispy white hair hanging around her sweating face. "We're sinking, we're sinking!"

Panic spread through the crowded cabin and seasickness was forgotten in this sudden and dreadful certainty of imminent, watery death. Most of the ladies added their screams to those of Lady Howard, and Mary, who had been thrown to the deck, tried her best to scramble back on her feet. But although the ship now seemed to be quite stationary, the angle made it impossible to rise. She was opening her mouth to quiet the women when Surrey's face appeared in the tilted doorway above her.

"Ladies, ladies! If you please!" A startled quiet followed his shout. "We have run aground at the mouth of the harbor," he explained, "but there is nothing to fear. Boats are on their way from shore at this very moment to take us into Boulogne, so may I suggest that you gather up your belongings"—he glanced around the disordered chamber—"and I will send down some men to help you up to the deck. If any of you are too ill to walk, they will carry you."

While he was talking he had helped Mary to her feet. Now he waited until she had straightened her tumbled skirts. "The first of the French boats should be alongside by now, Madame. Would you like to go ashore immediately, or shall we send some of the other ladies and gentlemen ahead?"

Mary laughed and made a face. "Now that we have all survived this grim crossing, I see no reason to linger in what has become a most unsavory cabin. I will keep my rumpled gown hidden under my boat cloak."

Within a very short time she was seated in a small rowing galley, watching the beach at Boulogne draw closer and closer. They headed for a wide stretch of sand where a crowd of her new countrymen stood, waving their caps and cheering lustily as the little boat cut through the morning surf.

"La Reine!" she heard them shouting. "La Reine! La Reine Marie d'Angleterre! Vive la Reine Marie!"

Surrey, who was seated forward, turned toward Mary with a worried face. "The beach shelves off so sharply here," he said. "I don't see how we can help you ashore without giving you a bit of a soaking."

Almost before he had finished speaking, Sir Christopher Garnish was overboard and standing deep in the water. He held out his arms to Mary. "If your Majesty will condescend—"

Without a word of protest or a moment's hesitation, Mary rose to her feet in the rocking craft, wrapped her cloak tightly around her legs and settled herself comfortably against his wide chest, gripping him firmly around the neck as they splashed through the chilly wavelets.

She was laughing delightedly when he put her down, and neither the Duc de Vendôme nor the Duc de la Tremouille, who had both been sent by Louis to greet his bride, was ever to forget the enchanting picture that Mary made as she took her first step on the damp sands of France. The cool wind had whipped a delicious pink into her cheeks, her blue eyes twinkled at them through lashes pearled with sea spray, a few vagrant red-gold curls had escaped the confines of her hood, and her dimples were busy at the corners of her red mouth.

"Ravishing!" whispered de la Tremouille to his companion. "What has our Louis done to deserve this?"

CHAPTER XVIII

MARY'S PROCESSION, as it moved slowly along the narrow, winding road to Abbeville, was the gayest sight the country people had seen in many a long year. From the new queen herself, in a handsome costume of silver and gold, riding on a snow-white palfrey in the middle of the snakelike column, to the last of her two thousand horsemen and three hundred archers, there was no one present who did not add a brilliant note of color to the whole cortege. Her thirty ladies and maids-of-honor wore beautiful gowns of crimson velvet, the French noblemen and noblewomen were attired in fine silks, satins and jewels, and all the attendants carried bright fluttering pennants. Even the Queen's glittering litter, empty today, and her three carved and gilded chariots, leading the humbler and more sober baggage wagons, looked unusually magnificent as they reflected the rays of the morning sun. It was a picture to delight the eyes of the little groups of gaping onlookers gathered along the side of the road.

Mary's own eyes, as her gentle mare trotted carefully under her, were on a tall, richly dressed, dark-haired young man who was approaching from the direction of Abbeville. For some time now she had noticed him guiding his glossy, spirited stallion past the large band of horsemen at the head of the column. To her surprise, he reined in beside the Duke of Alençon, one of the nobles who had joined her party at Nouvion, and they chatted a moment, glancing back at her as they talked.

Who, she wondered, could he be? All the French lords and ladies knew him; there was much nodding and smiling and calling to and fro as he and Alençon rode over to the Duke of Norfolk. Now, after a sentence or two, they were wheeling their mounts and coming towards her. Even at a distance she could see that this was no languid Gallic courtier; whoever he was, he was clearly a most masculine young man.

"Your Grace," said the Duke of Alençon as they arrived at her side, "I bring you a new kinsman. May I present François, the duc de Valois and Bretagne, the Compte d'Angoulême?"

Before he had finished all the impressive titles, the tall, long-nosed stranger was off his horse and down on one knee in the road, his thin lips on Mary's jeweled fingers. She thought quickly, as her blue eyes met his bold, black, hawklike, appraising glance. Francis—she translated the name to herself—Francis, the Duke of Valois, the Dauphin of France. He was Louis's cousin, the heir-apparent to the throne. And hadn't he recently married Louis's ugly little daughter Claude? He was more than cousin, then.

"Welcome to France, your Majesty." His English was slow but

his smile was so warm and gay that Mary felt they would be friends. "I am, believe me, your most humble servant."

"Thank you, my lord Duke—or should I say 'my dear son-in-law'?" Francis had addressed her in her tongue and she answered him in his. As she sought for the correct French phrase for son-in-law she tilted her head in its daring red hat and peeped out from under the wide brim, looking so much like a bright-eyed bird that Francis laughed with sudden delight.

So the stories of Mary Tudor's beauty and charm had not been exaggerated, after all! He had, rather reluctantly, come to escort her to the King at Abbeville, certain that he would find her either fat and stupid or thin and peevish. In any case, he was prepared to dislike the English Princess who might, so very easily, upset his claim to the crown. But the moment his eyes met hers he knew that he was going to like this golden-haired girl.

"Son-in-law. So I am!" He laughed up at her. "And you are my belle-mère. So very, very belle—and so ridiculously *not* mère!" As he rose to his feet and brushed the sand off his silk-stockinged knee, he gave her a look that made her blush hotly and turn away. A second later she was scolding herself for being foolish, for he had leaped back on his horse, slowed its pace to match that of hers, and was talking pleasantly and impersonally of the ceremonies and celebrations ahead of them and of her new husband, the King.

There was an affectionate, teasing note in his voice as he mentioned Louis that pleased Mary greatly. If he and the King were fond of each other, then she, too, could be easy with this decidedly attractive young man. With a little sigh of relief, she settled in her saddle and encouraged him to tell her about her new court and the life she would lead there. As a result, they were soon chatting and chuckling together as if they had known each other for years instead of minutes.

When they were only a mile or two out of Abbeville, Francis pointed to a cloud of dust ahead of them. "The King," he said.

Mary's heart began to thump with nervousness. But she wasn't supposed to meet him until after they had reached the town! She turned wide, questioning eyes on Francis. He leaned over and patted her shaking hands. "Come, come, little cousin, you have nothing to fear. Louis is the gentlest man I know. You will see."

Instead of pausing, as Francis had, to speak to his countrymen or meet Mary's lords and ladies, the King spurred his high-stepping, Spanish horse and rode right to her side, his gaunt, pale face alight with pleasure under the square-cut, iron-gray hair.

Mary checked her palfrey immediately and prepared to dismount, thinking it right to kneel before her lord and master in this rather awesome moment of their first meeting. But the King, guessing her intention, protested.

"No, no, my dear lady—my dear wife. We can forget formalities in this delightfully unexpected encounter! How fortunate that I happened to be hawking and caught sight of your entourage—"

Mary heard Valois smother a laugh as his cousin continued; he knew, apparently, that this meeting was *not* accidental. "I rode over to give you my dearest love," Louis was saying to her, "and to bid you welcome, so very welcome. And now, my dear Mary, if you will allow me one kiss I will delay you no longer. Au revoir—"

As he leaned toward her, Mary, remembering that she was wearing a most unsuitable red hat, flushed and pulled it off, tossing it to Francis. She turned a dutiful mouth up to meet her husband's first kiss and he, after touching it briefly with his, rode away.

For the next minute or two she sat very still and watched his thin, bent back jounce up and down on his elaborate saddle. She saw that he was wearing silver and gold, a costume that matched the one she had chosen for this important day. So that was why the Duc de Longueville had taken sketches of all her gowns to Louis!

For some reason it was not so easy now to talk and laugh together and the young couple covered the short distance to Abbeville in comparative silence. When they reached Notre Dame de la Chapelle, a little church near the gates of the city, the cortege halted, Mary's litter was brought to her side, she dismounted, took her place in it, and obediently changed her hat for a heavy, ornamented coif. Lady Guildford, who had ridden up to see that all was in order for her charge's ceremonious entry into the town, arranged the silver robe around her embroidered slipper tips, tucked one curl back into place, and drew the golden litter curtains close to their posts so that the people of Abbeville would be able to see their new Queen in all her beauty. With an approving nod, the older woman moved away again, and the procession started forward.

The clocks of Abbeville were striking five when they reached the gates, and a loud blast from a hundred waiting trumpets announced Mary's arrival. A moment later both the chiming and the trumpeting were drowned out by a terrific booming as the guns on the ramparts set off a whole series of volleys in her honor, and, in the ensuing noise and confusion, the cavalcade marched through the Marcade Gate and down the Chausee Marcade to the Church of St. Wulfran.

Mary leaned out of her litter, waving a friendly hand at the masses of cheering, shouting onlookers. She was heartened by their welcome and enchanted by the charm of the old town, made even more colorful today by the triumphal arches and picturesque tableaux set up on high scaffolds along her route; flags fluttered from housetops, tapestries and lengths of bright silk and brocade hung from most of the windows, and there was such a warm, holiday air about everything that she was moved almost to tears.

As peace between France and England had been proclaimed only three weeks before this eighth day of October, 1514, it amazed Mary to see that, far from showing signs of hostility toward her, the people were receiving her with open arms and the most enthusiastic approval. She would learn later that, in the face of youth, beauty, and royal romance, even of the May and December variety, the French were only too willing to forget yesterday's war. *L'amour*, she discovered, would always take precedence in France over *la guerre* or *la patrie*.

She stepped down out of her litter at the entrance of the old Gothic church and the dean, after a speech of suitable dullness, took her down the long aisle to the high altar, where he stood aside for a few minutes while she made her devotions. When she had prayed to God for strength to carry her through the ordeals ahead, she was immediately hurried off to the Hôtel de la

189

Gruthuse, where she was, supposedly, to meet her husband for the first time. It was here, too, that she and Louis would be married in person, early on the morrow.

The Duke of Norfolk was waiting for her at the door into the royal Presence Chamber, his elderly face a little concerned. "They have given your Highness no time at all to rest or ready yourself," he said. "Shall I ask his Majesty for a few minutes delay?"

Mary shook her head, and her jeweled hood sparkled brightly in the candlelight. "Unless you think me untidy, my lord, I see no reason to disturb his arrangements. I am as ready as I can be."

Without another word, Norfolk took her cold hand in his gnarled fingers and led her into the high handsomely decorated room. Louis sat on a dais at the far end of the chamber, surrounded by the highest ranking nobles of France.

Mary was glad to see some familiar faces among them; Francis, smiling encouragingly; Alençon, her friend of the last twenty-four hours; matchmaking de Longueville, whom she hadn't seen since he left her brother's court; and the Ducs of Vendôme and de la Tremouille, the two men who had welcomed her on the sands of Boulogne. The others were a blur of satins and velvets, jewels and glittering embroidery, beards and mustaches. She would learn their names later, she supposed; now she must officially meet her husband, the King of France.

She could hear Norfolk's voice, all pomp and stiff phrases as he presented her to Louis, but she was too busy making the proper obeisance to listen to what he was saying. When she straightened up again, she saw Louis regarding her with so much admiration in his tired gray eyes that she scolded herself for the feeling of oppression that hung over her heart. If she was to be a dutiful wife she must start by finding something about him to like; the fact that his touch made her shudder must not overshadow the good qualities praised by everyone here in France.

She had time, during Norfolk's long, dreary speech, to study her husband's aging face. She could see that he must have been a handsome man when younger, certainly his features were better than those of long-nosed Francis. But the folds and dewlaps around his cheeks and chin repelled her, as did the dampness of his hand when he led her into the banquet chamber.

He was limping so badly that she found it necessary to express concern for his obvious discomfort. "Don't worry about it, my lady," he said. "It's years now since I've been free from pain. You learn to live with it after a while. And some days are better than others." He seated her in the chair next to his and looked around at the other guests. "I suspect that every man here to-night would be glad to change places with me, pain or no pain."

As Mary accepted his compliment with a smile, and a dep-recating word or two, she realized that Francis of Valois was not at the long table. He was, the King told her, entertaining their English friends at his own hôtel. "They will join us later," she heard him say, "for the dancing."

A moment later he signaled to his wine bearer to refill his goblet. "My physicians have forbidden me wine," he said, "but I'm disregarding their orders tonight." Mary noticed his hand trembling on the stem of the glass as he gulped it down, and watched his thin cheeks flush.

She mentioned the incident later, when she was dancing with the Dauphin. Everybody she knew drank wine. Could it really have such a bad effect on King Louis?

"Everything pleasant has a bad effect on the poor man," was Francis's answer. "Rich food, wine, late hours, dancing—all the things that make life worth while. For months now he's lived the simplest way possible, bed at six, plain meals, fresh air, no strenuous exercise, never more than an hour in the saddle—"

Mary sighed. "How dull." By dropping her eyes, she hid the gleam that came into them. Surely a regimen like that meant that they would lead more or less separate lives.

"Of course," continued Francis, "he cannot obey those rules now. A young wife will make a difference."

Not knowing quite what to say, Mary turned her attention to her dancing and threw herself so wholeheartedly into the gay lavolta that Francis was forced to watch his steps, too, and to toss her higher and higher into the air. As they dipped, glided, and bounced around the mirror-like floor, more than one pair of eyes followed them enviously. Plain little Lady Claude, sitting on the dais beside her royal father, could see only too clearly how much the pair were enjoying themselves.

"Her Grace," she said to Louis, with bitterness in her voice, "dances with verve and skill. She and Francis are well matched."

The King agreed wistfully. In his day he too had been a vigorous and graceful dancer, and he would have liked to be partnering his young bride tonight. But it had been a long day and his gout was punishing him for being out of his comfortable bed. He stretched his leg out in front of him and hoped that it would not be as painful tomorrow. Tomorrow was his wedding day. . . .

He looked down at Claude and wondered whether he could persuade her to make friends with Mary. She had made her disapproval of his marriage very plain and, knowing how sincerely she still mourned her mother, he had said little about it to her. Perhaps a hint would be better, he decided.

"I hope"—he hesitated, not wanting to say "Queen" or "your new mother" to his frowning daughter—"the Princess Mary will not be too lonely here in what must be a very strange country to her. We must all try to be kind and friendly."

Claude sniffed, looking rather pointedly at Mary who was laughing blithely up into Francis's face, her eyes dancing and her cheeks flushed from the lively measures of the lavolta. "Lonely? I don't believe we need worry too much about that, Sire. My husband is doing his duty to her with what I would call enthusiasm, and I'm sure the other gentlemen in your suite will not prove too reluctant to be, as you suggest, kind and friendly. As for myself and my ladies, we are always your obedient servants; we shall try to do as you wish."

Although Mary opened her eyes the next morning and told herself that this was her wedding day, she couldn't seem to make herself believe it. Bess and Nan waited on her at breakfast, but no one said much and it was a hasty meal, anyway, as they must all dress for the nine o'clock ceremony. They both looked at Mary rather sadly when she dismissed them. It would be stupid, they realized, to wish her joy, and tactless to commiserate with her, so they ended by merely kissing her fondly and murmuring that they must hurry if they were to reach their seats by the appointed time.

When the door closed behind them, a tiring woman brought a gold basin filled with warm water, a soft linen towel and a piece of soap, and while Mary washed herself another woman carried in her cloth-of-gold wedding gown. It was made in the French style, the tight-fitting surcoat lavishly trimmed with snowy ermine and the skirt blazing with diamonds, but although Mary knew that it was the most becoming costume she had ever worn, she shivered a little as the two women helped her into it.

The room was quiet. Lady Guildford, who hovered around to make sure that every fold was in place, gave a few orders to the chamberwomen, her voice unusually soft and her manner lacking its customary briskness. Mary, still feeling oddly half asleep, obediently turned, moved, raised her arms, held out her small feet for the jeweled velvet slippers, and her fingers for the heavy rings. She was vaguely aware that Lady Guildford was brushing her long, red-gold hair, spreading it around her shoulders in a gleaming cape, and she held her head still while the older woman finished with the brush, then rubbed it with a piece of silk to make it gleam even more before setting the gemmed coronet in place.

She joined her lords and ladies who waited below, all attired in their most magnificent silks, satins, velvets, furs and jewels; she mounted her palfrey and rode through the covered way that led from the house where she had spent the night to the Hôtel Gruthuse, not even noticing that it was lined with her own English archers, standing stiffly at attention as she passed by.

She managed to smile when she entered the door of the huge salon and gave her right hand, as she was told to do, to the Duke of Norfolk, and her left to the Marquis of Dorset. While the three walked slowly up the long aisle to the dais where the King, her bridegroom, awaited her, Mary saw nothing but a blur of faces. The gasps of admiration, which caused Norfolk and Dorset to smile with pride, were a confused buzz in her ears.

When they reached the dais Louis stepped forward to meet her and the Duke of Norfolk put her right hand in his before moving away, Dorset following him. The King led his bride to the altar.

At the first touch of Louis's chilly, bony fingers, Mary woke to reality. The comforting mists drifted away and her heart began pounding in wild protest against this dreadful, irrevocable act.

Suddenly everything was much too clear and much too vivid. As she forced herself to make the proper responses to the ritual, she seemed to see everyone and everything in the crowded room. She noticed little things that she would never forget: a fat spider, hanging from the carved and gilded ceiling; a strangely shaped crack in the colorful mosaic floor; a fold that looked like a leering face in the cloth-of-gold covering the high walls. She saw that the King's collar of St. Michael sat crookedly on the rich marten trimming of his gold suit. She heard his shallow breathing. She realized that the Lady Claude was weeping as she knelt before her, Mary, and she flushed under the odd, hungry glance that Francis gave her before he knelt in front of Louis. All her senses had strangely sharpened. She smelt a sourness on the breath of the Cardinal de Brie as he conducted the wedding service, and heard one flat note among the true ones when the trumpets pealed at the end.

Having been informed that it was the French custom for a royal bride to remain in the seclusion of her own apartments, and to entertain only the ladies of her new family while the King made merry with the other wedding guests, Mary found herself looking forward to the long afternoon that followed the nuptial ceremony. It should, she thought, give her an excellent opportunity to make friends with her French kinswomen, the ladies who would be her companions in her new life.

She was distressed to find that this was not the easy and pleasant task she had anticipated, for the Lady Claude continued to be aloof, cool, and gloomy, and Louisa of Angoulême, the Dauphin's handsome, witty mother, while scrupulously polite, seemed to be watching the new young Queen with suspicious and critical eye. Only little Renee, Claude's prettier, younger sister, met Mary's warm advances with any enthusiasm, and with this mild conquest the English girl had to be content. "Thank God," she said to herself, "I will always have Gilly and Bess and Nan."

The hours, slow and dragging as they were, passed much too

swiftly for the unhappy bride. As the clocks struck—and then struck again and again—their hands moving inexorably on toward bedtime, Mary reminded herself that the ordeal facing her could not be too unbearable. A marriage of affection was a rare thing, after all. Most women married for other reasons and she had never known of one who had not survived her wedding night. But when Lady Guildford whispered to her that she must retire to the bedchamber for the formal disrobing and the benediction of the marriage bed, she felt her hands grow cold and her legs begin to tremble.

Having attended several weddings at home, she braced herself for the indignities to come: the noisy invasion of the bedchamber by a band of lords and ladies already more than half drunk, the public undressing of both herself and her new husband, which included the stealing of her garter and the flinging of her hose, and the loud ribald songs and coarse comments as she and Louis were bedded together.

But to her surprise and relief, she was spared all this. To be sure, the highest ranking noblewomen did flock in to help her disrobe, and some of their remarks did verge on the salacious. Still, these were merely whispered from one to another—nothing offensive was said to Mary herself. And King Louis and his gentlemen remained outside until her beautiful fur-trimmed brocade chamber robe (and this Lady Guildford saw to personally) was fastened securely around her silken bedgown.

When the last string was tied, Lady Guildford gave her a loving pat and an encouraging smile. "We are ready for his Majesty," she said to the other ladies. Under cover of the ensuing bustle, she leaned over and whispered in Mary's ear. "Courage, child. Gilly won't desert you."

Instead of the drunken ribaldry that Mary was still expecting, the King and his suite filed in quietly, followed by three handsomely robed prelates. With a word and a smile, Louis took his bride over to the great gilded bed, helped her up into it, and climbed under the blue velvet spread embroidered with roses that Mary had hastily pulled up to her armpits. With solemn prayers and a sprinkling of holy water, the Archbishop of Rouen, the Bishop of Amiens, and the Cardinal de Brie then proceeded to bless the marriage bed and the union of their King and the young Princess from England.

When they were finished, the King thanked them warmly. "And now," he said to the others in the room, "the Queen and I wish you a very good night. God bless you all."

In a very few minutes they were alone—except, of course, for Lady Guildford, who was busily locking up Mary's jewels. It was a lengthy affair. The jewels must be counted, re-counted, placed in orderly fashion on the velvet lining of the heavy casket, the box shown to her young mistress, the key fetched, and then, finally, turned in the lock. While all this was going on, Louis sat stiffly upright against the pillows, making strained conversation with Mary.

"If there is anything you want, your Grace," said Lady Guildford at last, approaching the bed, "don't hesitate to call me. I'll be in the next room. I won't be retiring for some time—"

"Thank you," answered Louis before Mary could open her mouth, "but I am quite sure we will not need you. You have had a long day, madam. I suggest that you go to bed."

With a last look around, as if trying to discover some task that needed her attention, Lady Guildford curtsied, wished them a good night, and backed slowly out of the room, leaving the door slightly ajar. The last thing she saw, as she disappeared into the antechamber, was Mary's pleading, frightened face.

CHAPTER XIX

MARY WAKENED WITH A START the next morning to find Lady Guildford hanging over her, her eyes streaming with tears and her face the picture of agitation and grief. She sat up abruptly.

"Good God, Gilly! What is it?"

Lady Guildford began to sob wildly. "I've been dismissed! His Majesty—and the Duke of Norfolk—" Her words were so smothered that Mary could hardly understand what she was trying to say.

"Dismissed? Nonsense, Gilly dear! There must be some mistake. You are in *my* service, you know, not the King's. Perhaps you misunderstood." She threw her hair back on her shoulders and pulled her old friend down on the bed beside her.

"No, no, no!" Lady Guildford shook her head vehemently. "It was all too clear. My lord of Norfolk says I must return to England immediately, immediately! And I'm not the only one—he's sending the greater part of your household home. My poor, poor child! You'll be almost alone here—" and she sobbed even harder. "How can I bear it?"

"You shan't have to! The whole thing is impossible. I know that his Majesty was very angry last night, Gilly, but I cannot believe he would dismiss my own people!"

The other woman sniffed and blew her nose, remembering, as Mary did, her well-meant but exceedingly indiscreet behavior after the King had sent her to bed. Instead of obeying him, she had invented several errands that took her back into the royal bedchamber, with the result that the aging monarch, already weary from his exhausting day, had finally retired to his own apartments. "Perhaps another night," he had said bitterly, "I will find a warmer welcome and a little more privacy."

Mary beckoned to a chamberwoman who was hovering around, doing her best to hear what the Queen and Lady Guildford were saying to each other. "Send a page for the Duke of Norfolk, Anne. I want to see him just as soon as possible. Then come and help me dress. I won't wait for my ladies this morning." She patted her distraught friend. "Leave me, Gilly dear. And try not to worry. I must take care of this affair myself."

Mary had just finished dressing when the Duke was announced. As he strode over and kissed her hand, she could see that he was pale and looked decidedly apprehensive.

"I think I know why you have summoned me, your Majesty," he said. "I was coming to you, anyway. I expect you have heard of the King's order to send some of your ladies and gentlemen back to England."

"A bewildering business, my lord." Mary's voice was low and controlled but she left Norfolk in no doubt of her anger. "Surely no one but myself has the authority to dismiss my own people?"

"I wish I could say so, your Grace. Unfortunately, as your husband his Majesty has the right to make what changes he wants in your household. And, of course, he *is* the King."

"But my ladies and gentlemen are English, not French!"

"He is still the King and this is his Court and his country."

"Who remains with me?"

"Your Almoner, one chaplain—"

"Which one?"

"Robert West."

"You mean he is sending John Palsgrave away?" Her tutor, her chaplain for so many years, her conscience—

Norfolk sighed dismally. "I'm afraid so. But you will still have with you one master of the horse, a physician, a cupbearer, a master of the pantry, carver, usher, three pages of honor, a groom of the robes, four maids of honor and two chamberwomen."

When Mary finished counting she stared at him in disbelief. Less than twenty out of her hundred attendants! "And which of my maids am I allowed to keep?"

After he had named them, Mary rose to her feet and began pacing up and down the room. "I cannot believe it, my lord. I simply cannot believe it. Lady Anne Howard—your daughter— and Lady Elizabeth Percy dismissed? The two ladies who have been with me the longest and who are my best friends? Leaving me with the youngest and least experienced of the maids—the Grey sisters, Mary Boleyn, Jane Seymour—I'm surprised he didn't suggest your young granddaugter Anne!"

"Mistress Boleyn is joining the household of one of our French kinsmen." He seemed to take her remark seriously. "And I would have protested, in any case, as I agree with your Grace that she is too wild and heedless. Mistress Seymour is very young, too, but she is quiet and dependable." He hesitated, then continued, trying to sound cheerful. "His Majesty is replacing your other ladies with members of his own family. The Lady Claude will be happy to serve you, he assured me this morning, and Madame d'Aumont, a most pleasant and jolly widowed noblewoman— I've met her, your Grace, and I'm sure you will like her—has been appointed in Lady Guildford's place. She will sleep in your bedchamber when the King is not with you, and can advise you on any little problems that may come up from time to time."

"I will agree to everything, if you say I must, but *not* to losing Lady Guildford. The others may go but I must have her. Will you tell his Majesty, my lord, or shall I?"

"Your Grace—" Norfolk all but wrung his hands in his agitation. "I assure you that any attempt to reinstate Lady Guildford will merely anger the King and do no good. He feels, and he spoke very frankly to me less than an hour ago, that her ladyship has assumed much too much authority in your household; that she behaves as if you were still a child and she your governess. It seems that she annoyed him very much yesterday by remaining constantly at your side. Even, he told me, when he wished to take pastime with you."

"But surely, my lord Duke, if I promise him that such a thing will never happen again—?"

Norfolk shook his head dismally. "It's no use, your Grace. I said as much myself, but he refused to listen to me."

"Then perhaps he will listen to my brother!" The young Queen's tone made it obvious that she considered the elderly nobleman of very little use to her in this difficulty. "You have my permission to retire, my lord!"

It was not easy, a few minutes later, having to tell Lady Guildford that she must, after all, leave Abbeville and set out for England. The two women clung together, crying openly. "But I am writing King Henry today, asking him to intercede for us," Mary assured her, "and as it will be some days before you actually set sail, Gilly dear, I am hoping that my courier will bring his answer in time to do some good. Surely my brother can change my husband's mind."

There was animosity in her voice when she said the word "husband" and there was animosity in her heart when she met him, later in the day. But she kept her feelings carefully hidden, saying nothing then about his dismissal of her suite. At all costs she was determined to control her temper and make what use she could of this wound he had inflicted on her so early in their marriage. If he could be unfair, so could she.

She pushed aside the thought that Gilly had behaved badly the preceding night—a word or two today signifying his displeasure would have been punishment enough. By dismissing three quarters of her household, Mary reasoned, Louis had put him-self very much in the wrong, and she laid her plans accordingly. To begin with, her own behavior must from now on be meticu-lous; he should have no further cause for anger, no reason to criticize her. She would be the perfect wife and Queen, attentive, sweet, affectionate in public, and—she smiled grimly to herself—very, very sensitive and easily upset in private.

When he presented her with a huge ruby, just before supper, she was extravagant in her thanks and praise of his gift. Never had she seen a larger, more flawless ruby! It was magnificent and he was much too good to her—much, much too good. She saw that the King was watching her with anxious eyes as she thanked him and she let a little sob, just barely discernible, escape. As he bent to kiss her she managed to turn her head away in time to avoid it, making it look to him as if she were hiding her emotion. A moment afterwards, she was holding the ruby up to the light, every inch the delighted bride.

Later that evening when the dancing began, the ruby looked so beautiful against her white bosom that Francis stopped her in front of a long mirror and showed her her reflection.

"By God, Mary," he said softly, "you are a lovely thing! A King's dream of a bride come true! What a Queen for France—and what a wife for my lucky cousin." His black eyes met hers in the mirror, a hot spark flashed between them. Mary felt first excited and then guilty. She frowned and tried to pull her hand away.

"No, no!" he said. "Look at us. Look at us. Aren't we a hand-some pair? There's a truly royal couple for France, little belle-mère; not you and Louis, or Claude and me." With a shrug of his shoulders, and a note of resignation in his speech, he finally let her go. "How very stupid of Fate to arrange things so clumsily!"

Mary was already in bed when the King's usher arrived to an-nounce to Madame d'Aumont that his master would be visiting the Queen in a few minutes. Having decided that Louis would find her alone tonight, the young Queen immediately dismissed her new lady-in-waiting. Madame d'Aumont, a fat, black-eyed Frenchwoman with a penchant for gossip and gaudy petticoats, was only too glad to slip away. Her appointment as Mary's senior attendant had come as a surprise, and she had plans of her own for the night.

The moment the door closed behind her, Mary faced the far wall and concentrated on sad thoughts. By the time Louis arrived at the bedside she was crying wildly, her shoulders heaving, and the satin pillow cover rumpled and spotted with tears. She started up, tried to smile, then gave another great sob and covered her face with her hands.

"Why, my dear lady!" Louis was genuinely distressed and obviously puzzled; Mary had seemed quite composed at supper and during the dancing afterwards. "Are you ill? Tell me what is wrong."

The girl shook her head and let a fresh torrent of tears stream down her cheeks. "F-forgive me, Sire. It is only that I m-miss—" She wailed, gulped, then went on. "I m-m-miss the Lady Guildford!"

"Oh." Louis shifted uneasily from one foot to the other, wondering if he had been mistaken in his decision to send the interfering old woman home. No. It was the thing to do; the only thing to do. It was difficult enough for a man of his age to be married to a maid of eighteen without a domineering busybody coughing behind screens and bursting into bedchambers at all hours of the night.

He leaned down and touched her still shaking shoulder. "There, there, my dear. You must trust me to know what is best for you, you know. For us both, I mean. Surely you cannot blame me for wanting to have my little bride to myself?"

Mary's only answer was to sob louder and burrow deep into the pillows. Louis waited a moment, wondering if perhaps he should allow her time to overcome her grief. Tonight, after all, did not seem to be a good time to press his suit.

"Would you rather be alone tonight, Madame?" he asked, hesitantly. "Shall I send Madame d'Aumont to you with a hot posset—to help you sleep?"

A rumpled head raised itself slowly and a pair of drowned eyes met his. "If—if—if you will be so kind, Sire. I sh-should be more myself tomorrow." Her voice broke, and seeing that she was going to weep again, Louis beat a hasty retreat, actually sighing with relief when he reached his own bedchamber. He was much too old, he decided, to make love to a crying, desolate young woman; too old by far for the task of kissing her tears away.

As he settled back in the comfort of his wide bed, he told himself that he should proceed more slowly for the next little while. He had forgotten, in his delight over Mary's beauty and desirability, that they were virtually strangers, and that she was a shy maiden, thrust into marriage with a man no longer young and attractive. And now he had hurt her by taking away her beloved lady-in-waiting.

He sighed in the darkness and made up his mind to court his new wife. It would be necessary to forget his doctor's orders, of course; he would ride with her, even dance with her, and do his best to seem gay. Then, when they were easy together and he had gained her affection, he would plan a romantic evening. Not send an usher, as he had done tonight, to announce that the King was visiting the Queen. No, he could see now that the formality of that approach might have frightened her. He would order a little supper by the fire, just for the two of them. The perfect wine, candlelight. . . . He smiled, thinking of it, and fell asleep.

While Louis, in his bed, was planning how best to make Mary truly his wife, she, her tears long since dry, was congratulating herself on her success and considering what to do next. If he came to take pastime tomorrow night, she could plead a bad headache, caused by tonight's grief.

"I shall be unusually quiet all day," she said to herself, "and try to look wan. If I refuse to dance and barely touch my food. . . ."

Louis gave a smothered groan as his attendants settled him on the divan which had taken the place of his throne chair on the canopied dais. He reached out his hand for Mary. "Sit with me for a few minutes, my dear, and then let me see you dance. This last week has been so dull for you that I feel guilty."

"Nonsense!" With a smile, Mary sat down on a low chair beside him and arranged her velvet skirts in folds around her slipper tips. "Let Francis lead the dancing with the Lady Claude tonight. I'd rather watch it here with you."

This was not entirely true; once the music started, Mary's feet itched to be out there among the other ladies and gentlemen. But, to her own surprise, she realized that she almost meant it. How, she wondered, could feelings change as much as hers had, and in so short a time? Thinking it over, she realized that her increasing fondness for Louis, and her genuine concern over his worsening health, probably stemmed from two things. First of all, there was her gratitude that he had not, after the night he had found her weeping, visited her bedchamber again. Without actually saying so, he had let her know that he was giving her time to feel more at ease with him, that he was hoping, first, to win her affection; and, in the days and nights of wonderful freedom that followed this decision, he had done exactly that.

Added to this was a most unpleasant sense of guilt, a nagging voice in the far corner of her conscience that said she was not only largely responsible for his increasing pain and weakness but that she had known only too well what she was doing.

When he had suggested that they ride all afternoon and dance all evening she had encouraged him, shutting her eyes to the weary pallor that crept over his face and to the twinges of pain that made him stumble and turn awkward as they danced. She shivered now, remembering how cruel she had been and how she counted each day a success that sent him off to his own apartments at bedtime, too exhausted to think of lovemaking.

The doctors had soon put a stop to poor Louis's spurt of gallantry and Mary was very glad of it. It was one thing to rail against the unkind fate that had tied her to an elderly invalid when her heart belonged to young and vigorous Charles; it was another to behave in a fashion that might hasten his death. Even wishing him dead was a terrible thing and she was suddenly grateful that her concern, now, was real. She honestly wanted his health to improve and his pain to lessen. From now on, she decided, she was going to shut her mind to her distaste for his person and play the affectionate, dutiful wife and companion. The future must take care of itself.

Stretched out on the elaborate divan beside her chair, Louis too was busy with his thoughts, deploring the abrupt and uncomfortable end to his courtship. When would he be able to resume it? When could he plan that supper in front of the fire, that dream evening that would bring about the consummation of his marriage and, perhaps, result in an heir to the throne? A son. . . . If he and this beautiful new queen of his could have a son!

Their eyes met and he urged her again to join the dancing. Again she refused, and the affection in her voice made him thank God that he had won her friendship, if nothing else. For a while he had despaired, thinking she would never forgive him for dismissing Lady Guildford and for refusing to reinstate her when both Henry of England and Wolsey had written asking him to do so. But somehow, even that cloud had passed and the girl seemed quite content these days with her French ladies.

Seeing him stir restlessly on the pile of pillows, Mary asked him what was wrong. "More pain, Sire?" She rose and adjusted one of the soft satin cushions behind his thin shoulders.

He nodded ruefully. "If we were only home in Paris, Mary! I feel sure, somehow, that once I am back at my own palace of les Tournelles that I will be stronger." He glanced around the elaborate salon. "The people of Abbeville have made us more than welcome, I know, but our stay has been much too prolonged. I planned to leave here days ago."

"I know," Mary tried to soothe him. "But it's a most pleasant place to be, my lord. Do try to curb your impatience and enjoy it. Once we start out on our travels we will be caught up in all kinds of exhausting ceremonies again."

"Exhausting or not, I want to see you crowned as soon as possible. And I'm eager to show you to our people of Paris. They will go mad over you, Mary. The Parisiens love beauty, you know."

Mary dimpled at him. "And all Frenchmen are base flatterers!" A moment later, with his permission, she stepped down from the dais and approached Francis and the Lady Claude, who were sitting side by side in two gilded state chairs.

"I'm afraid," she said to Claude, "that the King is tiring himself again. Will you two take our places on the dais and see that the dancing continues? I would like to accompany him to his apartments and be sure that he is comfortable for the night."

Claude's grateful look warmed Mary's heart. She was glad to be friends at last with Claude, and not the enemies they might well have been. She had been very, very wise to call a halt to Francis's gallantries—although she had to admit that she missed them. What a delightful rascal he was! As she bade him good night, she avoided his black eyes, knowing perfectly well that there would be provocation in them and that any answering smile might be misconstrued.

Two days after the royal party left Abbeville for St. Denis, where Mary was to be crowned Queen of France on the twenty-sixth day of October, they reached the ancient bishop's palace at Beauvais, where they would spend a night or two before continuing on their way. Surprisingly, Louis seemed to have stood the journey very well indeed, and as they passed through the narrow streets of Beauvais he ordered the curtains of his litter opened and smiled and waved at the cheering townspeople as if he were in the best of health. He greeted the leading citizens who were assembled to bid him and his bride welcome, and was still in good spirits when Mary ordered him immediately to bed.

"Your obedient servant, your Grace!" He beckoned to one of his gentlemen to give him an arm. "But I must wake in an hour or so to attend to some pressing business. Join me then, my dear."

It was nearer two hours than one when Mary was summoned. She changed into a blue velvet gown trimmed with ermine and pearls, tucked her curls into place, and hurried down the strange halls to her husband's apartments. One of his physicians came to meet her, a reassuring smile on his face.

"His Majesty is awake and has been asking for you, your Grace. He slept quite soundly for more than an hour and he seems to be feeling so much better that I'm allowing him to send some important messages on to Paris and to see some visitors from abroad."

"Can he possibly be strong enough, after our wearying journey?"

"If he doesn't attempt too much, yes. But watch him, your Majesty. If he tires, send for me. At the moment, I'm under orders to stay out of the room!"

The royal bedchamber was a scene of great activity, and, for a moment, she stood in the doorway, watching her husband at work. Two secretaries sat at a table near the bed, writing furiously as Louis, propped high against a bank of silken pillows, dictated orders. Beyond them stood a row of handsomely clad noblemen with their backs to a roaring fire, obviously waiting to confer with their sovereign. Some held documents, some were empty-handed. All looked impatient. Mary counted them in silent disapproval and shook her head. Too many; he could not attend to half of them, she was sure.

As she walked toward him, Louis glanced up and his thin face broke into a delighted smile. "Ah, there you are, at last! I've been missing you." He pointed to a chair drawn up so close beside him that it touched the heavy damask bed curtains. "Sit here, if you will, and don't scold! When I've finished with these gentlemen I have a surprise for you."

Mary settled into her seat and folded her hands in her lap. While she listened with one ear to the questions, answers, messages, plans—some pertaining to her coronation, some to the great jousts to be held in her honor later in November at les Tournelles, some concerned with foreign and some with domestic problems—she wondered idly what Louis's surprise could be. Another jewel, probably. She frowned at the thought. He had given her so many already. The last, a huge diamond called the "Mirror of Naples," was the most treasured gem in all France; it was worth at least thirty thousand crowns, was unbelievably beautiful, and was such a responsibility that Mary hated the sight of it. Why couldn't he simply give her a book or a new song for her lute?

Before she would have thought it possible, the last letter was signed, the final questions answered, and the room all but empty.

"And now," said Louis, "my surprise." He turned to a page and gave a quiet order. "If Milord of Cleremont has brought our guest from England, send him in to me."

As Mary waited to hear who their visitor was, he settled himself into a more comfortable position and pulled the rich velvet cover closer around his legs. Gilly, thought Mary suddenly; could Gilly be returning to her? No, Louis had said "him."

"At least," Louis went on casually, "I believe he is not a stranger to you. So close a friend of your brother's—"

206

The door opened and Mary's startled, incredulous eyes met those of the last person in the world she expected or could have hoped to see.

CHAPTER XX

"THE KING'S PLEASURE was that I should come to his Grace alone," wrote Charles Brandon to King Henry of England, the day after his meeting with Louis and Mary. "He embraced me in his arms and said that I was heartily welcome." And, Charles continued, when he thanked Louis, as Henry had told him to, for the great honor and love Louis had shown Henry's sister, the King of France assured him that there was nothing he would not do for Henry's pleasure, or in his service, as Henry had given him "The greatest jewel that ever one prince had of another!"

It was a long letter. A letter that must have made Henry very proud of Mary's conduct in an extremely difficult situation, for much of it was concerned with the wise and honorable way she was behaving. According to Charles, that was the opinion of all the noblemen of France who had seen her, and as for the King—! She had carried herself so winningly to him, he wrote, that Charles had never seen a man with his mind more set on a woman.

But although the letter so carefully described the scene in Louis's bedchamber, there was no mention in it of the light of rapture that Charles saw in the Queen's eyes when he entered the room, the joy of their secret meeting the next morning in the Cathedral of St. Pierre, nor the quick gesture with which he pulled her behind a pillar in that huge cathedral and kissed her until she gasped for breath.

"Charles! Charles! Behave yourself! We're in a house of God!"

"God is love," answered Charles, kissing her again. "And there isn't a soul in the whole place except that one verger away up there by the altar."

"But Jane Seymour will be joining me here in just a few minutes. I sent her back for my purse—it was the only way I could rid myself of her company."

"Then we shouldn't waste time." Charles smiled down on her and proceeded to be as good as his word. When he released her, it was to question her about her life with Louis. "Is the King as kind to you as he appears to be?" he wanted to know. "Or are you truly miserable, my darling? You must not send me away without a word or two of your welfare."

"He's been goodness itself," she admitted. "If I were his daughter instead of his wife, I'd love him dearly, poor man. But—quick, before Jane arrives. Do you love me still? Tell me, and then go."

Taking her in his arms again, he whispered over and over the three words she had been longing to hear, his lips touching her ear. Before he was through, her hood had fallen off and her hair was in danger of tumbling down; then a creak of the great carved door behind them gave them warning, and by the time Jane Seymour opened it and entered the cathedral, Charles was off in a far corner with his face hidden from sight and Mary was on her knees, deep in prayer.

Soon after this meeting, which was their only moment alone, the whole royal party left Beauvais, making their leisurely way through Picardy to St. Denis. It was a pleasant enough journey for everyone, although the countryside was growing bleak, but Mary, made content by the knowledge that Charles was a member of their entourage, enjoyed it more than anyone else. Even if she and Charles could only smile politely and exchange a careful word or two, he was *there*. She could see him. Occasionally, she could dance with him. She was free to compare him to the Frenchmen around her and be proud of him. He was within reach, and he was hers.

From his bed, his divan, and his litter, Louis watched Mary grow more beautiful as each day passed, and he chafed against the ill health that sapped his manhood. There was a new radiance about her, a softer pink in her cheeks, a lilt in her voice, a dancing motion to her step; she smiled with her eyes as well as her mouth, now, and those enchanting dimples were more often in evidence than not.

"She is happy here in France," he told himself, and conferred again with his physicians. "Can you do nothing to help me, messieurs?" He had been ill before and they had succeeded in restoring him; not to good health, certainly, but to more strength and ease than he was enjoying now.

"We warned you, Sire," was all the comfort they gave him. "You disobeyed all our orders and it will take time to undo the damage. Perhaps if you will return to your old, strict regimen, the moment the Queen's coronation is over—" But their faces were grave. After the coronation came the great tournament for the new Queen; it would be some weeks before all these festivities were concluded, and the King needed to be quiet *now*.

The day of Mary's crowning dawned at last, and long before the hour appointed for the ceremony in the old Cathedral at St. Denis, the huge building was filled and the streets around it were crowded with spectators. A loud flourish of trumpets announced the arrival of the new Queen at the great doors of the church, the people cheered loudly, and the audience inside fell instantly silent, their silks and satins rustling as they turned in their places to watch the entrance of the royal cortege. First came the nobles and noblewomen, all glittering jewels and sumptuous velvet and snowy ermine, then the Queen herself, her hand in that of Francis of Valois. The dark-eyed Dauphin was quiet and serious today as he led his young mother-in-law up the long aisle, perhaps wondering if he was destined to play such a role himself at some future time. Not that he would ever be crowned here at St. Denis, of course; France's kings were buried there but they were always crowned at Rheims.

When the handsome young couple reached the high altar, Mary knelt on the cushion provided for the purpose and Francis moved away. She prayed for a few minutes, then raised her head; the Cardinal de Brie, who had married her to Louis less than a month earlier, stepped forward, anointed her with the sacred oil, handed her the scepter and the rod of justice and placed a ring on her finger. Finally, as the silence around her deepened and she held her breath, he lifted the French crown matrimonial from its velvet pillow and settled it carefully on her red-gold head.

It was over so quickly that Mary, remembering how long it had taken to make her brother Henry the King of England, could hardly believe it. Before she had time to think of anything else, Francis was at her side again, with his hand under her elbow to steady her as she rose to her feet and made her way to the canopied chair of state at the left side of the altar.

Now the high mass began, and while the voices of the choir mingled with the chanting of the priests, Mary tried to sit straight on her throne. The crown was almost unbearably heavy but she knew she must hold her head high despite the discomfort. She was steadying the scepter in her right hand and the rod of justice in her left, tilting them so that her lap took most of their weight, when suddenly she realized that the crown was no longer cutting painfully into her forehead and that a warm, velvet-clad body was touching hers through an opening in the back of the high carved chair.

"Is that better, *ma petite?*" She heard an intimate, caressing whisper. "Sit quite still," Francis added, "or everyone will see that I am holding the crown."

At exactly the right second when the mass ended, he gently lowered the massive ring of gold and jewels into its place on her head, helped her up again, and steered her back to the altar, where she made her offering and was given the holy sacrament. Then, to a burst of loud music they turned, and, facing the standing congregation, paced slowly down the long aisle and out of the cathedral, followed by the same elaborately robed lords and ladies who had preceded them earlier. Mary's litter was standing at the huge door. She climbed in with a sigh of relief, hoping to rest for a little while.

"One moment." Francis reached in and pushed and shoved the cushions around and behind her back until they supported her in such a way that she could sit erect in comfort. "There!" He smiled into her eyes, patted her quickly on the knee, saw that the curtains were open, and signaled for the litter to move on its way.

Louis was waiting when she reached her temporary palace, looking tired and drawn but very proud and happy; and although it was obviously a painful thing for him to do, he walked slowly to the side of her litter and extended a shaking hand to help her out. For a moment they stood side by side, the King and Queen of France, while the crowds massed around the courtyard roared and threw their caps in the air.

"Vive le Roi! Vive la Reine! Vive la Reine Marie!" Mary's heart swelled and her eyes filled, but even as she waved her free hand and smiled gratefully through her tears, she had the odd feeling that all this was wrong. The oil on her forehead, the crown on her head, the ring on her finger—it was all a play, a pageant, a farce. She was not really "La Reine Marie"; she was the Princess Mary of England—a king's daughter and a king's sister, yes, but not a queen. Not a king's wife. . . .

After a quiet supper together, the King bade Mary good night and an affectionate farewell. He was slipping back into Paris ahead of her, and would not see her again until she joined him at the Hôtel des Tournelles.

"But why," asked his young wife, "must I enter Paris alone? Why should we not ride in together?"

"Because nobody wants to see me tomorrow," was his answer. "Every cheer and smile and wave will be for you, Mary. They want to see their new Queen. And that is how it should be. In fact, that is how I want it to be. Your progress through the city will be slow," he finished. "I should tire long before it was over."

As it turned out, so did Mary. She and her cortège left St. Denis by nine of the clock the next morning, and they warned her then that it would be at least six in the evening before they would reach the Palais Royal, her Parisian residence. Although her entourage was much smaller than the one that had escorted her to Abbeville, and could have moved much more swiftly, there were so many halts along the tapestry-hung route that the new Queen reached a point where she found it difficult to smile at the welcoming officials and pretend to listen to the little plays that were performed in her honor.

They were nearing Notre Dame, which was to be the last stop on their way, when one of the handsome litter horses stumbled slightly and Mary's crown slipped to one side. This was the tenth time it had happened and she swore a most unqueenly oath as she pushed it back in place with a finger stiff with glittering rings. Francis who, as the second gentleman of France, was again riding close beside her, laughed.

"I wish I could help you with that heavy thing as I did yesterday," he said. "But I cannot. All I may do, to ease your headache, is to tell you how beautiful you look with it on your head. When it isn't down over one eye, I mean." He leaned out of his saddle and gave her one of his long, admiring, searching glances that seemed to strip her naked.

"I suppose you realize," he said softly and meaningly, "that you must lead the dancing with me tonight. When Louis is absent it is my duty to take his place, and neither of *us* can plead ill health, I'm glad to say."

"I shall be terribly weary. I am already," answered Mary, avoiding his probing eyes. "You and the Lady Claude can very well—"

"Oh, no, we cannot! Make no mistake, Mary. This is one time when there can be no excuse. The new Queen of France will open the dancing with the Dauphin, and the Dauphin expects to enjoy every minute of it. This wifely devotion of yours is all very touching, *ma petite,* but it can become a bit ridiculous, you know." He laughed. "After all, I've ridden with you, laughed with you, danced with you, I've seen your eyes light up when they met mine, and watched your mouth all but ask me for a kiss!"

"Stop, Francis!" Mary sounded desperate but she was forced to keep on smiling at the crowds around them, waving her hand and sitting carefully erect. "How dare you say such things to me?"

He laughed again. "But I dare anything! Haven't you heard? And one day soon you will be very glad that I do. I promise you, Mary, that when these tiresome ceremonies are over we will find a way to be alone. There are places at the Hôtel des Tournelles—"

Mary broke in with a horrified protest, but before she could say more than a word or two the cavalcade drew up at Notre Dame and Francis had to help her out of her litter and lead her into the great Cathedral. She was still so shocked that she kept her eyes on the ground and saw none of its beauty; and it was only later that she realized that the long row of "Monsieur le Docteur This and That," bowing to her in their fur-trimmed robes, were Paris's leading scholars, teachers, physicians, and lawyers.

All during the short time allowed her to rest and change her gown for the evening's banquet, Mary fretted over Francis's behavior. Had she, with her playful, mildly flirtatious manner, led him to believe that she would welcome him as a lover? She admitted to herself now that it would have been wiser to remain stiff and aloof; but his warm friendliness when they first met, his constant consideration for her comfort, and his infectious good spirits had made formal manners seem unnecessary between them.

And suppose her pulse *had* quickened from time to time when he kissed her hand, whispered nonsense in her ear, helped her into her cloak with lingering fingers? She was young, after all; she had been lonely, she missed Charles, and she had forgotten that lesson learned so long ago at her brother's Court, that a Frenchman will read an invitation into almost anything that a pretty woman says or does.

Her heart sank. What would Charles think of her new predicament? Would he blame her? Scold her? Had she the courage to confess to him what had happened and ask his help and advice?

She would have been even more disturbed had she known that the Duchess of Angoulême, who had never before interfered in her son's affairs of the heart, had been watching his behavior with anxious eyes. She didn't care whether he had one mistress or ten, but the new Queen must not be one of them.

"You must be mad!" she told Francis that evening. "Don't you realize that if this—this English *poupée* succumbs to you, you may very well see your own son the next King of France instead of yourself?"

CHAPTER XXI

L'HÔTEL DES TOURNELLES, King Louis's favorite palace, was situated in the northern end of Paris, not far from the grim old Bastille. In fact, Mary discovered that by standing at one of the windows in a turret on that side of the Palace she could actually see and count the prison's eight round, forbidding and gloomy towers. But there was nothing forbidding or gloomy about l'Hôtel des Tournelles itself. Its turreted walls, beautiful reception rooms, long galleries filled with paintings and handsome furniture, and its many suites of charming, irregularly shaped private apartments reminded her so much of her brother's palace at Richmond that she very soon felt quite at home.

As the tournament would not begin until November 13, Mary had almost a week in which she was free to wander at will in the vast bare gardens and to mingle more informally with her English friends and the lords and ladies of her husband's Court. Even though she knew the long-awaited contest between France and England would be full of excitement, she was sorry to have the pleasant interlude end.

But November 13 dawned at last, a day both cold and clear; a perfect day for the jousters, everyone said, but a bit chilly for the hundreds of spectators. Mary, walking slowly up the steps of the high platform erected for the royal party, wished for Louis's sake that the sun was warmer. She tightened her hand under his elbow, helping him climb. How thin and sharp his bones were, she thought; how lank his hair, and how loosely his clothes seemed to hang today! He could be her grandfather, he looked so old and frail.

When they reached the gaily decorated dais, he paused a moment and smiled gratefully down into her eyes. "Let me catch my breath, my dear."

She nodded and they stood back in the shadows until a little color returned to his gray face. "Now," he said. Matching her step to his dragging gait, they moved forward, bowing from one side to the other as the crowds in the stands rose to welcome them.

"Vive le Roi! Vive la Reine!" The sound of their voices rose and fell in waves. It subsided while Mary and the Lady Claude, who had followed close behind them, settled Louis on the gilded couch and wrapped him carefully in fur robes; then it changed to a persistent cheering for Mary alone. Once, twice, three times before the formal opening of the tournament she was summoned from the King's side to acknowledge their enthusiastic shouts and the stamping of their feet on the bare boards of the scaffolds.

It continued until the Duchesses of Bourbon, Angoulême, Alençon and Nevers had mounted the platform and taken their cushioned seats around the Queen. The blare of trumpets announcing the entrance of the heralds quieted the uproar at last, making it possible for Mary to drop into her place beside Louis's divan and glance around at the picturesque scene spread before her.

The lists were in an open grassy clearing in the Palace park, a clearing that extended all the way out to the Rue St. Antoine. An elaborate triumphal arch had been built at the park end, not far from where the scaffolds stood, and, early that morning, the shields of the contestants and of the King and Queen had all been fastened to it, making a gay and colorful display.

The heralds, shivering noticeably and looking rather blue in new satin coats embroidered all over with the lilies of France, rode through the arch and reined up in front of the King and Queen. The trumpets blew again for silence, and the chief herald moved his mount forward a few paces to open the tournament.

"By the high and most puissant Prince, the Duke of Valois and Bretagne, for the joyous advent of the Queen to Paris, my said lord having had published through the kingdoms of France and England by Mountjoy, first and sovereign King-at-Arms of the French, and by the order of the most Christian King, our sovereign lord. . . ." Mary heard that much, her quick mind translating it readily, then Louis coughed loudly beside her and she missed the rest as she leaned over him and pulled the soft square of dark marten closer around his chest.

"Our 'most high and puissant Prince,'" Louis grumbled to her, "will be the death of us all. I warned that healthy young animal that the middle of November would be too cold for this business! But he would have it, whether we freeze or not." He took her hand and lifted it to his sunken cheek. "You seem warm, I'm glad to say."

Mary laughed. "If I am, it's for good reason. I'm wearing three heavy canvas underskirts and my thickest fur-lined gown! That's why I look rather like a wine barrel today. I've learned how to dress for these contests, my lord, because my brother likes to joust even more than our cousin Francis, and in England we hold tourneys all through the winter, regardless of the weather. But look, Louis! Here they come."

They were both silent as the contestants rode onto the field of honor, led by a great band of squires. Francis of Valois, and the Dukes of Bourbon and Alençon appeared first, representing France. After them came the Duke of Suffolk and the Marquis of Dorset. "For St. George and Merry England," whispered Mary to her husband. The four helmeted lords circled the lists twice, their brightly polished armor flashing in the noonday sun, bowing so low each time they passed the royal dais that their nodding plumes almost touched their saddles. This was a feat that brought a new burst of cheering from a crowd that knew well how extremely difficult it was for a man to maintain his balance when he was wearing so many pounds of unwieldy metal.

This first day's contest was to be by lance alone, the least difficult form of combat. The Duke of Suffolk accepted Valois's challenge and they moved back until they faced each other with the length of the field between them. At a signal from the King-at-Arms they spurred their mounts and galloped forward, their long lances raised. The pounding of their horses' hoofs on the hard ground was the only sound in the lists until they met with a clang a moment later, and there was a splintering of wood as they passed on, Brandon waving his unbroken weapon over his head.

Now it was his turn to challenge, and again, as he and Francis met, he splintered the Frenchman's lance. Five, six, seven—nine courses they ran, the excitement of the crowd mounting higher and higher as the visitor from England won seven times over

216

their own young Dauphin, the French Prince splitting Suffolk's lance only twice. The tenth challenge was Suffolk's, and this time, he lifted Valois's plumed helmet right off his head and tossed it to the ground in front of the scaffolds.

There was a moment's hush. Was the Dauphin injured? When, a moment later, Francis shook his dark head, straightened himself in his saddle, and galloped away, a great roar swept over the stands, a roar that grew even louder when the judges signaled that the honors for that course belonged to the Duke of Suffolk.

The courses had, so far, been run swiftly, one after another; now, for the first time, there was a delay, and then a new knight appeared to accept Suffolk's challenge.

"It's Alençon," said Louis in a worried voice. "Can Francis be hurt, after all?"

Claude, sitting on his other side, stirred uneasily. Mary could see that, although she was gripping the railing in front of them so tightly, her knuckles white, neither she nor Francis's mother, in her place nearby, allowed any trace of anxiety to cross their faces. Mary applauded them silently for playing their parts so well in the pageant; just so had she and Catherine schooled themselves many times while they waited to hear whether or not Henry was seriously injured.

Francis did not reappear until the jousting was over for the day; then, as the combatants, their visors raised, met in front of the scaffold to salute each other and the royal party, a burst of cheering broke out in the stands. The Dauphin was with them, head erect, his smile a bit grim, and his left hand swathed in a thick bandage.

"Poor Francis," whispered Mary to the King. "A hand wound may keep him out of the lists. How he will hate that!"

She was right. Valois's injury was minor, but the next morning France was represented by the Duke of Lorraine and Monsieur de Bourbon, while the angry young Prince, resenting every minute of his forced inaction and every one of the continuing triumphs of England's Duke of Suffolk, sat between Mary and Claude and tried not to groan each time his compatriots lost a match to his rival.

Mary, naturally, was delighted, and Francis, seeing the soft color and dimpling smile, to say nothing of the happy gleam in her blue eyes as they followed Brandon on and off the field, made a silent vow that this Suffolk, this commoner from England, this spoiled favorite of King Henry, this—this upstart, must be made to taste defeat. Mary belonged to France now; he would prove to her, somehow or other, that Frenchmen were stronger, braver, more irresistible. . . .

But as each day of the tournament followed the last, Francis discovered, to his discomfiture, that none of the French champions were skillful enough to win over the Duke of Suffolk. He was everybody's hero soon; everybody's, that is, except Francis's. His good nature made even the men he was defeating his admiring friends, and, as was inevitable, the ladies of the Court talked of little else. Whenever Francis saw a knot of French noblewomen chatting and laughing together, he could be almost sure that their subject was this handsome, invincible champion from England. Any lady with whom Suffolk danced was congratulated and envied, his lightest compliment was treasured and repeated, and there was constant speculation about the name of the fortunate Englishwoman to whom he was so exasperatingly faithful.

Mary watched and listened with a singing heart, longing to tell them that he belonged to her, but answering their questions, instead, with a shrug and a vague smile.

"Yes, my lord of Suffolk is considered very handsome. He's much admired at home. A widower, you know; a sad story—" She would let the idea dangle. "He and my brother the King have tilted together since they were boys, and tournaments are every day affairs for us. So it would be odd if he didn't excel."

Louis, who had hoped from day to day that he would be strong enough to watch some of the proceedings from his chair of state, finally rebelled against the cushioned couch.

"Surely," he complained to Mary and his chief physician, "I might try. There are only today and tomorrow left, and it is a sadly undignified thing for the King of France to huddle under rugs on a divan when his new Queen is being honored." With a sigh, he turned to her. "We should be sitting side by side, my dear."

The doctor shook his head firmly. "No, Sire. If you must attend this tournament, and you know how foolhardy I think it is for anyone in your condition to spend hours on an open platform in this weather, I insist that you remain on your couch and keep as warm as possible. And when this ordeal is over," he added to Mary, "I hope you will urge his Majesty to return to his old, simple regimen. Otherwise. . . ." He threw up his hands.

"Gladly, sir." Mary was more than agreeable to his request. "Our guests from England will leave us very soon and we shall be free to do as we wish. Do you advise us to retire to the country?"

"It would be a very good thing," was the answer. "The air at St. Germain-en-laye, which is less than fourteen miles from Paris, has always benefited his Majesty. Why not take her Grace there, Sire?"

Louis looked doubtful. "I suppose we could be comfortable enough; the royal apartments are still in fairly good repair. But the rest of the Palace is not, Mary, and it would mean leaving most of our lords and ladies here. I'm afraid you would be lonely."

"No I wouldn't, Louis." The young Queen shook her head vigorously. "Some of my happiest days were those I spent at Eltham with only Lady Guildford to keep me company. By all means let us go to this place and rusticate for a while. What do we do? Rise early, dine at ten, bed at six?"

"I'm afraid that is what I must do. But while I rest, my dear, you shall hunt. One thing we can promise you at St. Germain is good hunting. I must confess," he finished rather sadly, "that, much as I love Paris, I have found it a bit wearying recently."

"Then the matter is settled." Mary rose to her feet and smiled at the doctor. "We will obey you implicitly, monsieur, and his Majesty will soon be well and strong again." She glanced at the clock. "Come, Sire. I see it is time we started for the tiltyard. Our champions fight on foot today, and now that the Dauphin's hand is healed, I'm sure he will be the first challenger. I think he still has great hopes of defeating our Duke of Suffolk."

But when they were seated on the platform and the heralds proclaimed the tournament open, no one stepped forward.

"Where can Francis be?" murmured Louis.

Before Mary could reply, Charles Brandon, followed by the Marquis of Dorset, moved swiftly up to the barrier and announced to the King-at-Arms that he would be happy to fight all comers.

"Then Francis must accept the challenge for France," the King leaned forward on his divan. "What can be delaying him?" The spectators seemed equally bewildered; their chatter and laughter had died down to a puzzled whispering.

"Ah, here he comes at last!" But as Mary watched the tall, broad-shouldered figure striding up to the barrier, she began to wonder. *Was* it Francis? The man looked taller and moved with a firm, heavy step that was very unlike the Dauphin's long, easy lope.

"Louis," she whispered excitedly. "His visor is closed! Who could it be? They're supposed to keep their visors open until they start fighting."

While they were discussing the unknown warrior's peculiar behavior, the two Englishmen exchanged a word or two, Dorset stepped back, Brandon lowered his visor, presented his spear, and the close bout began. The stranger's first thrust was such a savage one that it brought onlookers to their feet and set them shouting.

Mary held her breath. There! Charles, thank God, was standing firm. Now he was beating his opponent back from the barriers, and she almost shouted, too. But there was such an unusual ferocity about the exchange of blows that she grew frightened; this was no mock combat, certainly, no mere tournament battle. Claude, she noticed, had closed her eyes. Mary managed to keep hers open until the stranger finally reeled, wavered, and staggered off to one side; then with an audible sigh of relief, she saw the judges drop the rail and call for a rest period.

When the rail was raised again, the combatants had swords in their hands instead of spears but after parrying a few wobbling thrusts from his opponent, Brandon suddenly threw his weapon down on the field.

"St. George and England!" He gave a loud shout that could be heard from one end of the arena to the other, reached over the barrier and caught the unknown giant by the neck. Before the reeling man could free himself, Suffolk had pushed the taller warrior's visor open with one hand and was pummeling him with the other. A great gasp went up from the crowd as blood spurted from the stranger's nose and he fumbled his visor shut again. At that moment, the barrier fell to end the struggle, and a French knight hurried the defeated champion off the field, leaving Brandon to receive, alone, the plaudits of the spectators.

"That knight was one of Francis's men," said the King to Mary, shaking his head in disapproval. "Most irregular! Well, whatever the boy has done today, he has given your superb champion an opportunity to shame all France. Your valiant fighters, my dear, have earned all the prizes in this tourney, and they have earned them more than fairly. They shall carry them back to England with my sincerest congratulations and my thanks for the pleasure they have afforded me and my friends."

Later that day the young Queen learned from one of the Grey sisters, a pair who seemed to hear all the news at Court, that the mysterious giant had been recognized by some of the French contestants as a German knight who was well known to be the tallest and strongest man in all France; and though no one said it out loud, the general feeling was that Francis had behaved shabbily in bringing him to des Tournelles.

Apparently Louis said as much, or perhaps more, to his young cousin, for when Mary met him at supper time, Francis insisted on defending his conduct to her.

"Your Duke of Suffolk challenged 'all comers,'" he said, his long face flushed and his dark eyes a little uneasy. "Don't you agree that he gave us the right to send in any defender we wished to do him battle?"

Mary raised her eyebrows a trifle scornfully but her voice was carefully casual. "Really, Monseigneur," she said. "I can't see what weight my opinion could have on such a matter. What do I know of French rules of chivalry? I confess that I was surprised when your visored knight appeared. In England contestants must submit their names to the King-at-Arms before the jousting begins. However, I have no doubt you arrange these things differently here. And"—she smiled so sweetly at him that Valois found himself writhing under her clear blue eyes—"I am sure that you, the King's own cousin, would do nothing dishonorable."

On Thursday the King and Queen bade most of their English friends Godspeed and with Lady Claude, the Dauphin, Suffolk (who had not finished all his Master's secret business with Louis), the other French princesses, and a few of the lords and ladies, prepared to set out for St. Germain-en-laye. Shortly before they left the Palace, the King arranged for Mary to return on the following Sunday and dine with the citizens of Paris at the Hôtel de Ville.

When the cavalcade was out on the open road to St. Germain he told her why he was sending her back to the city so soon. "It will be for only one night," he said, "I chose Sunday because you will have good company on the way. Milords of Suffolk and Dorset will be riding to Paris that day before starting home to England. And"—he indicated the nobles following his litter—"I shall ask most of our lords and ladies to accompany you, too, with the understanding that they will then remain in Paris until we send for them or rejoin them. But you must have some companions when you return to be with me. Shall we invite Francis and Claude to stay with us in the country?"

"If you don't mind, my dear lord," answered the girl, "I would rather have the Lady Renee. Why not let Francis and Claude play host and hostess at des Tournelles during our absence? When they are with us, we keep Francis so busy that he sees very little of his wife. They are, after all, still bride and groom."

What Mary really meant was that Francis should be forced to pay more attention to poor little Claude. As long as he had the excuse of the King's ill health to keep him at the Queen's side, he would use it, and she would again be forced to avoid his gallantries.

"Anything you wish," was Louis's reply. "I will be very content to spend my days with you and Renee."

As it was growing dark when the royal party climbed the hill at St. Germain, and then rained heavily all day Saturday, Mary didn't see how beautifully the decrepit old Palace was situated until she left it on Sunday morning. The rain had stopped during the night, the day was cool and clear, and as she and her party descended the steep slope she found herself looking down on a magnificent panorama. Directly beneath her was the Seine, curling around the base of the hill, and she could see that their road followed it all the way to Paris. The city, a jumbled mass of

222

slate roofs and pointed turrets and towers, was clearly visible from the terraces at St. Germain.

She sniffed the invigorating air. No wonder Louis's doctor had suggested they come to this wonderful hilltop! Francis, riding beside her, laughed. "It doesn't smell much like Paris, does it, my sweet? The streets there are rank, even in the winter. During the summer the odor is almost unbearable."

"London is the same," answered Mary. "It drives us all away during the warm months." She glanced back at the princesses behind them and then ahead at Charles, Dorset, and the other gentlemen. It was a small cavalcade today and everyone was on horseback. No swaying litters to hamper them. They would cover the fourteen miles fairly swiftly. She waited until they were well on their way, then she interrupted the Dauphin's stream of amusing chatter to suggest that he give his place to the Duke of Suffolk.

Still smarting from his defeat at Brandon's hands, Francis refused hotly.

"But I have some messages for my brother," Mary said. "I'm afraid that once I reach Paris I will be too busy to do more than wish my friends farewell."

"Nonsense," was Francis's answer. "This is just another excuse to avoid my company." He met her exasperated look with stubborn eyes. "Give me your messages and I'll be happy to pass them on to Suffolk." Making a grimace, he explained himself further. "I mean that I will be happy to act as courier for *you*. No one, I'm sure, could enjoy talking to that mountain of muscle, that—what is your word—lout?"

Mary flushed angrily. "I've heard him called many things here in France, and particularly by your ladies, but never 'lout!' "

Francis shrugged. "Our ladies are easy to please."

Suddenly remembering that she was, after all, a princess of England and the Queen of France, Mary bit back the sharp retort on the tip of her tongue and fell silent. She was aware that he was studying her face as they rode along, so she kept it impassive, her gaze on the road ahead. After a few minutes she spoke again, in her most formal voice. "It is my wish, your Highness, that you join the other gentlemen for a little while. Leave

223

me immediately, please, and request his Grace of Suffolk to bear me company during your absence."

She turned, and he saw that her eyes were the color of steel, her mouth set. "Immediately, my lord!"

When Charles reached her side a few moments later, her face was still stormy; but as she was very conscious of the ladies riding close behind, for she had slowed her horse to allow Charles time to fall back, she greeted him quietly. While she widened the gap between them and the group following her, she gave him several messages for her brother and sister-in-law. "I thought," she told him, "that this might be our only chance to speak privately."

"Then what must I tell Henry about your husband's health?" he asked her. "What do the doctors say? He looks very ill to me."

"Just what they've always said to me—that all he needs is rest. Rest, simple food, early hours. That's why he's sending so many of his Court back to Paris today, so that we can be quiet for a while. And, much as I want to be free, Charles, he's been so kind to me that I cannot wish him ill or dead. I find myself actually hoping the physicians are right. . . ."

"I'd be a monster myself if I didn't feel the same," he answered. "Louis is as gentle a man as I ever met, and I hate to see him suffering. We must go on being patient, my love, and let the future take care of itself for a while. We're young, thank God! But it's hard to leave you here in France, my darling, wondering how many months or years will pass before we meet again. . . ."

They rode along awhile without saying anything more. Then Charles asked her what Francis had done or said to make her look so angry. "At least, I assume it was Francis."

"I had to *order* him to leave me and send you back here!" She flushed and dropped her eyes. "I—I don't know what to do, Charles. I think he fancies himself in love with me, and he's so used to having his way with women that it frightens me. I keep wondering what would happen if Louis *should* die and I were alone here in France. He'd be King, you know." She glanced quickly at him through her lashes; his face was so grim that she was almost sorry she'd told him.

"So?" he said, finally. "That explains many things, Mary. I see now why our fine Prince was so determined to win the tournament. Believe me, if I'd known of this earlier, he would have left the field with more than an injured finger! But is it possible? He already has a mistress to whom he's devoted; I know, because he arranged for me to stay in her house, those first days in Paris."

Mary looked ahead at the Dauphin, now chatting gaily with the Marquis of Dorset. "Perhaps I was exaggerating when I said he was in love with me. It may very well be that he regards me merely as another woman to be seduced and tossed aside. He has a long list of romantic conquests, I hear, and he's only twenty. But no matter what his motive, Charles, I'm frightened. Would you come back to France if I needed you?"

"Mother of God, Mary! Of course I would! How could you doubt it?" With a quick gesture he stripped a ring from his finger, made sure that no one was watching them, and slipped it into her hand. "Take this, sweetheart. If such a time should come, enclose it in a letter to Wolsey or Hal, saying that one of the servants found it in my apartment at St. Germain. It's my seal ring, so you can ask to have it returned to me without delay, as you think I must be missing it."

"How clever of you!" Tucking the ring into the pouch that hung from her belt, Mary smiled gratefully up at him. "I feel much more comfortable now. But"—and her smile faded—"I suppose I should be sending you away. And, as you said, it may be months or years before I see you again. Surely, before you leave me, you are going to tell me. . . ."

Charles told her.

CHAPTER XXII

"IF YOU WOULD tilt your head a little more this way, your Majesty—" The young artist adjusted a fold in Mary's ermine mantle and watched her lift her chin. "Yes. Exactly. Now we begin,

225

your Grace." As he picked up his palette and his brush, the young Queen glanced over at Louis, half asleep in his great tester bed, and a cloud crossed her face. Their ten quiet days here at St. Germain had not improved his health, as they had hoped. No, it was painfully obvious even to her that he grew weaker instead of stronger.

They had obeyed every one of the doctors' orders and suggestions, but nothing seemed to help. Because the King was too ill to leave his bedchamber, for many days Mary had risen early to join him here, ready to amuse him as best she could, reaching for her lute when he was too tired to talk, and for her needlework when he felt well enough to reminisce about his early years on the throne of France, the only subject that still seemed to interest him.

She rode in the palace park and adjoining forest while he slept each afternoon, and occasionally, but only when he insisted that she do so, she dined with some of their noble neighbors, returning early, for her supper was always served to her at his fireside. But even this small pleasure, as his appetite dwindled, meant less and less to him.

Recently, because he was too frail for either music or conversation, Mary had the two artists whom Louis himself had ordered to paint portraits of his new Queen, bring their paints and easels to his room; for as long as she was able to hold her pose the work would go on, giving the ailing monarch something to watch, and giving her a quiet occupation.

But today she was aware that his eyes rarely turned her way. She saw him frown and pleat the bedcover in his wasted fingers; she noticed that he shivered once or twice as a draft blew in around the window frame near his bed and set the heavy tapestry stirring on the wall. With a sigh, she stepped down from the little platform and dismissed the artist.

"I'm sorry, monsieur," she said softly, "but I think that must be all for today."

When he had left the room, she untied the fur mantle and tossed it on a bench, realizing as she did so that the bedchamber was much colder than usual. The old Palace, high on a hilltop, was at the mercy of all the December winds.

"Mary—" Louis's voice was urgent.

She hurried to his side. "Yes, dear lord?"

"Mary," he said again, "I think that we must return to Paris. And soon. As soon as possible."

The doctors, realizing that only a miracle could save the King now, let Mary take him back to the Hôtel des Tournelles. The small cavalcade traveled slowly over the winding road, spending a night at Bougival and covering the rest of the distance the following day. The Lady Claude was waiting for them when they carried Louis's litter into the Great Hall. After an involuntary gasp at the sight of her father's emaciated face, she managed to control herself and hurried over to give him a welcoming kiss.

"Francis," she told him, "is off hunting. We sent for him the moment your courier arrived here, telling us of your coming, but it may be some time before they find him."

Louis laughed feebly. "Hunting in December! Well, well, I used to do it myself in days gone by. The very thought makes me shiver today. However, I'm glad the boy is well and enjoying himself."

While the ailing monarch was being settled into his familiar rooms, attended by both his daughters and all his physicians, Mary fled to hers, grateful for a little time to herself. Here at des Tournelles life would be easier for her, as even a very sick king must bow to custom and admit a great many of his lords and ladies into his presence.

She found Madame d'Aumont, who had not accompanied her to St. Germain, waiting in her withdrawing room, a letter in her hand. "From England, your Grace," she said, after greeting her mistress. "A courier brought it a short time ago."

Mary took it to a window and read it. It was from Wolsey. He had heard, apparently, of Louis's increasingly grave condition and it was a letter of good advice, telling her what she should do and what she should not do if her husband died. Folding it carefully, she locked it up with her private papers; she might need it soon. . . .

During the next few days Louis seemed a little stronger; the change of scene raised his spirits and he was happy to be in his beloved Paris again. But by Christmastime he was so ill that the occupants of the large rambling Palace let the holiday slip by almost unnoticed, and if Mary had a few wistful thoughts of England and Charles and happy Yuletides, she pushed them firmly aside and turned her attention to her dying husband.

Francis, obeying the warm heart under his flippant manner, stayed within call all week, on the chance that his cousin might need him. On December 29 he was, indeed, called in, and spent a pleasant hour watching Louis write a letter to King Henry in which the French monarch again described his delight in his English bride, assuring him that he loved and honored Mary more each day.

Because composing a letter was no light task for a man in the King's condition, Francis became convinced that his cousin's health was taking a turn for the better, and, early on New Year's Day, persuaded himself that there was no reason why he should not slip out of the Palace to visit his mistress. Neither Claude, Mary, nor Renee, who were already at the King's bedside, knew that he had left des Tournelles. Nor, although the rain was lashing at the windows and wind howling through the palace turrets, had they any idea that Paris was in the grip of the worst storm it had suffered in many years.

All three women had been roused early that morning with the news that Louis had passed an unusually restless night and that he was much weaker. Their one thought had been to dress, snatch a bite of breakfast, and hurry to his bedchamber; and now, seeing his white lips and hearing his heavy, difficult breathing, they exchanged frightened glances. After a little while, he opened his eyes, smiled faintly at them, and murmured, "Francis . . . ?"

One of the noblemen present nodded and left the room. Louis's confessor moved a little closer to the bed, but the King shook his head. Expecting the Dauphin at any moment, the Queen and the two Princesses walked quietly over to a far window, where they talked in a low whisper, their faces pale and their eyes wet.

When fifteen minutes had dragged by and Francis had not yet appeared, the Lady Claude returned to her father and sat close beside him, her lips trembling as she prayed for his soul. After a little while more she bent, kissed his hand, motioned to

Mary to take her place, and left the room, intent on discovering what could possibly be delaying her husband.

She found the Palace in a turmoil. The huge rambling building had been combed from top to bottom and Francis could not be found anywhere. No one, apparently, knew where he had gone. No one except, perhaps, his valet, who, they told Claude, had appeared in a thick cloak, demanded a horse, and ridden off into the storm, after promising to bring his young master back to the Palace.

"Pray God he does, and soon!" Claude said in a shaking voice, her anger at Francis's absence almost stronger, at this moment, than her grief. As she stood at the foot of the wide, malodorous staircase, not knowing whether to wait, send out a further search party, or return to the royal apartments, she heard a great bustle down the corridor, the sound of excited voices and hurried footsteps, the opening and shutting of doors.

She was still standing there when Francis appeared. Water dripped from the soaked plume on his hat, from the end of his long nose, from the hem of his riding cape, and even from the limp fringe on his heavily embroidered gauntlets. His valet, equally soggy, was at his heels. Claude stopped them both with an imperious hand.

"Don't waste time telling me where you have been, my lord, or why. Just strip off those soaking garments and come with me. My father is dying. You may already be too late."

At the King's bedside, Mary sat holding her husband's hand. It was icy cold in her warm fingers, so cold that she wanted to drop it and run away and hide. She could feel death creeping over him and she was frightened, but until Francis arrived she knew that, frightened or not, she must remain.

When the door opened at last, she rose and gave the Dauphin her seat, noticing as she did so that he looked almost as terrified as she was feeling. As he sat down Louis opened his eyes again.

"Thank God you've come, Francis. I'm dying."

"No, no, cousin," the young man protested. "If you rest, Sire, and—"

"Nonsense, my boy. I'm dying. I know it. I sent for you to say farewell and to tell you that I leave France in your hands. France and my daughters and my wife—" The Dauphin had to lean over the bed to hear what he was saying. After a word or two more the dying King asked for his confessor, and with a muttered "God bless you, my dear lord!" Francis surrendered his place to the hovering priest, and joined the crying women.

"May God rest his kind and gentle soul," he said to them. "A good man and a fine King. I hope I'll have as little to confess when I lie there."

The heavy rains stopped some time later that night and when Mary quitted the Palace des Tournelles early the next morning the roads were so muddy and so wet that she had to guide her mare over them with the greatest care. The Rue St. Antoine was not so bad, but when she and her little train of archers and attendants turned off onto the narrow road that led to the Seine, they found it pitted with deep, water-filled potholes.

She was vividly reminded of the morning after her father's death, almost six years earlier. That was a cold day too, and her thoughts had been filled then, as they were now, with the macabre picture of a king on his deathbed, making his farewells to those he loved and his peace with God. Just as she and her brother had left Richmond for the Tower of London, resigning their father's remains to the impersonal hands of the embalmers, so now was she forced to hurry away from des Tournelles, never to see her husband again either in life or death.

It was young Renee who had told her, soon after Louis drew his last breath, that, as his widow, she must go to the remote Hôtel de Cluny and remain in strict retirement there for the next six weeks.

"Didn't you know, your Grace?" She was surprised when Mary merely looked at her in astonishment. "I thought, surely, that it would be the custom in England as it is here in France. How else can they be sure—? Although in your case it is, of course, ridiculous and unnecessary. But there may very well have been queens in the past—" She blushed and stammered a little. "Well, what woman wouldn't like to be the mother of the heir to the throne, after all? I mean—"

And she struggled on with her halting explanation until, at last, Mary understood what she was trying to tell her. Now that she, Mary, was the widow of the late King of France, she must be so strictly guarded that if, in the next month or so, she should prove to be pregnant, there could be no question raised concerning the baby's paternity.

Two other ladies besides Madame d'Aumont had slept in her bedchamber the night before, two noblewomen whose word could never be questioned. They were the Duchesses of Alençon and Nevers, and they were riding behind her now. They had never left her side since the moment they had been sent to her private apartments, less than an hour after the King's death. And they would remain with her, Mary had been told, until she was safely shut into seclusion at the Hôtel Cluny, some distance away on the other side of the Seine.

When the sad little cavalcade reached the bank of the river and climbed aboard the sable-draped barge, the ladies, looking rather like a flock of black crows, gathered around Mary, whose royal white mourning garments seemed even whiter among all their dimness, to point out anything of interest that they might pass on their way.

The sun was breaking through the clouds and, as they slid around the tip of the Ile de la Cité, it gleamed, for a breathtaking moment, on the beautiful windows of Notre Dame Cathedral, towering close above them. Now they moved swiftly westward between the left bank of the river and the narrow Ile, passing under a bridge built solid with what looked like tall houses. "The Pont l'Hôtel de Dieu," said the Duchess of Alençon. "And that," indicating a pile of gloomy buildings to its right, "is the Hôtel de Dieu itself, our great hospital for the poor. If you will look ahead, your Grace, you will see there, at the far end of the Ile, the Palais Royal where you stood the night of your coronation. But"—she pointed to the left—"see, we are landing. There are horses waiting for us."

Once in their saddles, they swung away from the Seine, riding through almost open country, with little to see except a farm here and there or a sprawling monastery. Finally one of the other ladies showed Mary a much larger edifice, clearly visible through the leafless trees. "The Sorbonne," she told her, "where our priests study theology. The Cluny is that smaller hôtel near it—the one with the Gothic windows and pretty stone parapet."

231

Mary was glad, afterwards, that she took this opportunity to observe the outside of her new residence, for she was not to see it again for six long, dull weeks. It was a handsome building, erected shortly before the turn of the century by Jacques d'Amboise, Abbot of the Order of Cluny, and it was still used by the abbots as a temporary country residence for themselves and their guests. A Cluniac brother helped Mary down from her palfrey and bade her welcome, bending his knee and bowing his hooded head over her hand, then slipped away as Madame d'Aumont, who had ridden through the rain the night before to make sure all was in order for her mistress, appeared to guide Mary to her apartments.

They walked through a long covered arcade beside the open Court of Honor, into a tiled passage, up a narrow staircase, and along an open balcony. When they reached a handsomely furnished retiring room Mary looked around it with pleasure, thinking it a most comfortable place. If all her apartments were as pleasant as this one, life here would not be too disagreeable. She turned and said as much to the other ladies who had followed her into the pretty chamber.

Without answering her, the Duchess of Nevers threw open a door on the left-hand wall and asked her to step inside. Mary did so, blinked, and gave a startled gasp. It was a small room with rather low ceilings. Everything in it was pure, stark white; white arras covered the walls, white curtains hung at the mullioned casements, white fur rugs were scattered around the floor, and the bed furnishings—tester, hangings, coverlet—all were white.

Seeing her shiver, the Duchess of Nevers tried to explain. "It is a royal custom," she said. "A custom that goes so far back into mists of the past that no one remembers now why it was considered necessary. It is not enough for our widowed queens to wear white! During this first period of their mourning they are called 'La Reine Blanche,' and everything around them must be white."

Dipping a curtsey, she spoke again. "And now, your Grace, I am afraid we must leave you here in the care of the good brothers, Madame d'Aumont, and your own English ladies. Send for anything you may wish to help you pass the time—books, needle-work—"

She threw open the nearest window and leaned out. "See, your Majesty? Fresh air and a lovely view of the garden." Crossing swiftly to the adjoining wall, she opened another. "This one looks down into the chapel. If you stand here you will be able to follow the service."

Mary was frankly bewildered. "But I would much rather walk in the garden itself and attend the services in the chapel."

The older woman shook her head regretfully. "I'm sorry, your Grace. I see no one has told you. No, you cannot walk in the garden or go down to the chapel. For the next month or six weeks you must remain within the four walls of this room. Even the adjoining rooms are forbidden you. I know it will be tedious but it is the law. What can we do?"

Mary had dragged her way through other wearisome months in her lifetime but it seemed to her that this particular one would never pass. Had she been the kind of young woman who enjoyed lying idly on a pile of cushions, spending the hours napping, yawning, gossiping—reaching out a lazy hand to fondle a spaniel or convey another sweetmeat to a greedy mouth—she might have been supremely content at the Cluny. But as she was, instead, a true sister of an energetic Tudor brother, accustomed to afternoons in the saddle and evenings of swift and nimble dancing, this enforced imprisonment was torture.

It was not so unpleasant for the first few days for she was exhausted from Louis's illness and death and was suffering from such mixed emotions that she was glad to have her chamber darkened and her ladies silent while she alternated between weeping into her pillows for her husband and dreaming hotly happy dreams that might now come true. But this lasted only until she was thoroughly rested and her young body began crying out for exercise and fresh air. Before long she and her ladies could find nothing new to talk about; her eyes smarted from continual reading and embroidering, and the small white room closed in around her like a dungeon cell.

"How many days have we passed now?" she would ask Jane Seymour or Anne Grey.

"Ten—fourteen—twenty—" The answers were as unsatisfactory as the slow movement of the hands around the face of her clock.

The young Queen walked to the leaded casement window and stared down into the wintry garden, sighed drearily and returned slowly to her chair by the fire. Her head ached; Mary Boleyn had been quarreling with Madame d'Aumont; her feet were cold, and she had nothing to do. She tried to count the days on her fingers and failed.

"Jane!" She called suddenly to Jane Seymour.

"Yes, your Grace?"

"What is the date, Jane?"

"The twenty-sixth day of January, madam."

"Then we have been here almost a month. It has seemed at least a year!" She picked up her needlework, then flung it down again. "Mother of God, how my head aches!"

As Mistress Seymour tossed aside her book and rose to come to her, loud footsteps sounded in the adjoining room and a scratch at the door.

"Our dinner, I suppose," said Mary listlessly, pressing a hand to her forehead.

A moment later she was on her feet, her fingers tingling under the lips of the new King of France. "Sire!" she gasped. "I didn't know—I didn't expect—"

His black eyes smiled into hers. "They wouldn't let me visit you until today," he told her. "Everything goes by strict rule, it seems. No male callers for La Reine Blanche until such and such a day, then, on this particular date, I was told that I should come to you and ask you a question."

"A question?"

He nodded. "And as it is an extremely private kind of question, I wonder if we might request your good lady here to retire to the other room? Leave the door open, of course, if you will. Her Grace's period of seclusion will not come to an end for another two weeks."

When they were alone, he drew a chair close to Mary's side. "You can have no idea, my sweet," he said, "how much I have longed to be with you. I can imagine how dreary this last month has been for you; indeed, I have thought of little else since we said farewell." He took her soft hand and kissed it again, this time letting his mouth stray around her wrist and up under the lace of her sleeve.

She pulled it away. "Stop it, Francis! If this is your private question I will recall my prim little Jane."

He laughed. "Perhaps we should attend to business first! But I find it hard to think of the right words." After pausing a moment, he went on. "Tell me the truth about this, Mary. If there is any doubt still, I must know. Am I truly the King of France?"

"But of course you are, my lord. What other king could there be but you? If, as I assume, you are asking me whether or not I am enceinte, I can assure you that I am not. And this whole situation is ridiculous, Francis! I could have told you when Louis died that I could not possibly be carrying a child. He and I never—Louis was too ill—" As she floundered, her face flushed a bright pink.

Francis whistled softly, and an excited expression crept into his piercing black eyes. "So it was that way, was it? Poor Louis— poor man! I suspected that it might be so, but I couldn't be sure, of course."

He reached for her hand again. "Well, if there is no infant to consider, we must think about your future. Did you know that your brother is planning to renew your old contract with Charles of Flanders? Would that alliance please you?"

Mary looked at him with horror. "Charles of Flanders? I won't! Henry knows perfectly well that I won't. He can't be thinking of such a thing!"

"But he is, Mary." Francis shrugged his wide shoulders. "And it's not just idle gossip, I promise you. Now if I had my way, we would keep you here in France, and my advisers have already suggested that you wed either the Duke of Lorraine or Charles, the Duke of Savoy."

"No."

He twinkled at her like a merry, long-nosed fox. "No?"

"No. No, no, no!" In a state of complete agitation, Mary jumped up and ran to the window, turning her back to the King.

He was with her in a flash, his arm around her waist. "Why be angry with me, *ma petite?* I don't think you should marry them, either." He reached out a long finger and tipped up her chin so that he could look into her eyes. "I have a better plan, Mary. Marry me!" Before she could utter even a word of protest, he was kissing her passionately, her lips, her throat, the cleft between her soft white breasts—

With a gasp, she tore herself free. "Have you gone mad, Sire?"

He reached for her again, but she ducked behind a tall chair. "No, Francis! You *must* be mad!"

"If you mean because I am married to Claude, I see no reason why that marriage should not be set aside. No, listen to me, Mary! I'm extremely serious about this! Louis dissolved an early union with Queen Jeanne because she was weak and malformed. Claude is frail, as she was. And if you were never truly Louis's wife, why I'm sure the Pope would grant us a dispensation—"

His face was alight with excitement and his voice suddenly tender. "I keep thinking of us as the King and Queen of France, my darling. Just imagine us—happy, healthy, bearing wonderful strong princes and beautiful princesses. It would be magnificent —a dream come true!" Then, seeing her recoil and turn white, the animation died out of his eyes. "Have I frightened you? I didn't mean to. Perhaps I should give you a little time to think about it before pressing you further." He took a step or two toward the door, then stopped again. "But I meant every word of it, Mary. I'll come again as soon as I can."

The moment he was gone, Mary threw herself on the bed and burst into an agony of sobs. Were her troubles beginning instead of ending? His proposal had shaken her, as had his news of her brother's treachery. Hal, she told herself for the hundredth time, had *promised* her that she could now wed as she pleased!

Then she reread certain passages in her last letter from Wolsey, the one that arrived shortly before Louis's death. ". . . the King, your most loving brother, will never forsake, but most fastly stick unto you, in all your needs." Would he, indeed? "Never do anything but by the advice of his Grace; referring all things to him whatever fair promises, words, or persuasions shall be made to the contrary; having always a special regard to his common honor, and letting nothing pass your Grace's mouth whereby any person in those parts may have you at any advantage. And if any motions of marriage or other thing fortune to be made unto you, in nowise give hearing to the same. And thus doing, you shall not fail to have the King fast and loving to you, and attain to your own heart's desire and return again to England with as much honor as ever woman had."

Well, certainly "fair promises, words or persuasions" had been made, and "motions of marriage." Setting her mouth firmly, she sent for a courier and reached for paper and ink. After she had told Henry about Francis's various proposals she assured him that she had no intention of yielding to his entreaties, urged her brother to tell her when she might return to England, and reminded him of his promise. "I beseech your Grace," she ended, "to be good lord and brother to me; for if your Grace will have me married in any place, saving where my mind is, I will be there whereas your Grace nor any other shall have any joy of me; for, I promise your Grace, you shall hear that I will be in some religious house. . . . You know where I purpose to marry, if ever I marry again."

Before she sanded it, she went to her jewel casket and touched a spring on the side of the gilded wooden box. A secret drawer sprang out, her fingers found Charles's heavy seal ring, and she returned to her desk.

"You will find here in my letter," she added to her note, "a ring that was found in the apartments occupied by the Duke of Suffolk. . . ."

CHAPTER XXIII

SEVERAL DAYS WENT BY before Francis returned to the Hôtel Cluny—days of sheer torture for the young dowager Queen of France, as the morning after his first visit he had replaced all her English attendants with Frenchmen and Frenchwomen, a move that frightened her. Was he planning to force her to his will? Was he intending to intercept any letters she might send to England? When this possibility occurred to her she was glad she had wasted no time in dispatching that important note to her brother. Had she been wrong in thinking Francis kind and friendly? Did that gay and charming surface hide a man who was willing to toss honor and scruples away in order to gain what he wanted?

Hand in hand with these disturbing thoughts was the fear that some mischance might keep Charles from answering her summons. Her brother might forget to give the ring to him, letting it lie unnoticed on some table for weeks and weeks. Or, if he did deliver it safely, there was always the chance that he would forbid Charles to leave England. And, if neither of those things happened, storms might delay him until it was too late.

All day, every day and during most of the long nighttime hours, Mary fretted, eating little and sleeping less, calling for candles and her solitaire cards in the middle of the night, and often waking her ladies in the early morning because she needed someone to talk to, even in French. Anything, she found, was better than enduring a silence that left her at the mercy of her overactive imagination.

She was so tired and nervous by the time that the new King visited her again that she actually considered pleading ill health and sending him away unseen. Then her common sense returned and she remembered his good-natured assistance during her first meeting with Louis, her marriage, her coronation, and her early trials at her new court. She must see him, she decided, and refuse him firmly. Then, if he showed any signs of being reasonable, she would throw herself on his mercy and ask for his help.

The moment he entered her room and dismissed her ladies, Mary knew what she should do; for although he led her to the window on the garden side of the chamber, one of the few spots where they would be unheard and unobserved by whoever might be in the antechamber, she could see that he was not the tempestuous lover of their previous interview.

"You look very tired and white, Mary," he said, glancing at her down his long nose. "Have you been worrying over my proposal? Is the thought of wedding me that distasteful to you? Was I so very wrong in thinking you found me a good companion and might welcome me as a lover—a husband?" While he was questioning her, Mary noticed that his black eyes held something new, a hint of anxiety, a hesitation, a shadow that she could not understand.

"My dear Lord," she spoke slowly, seeking the right words, "I must tell you that, regardless of any feeling I may or may not have for you, I could never allow you to divorce Claude for my sake. If you did, and we wed, I know I would soon hate both myself and you—and I would always have uneasy doubts as to the legitimacy of our children. So, in love with you or not, my answer is no. And, dear Francis, I am fond of you, I find you a delightful supper and dancing partner; I know a flirtation with you would be excessively enjoyable, but, as it happens, I am *not* in love with you."

When Francis made a move and opened his mouth as if to protest, Mary interrupted him. "Be my friend, instead, Francis." Her eyes filled with tears. "Please, please! I need one so desperately!"

"Haven't I always been that?"

"I thought so, Sire, before—well, before. And that's why I dare ask you now to help me." She fell on her knees and held out her hands in a beseeching gesture. "But if you *will* help me, you must promise to keep my counsel—by your faith and truth as a true prince, Francis. My problem is a—a very delicate one."

Francis laughed and raised her to her feet. He led her to a chair, dried her eyes on his lace handkerchief, and seated himself beside her.

"I will do better than that," he said. "I will promise you as a *king* to help you and keep your counsel. Sweethearts or not, my dear Mary, we will always be friends. So tell me your secret, *ma petite*, whatever it is." He laughed again and kissed her hand. "If ever I saw a small woman bursting with a large secret, that woman is you!"

Encouraged by his soft mood and his promises of faith, Mary told her story. She had fallen in love with a knight's son, she said, and had hoped to marry him. When Henry insisted on her wedding Louis, they had made a bargain. "I refused to come to

239

France," she went on, "until my brother promised me that if I should ever be free to marry again I might choose my own husband. So you see why I was so angry when you told me that Henry was considering another foreign alliance for me."

"Surely you don't mean that you, the sister of the King of England and the widow of the King of France, can be thinking seriously of a union with some insignificant, lowborn commoner?"

"He's hardly that," Mary raised her eyes defiantly. "He's a duke now, and known in your country and mine as what you would call *'un homme formidable'!*"

He looked at her for a moment, then laughed grimly. "So! And you are strangely reluctant to name him, are you not? You know how difficult it will be for me to play the friend to the Duke of Suffolk. No wonder my hackles rose every time we met!" Rising to his feet, he strode around the room. When he returned to her side, his eyes were still angry. "This is a bitter pill you have given me to swallow, little belle-mère. Must it be Suffolk? The man who defeated me in the eyes of all France?"

"Please, Francis! I've loved him for many years and he's all I want. All. I never wanted to be a queen! And I've just told you that I don't know—" Taking her courage in both hands she described her romance from beginning to end, and was rewarded, at last, with a more sympathetic smile.

"Well, I gave you my promise, and I will honor it. But believe me, if the doctors hadn't told me yesterday that Claude is enceinte, I wouldn't be succumbing so easily."

"Claude enceinte?" Mary's face lit up. "What wonderful news, Francis! An heir for France! So, everything arranges itself, as you would say." Giving a delighted chuckle, she dimpled at him. "What would you have done if I'd greeted you with open arms today with the announcement that I would be happy to have you annul your marriage to her so that you could wed me?"

The King looked sheepish. "I hadn't made up my mind. It would have been a little uncomfortable, wouldn't it?"

After they had laughed together, he returned to her problem. "With my promise and Henry's," he said, "your way is surely clear. I will not put any obstacles in your path to prevent you from returning to England, and, once there, you will be free to remind your brother of the bargain he made with you."

Mary dropped her eyes and studied the floor. "Yes—but Henry's a king first and a brother second. He might very well break his promise."

"I see." The young French ruler was thoughtful but not too surprised. "Then how can I help you? Send for Suffolk on some pretext and arrange a secret marriage for you? If Henry refuses his permission, I mean? Once you are wed he should come around. Or"—he shrugged—"suppose he doesn't. You are Louis's widow, after all; the dowager Queen of France. Live in France with your Brandon, if you must. I don't promise to like him, Mary, but I will try for your sake."

"Francis!" Throwing her arms around his neck, Mary gave him an impulsive kiss. "Bless you! Bless you! I'll love you all my life for this."

"But not the way I want you to." He returned her kiss gently. "Well, never mind, sweet, never mind. Now, how do we spirit your doughty champion over the Channel?"

"Unless he failed to receive the message I sent within an hour of your last visit here, Francis, he should be on his way to me at this very moment."

"To rescue his lady in distress I suppose. With a fire in his eye and his sword in his hand! Well, we can only hope, then, that no blood will flow!"

After that, Mary had little time in which to worry or wonder, for on February 3 Charles arrived openly in France as an accredited ambassador from England, accompanied by two others, the Dean of Windsor and Sir Richard Wingfield. Instead of his sword, he had letters of condolence and congratulation in his hand when he and his companions met the new King of France at Compeigne.

To his great surprise and open bewilderment, Francis immediately invited him into the royal bedchamber for a confidential chat. As his attitude was unusually friendly, Brandon followed him warily, wondering if he were walking into some kind of trap.

His first words convinced the Englishman that he had. "Have

you come to France to marry the Queen?" Francis put the question bluntly.

"Good God, Sire!" Brandon sounded as horrified as, indeed, he was. "Surely you cannot think me so foolish as to come into a strange realm and marry her Grace without your knowledge or her brother's consent?"

"If I were in your shoes," said Francis, "I would wed Mary at the first opportunity and worry about King Henry and me after the deed was done."

Charles flushed, his head whirling with questions and speculations. How had Francis learned their secret? Had he frightened Mary into revealing it? Was that why Mary sent him his seal ring? Or was Francis merely guessing and baiting him into making some admission?

Francis watched him flounder, wondering again how Mary could prefer this Englishman to *him*. It was rather amusing to see him squirm. . . . But if he was to keep his promise to the Queen, he must, he supposed, set Brandon at ease.

"Come," he said at last, "let us understand each other. Her Grace has confided fully in me, and I have promised to stand your friend. In fact, I have vowed faithfully to help and advance the matter between you with as good a will as if I were doing it for myself, either by seeking Henry's permission for you to marry her here in my kingdom, or, if necessary, by arranging a secret marriage without it."

When Brandon still hesitated, Francis smiled rather maliciously. "You kissed the lady first beneath a withered branch of mistletoe. There! Does that convince you that she and I have no secrets from each other?"

Although he could not yet understand Francis's change of face and offer of friendship, Charles knew now that Mary must have taken him completely into her confidence. So, after thanking him warmly for his kindness, he assured the French ruler that his one aim in life was to make the widowed Queen his wife. "But I must inform you, Sire," he added, "that I am here only because I gave King Henry a solemn oath that I would not wed her Grace without his permission. I must take her back to England unmarried and await his Majesty's pleasure."

Francis whistled softly. "So? That makes the problem even

more difficult. We will have to walk carefully, my lord, I can see that. First, I think, we should visit the little Queen and discuss it all with her."

Mary, alone in her white prison, stood clutching the tall gilded bedpost. The sound of the King's trumpets in the courtyard had sent all her ladies rushing into the antechamber to make sure that everything was in readiness for their visitors. The servants had set up a long table there for their dinner, and the kitchens below were in a flurry of preparation. Cooking for a handful of women was one thing, the chef had said; it was another matter entirely to provide a suitable dinner for the King of France and three ambassadors from England. Mary had conferred with him, earlier in the day, and had made several suggestions to her ladies about how the other room should be arranged, but as she was still confined to the four walls of her bedchamber, and would be for another week, there was nothing she could do now but stand here and wait.

With her free hand, she stroked her white velvet robe, a gown lavishly banded in ermine and embroidered all over with sprays of pearls. She had chosen to wear it today because of something Ann Grey had said, the first time she had seen it. "Why, your Grace"—she had run an admiring finger over the jeweled sprays —"these could be sprigs of our mistletoe!"

"Meestletoe?" Madame d'Aumont raised her eyebrows.

"A winter berry," Mary had explained to her. "We hang it overhead at Christmastime, and any maid caught under it forfeits a kiss."

Mary was remembering the incident, and thinking of the part that the little white berries had played in her romance, when she heard heavy footsteps, a page's piping voice announcing her royal visitor, and a great bustle of men and women greeting each other in French, English, and a mixture of both. It brought her into the doorway, her heart in her mouth.

There, just behind Francis, loomed a tall, broad-shouldered man—a man handsomely garbed in gold velvet and marten. A man who was smiling at her. As her eyes met his, the room swam around her. The moment it steadied, she dropped down in a deep court curtsey, bade her guests very, very welcome, and invited them into the bedchamber.

"I'm still a prisoner here, my lords," she told them.

After a few minutes of general conversation, Francis suggested that he and Mary's guests retire to the adjoining room and have their dinner. "My lord Duke," he told her, "brings you messages from King Henry, and there are certain arrangements for your future that he and I must discuss with you in private. With your permission, your Grace, we will return to you here when we have dined, leaving our other friends from abroad to entertain your ladies with news of their families and friends."

Mary, her solitary dinner soon eaten, thought the meal that was being served in the antechamber would never end; even little Jane Seymour, after carving her mistress's meat and filling her wine glass, had hurried in to join the others, and Mary felt lonely and unwanted. She was sitting in a tall chair near the fire when Francis entered at last, followed closely by Charles Brandon. He tossed a last gay word to the diners, still seated at the table, closed the door between the rooms with his own hand, and motioned to Mary to remain where she was.

"We may forget our manners for a little while," the young King said to her, "as my chief purpose in coming here is to tell you that I have taken my lord of Suffolk into our confidence, and to arrange, if possible, for you two to have a moment alone. But how?"

Striding across the room, he pointed to a small door in the far corner. "What is behind that door?"

"The staircase to the chapel," answered the girl.

"Splendid." He opened the window beside it and looked down. "Empty. I think perhaps I should slip down and pray for the success of our venture." With a mocking smile, he disappeared.

Almost before the staircase door was closed behind him, the two lovers were in each other's arms and lost to the world around them. Mary drew away at last, her mouth deliciously bruised and her heart singing.

"We must talk, Charles. There will be little enough time before the King returns. What have you and he decided? When do we wed?"

Charles shook his head. "I'm afraid I must take you home to

244

England first, sweetheart. I had to swear a solemn vow that I wouldn't marry you without Hal's permission."

"Charles! Why did you do such a thing? You've tied our hands!"

"You sent for me, Mary, and Hal wouldn't let me come to you until I promised. He had planned to send Surrey on this mission, not me, and he was most reluctant when I begged for the privilege. It's not an easy task he's set me, and he thought Surrey a better man for this particular piece of work." Brandon sighed heavily. "Bringing you back unwed, and with all your dowry and French jewels—"

"Then he must mean to break his promise! He *is* planning to marry me to Charles of Flanders! Francis said he was, but I kept hoping it wasn't true. I tell you, Charles, I will not do it—I will not. Hal promised me *faithfully;* once in front of Wolsey and again on the sands at Dover!" She stamped her foot and her voice rose in anger. "Oath or not, Charles, you must marry me now. Francis will arrange it."

"Mary, love. . . ." Poor Brandon's face was flushed and he was obviously miserable. "Listen to me, sweetheart! I swore that oath to the King of England. Don't you understand, my darling? To break it might be considered treason."

Mary burst into tears. "Oh, it's all so dreadful. How can I bear it? I thought I could be happy at last, and now—now—"

Charles was trying to soothe her when Francis rejoined them. Mary pulled away and hurried to the French King's side.

"Help me, dear Francis. You said you would. What shall we do?"

He put his arm around her shoulders and smiled bracingly down into her tear-stained face. "I suppose, in the face of Suffolk's delicate position, we must write King Henry and ask for his permission to let you two wed. If I point out the fact that this is my first request as the King of France, he may consider himself in duty bound to grant it."

"I doubt it," answered Mary grimly. "Henry rarely thinks himself in duty bound to do anything he doesn't want to do. However, I am willing to try. I will write him, too. I think I'll write Wolsey as well. And I'll wait for their answers." She swung back and faced Charles. "But I'm not going to sit here for months while letter after letter goes back and forth from France to England, and give Hal time to maneuver me into another political marriage. That I will not do! If his answer to our request is no, Charles, and you are afraid to wed me then, I'll give you up and retire into a nunnery, I mean it! I've already told my brother that."

"I'll send my courier for your letters, Mary," said Francis hurriedly, "and dispatch them with one of mine before I sleep tonight. And now I think we have conferred for as long as we should—your other guests will be growing restive."

Although the February seas were unusually calm, and Francis's couriers swift, the exchange of letters took longer than Mary had hoped. Fortunately for her, she was free to come and go after the twelfth day of the month, and this made her period of waiting a little less wearing than it might have been; now she could ride, walk, and establish herself more comfortably at the Cluny, where she was to remain until her future was settled. After consulting with Francis, who rode over to celebrate her release from captivity, it was decided between them that she should dismiss Madame d'Aumont and keep only her English attendants, returned to her long since, at her side. The young Queen and the jolly Frenchwoman were good friends but Madame d'Aumont had a pair of unusually sharp eyes and a weakness for gossip, two things which might cause trouble later.

"As long as there is even a possibility that you and Suffolk may have to wed secretly," Francis said, "your household must be arranged so that there are not too many obstacles in our way. Make it a habit to share your bedchamber with the two maids you trust the most, and establish the others in quarters a little distant from yours, so that if Suffolk and I have news for you we can call late in the evening without setting too many tongues wagging."

"Then it will have to be Jane Seymour and Mary Boleyn," answered Mary. "My other two maids are sisters and tell each other everything. Jane is very young, I know, but she's quiet, discreet, and, I think, devoted to me. Besides, her brother Edward is my page of honor, and would be the one to carry messages or guard doors." She nodded at the King, sitting beside her.

246

"I shall do exactly as you suggest, Francis. As you know, I have little hope that Henry will change his mind."

Mary was still up and sitting in her withdrawing room, having sent everyone to bed except Jane Seymour, when Edward scratched on the door. "It's his Grace, the Duke of Suffolk," he announced to his sister. "He's waiting below with letters from his Majesty, King Henry. If the Queen has not retired he would like permission to bring them to her."

"Tell my lord Duke that I will be happy to see him." Mary rose and came to the door herself. "Bring him to me, Edward, and send a lackey with wine, saffron cakes, and more wood for the fire."

Under cover of this normal bustle and activity, Mary was able to greet Charles as if his call was nothing out of the ordinary, and as if the letters in his hand were not the most important things in the world.

"Warm yourself by the fire, my lord," she said, "and let Mistress Seymour pour you a glass of wine while I read my letters. They may contain some messages for you from my brother."

Charles watched her face as she scanned Henry's answer to the French king's plea on their behalf and then opened hers. She looked up, a moment later, met his eyes and shook her head, her mouth set. Then she read them both again, more slowly this time, before handing them back to her lover. "Please read them, my Lord."

"I wonder, Jane," she turned to her little maid while he was so occupied, "if you would mind taking your needlework into the bedchamber for a few minutes? But stay within call, my dear, as I will be needing you again very soon; my letters contain a private matter that I must discuss with my lord of Suffolk, but it will not take us long."

With a smile and a curtsey, smooth-haired Jane slipped away and closed the door behind her, leaving Mary and Charles alone. The young Queen waited until he had finished reading, then rose from her chair and stood in front of him, her hands spread wide in a gesture of hopelessness.

"You see, Charles? It's no use. No use whatever. My brother hasn't the slightest intention of letting us wed!"

"He doesn't say *that,* Mary." Charles put the papers down on a table and drew her onto his knee. "He refuses to allow us to marry here in France, my darling, but he doesn't say we may not wed after we've returned home. I admit," he added thoughtfully, "that I find it difficult to be sure just what he *does* mean in these two letters."

Mary snorted. "He means nothing, absolutely nothing. He's ambiguous and vague—purposely, I would say—so that I'll have nothing in writing to use either now or later. I know him and his trickery and so do you."

"Then we'll have to write him again. Francis feels as you do, that Henry is being evasive."

"We will *not* write him again," said Mary firmly. She rose and faced him. "No, Charles. I said I would wait for his letters and no longer. Now we shall have to take matters in our own hands and be married here in France. Immediately."

"But, Mary! I gave Henry my *word!*"

"And he gave me *his* word." The Princess looked with stormy eyes at her lover, who had joined her near the fireplace. "Not once, Charles, but twice. Henry's promises came first, and having given them to me he had no right to ask for yours. He knows perfectly well that it's you I mean to marry, and that's why he made you vow to bring me back to England unwed. It's just another proof that he means to break his bargain with me."

She was trembling all over, but she managed to keep her voice steady. "I carried out my part of our agreement, didn't I? I married Louis and I tried to be a good queen to him so that my brother would be pleased and proud of me. And so that England need not be ashamed of its Princess!"

"I know. I know. And you succeeded wonderfully, my darling. Everyone in France loves and respects you and so does everyone at home. Believe me, they know how difficult it was for you. . . ."

"Then I want my reward." As Mary's eyes met his, all the color drained out of her face, leaving her so white that Charles, thinking she was about to faint, moved toward her.

"No, don't touch me!" She put up a hand to stop him. "I have something else to say and I want you to listen, Charles, because I mean it. It's this: You must marry me within four days or I will never see you again." Her voice broke. "Never. I—I've reached the end. I can't wait and wonder and worry any longer. If you want me," she began to sob, "you m-must take me now!" At that moment Mary's last bit of control disappeared. The long months of strain had been too much; her wedding, Louis's illness and death, her incarceration here at the Cluny, Francis's proposal, and the days of suspense, waiting for Henry's answer to their letters. . . .

"All my life I've been waiting—and waiting—and waiting!" She was almost screaming now. Giving in to hysterics for the first time in her eighteen years, she rocked back and forth in an agony of tears and sobs; she covered her face with her shaking hands and leaned helplessly against the wall, trembling so that she could barely stay on her feet.

When Charles took her in his arms she gave a wail of protest and pushed him away. Thoroughly frightened, he ran and opened the bedchamber door.

"Mistress Seymour! Mistress Seymour—please! The Queen!"

Jane, who had been listening to Mary's wild weeping and wondering what to do, rushed in and led her mistress to a chair. "Some wine, my lord, quickly!" Loosening Mary's gown, she produced a small flagon of aromatic vinegar and held it under her nose. But Mary's sobs only increased, and when Charles tried to make her take a sip of wine she thrust it aside so roughly that it spilled down the front of her gown and on the floor.

With a groan, he knelt at her feet and caught her frantic, twisting hands in his, oblivious to the fact that they were no longer alone.

"Mary, beloved! Mary! Listen to me, Mary! I'll do whatever you wish—anything, anything. Only stop weeping, my darling. Stop weeping. I can't stand it. I can't stand it! For God's sake, *stop weeping!*"

CHAPTER XXIV

THE ABBOT OF CLUNY, the obvious person to perform the marriage ceremony, had readily agreed to do so, and Charles had heard Francis only yesterday swear him to secrecy. At the King's suggestion, Claude had invited the Grey sisters to spend several days at des Tournelles, leaving Mary with the two maids whom she and Francis had already chosen as the most trustworthy— Jane Seymour and Mary Boleyn. And the custodian of the chapel here at Cluny had received royal orders to leave a convenient outside door unlocked from now on, and to turn his back if he saw a cloaked figure slipping through it at odd hours.

It was surprising that a man of only twenty summers, and a king to boot, could arrange a clandestine wedding with such ease. Only four other people had been taken into their confidence: Mary's two chamberwomen, Edward Seymour, her page of honor, and Charles's own squire.

Brandon caught Francis smiling at him and, as he smiled back, he pushed aside his doubts about the wisdom of what he was doing today. Whether Henry forgave them or not, he told himself for the hundredth time, he and Mary would have their happy hour.

A clatter of feminine feet on the stone steps took Francis to the open door of the staircase, and Mary emerged a moment later, looking so entrancing that Brandon's heart stood still. She was wearing a pearly white velvet gown, deeply banded in ermine; a gown that seemed familiar to him, although he wasn't sure just when he had seen it before.

Her rippling red-gold hair was unbound, hanging freely over her shoulders, and confined only by a narrow fillet of gold set with pearls. She was at his side, her hand in his, and the Abbot had already begun the ceremony before the significance of this reached him. His beloved Mary was to be his, and his alone— not only from this day forward, but also from this day backward, to love and to cherish, in sickness and in health, as long as they both should live! At Mary's request the English ritual was used to make them man and wife, and they both made their responses clearly, firmly, triumphantly.

When the last prayer was prayed, the new Duchess of Suffolk kissed everyone within reach—Francis, Jane, Mary Boleyn, her husband—for a moment Charles thought she was going to embrace the Abbot. She was all but dancing as she held out one hand to Charles and one to Francis, and led them toward the staircase to her rooms.

"You must have a glass of wine with us, your Majesty," she said, "to wish us happiness." At the foot of the winding stairs, she laughed, dropped their hands, and folded her velvet skirts closely around her legs.

"It's such a narrow stairwell," she explained. "Our gowns brush the walls if we aren't careful."

"But such a useful one," answered the King, mockingly. "And I suspect it will be even more useful from now on."

As the little wedding party passed through the Queen's bedchamber on their way into the anteroom, Francis paused long enough to comment favorably on the changes Mary had made in it. "You were wise," he said, "to send for your own tapestries and bed hangings. All that white was oppressive."

Mary shivered. "I never felt really warm. Not even when the fire was blazing."

"You've made this room more comfortable, too," he said, when they reached the antechamber that adjoined it. "No, nothing to eat, thank you." He waved away the delicious food that Mary's maids-of-honor were offering him. "A goblet of wine, please, Mistress Seymour, to toast the bride and groom. But nothing else. I dine with a large company at the Palais Royal within the hour. And so do you, my lord Duke." He turned to Charles and smiled wickedly.

"But—" Mary began protesting, her face suddenly pink. "You can't mean to take Charles away now, Sire?"

"But of course," said Francis. "Why not? The wedding is over."

"Well," she stammered, "I thought surely—"

He burst into delighted laughter. "Don't worry, little belle-mère! I promise to send your husband back to you as soon as darkness falls. But seriously, Mary, if we are to preserve our

251

secret, my lord of Suffolk must take his part in all the festivities planned to honor him and the other ambassadors."

Lifting the tall Venetian goblet, he smiled from Mary to Brandon. "And now, your very good health. May you live, as they say in the romances, happily ever after! In England, if my cousin Henry forgives you, or here in France, if he proves obdurate. For my sake, I hope he will."

The newly married couple knelt as they thanked him, and Mary's eyes filled with grateful tears. Before she could say anything more, Francis emptied his glass and handed it to Mary Boleyn.

"We must be off, Suffolk." He strode to the door.

Brandon gave Mary a hurried kiss. "I'll return at the first possible moment," he whispered. He was just leaving the room when Francis returned.

"I was forgetting a last bit of business that I must conclude with her Grace," he said. "Wait for me below, will you, Suffolk? I won't be a moment."

As Brandon's rather reluctant footsteps were receding down the hall, Francis ordered the two young ladies-in-waiting into the bedchamber. "I want a word in private with your mistress," he told them.

"Dear Francis," said Mary, as soon as they were alone, "before you talk of anything else, I must try, again, to say how grateful I am. How can I ever thank you for making me so happy?"

Before answering, he snatched her up into his arms. "You can thank me," he said savagely, "by remembering this!" Then, holding her struggling body firmly against his with one strong arm, he twisted his free hand in her cloud of hair and forced her head back. For a long moment his hot black eyes searched her face. Then with a groan, he began to kiss her—her dimples, her eyelids, her forehead, and, finally, her protesting, stubborn mouth. She clenched her teeth and tried to jerk away from his searching lips; but it was no use. Francis merely pressed closer, found her mouth again and caressed it with his, sweetly at first, gently, then more and more passionately until Mary, betrayed by her own young and responsive body, gave a little gasp and felt her lips quiver under his kiss.

He raised his head and touched hers with a suddenly tender

252

hand. "There." He sounded shaken but triumphant. "Remember that kiss, Mary," he said as he released her. "On some dull, distant evening, when your beloved Charles has grown fat—as he will, Mary, as he will!—and is thinking only of his supper, remember it and think of me. Think of me then, *ma petite*, and be sorry that I did not claim *le droit de seigneur*. When we grow old, you know, we regret only the sins we did not commit."

Long before Mary heard Charles's step on the stairs she had changed from her white velvet gown into her loveliest blue chamber robe; she had dismissed her chamberwomen, arranged for Jane to sleep in the anteroom, and locked the connecting door. A small supper for two was set by the fire; some fine French wine, a beautifully roasted little bird, a delectable jelly and some flaky pastries. The curtains were drawn, shutting out the darkening, chilly skies, and a good supply of wood was piled by the fire.

Tonight there should be no ringing of bells, no summoning of chamberwomen and lackeys, no formal disrobing by ladies-in-waiting. She and her husband—Mary caressed the word in her mind—her husband and she would wait on themselves. They would be alone as they might never be again.

There! He was mounting the staircase now; she could hear his firm tread on the stone steps. The girl flew to the little door set in the corner of the bedchamber and threw herself into his arms.

"Beloved!" A long kiss, and then that door was locked, too, and they stood for a quiet moment, smiling at each other.

Mary indicated the table. "Supper, Charles? I waited for you." And she reached for the knife, to serve her lord and master as any new young wife should. If her carving was a little uncertain and she spilled a drop or two of wine, neither of them noticed or cared. But to her surprise, Mary's appetite suddenly failed her and she fell silent as she watched Charles empty his plate. She had waited so long for this moment. Why should she be frightened now? And although she fought it, the memory of Louis's cold groping hands flooded over her again and she shuddered.

She looked across the table at Charles and their eyes met.

Without a word he set down his wine glass, rose, and knelt by her side. He reached up and touched her hair that still hung freely on her shoulders.

"Mary—" His voice was hesitant and almost shy. "You wed me with your hair unbound. Did Louis never make love to you, then?"

She shook her head. In a few faltering words, she told the story of her short married life. When she was finished, he lifted her in his arms and whispered his love and thankfulness in her ear. "God has been good to us, love," he said.

He tightened his arms around her, carried her a few steps toward the bed, and stopped. No, he told himself—not yet. Before he and Mary shared their marriage bed he would blot out, forever, her memories of that other wedding night.

"The fire is so beautifully warm," he said to her. "Why should we leave it?" And setting her down, he moved to the cushioned divan that stood at the foot of the tall, gilded bedstead. He dragged it over until it faced the flames, then he laughed, scooped up two white fur rugs from the floor, and spread them over the pillowed couch. "There! A soft nest for us."

Turning away for a moment, he stripped off his silver satin Court clothes and returned to her side, wearing only his white silk shirt and hose. He led Mary close to the hearth, unfastened her chamber robe with gentle fingers, pulled it off her white shoulders, and tossed it aside. Mary glanced down at her almost transparent linen shift, gave an involuntary murmur of protest, a protest that died away as her husband caught her in his arms. His first kiss sent the blood singing through her body and every fear was forgotten.

"There, Charles," she said, her voice a blend of rapture and triumph. "Loving each other *is* heaven! You see, I was right, after all!"

For the next few weeks, the Duke and Duchess of Suffolk were very, very busy. Between nights of stolen lovemaking, and days worrying over the letters they were writing to England, there was little time for sleep or anything else. They were equally determined to shoulder the lion's share of the blame, if blame there was to be for their secret marriage, and they were also equally eager to win King Henry's forgiveness. And when they learned, almost immediately, that there was indeed going to be a great deal of blame, both Mary and Charles wrote again and again, first to Henry and then to Wolsey, trying desperately to justify their rash action. Much as they liked France and its young King, they wanted to go home.

Across the Channel, the irate King of England gave their long, labored scripts very little attention, tossing them aside with a string of colorful oaths, his threats to the punishment to be meted out to the two sinners growing more and more violent. Would he never relent? Wolsey wondered, as he watched Henry's purple face and listened to his furious ranting. Should he advise the young couple to give up hope and settle down in France?

He was considering it very seriously one day when another letter arrived from Charles Brandon, addressed to the King. Henry ripped it open, glanced down the page, stopped, read a sentence again, and suddenly burst into a great roar of laughter.

"Poor Brandon!" He gasped through his noisy mirth. "That poor, miserable, henpecked dog! Listen to this, Wolsey—" And he read aloud the few short words that had somehow succeeded where all the lengthy pages and paragraphs had failed. By accident, Suffolk put into eight words the whole story of how he had come to break his solemn oath to the King of England.

" 'She wept. I never saw woman so weep.' " Henry threw the letter down and laughed again. "I tell you, Wolsey, women are hell. What could that poor devil do?"

He was still chuckling when he broke the seal on the letter of Mary's that had arrived at the same time. Amused now instead of angry, and with the picture of his stubborn little sister winding great, strong Charles Brandon around her smallest finger, he read it with an open mind. As it happened, it was Mary's most eloquent plea, her reminders of the bargain between them strongly phrased and her love for her brother obvious in every word.

He was thoughtful when he finished. He sat and drummed his fingers on the table. Finally, he turned to Wolsey, a sheepish smile on his broad face. "I think I'll let them come home, Wolsey. I don't mind confessing to you that I miss them both. But if they are to have their way, and keep their heads still on their shoulders, they shall pay—and pay dearly! I must have every last pound of Mary's dower rights, and all her French jewels. See that they bring me every diamond, every pearl! Do you hear me, Wolsey? Everything!"

On the thirteenth day of May all of England's noblest lords and ladies gathered at Greenwich Palace to see the King's little sister wed, again, to the tall, handsome man she loved. It was perfect spring weather, the kind of warm, sunny day that sets poets to scribbling, birds to singing, and bees to humming; the hedges were snowy with the May, the season's new lambs frisked around their mothers in the meadows nearby, and a few roses, deceived by the bright sunlight into thinking it was June, burst into bloom.

Inside the Palace chapel, King Henry smiled to himself at the look of rapture on Mary's face when he placed her hand in that of her bridegroom. His own fingers, freed now, caressed the huge, glittering "Mirror of Naples" that hung around his thick neck, and before stepping aside, he bent and kissed his sister's glowing cheek. As he raised his head, his eyes met Brandon's. Henry chuckled softly.

"No more weeping for a while, eh, Brandon?" But the King never knew whether his whisper had reached his friend's ear, for at that moment the wedding ceremony began and Mary Tudor, the Princess of England and the Dowager Queen of France became, in the sight of God and everyone she loved best on earth, the Duchess of Suffolk.

GREENDALE BRANCH

Mary Tudor, sister of Henry VIII